WHITE CROCODILE

WHITE CROCODILE

K. T. MEDINA

MULHOLLAND BOOKS

LITTLE, BROWN AND COMPANY

NEW YORK   BOSTON   LONDON

For Paul Jefferson, the inspiration
for this novel, and a truly inspirational person
For Isabel, Anna and Alexander

Copyright © 2014 by K. T. Medina

Mulholland Books/Little, Brown and Company
Hachette Book Group
1290 Avenue of the Americas
New York, NY 10104
mulhollandbooks.com

First North American Edition: June 2015
Originally published in Great Britain by Faber & Faber, August 2014

Mulholland Books is an imprint of Little, Brown and Company, a division of Hachette Book Group, Inc. The Mulholland Books name and logo are trademarks of Hachette Book Group, Inc.

The publisher is not responsible for websites (or their content) that are not owned by the publisher.

The Hachette Speakers Bureau provides a wide range of authors for speaking events. To find out more, go to hachettespeakersbureau.com or call (866) 376-6591.

ISBN 978-0-316-37400-2
LCCN 2014959304

10 9 8 7 6 5 4 3 2 1

RRD-C

Printed in the United States of America

Day 1

I

Tian was woken by a noise. A brief cry, like the sound her mother let out when she saw a rat between the huts at dusk. Silence followed, and she wondered if she had dreamed her mother's voice. But sleep wouldn't come, even when she tugged her sarong right up to her chin and closed her eyes.

She could picture Mummy sitting motionless on the top step with the empty look she got in her eyes sometimes, on those afternoons when Tian would call and call her and she wouldn't hear. She pulled the sarong down again and sighed. Night was framed in the glassless square of window above her.

Jumping up, she pushed the cloth curtain aside and tiptoed across the hut. The doorway was empty. The moon slid from behind a cloud, lighting a bare sleeping roll.

No Mummy.

For a few seconds, Tian stood there mystified.

Mummy?

She turned and scanned the room. It was barely seven metres across and her eyes ran along the walls, searched every corner.

Outside the doorway, the night was black and full of the trill of cicadas.

'*Meak?*' Mummy. Just a whisper.

She took a step forward.

'*Meak. Meak!*'

Tian hugged her arms around herself. Biting her lip, she

began to walk towards the doorway.

On the top step she paused. It was colder outside than she had expected. A light wind rustled her sarong and brushed grey clouds across a sliver of moon. The rough wooden boards chilled the soles of her bare feet.

Her mother had warned her never to bother the neighbours. Even at six, Tian knew that she and her mother were not like the others. Bastard. She had heard the word and though she didn't understand its meaning, she recognised the contempt.

But where else would Mummy be?

It was only twenty metres to the next hut, but there was no light. Tian glanced in the other direction. There was just enough moon for her to see the still edge of the jungle. Quickly, she dropped her gaze down to the five wooden steps between her and the ground. Something glistened on the bottom step. She bent down. It was a knife, its blade glassy in the moonlight. Recoiling, she sucked in a breath. She would run, as fast as she could. Ten seconds and she would be there, safe inside the neighbour's hut with her mother. Then she noticed something else next to the knife, something carved into the wood of the bottom step, the gouges deep and uneven. She couldn't quite see what it was at first. But it stirred a memory.

Instead of running as she had planned to, she sank into a crouch, wrapping her arms tight around her knees, feeling the chill on her bare shoulders. She remembered why she recognised the carving. The last time she had seen it, it had made the men of the village fall to their knees and pray.

Day 2

2

The sign was a square of painted wood nailed to a post at the edge of the minefield, hanging crooked, as if it had been hurriedly tacked up. The stick figure of a reptile daubed on a black background. Needle-sharp teeth, a splash for an eye.

Tess realised that her hands were tattooing a rhythm against her thighs. Curling them into fists, she jammed them into her pockets. There was something written in Khmer beneath the drawing. She couldn't read it. But she knew what the thing meant.

'White Crocodile minefield.' A Khmer in mine-clearance fatigues was standing watching her, his flat brown face expressionless. 'You heard about the White Crocodile?'

Tess shook her head, and thought back six months to an English spring morning: trailing a hand along the sleek lines of a young man's coffin.

'No.' She was surprised at how steady her voice was. 'What's the White Crocodile?'

The Khmer slotted some betel nut into his mouth, his saliva reddening as he chewed. 'It come to Cambodia at time of important change. Present at birth of Cambodia. When Khmer Rouge took country, White Crocodile seen. This minefield.' He gestured towards the red-and-white warning tape. 'When this minefield found, White Crocodile here.' He stared past her, out across the spoiled fields. 'Seen here.'

'So it represents fate, does it? Is that what people in Cambodia think?'

The mine clearer levelled his gaze at hers; he hadn't understood.

'Fate,' she repeated. 'Something that is meant to be. Something that you can't change whatever you do.'

'*Bhat.*' Sudden understanding lent a gleam to his dark eyes. 'Fate. The White Crocodile is fate.'

*

The call had come early one morning.

She had stayed up late the night before because it was a Friday, a precious evening before a weekend with no training, no exercises, the end of a gruelling week where her troop had spent four days in the field sleeping rough.

The phone woke her just before five, still almost dark outside, the white curtains beginning to turn grey-tinged pink. She fumbled for it, dragged from a dream that disappeared from memory the moment she woke, just the wisps of something warm and comfortable remaining. She was about to ask Luke if he knew what the *hell* the time was – let alone why he was calling her anyway – but when she pressed the receiver to her ear there was no static crackle, no pause while she waited for the words to lurch down the line from thirteen thousand miles away.

The memory of what happened next was as clear in her mind as if she'd received the same call every morning since.

*

'Don't listen.' A voice cut in, a confident English voice, and a muscular arm folded around her shoulders. Johnny leaned into her, his breath hot on her cheek. 'It's just peasant bullshit.'

Tess twisted out of his grasp, raising a hand to shield her eyes from the sun, meeting his gaze and catching his grin.

'Jonathan Douglas Hugh Perrier – our resident toff!' Bob MacSween, the MCT boss, had told her yesterday, taking her through the staff photographs tacked to the team-room wall. 'Parents own a couple of thousand acres in Shropshire. My parents' estate is a two up two down in the arse end of Glasgow. He's a bit of a joker; comes with the posh-boy domain, I suppose. Never needed to take life seriously. Johnny swears he wires his house with trip wires, changes their position every few days just to keep himself on his toes.'

MacSween had laughed when he'd said it, but Tess had sensed a slight unease. Jokes and mines: it was dangerous territory. She lowered her hand to her cheek, smearing Johnny's breath into her palm. His touch had felt too personal; she hardly knew him.

'What's bullshit? The Crocodile?'

'It's a Cambodian myth. A stupid five-hundred-year-old myth that's got completely out of hand.' He rolled his eyes. 'They have crocodiles running around in their heads. The betel nut they all chew is hallucinogenic.'

'Is that what the sign's about?' She tilted her head towards it.

'I've no idea who put that up. I was going to come out here with a tin of paint and give it one less leg and a crutch, but

MacSween would kick my arse if he found out. He's into the locals and their idiosyncrasies.' Smiling, he pulled a packet of tobacco from his pocket, rolled a cigarette and lit it. 'Actually MacSween's furious because he chose that fucking croc as our logo when he set the charity up five years ago.' He pointed to one of the Land Cruisers where a sleek white reptilian insignia wound around the navy-blue letters, MCT, on its bonnet. 'And now the villagers see it as their harbinger of doom. Not quite the image he was trying to create. Personally, I don't care what the villagers think as long as my Khmer clearers don't start believing that shit too and getting jumpy.' He caught her eye and suddenly seemed to sense her anxiety. 'You're a bit edgy as well, aren't you? Has something upset you?'

'No. I'm fine. Just a bit spaced out by the time change.' Her hand rose to finger her ear as she smiled up at him, a smile she hoped reached her eyes. 'I should be going to bed about now.'

Johnny nodded, measuring her denial with a steady gaze.

'Don't worry,' he said finally. 'You're only stuck with me for the week until you're used to the foibles of the Cambodian fields, then you get your own troop.' Taking a final drag of his roll-up, he dropped the butt and crushed it under his heel. 'So let's try and make it interesting for you. See what we can find.'

He looked past her. She followed his gaze, checking out the field as a mine clearer this time – a professional – trying not to look at the black sign with its crude drawing. Below them was a huge expanse of mined land that took in jungle, waterlogged paddy fields where rice once grew, cassava, maize and soybean fields, grazing land for cattle, dirt roads and pathways, and two deserted schools, the buildings derelict, windows blank. The land stretched five kilometres north to south, three east to west, linking a network of twelve small villages, each at starvation level, ravaged by the lack of safe land to farm.

It would take years to clear fully. Every centimetre – jungle, flooded paddy fields, footpaths, thigh-high elephant grass – had to be covered by a trained clearer, sweeping his detector from side to side across a metre-wide clearance lane, bending to investigate any alarms by hand, probing the earth with a steel wand to see if he could make contact with metal. When that happened, a hand would go up, and all the teams would have to pull back to safe ground while the clearer lay on his stomach and gingerly uncovered the suspected mine with his trowel and his fingers. If a land mine was found, it was marked with a red cone, the clearance lane closed for the rest of the day and the clearer taken to a different part of the field to continue work. At the end of the day, all the mines found were wired with explosives and detonated *in situ*.

It was early. Mist still clung in hollows. Johnny's Khmer clearers, slight figures in pale blue MCT fatigues, were already working in their lanes, flak jackets and helmets on, visors down, eyes locked to the ground. Total concentration, and just the ambient hum of insects to mar the silence.

'Tess.' She felt Johnny's hand on her arm. He had fastened his flak jacket. 'I'm going to check something out in the field. One of my clearers has seen something in the lane next to his that he wants me to have a look at. Huan, the guy who's clearing that lane, isn't here today.'

'What's he seen?'

'Nothing, probably. It's usually nothing with these guys in this damn field. Are you happy to wait here and keep an eye on the rest of my teams?'

'Yes, of course. But what is it? What's he seen?'

Johnny had crouched down and was checking his detector, passing his hand around the metal coil to ease off the dirt, tracing his fingers up the shaft to the test button, which screeched a warning signal into the silence. She thought he hadn't heard her.

'Johnny, what's—'

'He thought it was a skull,' he said, straightening.

A tight little laugh caught in her throat. 'A skull? A human skull?'

'That's right. A human skull.' Johnny grinned. 'You've heard of the Khmer Rouge, haven't you?' His voice was heavy with sarcasm.

'Of course I've heard of them—' She broke off, aware that her own voice was rising, becoming shrill. He'd start wondering again – why she was so anxious – and that was the last thing she wanted to happen.

'They killed millions. Marched their countrymen out to fields just like this, made them kneel and beat them to death with wooden clubs so they didn't waste bullets.' He pulled a face. 'It's probably just a fucking rock. So sit back and sunbathe and I'll be back in a minute.' Shouldering his detector, he turned towards the minefield. 'Just don't get burnt,' he cast back over his shoulder. 'I certainly don't intend to.'

3

Tess watched Johnny cross safe ground to the edge of the minefield and the start of Huan's clearance lane. He looked relaxed, his detector swung over his shoulder, visor propped over the top of his head. She almost called out to him – told him to pull it down before he entered the field – but she thought better of it.

Her gaze moved past him to the lone tree in the middle of the mined land. Its tight mass of branches and leaves cast an almost perfectly circular disc of shade, so dark that in this bright light it looked like a stain on a projector image. Beyond the tree, Johnny's clearance teams were still working silently, the heat staining their armpits with circles of sweat even though it was barely 8 a.m.

Tess hadn't noticed the heat while she'd been talking with Johnny, but now, standing alone, she felt its intensity. She dragged a hand across her forehead, wiping sweat into her hair. Somewhere near her ear an insect buzzed. She swiped at it, heard its buzz fade then become louder. Then, out of the corner of her eye, she noticed a mine clearer standing looking towards her, his hand raised in dumb show. A mine had been found. Pulling her visor down over her face she walked swiftly towards him.

The explosion was just a muffled, insolent little bang.

*

Later, the only thing Tess would be able to recall clearly was the lack of noise: the absolute silence. She had been here before, in this exact moment, in this exact minefield, but with another man dying, over and over.

Each nightmare had been different.

Sometimes the colours were extraordinary, the ravaged grass in the mined paddy fields an unfeasible shade of emerald, silvers and golds ringing the burnt-out craters. At other times, the landscape had been washed to watercolour by a monsoon rain. Still others, the scene had been monochrome – one man, alone, bleeding his life into a strange lunar wasteland.

But whichever dream, there had never been this overwhelming silence. She realised, when she was able to think back, that it must only have lasted for a second or two, but in that moment – the moment after Johnny stepped on a mine – each second had stretched and gaped.

Gradually the sound of her own ragged breathing crept around the edge of her consciousness. And suddenly there was mayhem. Panicked mine clearers dropped kit and sprinted down their lanes towards safe ground, some screaming and stumbling, others running, silent, fast. The smell of TNT filled the air. Somewhere to her left she could hear someone yelling – helicopter, *helicopter*.

And there, twenty metres in front of her, lying under the lone tree in the middle of the field, was Johnny, moaning, broken. His right leg twisted and sheared off mid-calf. Shrapnel wounds ploughed his face and neck and even from

this distance she could see that his skin had gone dead white.
His eyes were wild with panic.

Move, Tess, move. Her flak jacket felt heavy, constricting,
a buoyancy aid filled with sand instead of air, a sensation, a
memory she hadn't had since home: a frivolous memory of
dancing around the living room in Luke's flak jacket, nothing
else on but red lace knickers and a wicked smile.

Metal detector? Where was her detector?

But she couldn't see it, and now that she was moving her
blood began to pulse again, bringing with it energy – pure adrenalin. As if her legs belonged to someone else she felt herself
begin to move, one foot and then the other, carrying her forward, towards the edge of the minefield, towards Johnny.

Hands grabbed at her suddenly, hauling her back.

'No.' A voice was screaming in her ear. 'You no go in.'

She fought to free her arm. 'We have to get to him now.
He'll die.'

'No. Stop! You no go in. *No go in!*'

She could see Johnny panting now, gulping, as if there was
not enough air in the world. His chest heaved and lifted and
heaved again and then he was sobbing.

The other clearers – his clearers – were huddled in silence
around the Land Cruisers. No one was moving. Why was no
one doing anything? What the fuck were they waiting for?

The young man holding her arm had a face distorted with
fear. She jerked back, fighting against his hands.

'Wait? Wait for what?'

'Lady. Listen – you listen.'

'No! For God's sake, we have to get to him now.' She was
yelling, she realised, her throat raw with it. She could see the

other Khmer men drawing back, retreating from her, shutters closing over their faces.

'Lady, this field. The White Crocodile came here.' He was pointing at Johnny. 'Twelve times. Mr Johnny thirteen—'

She wrenched her arm from his grasp, shoved past him and broke into a run, her feet slipping, heavy combat boots dragging at her legs, flak jacket pressing against her chest, making it hard to breathe. Her heart lurched as she passed the red-and-white mine tape marking the edge of the field, but she didn't stop.

He looked calm now. *Sit back and sunbathe. Don't get burnt.* His eyes were closed and he was silent, his breath slow and shallow. *I certainly don't intend to.* Only the blood didn't fit. She couldn't believe how much there was.

It poured from the ragged remains of his calf and the shrapnel wounds on his face and neck, slick underneath him, forming a glossy halo around his head. His skin had darkened to navy blue around the edges of the wounds. A stain was spreading across the front of his shorts. The burnt, twisted case of the anti-personnel mine lay a couple of lanes away, and next to it, a boot – a splintered, sopping boot.

Forcing her mind to blankness, Tess lowered herself gently down beside him. Knelt in his blood. Smelt scorched flesh and fear. Felt the shade of the tree on her face. Gripped his hand. Gestured for the first-aiders to come forward – *It's clear! I just ran down the fucking lane, there's nothing else here! It's clear!* – listened to the slop of their boots in the mud, to the rustle of the stretcher, to the static from a radio somewhere in the distance, to Johnny saying something that didn't come out as words, just babble, before he groaned and coughed a red mess on to his flak jacket.

She looked from his jacket to his face and saw that his eyes were open now, flickering blue lights that were brightening, dimming.

4

The complex was situated on the fringes of central Battambang, on a potholed road, tree-lined and oddly peaceful given its location. Tess drove through the gate into a dirt courtyard shaded by palms and a huge, spreading frangipani tree, and hemmed in on three sides by shabby, single-storey whitewashed buildings. Each building was rectangular, with a deep covered veranda running down the side that faced the courtyard. Their glassless windows were dark behind mosquito mesh.

Cutting the engine, she slumped forward, pressing her forehead against the steering wheel and closing her eyes. The pain in her skull, which had come on the moment she'd seen Johnny loaded into the ambulance, refused to subside. She fought a wave of nausea, panicky at the thought of seeing him again, maimed – *bitten*, she found herself thinking, remembering the boot. She had tried to maintain her professionalism at the field – ducking behind a Land Cruiser, out of sight, to throw up – but she knew that she must stink of it. Vomit, and his blood, which had dried to brown paste on her trousers.

Sitting back in the seat, she opened her eyes and took a few long breaths, sucking the hot air into her lungs. For a moment, her mind flashed back to England, where winter would now be approaching. She suddenly yearned to be cold. Flipping the rearview mirror down, she glanced at her reflection. Drawn and pale. She shoved a strand of hair behind her ear, moistened her fingertips with her tongue and scrubbed at the tracks on her cheeks, until the lines merged into the rest of the dirt. She detested herself when she cried, couldn't start out in Cambodia like this, whatever had happened. The woman who cried had to be left behind with the bills on the mat and the rancid milk she'd forgotten to empty from the fridge. Giving herself another quick glance in the mirror, she climbed out and slammed the door.

The three buildings facing the courtyard were nearly identical. The one to her right was in semi-darkness, wooden slat blinds pulled low over the windows. The building at the back of the courtyard was also deserted, but a couple of metal chairs rested on the veranda and two lines of faded washing hung listlessly. To her left, doors were open and she could see the outlines of people moving around inside, hear the gentle hum of conversation. Two Khmer men were sitting on a low bench in the shade of the veranda, watching her in silence. She made her way over.

One was young, in his teens she guessed, with dark curly hair. The leg-hole of his green shorts sagged around a pinched stump; his other leg was pitted with scars. The other man was old, white hair, eyes glazed by cataracts. His right arm was a knot of rough skin hooked over a wooden crutch, his left ankle a swell of distorted flesh, with no foot attached.

'A man, a white man, *Barang*, was brought in here a few hours ago. He trod on a land mine. Could you please tell me where he was taken?'

The young man gave a shy smile, the old man nodded and grinned, but it was clear that neither had understood.

'*Un homme blanc*. Accident. *Il arrive ici, deux heures ...*' She waved her hand. 'Ago ... Where ... *Où? Où est-il?*'

It was poor. She waited, chewing her lip. Slowly a hand was

raised. The old man pointing, with his good arm, across the courtyard.

'*Ça c'est l'hôpital.*'

*

At the far end of the building, the corridor opened out into a small waiting area, where narrow wooden benches were set against the wall.

A dark-haired man was slumped on one of the benches, legs stretched out in front of him, head hanging, smoke curling from a cigarette in his hand. Butts made a pile on the floor by his feet. He was wearing navy-blue MCT fatigues, shorts and shirt, long-sleeved despite the heat, faded and stained with tidemarks of sweat. As she walked through the doorway, he lifted his head and she recognised him from his photograph on the team-room wall. Alexander Bauer: early thirties, dark brown hair, eyes so dark they had looked almost black. 'Croatian,' MacSween had told her. 'Keeps himself to himself. But he's good. Tough, reliable and knows his shit.'

In the photographs he had seemed a broad, tall figure. Here in the hospital waiting room, his size was magnified – the bench he was sitting on seemed absurdly small and delicate by comparison.

'Alexander, Alex? I'm—'

'I know who you are.'

He took a drag of his cigarette and blew the smoke slowly through his nostrils, dark eyes fixed on her face.

'What's happening?' she asked. 'Where's Johnny?'

He answered with a tilt of his head. She glanced towards closed double doors on the far side of the waiting area, which bore a sign written in Khmer.

'Operating theatre. No entry. Operation in progress,' he read, slowly, sardonically.

'How did you hear about . . . about Johnny?'

'Radio, it is open band. We all heard.'

'Do you know where MacSween is? Is he coming?'

'He's meeting local military commanders. Sweet-talking. He won't know yet probably. When he does, he will come.'

She nodded. 'I followed as soon as I could.'

'You didn't need to.' His eyes were hard.

Tess slumped down on one of the benches; Alexander stayed where he was, smoking, looking at his hands.

The double doors to the operating theatre swung open and a small Khmer in green surgical robes slipped out. Head down, eyes fixed on the floor, he hurried up the corridor, and returned a few moments later clutching two transparent sacs of blood.

Alexander held out his arm. '*Ohm.*'

The orderly paused; Alex spoke quietly in Khmer. The orderly replied in monosyllables. When they had finished speaking, he whirled past Alex and into the operating theatre.

'What did he say?' she asked. 'How's Johnny? Did he tell you?'

Alex stood without answering and moved over to the window, where he raised his arms, using splayed fingers to rest against its frame, staring through the mosquito netting.

'Is he OK? Is he alive?'

Alex nodded. 'Alive.'

She fell silent, stared at his back, at the contours of his

shoulders and arms tense against the material of his shirt. Her gaze slid past him to the outside, where a group of Khmer mine victims were walking around a brightly painted obstacle course, some stumbling at every hurdle, others coping better on their prosthetics and battered wooden crutches. Alex watched them. After a while he cast the butt of his cigarette to the ground, reached in his pocket for the packet, opened it, but didn't take one. Instead, he turned back towards Tess, leaning against the windowsill.

'Why are you here?'

'What? In Cambodia? Or in this hospital?'

'What brought you to Cambodia? Why are you doing this?'

Tess waited a beat before answering. She had never worked for a humanitarian mine-clearance charity, but had five years in the Royal Engineers under her belt, including three tours of duty clearing mines in Afghanistan. She had more than enough experience to make her valuable to a small charity like MCT – and to provide a convincing cover story for her being in Cambodia. She wasn't about to open up to Alex, or to anyone else, about the real reason.

'Why not? There's nothing else I'm good at.'

He was studying her face, searching it for clues. She met his gaze unblinking. There was truth in what she'd said, and the rest was none of his business.

'What about you? Why are you here?'

He didn't speak for a few moments. 'It's a long story, and not one that is very interesting.'

'You've never been injured clearing?'

He shook his head. 'I've been lucky. But once, almost—' He broke off, turning back to the window. It had begun to rain, a soft patter against the mesh. Somewhere out in the street a tinny radio blared hip hop, and a rooster squawked. 'I got too close to someone else's fuck-up.'

Her mouth was suddenly dry. 'What happened?'

'Not important.' His fingers tapped against the window-frame. 'You should go home.'

She shook her head. 'I'm happy to stay.'

'Go home. There is no need for you to be here.'

'I want to stay, see that Johnny's OK.'

'*Go*,' Alex hissed. 'Just go. This has *nothing* to do with you.'

*

He watched her walk across the yard to the Land Cruiser, watched the tense set of her shoulders. He had watched her come too, had felt the extraordinary pull of those green eyes, of her aloofness and her vulnerability. She was wound as tight as a spring. She was everything he'd expected.

Holding the cigarette against the back of his hand, Alex watched the dark hairs curl and melt, the flesh start to blister under the red-hot ash, felt the heat sear right through to his nerve ends. He held it there longer, closed his eyes and ate up the pain, feeling the tide of anger and guilt receding. Lifting it free, he gazed dispassionately at the other burns on his hands and the scars of knife marks threading their way up his wrists to the cuffs of his shirtsleeve, as though they were words set down in a language he'd forgotten how to read.

5

Luke had come into the kitchen one morning last summer, mud from his boots flaking on to the lino, smiling, self-conscious, contrite.

'I've got something for you.'

She had tried to smile back then, reading his mood. Her mouth still tasted of blood and her lips felt puffy and lopsided. But it was easier to move on, pretend nothing had happened. Her brain processed quickly, running through a range of low-risk answers, stopping to select, like a sixties jukebox picking records.

'A present?' she murmured, aware that her thick lip was making her slur a little, hating herself for it. 'Diamonds, maybe?'

He smiled and stepped towards her and automatically her back went rigid, her pulse rose a few notches. He sensed the change and hurt flashed in his eyes. But the walk had calmed him and he was obviously determined not to spoil the moment; his voice didn't falter. 'Close your eyes and hold out your hand.'

She watched through the crack of her eyelids as something soft fell into the palm of her hand. 'What is that?'

'A sock. A baby girl's sock.'

'Where did you get it?'

'I found it on Salisbury Plain. Lying on the ground.'

'And you just picked it up?'

He shrugged and grinned, relaxing into the moment, conscious now that she was going to let him move on, pretend his outburst an hour ago had never happened.

'It's a good omen. I know it is. It's going to happen, soon.' He smiled, his eyes growing warm again. 'It's what I want . . . what we *both* want, isn't it?'

Tess forced a smile of acquiescence, her heart fluttering in her chest. 'It's filthy. And you're nuts,' she whispered, regretting it immediately.

'Of that,' Luke said, with a tiny smile, 'there is no doubt. But you're crazy too, Tess. That's why we love each other so much.'

Tess shivered. 'I'm throwing it away.'

But for some reason, she hadn't. She'd made up some excuse about having to get dinner on, to get away from him, and left it on the hall table. When she had remembered and come back, it had disappeared. He had taken it.

The next time she had seen the tiny pink sock was in a battered envelope with a Cambodian stamp on it, which had landed on her doormat a month after Luke was dead and buried.

The address was typed, and there was nothing else on the packet to betray who had sent it, and nothing else inside. She had turned the envelope upside down, and shoved her hand right up inside to make sure. Luke had gone to Cambodia as a single man, knowing their marriage was over, that she had finally found the guts to leave him. Who there knew about her? Who cared?

And then she had noticed, on the other side of the envelope from its stamp and postmark, a tiny scribble. It had meant nothing to her at the time: a doodle of a reptile, like a pictogram, so small that she couldn't even tell exactly what it was supposed to be. A gecko? A lizard?

The sock was here now, on the coffee table in the centre

of her room in the boarding house. She bent and curled her fingers around it.

The room was large and airy, with a small kitchen and white tiled bathroom leading off it, on the first floor of a two-storey new build, set back from the road in a walled garden, and overlooked by a jostling crowd of palms. The walls were white-painted and bare: she had nothing personal to hang up, and the floor, bed and sofa were clear of scattered belongings.

She had forgotten to close the balcony doors when she had left in the morning. Orange light streamed through the glass, casting twin rectangles on the floorboards. There was a puddle of rain-water on the wooden floor and the bottoms of the white curtains were opaque with damp. Beyond them the sun was sinking.

*

'I know I shouldn't be calling,' Luke had said, the first time he telephoned from Cambodia. 'I know we agreed. But I wanted to speak to you. That's OK, isn't it? Just sometimes? You know that I don't have anyone else.'

She had been on the verge of telling him that he didn't have *her* any more either, but now that he was on the line it felt petty, vengeful. She had assumed, after all that he had done to her, that her anger would never subside. That she would be able to close him off – be rational and emotionless in their dealings. But the reality was far less binary. There was history and memory. Love – gone now – but more intense than she had felt for anyone else, ever.

He had been so self-contained the first time they had met,

at a summer ball in the officers' mess four years ago. She had noticed him immediately: something to do with his height perhaps. He was half a head taller than most of the other men in the room, and well built, not in a body builder's way, but loose and athletic. He had sandy blond hair, cut short, and the palest blue-grey eyes she had ever seen, the colour of a clear winter sky. But, attractive as he was, his physical features weren't the main reason she had noticed him. He was standing alone, and what drew her to him was how comfortable he was in his self-containment, surrounded as he was by a heaving mass of drunken extroverts. She had seen a reflection of herself in him. That same distance, that same separation she felt from other people. The image she retained of their meeting brought to mind the Robert Doisneau photograph of lovers kissing, freeze-framed against the blur of a busy Paris street.

She had felt a fierce love for him virtually from the moment they met. She realised, soon after they were married, that the love she felt had blinded her to the reality of his personality. Controlling behaviour had seemed protective; overly intense and uncompromising behaviour, adoration and concern; introversion and suspicion of others, mysteriousness. As the only child of a single father overwhelmed by his parenting responsibilities, who had farmed her care out to friends and an ever-changing roll call of nannies, she wasn't used to being the centre of someone else's world, and that feeling had been intoxicating.

Now she just felt exhausted by it all, empty.

Why did it matter if he called her? She was never going back to him. Distance protected her, made her strong enough to resist. She could speak to him without being sucked back into that same old pattern of needy love, violence, guilt and apology. She placed a hand against the flat of her stomach.

'It's fine, Luke.'

He was managing a troop of thirty Khmer clearers, teaching them Western military disciplines so that, in time, they would become skilled enough to be self-sufficient. He sounded softer, more relaxed than she'd known him in a long time, and she felt relieved that he had found a life beyond her that might make him happy. But a couple of months after he arrived, his tone began to change.

'It's different when you get under the surface,' he said one time, his voice rising against the static crackle on the line. 'You start to see the other side.'

'What do you mean? What other side?'

'You remember when you called me outside because there was a cat in the garden? What, two summers ago?' She was baffled by the non sequitur, and then a burst of interference and the faint words of someone else, another conversation, crossed the line.

'Luke, I can't hear you.' The memory came into focus though. A stray cat hanging around in the back garden one morning. When they'd approached it, they'd seen the fur on one flank stirring, the pale, bloated bodies of maggots. It watched them with unperturbed green eyes; leapt the fence when Tess had tried to tempt it close enough to catch with a saucer of milk.

She heard a sigh, pixellated by the crackle. He was talking about the UN brokering peace after the fall of the Khmer Rouge. 'They did it, sure. But at the same time they screwed around, didn't bother to use condoms and kickstarted AIDS. They were out here to help, for fuck's sake. Like that cat. Perfect one side – then you see the other, the hidden side.'

She drew a long breath, closed her eyes. 'But that was almost thirty years ago, Luke?'

He laughed bitterly. 'Cambodia has an AIDS epidemic, now. So they've not just got the mine problem they started with, they've got an AIDS problem too, caused by the bastards who were supposed to be helping.' She heard the familiar anger rising in his voice, and shivered despite herself. 'And that attitude, that disregard for people's rights, for their *lives*, it pervades everything out here. Khmers have a weird fatalism.'

The tone of his voice, slightly distorted by the distance, made her skin tingle. Sliding the chair back from the desk, clutching the receiver to her ear, she had moved over to the window, stared over the endless green of Salisbury Plain. A man and his dog appeared over the brow of a distant hill; a pair of buzzards circled; the white wisps of a jet engine's contrail streamed across a cloudless sky. Everything felt so normal, so dull and predictable and achingly safe, that she just wasn't able to go there, to push her mind to the place where Luke was. Wasn't sure that she even wanted to.

It was when he called the following week that she realised he was frightened.

A few weeks later, he was dead. And she had known, in that instinctive, organic way that someone so familiar with another person knows, that, despite what she had been told, his death couldn't have been an accident. He was too controlling for that. Too *good*. One of the best mine clearers that the army had ever seen, precisely because he was so controlled and precise, *every single time.*

And now Johnny. Another army-trained, experienced mine clearer, in the same minefield, just a few months later.

A coincidence? No. She didn't believe in coincidences.

6

Manchester, England

From Rose Hill woods, Detective Inspector Andy Wessex watched the sun edge up into the sky beyond the M60, the light glancing off the windscreens of cars speeding southeast. It reminded him of Morse code exercises he used to play as a boy: his older brother hiding in the branches of the copper beech at the foot of the garden, him leaning out of their bedroom window flashing a torch to signal. Dot dot dot. Dash dash dash. Dot dot dot. Save Our Souls. The imaginary enemy massed below them on the dark lawn.

Rose Hill was an offbeat description for this parallelogram of scrappy woodland jammed between two motorways, this one and the M56, the hum of traffic a reminder – even cocooned in the trees as Wessex was – that it was slap bang in the middle of south Manchester, surrounded by industrial estates and a spider's web of terraced streets. The wood was predominantly conifer, with some ancient oaks scattered amongst the evergreens, their remaining leaves curled and yellow.

'Morning, sir.' Detective Sergeant Harriet Viles joined him, rubbing her hands together and shivering.

He stifled a yawn. 'I hope you haven't had breakfast yet.'

'That bad?'

Andy tapped a finger on his nose. 'Looks like something's had a nibble.'

'Just what I wanted to hear. Teach me to nip into the service station for a bacon sarnie on the way here.'

'You've got a cast-iron stomach, Viles.'

They had to stop talking while an aeroplane roared over-head, its wheels lowered for landing at Manchester City Air-port, just a few miles south; so low that Andy felt he could stretch his fingertips up and touch its shimmering underbelly.

'Be a bugger to live around here,' Viles said. She lived in a tiny house in Saddleworth, in the Pennines, with her girlfriend and six rescue cats. Wessex had been there once when they'd first started working together last year, to collect her when her car had failed to start. She'd invited him in for a coffee to meet Serena, but he'd had to leave after five minutes because he'd broken out in a rash from the cat hair on the sofa. Back in his spotless warehouse apartment, sandwiched between bankers and lawyers, as central as he could afford without living with the tramps in the city station, he shuddered to think about the mess in that house.

'So what have we got, sir?'

'Young female, teenager or early twenties, Pakistani or Indi-an most likely, though it's hard to tell without an autopsy. Been here a few days from the look of her.'

'Who found her?'

'Dog walker.'

'Ah. Who'd be a dog walker? As I've always said, cats are the way forward. Just remember that when you finally cave in and get yourself some live-in company for those lonely weekends.'

He clapped a hand on her shoulder. 'I crave lonely weekends. Come on. Let's take a look at the crime scene, and then I'd like you to drive the dog walker back to the station and get a prop-er statement from him.' Wessex inclined his head towards the command vehicle, where an elderly man in a tweed coat and hat stood holding the lead of an overweight brindle Staffordshire bull terrier.

'Fine. Who is he?'

'Name's Derek Taylor. He runs a printing company out of a unit in Sharston industrial estate. He said he comes here every morning to walk the dog before work.'

They moved slowly through the slippery, rotting leaf mulch, towards the forensic team who looked like forest ghouls gliding through the trees in their white plastic overalls. As they went deeper into the trees the hum of cars on the M60 faded. A roar and another aeroplane flew overhead, landing lights washing them white as it passed.

'How did he find her?'

'The dog ran off, wouldn't come back when he called. She's quite old, the man said, and pretty obedient.' Andy stretched and rubbed a hand across his stubble. 'But greedy. When she wouldn't come back, he followed the dog's tracks and found her pulling at something. The body was partially covered in fallen leaves, so he took a moment to realise what it was. I don't think the image will be leaving him for a while.'

They moved over to the edge of the police tape that a couple of uniforms were stringing between the trees to fence off the crime scene, and Wessex pointed.

'There. See her? Lying on her back.'

'No, I can't see her.'

'Just the torso is visible. Her bottom half is covered in leaves, that orangey-brown mound.'

He shifted closer, so that she could peer down the length of his arm.

'The oak. See the oak. Follow the trunk down, and she's a couple of yards to the right of that.'

'OK, I . . .' She put a hand over her mouth. 'Fuck.'

'Yes. Not the most pleasant.' He laid a hand on her shoulder. 'And just for the record, the puke's the dog walker's, not mine.'

Day 3

7

Hammering. It took Tess a moment, fighting the mugginess of sleep, to recognise the noise as knuckles on wood. Turning her head, she glanced out of the window. The sun had risen, but the air in the room was still relatively cool. Throwing back the sheet, she climbed out of bed, extracted a T-shirt and shorts from her suitcase and pulled them on. By the time she reached the door, her landlady was halfway back down the stairs.

Madam Chou turned: 'Ah. Miss Tess. I thought you out, *gone*.' She waved a skinny arm in the direction of the gate. Hitching up her lemon-yellow sarong, plastic flip-flops slapping against her soles, she retraced her steps. 'I got mes'age from mines work. Man say got be there for seven. Mee'ing, seven.'

Tess glanced at her watch. It was just past six, so she had an hour. An hour to mainline coffee and get her head straight. The meeting would be about Johnny. Raking, in painstaking detail, over yesterday's explosion. Trying to work out what had gone wrong in a lane that was meant to be clear. It would be vital to her too – it might give her a pretext to ask more about Luke.

She felt Madam Chou pat her arm. 'Worry mee'ing later. I make breakfast.'

'Thank you, but a coffee's fine.'

'Coffee no breakfast. You must eat.' She reached out and plucked at Tess's arm with two bony fingers. 'You skinny enough already.'

Tess smiled, despite herself. 'It's expensive to be this skinny where I come from.'

'In Cambodia, you skinny you poor.' Madam Chou's wrinkled brown face split into a grin. 'Or old, like me. See you breakfast.'

Turning, she slap-slapped her way back down the stairs to the kitchen.

*

The headquarters of Mine Clearance Trust was in a crumbling French colonial mansion overlooking the river Sanger. Evidence of Cambodia's French heritage was everywhere in Battambang's architecture. The mansion was ringed by overgrown lawned gardens, shaded by a giant banyan tree and crowded with heliconia, orchid and lotus flowers. A row of aged Land Cruisers snaked along the edge of the cracked gravel carriage driveway, which cut in a semicircle from rusting iron gates. The mansion itself, once opulent, was decayed: plaster flaking off the walls exposing the brickwork beneath, white paint peeling from windowframes, glass filmy with grime. Two stone statues, armless women in skimpy robes, had once guarded the foot of the stone steps which led to the massive black front door. One remained. The other had toppled off its base and lay tangled in undergrowth, features crude with moss.

Tess made her way up the drive, past the row of silent Land Cruisers. She'd imagined a scrum of early morning activity here, like yesterday morning, but the place was deserted. The lament of the front door when she pushed it open made her wince; the hall she entered was cavernous. Six doors, all of them closed, led off the huge atrium, and an ornate staircase which looked like something from the set of *Gone with the Wind* rose up the wall to her right. She could almost imagine a Southern belle sashaying her way down the stairs, dressed in miles of lilac silk and lace. But the smell quickly put paid to the image – musty-hot and stale – motes of dust floating in a stream of sunlight cutting in from the huge picture window on the landing above her.

Faint sounds of voices were floating down the stairs. She climbed towards them.

Bob MacSween was sitting at his desk, hands clasped behind his head, the expression on his face pure exasperation. He released his hands when he saw Tess in the doorway and motioned her in. There was another man in the room, she saw now, standing in front of the window – tall, thin, with blond hair slicked back from a pale face.

'Tess,' MacSween said. 'Good of you to come.' Glaswegian accent, mellowed with absence. He had told her yesterday that he had left to join the army thirty years ago, and never been back. 'No reason to. Just an alcoholic cunt of a father – 'scuse me, love – mother long since legged it, and my brother, the sensitive soul of the family and the only one I cared about—' He had shrugged. 'Well, Cameron's long gone too.'

MacSween was a huge man, with a latent strength and fitness that could have belonged to someone far younger. Only the lines on his face and the grey peppering his dark crew cut hinted at his age; late fifties, she'd guessed. A tough ex-army sergeant with a veneer of lassitude: as if he'd seen too much of the world already and was no longer impressed with any of it. 'Grab a seat, Tess.'

The only other chair in the room was stacked with papers. She lifted them and, when he gave her no indication where she should put them, laid them on the floor at her feet. When she sat down and glanced around the room, she realised that it wasn't just the chair he was using as a makeshift filing cabinet. Files littered every surface. The cupboard hung open, doors forced apart by its ballooning contents: folders, stacks of paper, books and files, and even a bundle of clothes shoved in one corner. The notice board behind him was covered with scraps of paper and scribbled Post-Its laid one on top of another like crazy paving. A pot of old coffee had leaked its black contents over a stack of folders on the corner of his desk.

MacSween watched her eyeing the room. 'There's a wee bit of method in my madness, though on first inspection you may be hard pressed to see it.' He pulled a face. 'Now, let me introduce you to Tord Jakkleson, my second-in-command and the man responsible for all the admin in this place.' The faded tattoos on his bicep blended and separated as he lifted an arm to gesture towards the man standing in front of the window. 'The Professor, we call him, because he's so goddamn anal.' He winked at Tess. 'Which suits me just fine. Jakkleson, Tess has just left the British Army. She was a combat engineer – a troop commander – with a couple of tours in Afghanistan under her belt. This is her first foray into humanitarian clearing, though I doubt there is much we can teach her about mine clearing after five years with the Sappers. Except how to do it with no damn cash, mebbe.'

Jakkleson stepped forward and held out a hand, briefly flashing a micro-thin gold wristwatch from the cuff of his white linen shirt.

'Good to meet you,' she said, taking his outstretched hand. It was like squeezing marble. His eyes were the palest shade of blue.

'So, Tess, first let me apologise,' MacSween said, when Jakkleson had returned to the window. 'You had a proper shit-show of a day yesterday. Not the introduction to MCT, or this beautiful country we're working in, I would have liked. How're you feeling?'

She managed a smile. 'I'm fine.'

MacSween watched her silently for a moment. 'Come on, Tess.'

'It wasn't great, obviously. But you don't need me to tell you that.' She cast her gaze to the floor. 'Have you seen him? Is he OK?'

'Aye. I dropped by the Red Cross Hospital last night, soon as I heard. He's in a mess, but Dr Khouy Ung, the surgeon who runs the place, says he'll pull through. Johnny was lucky you were there. His Khmer clearers wouldn't have gone in if you hadn't, not after that. Not with the reputation that fucking field is getting. Though it also sounds as if we were lucky not to be carrying two people out on stretchers. Charging into a minefield without even a bloody detector in your hand isn't the best idea, lass. Be careful, eh.'

Lifting a hand, he massaged his eyes, scratched his fingers through the grey-brown stubble on his chin. 'I'm going to be straight with you, Tess, and then I need you to tell us everything – *everything* – you can remember about yesterday. We had another accident six months ago. A fatality. Same minefield. Koh Kroneg it's called, though I'm sure Johnny told you what the locals call it. A very good guy died. I was down in Phnom Penh, so I never got to see him.' His voice faltered. 'The second time in six months we have a serious accident and I start to get worried. It happens in other agencies – this isn't a cosy job. But I still don't like it. I spent the night interviewing the Khmer guys, Johnny's teams, but I didn't get much from them. They're being rather . . . obstructive isn't the right word, but they're jittery as hell. I couldn't seem to get a straight piece of information out of anyone.' His eyes hung closed for a moment. 'Start from when you first arrived at the minefield and *don't miss anything out.*'

Tess dug her bitten nails into her palms and forced herself to hold his gaze across the desk.

A fatality. *Luke.*

She glanced at Jakkleson, framed in a halo of sunlight by the window.

She talked them through what had happened: that there was mist clinging in hollows but, apart from that, visibility was good, that Johnny's teams were sweeping their clearance lanes, all focused, all calm, that it was still early, eight or so, and that no mines had yet been found.

'What was Johnny doing?' MacSween interrupted.

'He was watching his teams.'

'How was he feeling?'

She shrugged. 'Obviously I'd just met him, but he seemed fine, relaxed. He was joking with me.'

'What about?'

'The minefield.'

MacSween raised his eyebrows.

'The White Crocodile,' she corrected. 'The myth.'

'What was he saying?'

'He was talking about the sign, the one that looks like a cave drawing. He was joking about getting a can of paint and giving the crocodile one less leg and a crutch. He said he would have done it, but that you wouldn't be happy. "He would kick my arse" were the exact words he used.'

She saw a flicker of a smile cross MacSween's face. 'It means something in Cambodia. We believe in God, in Father Christmas, in—' He raised his hands, let them fall back to the desk. 'In whatever. Many Khmers believe that the White Crocodile is a bad omen. It's easy to slag it off. Johnny can be flippant but there's a time and a place for that kind of thing. The distinction gets blurred with him sometimes.'

She nodded, listening hard. There was history here. She'd thought that before, when MacSween had told her about Johnny rigging his house with booby traps. She caught his eye, but he didn't smile this time. 'Go on,' he said.

'Johnny's teams had been working for about ten minutes. Then he said he was going into the field to check out a skull that one of the mine clearers had seen in the adjacent lane.'

'A skull?'

'Yes.'

'Human?'

'That's what his clearer said.'

'You went in, didn't you?' Jakkleson interrupted.

She started and glanced over her shoulder at him. It was the first time he'd spoken and she'd got used to the idea that he wouldn't be saying anything. 'Yes.'

'So you saw the skull.'

'No. I didn't see it.'

'Why not?'

She swivelled around in her chair to face him, lifting her hand to shade her eyes from the sunlight.

'I guess I had other things on my mind.'

He seemed about to say something else, but MacSween waved a hand in Jakkleson's direction, silencing him. 'Forget the skull, for the moment at least. We've been told it was Huan's lane. Is that right?'

'Yes, that's what Johnny told me.'

'And Huan was where?'

'Johnny just said he hadn't turned up.'

MacSween looked questioningly at Jakkleson.

'I'll find out,' Jakkleson said.

MacSween nodded. 'Huan. He's been with us for a while.' He wrote something down on a pad of yellow paper, already covered in his notes.

'Where was the mine Johnny stood on?' he asked, looking up. 'Did he miss the marker somehow and walk too far down the lane into ground that hadn't yet been cleared?'

'I'm not sure.'

'It's important. Take your time. Think about it.'

Tess dropped her gaze, trying to picture the field in the seconds leading up to the detonation. Mine tape. Johnny, confident, cocky even. The quiet bang that was the mine exploding. The tide of panic. Clearers running. Mud. Heat. Blood. The screaming. The taste of fear like tinfoil in her mouth.

What else?

Where was the metre length of wood – painted red and white – that Huan would have laid across his lane to indicate how far he had cleared?

'The marker—'

'Was where?' MacSween prompted.

The grip of a hand on her arm. Men huddled shock-faced around the Land Cruisers. Her combat boots dragging at the muscles of her legs. The leaves of the tree casting flickering shadows over Johnny's face. The splintered bones of his leg visible through rags of flesh—

'What else?'

She shook her head.

'*Oh, come on.*' Openly scornful now.

'Jakkleson.' A warning tone from MacSween.

She met his gaze. Then she sensed someone else. She glanced behind her and saw Alex leaning against the filing cabinet by the door. He was wearing the same clothes she'd seen him in at the hospital yesterday and he looked wrecked.

She turned back to MacSween. 'I'm sorry. I didn't see it. But I didn't pass it.'

'The marker?' he asked.

'Yes, the marker. I didn't pass it.'

'Are you sure?'

'I was looking down as I was running. I definitely didn't pass it.'

'A hundred per cent sure?'

Tess nodded. 'A hundred per cent.'

MacSween leaned back in his chair. 'So if you're sure you didn't pass the marker, either someone had moved it, which is unlikely, or the mine Johnny stood on was in ground that had already been cleared. So maybe Huan missed a mine.' He steepled his fingers. 'And if he had only cleared just beyond it, he wouldn't have walked over it, wouldn't have had a chance to set it off himself. There are quite a few minimum-metal plastic anti-personnel mines out here that are fucking hard to detect.' He sat back and sighed. 'That's one theory at least – a sensible one. Anything else?'

'No,' she said, then paused. 'Yes, one thing.'

MacSween tilted forward, laying his hands flat on the desktop. 'What?'

'The helicopter. It didn't come. We radioed it from the field but it didn't turn up. We radioed again but there was no an-swer. So Johnny had to be taken to hospital by road. Our first-aiders bandaged his wounds as best they could in the field, but it's still a miracle he didn't bleed to death during the journey with the extent of his injuries.'

MacSween turned to the window again. 'Jakkleson?'

Jakkleson shrugged.

'Check it out. I know we don't own the bloody thing, but we pay those fucking fly boys enough to be there when we need them.'

Jakkleson nodded. MacSween turned back to Tess. 'That it?'

'Yes,' she said with a nod.

'Sure?'

'Yes,' she repeated, holding his gaze across the desktop. 'I'm sure. There's nothing else.'

Except Luke.

MacSween sat back. 'OK. Well, I'll need to talk to Huan, but a missed mine sounds the most probable scenario. And if that's the case, then Johnny's accident was just that – terrible and totally avoidable, but an accident all the same.' He looked towards the door. 'What do you think, Alex?'

Alex pulled at one of his shirtsleeves as if the material was chafing his skin, and gave a half-shrug. 'Makes sense.'

'Jakkleson?'

'It sounds like a sensible conclusion.' There was an edge to his voice. 'But—'

'But what?'

'But you know what Johnny's like.'

Tess caught the warning look that MacSween shot him.

'Oh, come on, MacSween.'

'Jakkleson.'

'He's a maverick. You *know* what he's like.'

'Jakkleson, enough.'

Pushing himself away from the window, Jakkleson stepped forward, his face tight with anger. 'You know that Johnny's a complete bloody liability, MacSween, so why the *hell* are you—'

'*Goddammit, Jakkleson.*' MacSween exploded from his seat. 'I said *enough*. I will *not* have that kind of talk.'

They faced each other across the desk, the air in the small room crackling with animosity. Finally, Jakkleson turned away, his shoulders rigid. He made his way back to the window and stood, staring out, arms folded tight across his chest. MacSween slammed both hands down on his blotter, then, as if he had short-circuited, he slumped, silent and glazed, into his chair. It was some time before he spoke again.

'This is a bloody tough country to work in. It's corrupt. It's dangerous. There are a hell of a lot of people out there –' he gestured irritably towards the window – 'with their own agendas. Cambodian military and government who would seize any opportunity to cause trouble for NGOs like MCT if it meant more money to line their own damn pockets. Donors who'd run a mile if they got a whiff of anything they didn't like. We're in the middle of it, trying to keep everyone happy *and* trying to make some kind of a difference for the poor bastards who have to live in this country. This whole Johnny issue could be a complete *nightmare* for us.' He sighed, a man on the edge of his patience. 'It sounds harsh, but I have to protect the operation because we're making a real difference out here. And I *know* it's what Johnny would want. If we start using words like maverick, we open ourselves up for every dickhead to take a pot shot at us. Does everyone understand that?'

He looked from one face to the next. When he met Tess's eyes, she looked back evenly and nodded.

'Good, right. I'm glad we've got that straight.' He sat back. 'I'm going to suspend clearing for a couple of days until everyone calms down. We need to protect our Khmer mine clearers – keep them sensible – so I'm going to move Johnny's troop from that part of the field.' Hefting himself to his feet, he turned to look at a map of Battambang Province tacked to the wall behind him. The minefields were marked on it in red, so many that the map looked diseased – Koh Kroneg the largest by far. He traced his finger side to side before planting it. 'Here, they can join Alex's troop at Sung Pir village on the eastern edge. Their case is urgent and there's a lot to clear. A kid lost his foot in the grounds of the school last week. The village is at the bottom of a steep valley, which has been deforested. There's a logging operation up there. Illegal, of course, like most of them are. I reckon some of the mines are moving into the village with the floodwater. We're at the tail end of the rainy season now, so the ground is already sodden. The forecast's for more rain, which is going to make things even more fucked up than they already are. Tess, I'm going to ask you to take over Johnny's troop, for the moment at least.' He twisted back to face them. 'That OK with you?'

She nodded.

'Good. As I said, I've given the Khmer lads a couple of days off to get their heads back in order, so I want you lot to take time off too. Go home. Take a day off.' He glanced at Tess and rolled his eyes. 'One day on, one day off.' His gaze found Alex. 'Get some bloody sleep. And we'll start again the day after to-morrow. Now get out of here. *Go.*' He swivelled to face the window. 'And Jakkleson—'

'Yes?'

'Cut the divisive crap.'

*

Tess stood leaning against the windowsill on the landing and watched Alex climb into one of the Land Cruisers below and drive off. A minute or two later, as she pulled open the front door, MacSween caught up with her. He seemed to have shrunk a couple of inches and aged a couple of years in the time it took to reach the bottom of the stairs.

'I'm going to the hospital to catch up with Dr Ung, see how Johnny is. Want to come along for the ride?'

She turned to face him, her hand on the doorjamb. 'I've already ticked the hospital off my list of places of interest to visit in Battambang.'

MacSween met her gaze with a weary smile.

49

'I'm only going to stay for a few minutes and then you get to sink yourself into a bottle of gin, or whatever you're planning to do for the rest of the day. There's a kid, Ret S'Mai, who works there helping out Dr Ung with odd jobs. I have a little gift to give him. I'm sure he'd like to meet you, and it would be interesting for you to meet him too. He's a bit of local colour, if I can put it that way. He's a good kid who's had a bad run of luck.'

What she really wanted to do was to go back to Madam Chou's, lock the door and sleep for a year, then sit and think for the next two, but time spent with MacSween meant time to talk about MCT.

'So you're using me as some sort of consolation prize?'

'They don't get to see many Western women out here.'

'He'll have posters of Cameron Diaz and Emily Blunt stuck on his wall. Don't you think he'll be a tiny bit disappointed when I turn up? All dolled up and not a hair out of place. I'm afraid that I forgot to pack the red one-piece, or the blond wig for that matter.'

'A bird in the hand, as they say.'

'Is worth two stuck on the wall. I hope that's not supposed to be a compliment.'

With a wry smile, MacSween held out an arm and guided her down the drive to his Land Cruiser.

'Local colour?' she murmured, as he opened the door for her.

'Aye. You'll see.'

*

He found first gear and hauled the Land Cruiser out of the

drive. Scenery flowed backwards past the open windows: huge, crumbling colonial houses to their right, many of them bases for other NGOs; flashes of sunlight on the river to their left through the bushes and trees shading its bank; a pack of skinny dogs fighting for scraps in a stinking mountain of rubbish; two children leading a grey cow down the side of the potholed road, all angles and dirty stretched skin. It was 10 a.m. It was hot. The Land Cruiser was a rusting hulk, like all the others MCT owned. Tess's back was slippery with sweat before they'd even reached the end of the street, and she didn't need to ask to know that the air conditioning was broken.

She tuned into what MacSween was saying: 'This province is known as the rice bowl of Cambodia. It's all small villages, paddy fields and farmland, incredibly fertile. There's few tourists who bother to come up this way though, so you'll get to see the proper, unspoilt Cambodia. Problem is it's also mined up the yin-yangs.' He took a hand from the wheel to mop at his forehead with a handkerchief. 'As far as I see it, lass, the land-mine problem is by far the biggest problem Cambodia's got. It drives everything else. Your typical Khmer doesn't have enough to eat because the land mines stop them working their fields. And there's no social security or any of that nonsense. No opportunity to sit around watching *Coronation Street* and drinking Special Brew while some other bugger pays for you and your kids. Out here, they either find a way to feed themselves and their family or they starve. Eighty thousand kiddies a year dead from fucking malnutrition and sicknesses. That's the ones who aren't being exploited.' He turned to glance at her. 'And the Western world – the moneyed world – sees land mines as just another trendy cause. We were top of the tree fifteen years ago when Princess Di was around, but now we've been shoved out by one-legged lesbians or whatever the fuck the donating public is into this week. And we can't do shit without money.'

He braked suddenly, cursing, as a moped with an unfeasible number of squawking, flapping chickens tied by their ankles to its pannier swerved wildly into their path.

'What do you mean they get exploited? Who exploits?' she asked, when they were back on the road, the moped cackling and wobbling into the distance behind them.

'Other Khmers: corrupt military, police, government officials. Sexual tourists and paedophiles from the West.' He nodded at the maze of streets beyond the window. 'Cambodia is full of the fuckers. International corporations who see things like the logging potential here and realise they can strip the forests for a pittance because the Khmers in power are so corrupt. Foreign governments and NGOs who think they know what's best for countries like this, but who often have their own agendas, or simply don't have a damn clue. When a country is in this much of a mess, everyone wants a piece—' He broke off to brake, controlled this time, and slowed almost to a crawl as he changed down and swung left on to the narrow concrete bridge crossing the Sanger. Crammed together on its southern bank, like cardboard boxes on a landfill site, was a shanty town of bamboo huts, many on stilts over the water. The edge of the river was clogged with rubbish, and a couple of streams of dark brown filth wound their way from the huts to the water – the river where they met ballooning, thick and coffee-coloured. A little girl was squatting naked, relieving herself by the water's edge, oblivious to Tess's gaze.

On the other side of the Sanger was the main part of the town, still touched by faded grandeur: more ornate two- and three-storey buildings, their facades crumbling; potholed boulevards streaming with mopeds and bicycles, a few cars trying to force their way through; the huge, low building housing the marketplace, churning and chaotic, bustling with people, animals, colour and noise. The smell of sewage mixed with spices, incense and tobacco, wood smoke from cooking fires, the charry stench of fumes from countless exhausts.

'And your Khmers in the street,' MacSween continued, 'from the old to the very young, kiddies, bairns for Christ's sake, have to put up with exploitation and abuse.' He lifted a hand to express their helplessness, then slammed his palm back on the wheel with a force that made Tess jump. 'So that's what we're trying to do, lass. Eliminate the land-mine problem, change their fate.' He glanced across. 'And you need to keep that in mind, or you might start wondering whether the hell it's all worth it. Because none of this is easy.'

8

Five minutes after MacSween's Land Cruiser had disappeared down the road and out of sight, Jakkleson stepped on to the landing. Laying his feet heel to toe, so as not to make a sound, he moved over to the banister and stood for a moment, listening. MCT House should be empty, he knew, but for what he was about to do he had to be certain. He stood motionless for a few moments, his ears straining to pick up even the tiniest sound. And when he was satisfied there was none, he retraced his steps and pulled the door shut.

Moving over to the window, he cast one last look around the garden: deserted. His hands were trembling slightly as he drew the shutters across the window, blocking out the sun and the limp still forms of the trees sweltering in the heat. Then, in semi-darkness, he made his way across the room to the filing cabinet. Ignoring his beautiful blonde wife and his two perfect daughters smiling out from their silver frame on its top, he withdrew the cabinet key from his pocket and slid it into the lock.

Passing over the top three drawers, he bent straight to the bottom one. Pulling it out as far as its runners would allow, he hooked his hands underneath it and, with a combination of lifting and wiggling, managed to free it from its track. Breathing a little more heavily now, he lifted it clear and laid it on the floor to his side. Then he reached back and scooped up the file that lay flush with the bottom of the filing cabinet.

Still crouching, he flicked quickly through it, just to make sure that its contents were complete. He gave a brief, satisfied nod. It was all here. Nothing disturbed, nothing missing.

Moving back to the desk, he dug in his pocket for a lighter. The blue flame leapt to meet the bottom of the sheaf of papers. He held his hand steady as the papers blackened, the flame unnaturally bright in the half-light as it caught and raced up the edge. Dropping the burning papers into the metal bin at his feet, he stood and watched until he was absolutely sure they were nothing more than ash. Then he returned to the filing cabinet, carefully slotted the bottom drawer back into place and locked it again.

9

The hospital grounds were silent apart from the buzz of insects cutting intermittently through the hot air and the sound of the Land Cruiser's engine groaning as it cooled. MacSween opened the boot and took out a framed sheet of parchment-style A4 paper: gold letters scrolling across the page, the Mine Clearance Trust logo, navy blue and white, embossed at the top, a name written in fountain pen across the centre of the page. He locked the Land Cruiser and together he and Tess started across the courtyard towards the common-room building.

'Is that the gift?' she asked, as they walked.

'Aye. It's a certificate, a mock certificate, if I'm being accurate, for graduating from MCT mine-clearance training.'

'Why are you giving him a mock certificate? Did you fire him and feel guilty?'

MacSween rolled his eyes. 'Such a poor impression of me already. I got him a certificate because he was desperate to become a mine clearer and couldn't. Him and his dad. They were both halfway through training with us.'

'Why didn't they finish?'

'Ret S'Mai and his father were on a moped which was involved in an accident. Dad was killed. Ret S'Mai's hands got caught in the back wheel while it was still spinning.' He raised a hand and made a slicing movement with the other across the base of his fingers. 'His fingers were torn off – all of them on one hand, three on the other.'

Tess met his gaze. 'That's terrible.'

'Aye. It wasn't pleasant. So that's why I had the certificate made. To try to cheer the kid up. Also I feel a bit—' He tailed off with a shrug.

Tess glanced across; there had been something in his tone. 'A bit?'

'You're nosy, aren't you?'

'It comes with the female territory, I'm afraid.'

'Aye, well. I feel a little responsible, I suppose.'

'Responsible? Why?'

They had reached the common-room building. MacSween stopped, his hand on the door.

'It was an MCT Land Cruiser that hit them.'

'What?' She paused as the information sank in. 'You were – *were you driving?*'

'*No.*'

'Then who?'

He had begun tapping his fingertips against the doorframe, just gently. 'Johnny was driving.'

'Was it Johnny's *fault?*'

'No. It was . . . one of those things. Ret S'Mai's dad had been drinking. Johnny had also had a few. It shouldn't have happened and the consequences were fucked up for Ret S'Mai and his family, but no one was to blame. This is Cambodia. The Green Cross Code doesn't apply out here. Drink-drive laws don't apply out here, and we live with the fallout.'

The room they entered was light and airy and ran almost the entire length of the building. Tables and chairs crowded the near end; the wood floor at the far end was covered with blue mats, gym bars climbed the walls, and soft shapes and exercise balls of various sizes were scattered around. Double doors in the opposite wall were propped open and through them Tess could see the obstacle course she had noticed yesterday from the window of the hospital building.

Groups of Khmer mine victims were gathered around the tables, chatting and laughing. They quietened when they noticed her and MacSween.

'*Johm riab sua.*' He raised a hand. '*Neuv ai naa, Ret S'Mai.*'

One of the men pointed to the obstacle course. Outside, a young boy was helping a middle-aged woman with a thigh-length prosthetic climb the wooden obstacle-course stairs. Her expression was a blend of concentration and fear as she clung to the banister, hauling herself up each step more with her arms than her legs.

'That's Ret S'Mai,' MacSween said in a low voice. 'Dr Ung's done me a favour and given him a job here helping mine victims with their physiotherapy. Cambodians believe that anyone who's lost part of their body has also lost part of their mind, so it makes mine victims both an object of ridicule *and* unemployable. It's incredibly tough for them to find jobs. And if they can't work, and don't have relatives who'll support them, they starve.'

They waited while the woman completed her ascent and stopped to lean against the rail at the top, chest heaving. After Ret S'Mai had helped her down and to a chair, he trailed across the yard to join them. He was so tiny and slight that he could have passed for ten had he been a Westerner, but MacSween had told Tess that he was fifteen. His head was disproportionately large – but his features were tiny, nose a folded stub of skin, mouth a pucker. MacSween clapped him on the shoulder, almost tilting him off balance with the force of his hand.

'Working hard, I see.'

'*Baat.*' He smiled shyly and tiny black eyes skipped from MacSween to Tess and back.

'Ret S'Mai, this is Tess. She's joined us for a time to help train more local mine clearers.'

Tess extended a hand – stopped short – silently cursing herself for her stupidity. But Ret S'Mai just grinned and raised a skinny arm. The fingers on the hand he had raised, his right, were missing completely, as if someone had ripped them out with a pair of pliers leaving him with nothing but four pale dents and a twisted thumb.

MacSween stepped forward, holding up the certificate to cover her embarrassment. 'I've got a wee present for you, lad.'

Ret S'Mai was trembling as he leaned forward to study it, trailing his thumb over the gold embossed letters, over the blue and white of the MCT logo, pinching the frame between his thumb and the flat of his hand and tugging it from MacSween's grasp.

'How are things, kid?' MacSween asked, when Ret S'Mai had finished studying the certificate.

'I very busy. Many mine victims here.' His big head bobbed. 'Dr Ung tell me about Johnny accident. I sorry. Very sorry.'

'Thank you, Ret S'Mai. It was a hell of a shock.'

'He going to be OK. Dr Ung says.'

'I'm going to talk to Dr Ung now. See what he has to say.' He reached out and ruffled Ret S'Mai's hair. 'Look after yourself, kiddo. *Juab kh'nia.*'

'*Lia suhn hao-y*, Mr Bob,' Ret S'Mai said. Then he turned

to Tess. Tiny black eyes stared up at her; the stump of a blunt palm felt its way into her hand. 'Come again. Please. I like you come.' A grin parted his small mouth.

Tess shivered, despite herself. 'Of course I will,' she said, with a brief smile. 'It's nice to meet you.'

10

Running, which in her early twenties, before she met Luke, had been about burning off excess energy, had become Tess's way of escaping, of letting her body and mind float free. Ducking out of the hospital gates, she stood on the quiet street for a moment, sucking in a couple of breaths, jiggling her arms and legs to get the blood flowing. The sky was that rare, perfect blue over a green English field. But it was fiercely hot: the dense heat peculiar to Asia that made every breath an effort, even when standing still.

Sweat ran into her eyes and darkened her T-shirt as she ran down the road, dodging the steady stream of bicycles and mopeds, whose drivers honked and shouted encouragement; a couple of women washing clothes in a plastic bucket, who raised their eyebrows at her; a gaggle of tiny children who danced in front of her waving and pulling faces, dodging out of the way, giggling, just as she reached them. A dog slunk out from behind a fence and kept pace with her for a few steps, but it must have been too hot and lethargic to put up a proper chase because when she looked back it was lying on the kerb, its tongue lolling.

She crossed straight over the intersection, following the curve of the river on the quieter, southern side, past white-painted two-storey houses and traditional bamboo huts leaning drunkenly on stilts over the water, all somnolent in the midday heat.

Though she tried to focus only on the sound of her soles hitting the cracked tarmac, her mind kept orbiting back to Luke, to Johnny.

Luke who couldn't go to bed until every light had been switched off, every appliance unplugged, every lock checked and double-checked. Luke who couldn't leave the bathroom until the towels were hung on the rail in perfect rectangles, the shampoos ranged from small to large on the shelf above the bath. Luke who had to load the dishwasher because Tess could never do it right. Luke, who was so controlled, so *controlling* – because he was making up for all the years of childhood during which, as the son of a drug-addicted single mother with a ruinous lifestyle, he had no control over anything, even his own body.

She slowed to a walk – shaking out her arms and legs as she went – turning right across the bridge over the Sanger, letting her eyes skim along the water. In the middle of the bridge she stopped and leaned against the concrete parapet, tilting forward so that she could see the muddy water below. From where she stood there were two towns. One hemming the banks of the river: alive, moving, a flood of cars, mopeds and bikes, people walking, running, shouting, jostling, lights, colour and noise. Its reflection, the silent, phantasmal twin.

Coincidences were for romantic comedies, not real life, and as such she was pretty sure that Luke's death and Johnny's injury were connected. But how had Johnny been targeted? How had the person who laid that mine make sure that Johnny, not somebody else, would step on it?

She looked back down at the water below her, and she pictured him walking towards Huan's lane, his detector slung over his shoulder, visor propped over the top of his head, casual, too casual because he'd done it a thousand times. Because he was arrogant and flippant. *He's a bit of a joker – goes with the posh-boy territory, I suppose.*

The skull: *It's probably just a fucking rock.*

Whatever she thought of her profession, she knew that at its most basic level it was a game. A game in which the mine clearer needed to be cleverer than the person they were playing against, the one who laid the mine. Whenever a mine clearer felt they were being led, they needed to ask why? Because what normally works is the simple things.

She remembered an incident the Royal Engineers had faced during her most recent tour of duty in Afghanistan last summer – the incident which had finally made up her mind to leave the army when her five-year service commission was up a year later. It had stayed with her for months afterwards.

Their Engineers' company had been on a route-clearance operation in Helmand Province, a land with few roads, where routes were easy for the Taliban to predict and target with land mines and IEDs. One critical Engineers' role was to check and clear these roads before other troops used them.

Their company had barely left the base, were nowhere near their target, so were driving fast, on a tarmacked road which was in constant use and considered safe as houses. She could see it now: the road, a thin black strip cutting through the pale landscape, on one side a desert plain, endless and featureless, on the other a rocky overhang. Through the grimy glass of the windscreen, she watched the Land Rover in front, its desert camouflage colours pale against the black tarmac, the soldiers inside young – most not yet out of their teens – and full of bravado. Beyond the Land Rover, she saw a landslide blocking the road. She thought it was trying to tell her something, but in the speed, heat and dust of the moment she couldn't think what. She saw the soldiers laughing, saw the flash of brake lights as the Land Rover reached the landslide and slowed, saw it turn off the tarmac and put two wheels on the sandy verge. The sound of the anti-tank mine exploding drowned out the sound of her screaming at them to stop.

The skull.

Planted by someone who knew that a cautious Khmer mine clearer, jumpy as hell, his mind full of myth, would call in his boss when he saw it, particularly if it wasn't in his lane. That he wouldn't want to deal with it himself. Planted by someone who knew that the boss had a weakness, knew exactly how to exploit it. Planted by someone who knew that the boss, in the White Crocodile minefield that day, was Johnny.

11

As she left the outskirts of Battambang, lightning snapped across the sky, illuminating gathering storm clouds with flashes of neon white. A crack of thunder sounded, barrels rolling down stairs. Another, closer. The countryside was a depthless sea green under this brooding ceiling. The long grass in the paddy fields rippled and bowed and the palm trees were beginning to sway, their broad leaves heaving and dipping in the wind. A branch blew across the potholed road in front of the Land Cruiser. Tess braked, the wheels screeched, and for one heart-stopping second she thought she might lose traction and skid off the road into the waterlogged ditch beside it. But the huge tyres held and she accelerated away again, her heartbeat slowing as the wheels ate up the tarmac. She passed a family of peasants wheeling a wooden handcart piled high with cut bamboo, glancing up at the sky with harried expressions. She beeped her horn and caught sight of the family in her rear-view mirror, the children dancing and waving, the parents herding them along, faces unchanged in reflection.

The storm broke and a curtain of rain swept across the fields, flattening the long grass in its wake, engulfing the Land Cruiser. She slowed and flicked the wipers to maximum. They fought against the downpour, sloshing water from the windscreen, clearing visibility, losing it again. She was still driving too fast, but she had to get to Koh Kroneg before dark. Going into a minefield after sunset would be madness.

This was madness anyway, she knew. But she had to get another look at the clearance lane where Johnny was hurt.

Forcing her attention back to the road, Tess drove on, squinting through the windscreen, trying to pick out landmarks. At first she could find nothing familiar, but then, just as she began to feel uneasy, a village she recognised swung into view. Twin palms swaying in the wind, rickety huts clustered tightly around a corral of animals. One hut on the edge of the cluster, its walls blackened and burnt-out. The track was a kilometre or so further on. She slowed again and wound down her window. Rain lashed into the car, freezing cold down her cheek, but at least she could see. A track wound off to her left – not the one. Another – too narrow. Then, a few hundred metres further on, she saw a third, just wide enough to take a 4 x 4, bearing heavy tyre marks flooded with rainwater.

Changing down, she eased her foot off the accelerator, minimising the revs. The Land Cruiser leapt off the road and sank into the mud, bucking and slithering like a rodeo bull, but its wheels kept turning, pulling her forward. Tangled bushes on either side dragged against the windows; the mud sucked at the tyres. A hundred metres further and the front wheels bit deep into a rut and span uselessly.

'Fuck.' She couldn't get trapped out here alone, in the dark. And what the hell would MacSween say when he discovered one of his clearers and one of his Land Cruisers were missing? Reducing the revs, she reversed a fraction, jammed the vehicle into second gear and crawled forward. 'Come on, damn you.' The tyres slipped and grabbed, lost their traction again, and the Land Cruiser slumped back down into the rut with a metallic groan. Pushing back panic, she tried again, easing her foot gently on to the accelerator, just giving enough revs to get the wheels moving without turning them so fast that they lost grip and span. 'Please, *please, come on.*' Finally, the Land Cruiser bit into the muddy bank of the rut and hauled her upwards. She exhaled in a burst of pent-up tension.

Just beyond the third village, Tess turned off the track and cut the engine. She sat for a moment, squinting out through the steamed-up windscreen. The landscape was already familiar. Koh Kroneg, shrouded in a mist of warm rain. She looked towards the village. Deserted. The animals were huddled together beneath the huts, ears flattened against the weather, huge eyes watching the metal intruder warily.

Hauling herself into the back seat, she slid the flak jacket over her head, squirming to fix the fastenings in the constricted space, then grabbed her detector and battery pack. The rain was still tapping on the side of the Land Cruiser, but lighter now, easing off. Nervous, limbs tingling, she swung the door open and eased herself to the ground.

There was a movement at the front of the Land Cruiser – one of the animals? Her detector held in front of her like a club, she made her way around the vehicle. A tiny girl – five or six – was standing by the bonnet. She had a soft oval face the colour of chocolate milk and huge, solemn dark eyes. A torn purple T-shirt, much too big, flopped off one shoulder; its hem sagged around her ankles. Where had she come from? She hadn't been there as Tess was pulling in.

'*Johm riab sua,*' Tess said gently, squatting down.

'*Johm riab sua.*' Her voice was only just louder than the whisper of rain. Her head dipped and a curtain of matted hair fell across her face. Both feet were bare, caked in mud, one balanced on top of the other in an agony of shyness. One skinny arm trailed across the Land Cruiser's bonnet; her tiny fingers rested on the MCT logo.

'Whiecocodi,' she said suddenly, still looking at her feet.

Tess leaned forward. 'Sweetheart, tell me again. What did you say?'

'Whie Crocodil.' Her tiny index finger began to pick at the logo. '*Laan ch'nual. Pel yohp.*' Her other hand was missing, the arm finishing in a messy brown scar just below the elbow, the skin of her upper arm stretched and ridged like overstressed elastic.

'I don't understand,' Tess said, gently.

The little girl was trembling. She was so thin; so exposed. '*Laan ch'nual. Pel yohp,*' she repeated and this time her gaze slid towards the minefield. 'Whie Crocodil *laan ch'nual.*'

Tess glanced over her shoulder, following the child's gaze, and saw the red-and-white mine tape fencing the mined land. She turned back to face the girl, suddenly horribly conscious of the time.

'It's OK. I know about the White Crocodile, but I'll be safe because I'm a mine clearer.' She pointed to her flak jacket. She had to get moving. 'Sweetheart, go back to the village. You must go back home. *Now.*'

Tess laid her hand on the girl's shoulder and tried to turn her, but the child resisted with surprising strength. Her mouth formed a firm line and she looked up, meeting Tess's eyes fully now for the first time.

'*Whie Crocodil laan ch'nual. Night-night! Laan ch'nual. Pel yohp. Pel yohp.*'

Then she pushed Tess's hand away gently, turned around and

walked back towards the village, soon lost in the twilight.

*

Tess crossed the sodden grass to the field through the drizzle. Suddenly disconcerted, she stopped. The lone tree – Johnny's tree – with its knot of branches and thick, dark foliage, looked different; the contours of the mined land rose and fell with a rhythm that felt totally unfamiliar; the clearance lanes weren't placed in a pattern that matched her memory. And – the sign had gone.

She looked back over her shoulder to the solid, safe shape of the Land Cruiser, and the village beyond it. The sun was low now, dipping below fast-moving grey clouds, skimming the roofs of the wooden huts, orange deepening to red. A pall of smoke rose from one hut, candlelight flickered in the window of another, and a distant peal of laughter rang out. She was infused with a sense of weightlessness – of how easy it would be to turn back.

Ducking under the warning tape, she inched up to the start of Huan's lane.

It *was* the same. The same tree, the same curves and undulations that she had seen yesterday morning. The same soft ground: grass, mud, puddles reflecting a fiery sky, the imprint of running boots. She gripped the metal detector.

'You know it's clear,' she whispered. 'Just walk.' But it didn't feel right, walking into a lane – *this* lane, in *this* minefield – without checking every square centimetre of it first. She didn't have the time.

Trying not to think too much about anything, she stepped forward, slotting her boot softly into one of the footprints. Nothing. *Well, what did you expect?* She took another step and another. The ground slurped as it caught and released her boots. Every few steps she stopped and looked around her, compelled by an urge to keep checking she was alone.

By the edge of the crater under the tree, she stopped. Cloudy water was pooled at the bottom. The sides glistened red in the dipping sun. Hesitantly, she reached out and started tracing her detector in circles around the crater's rim. The circles became smaller and smaller. Sliding the detector into the puddle at the bottom of the crater, she pressed until she felt it snag on mud. The detector screeched, and her heart almost jumped out of her chest. Dropping it, she fell back on to her knees, staring down into the pool of water. This was the epicentre of the anti-personnel mine's explosion. There *couldn't* be anything else down there. But if she really believed that, what had brought her back here in the first place?

Pulling the detector from the crater and laying it aside, she slumped to her knees in the mud, rolled up her sleeves and leaned into the puddle, splashing handfuls of water over the edge on to the ground behind her. Grabbing the detector once more, she passed it over the base of the crater. The same screech. There was definitely something there, and not just a mine fragment. This was something big, heavy with metal.

Lying on her front, the thin shaft of her mine prodder in hand, Tess slithered to the edge of the crater, just far enough that she could reach to its base without putting any pressure there. She slipped the prodder into the muddy soil. It snagged on a solid object immediately. She pulled it out and moved it a couple of centimetres to the left. Something solid, again. Dropping the prodder, she started scooping at the earth with her fingers. Her hand sliced on something sharp. She snatched it away, saw a cut pop red against the damp white of her skin; licked it, tasting blood and dirt. Ignoring it, she reached back into the crater and began digging again, her heart slamming in her chest.

It took her a few more minutes to uncover the whole thing. Olive-green metal, black stencilled writing. She wiped her fingers across the letters and stared in disbelief.

An anti-tank mine, Jesus. She pushed herself on to her knees, wiped a muddy hand across her eyes and looked again.

Its fuse had been removed. Someone had laid this thing *under* the anti-personnel mine that blew Johnny's foot off, with the idea that it would sympathetically detonate when the anti-personnel mine triggered. Johnny would have been vaporised if the anti-tank mine had blown. But something had gone wrong, the sympathetic detonation hadn't worked – which was why he was still alive. And there was no way Huan could have missed this. It would have sent his detector haywire.

Tess unearthed the rest of the device, lifted it gingerly from its muddy bed and started back towards the Land Cruiser, the weapon cradled under her arm. Though she knew it wouldn't explode – it had no detonator – her muscles were still stiff with fear. Stowing the mine carefully in the Land Cruiser's boot, she took off her flak jacket and tucked it gently underneath, so it wouldn't thump against the floor of the boot on the long drive home.

The orange of the sky had faded now and the sun had dipped

behind the trees, a claret glow in the distance. A couple of water buffalo were watching her from an adjacent paddy field, their coats russet in the waning light. She waved a hand at them. They ignored her, big brown eyes impervious. On an impulse, she jogged towards them, waving both arms. They lowered their heads and backed away until the ropes around their necks snagged taut. She stood and watched them for a moment, regretting having frightened them, then turned and walked slowly back to the Land Cruiser.

12

Manchester, England

The Brookses' house, with its bay window, new plastic double glazing, neat square of lawn and gravel drive, in a leafy Altrincham street, was textbook middle-class. Andy Wessex stood outside for a few moments, shuffling his feet in the slushy sleet on the pavement, clutching Carly Brooks's passport – the only identification they'd found on the girl's body – and getting his thoughts ordered before he pushed open the wrought-iron gate.

The Brookses must feel happy here, he thought, among their own kind. Hard to imagine tragedy lurching down these suburban streets.

He was from a different world – he'd grown up in a council flat on Lancashire Hill, just outside the centre of Stockport. The middle of three boys in an all-male household. It hadn't predisposed him to be relaxed socially with women, or to understand them, and he was very comfortable in the knowledge that, at his age, marriage and children, a house in a quiet street like this one, had eluded him. He could never help thinking about quantity at a time like this, though he knew it was coming at the problem from the wrong angle. Did the Brookses have more than one child? He hoped for their sake that they had. But did it mean anything? Could you balance the life of one against the death of another, and come out even? Or didn't it work like that? He genuinely didn't know.

Wessex hadn't had time to form an impression of what the

parents might be like. But the man who answered the door was exactly what he would have expected if he had: mid-forties, running to fat around the middle but otherwise in decent shape, a blue-and-white striped shirt, the cuffs rolled up a couple of times, tucked into navy-blue suit trousers, greying hair neatly clipped. Questioning hazel eyes met Andy's.

He held up his warrant card. 'DI Wessex, South Manchester CID. May I come in?'

They had a brief dance on the doorstep, Wessex trying to step in, Mr Brooks still grappling with his confusion at what a policeman might want with them.

'Who is it, Bill?'

A tiny Asian woman with a round face and huge, gentle brown eyes appeared in the hall behind Mr Brooks. She was wearing a hot-pink T-shirt and an ankle-length skirt that could have been stitched from Joseph's Technicolor dreamcoat. The contrast between her and her husband was startling, as if he had plucked her from a flock of exotic rainforest birds.

'The police. My wife, Jintana.'

'Detective Inspector Andy Wessex.' He addressed himself to her, reaching past her husband to shake her outstretched hand. 'May I come in?'

'You already have. But – yes, of course. That's fine.'

Wessex followed them down the hall, past a row of A4 photographs in black frames: the Brookses on their wedding day, framed in the arched doorway of a church; an older couple, his parents by the look of them; the daughter sitting cross-legged on a sofa, unmistakably Asian-looking, the British half of her genes coming through, in appearance terms at least, only in her soft hazel eyes. Indisputably the girl whose passport he had in his suit jacket pocket.

He couldn't see signs of any other children.

Entering the sitting room was like stepping into a page of *Living* magazine, all muted beiges and creams. Two beige linen-covered sofas set at right angles to each other on the cream carpet, the three-seater facing a credit-card-thin plasma TV, a glass coffee table bearing a big colour edition of *Flora Britannica*. Every door he stepped through to do this – to break this news – opened on to a complete world, like a stage set. He'd done the same only last week in Longsight, the mother of a junkie. Different decor. Hadn't been any easier.

Mrs Brooks perched on the edge of one of the sofas and gestured for Wessex to sit down.

'I'm fine standing, thank you. But you sit down please, Mr Brooks.'

The couple exchanged glances.

'I'd rather not. Can't you just tell us what this is about?'

Wessex shuffled his feet. The first time he had told someone that their child was dead, he had skirted around the issue, believing that it was easier to let the bereaved acclimatise degree by degree. By the third time, he'd realised that getting straight to the point was kinder.

'We've found the body of a girl in woods in south Manchester. I'm very sorry, but we think it's your daughter, Carly.'

Mrs Brooks stared resolutely back at him. 'It can't be her.'

Wessex suddenly felt immensely sad. 'I'm sorry. There hasn't been a mistake—'

She lifted her hands to halt his flow, let them fall back to her lap. 'No, really it can't be.'

'Mrs Brooks—'

'We spoke to her this morning. On Skype. She called from Sri Lanka. She's staying with my brother and his family. They run a wildlife project, protecting turtles. She's taking a year off travelling before starting university next September.'

'But I have her passport.' He pulled the passport from his pocket. 'The photographs in your hall . . . it's definitely your daughter's.'

'May I look?' Reaching out, she took the passport from him; looked at the cover briefly before flipping through the pages. 'Yes.' A tiny smile tipped the corners of her mouth as she studied the photo. 'Yes, that's her. The name, date of birth, everything – it's definitely her passport. Or identical to hers if it isn't.' She passed it back to him.

'How did she get to Sri Lanka without a passport?'

'She has dual nationality. She travelled on her Sri Lankan passport.'

'Did she tell you she'd lost her British passport?'

'Yes. She was planning to take both with her, but we couldn't find her British one, so she just took the Sri Lankan.'

'And you didn't think to report it stolen?'

'We were pretty sure it would turn up somewhere in the house,' Mr Brooks cut in, joining his wife on the sofa. 'She's not the most organised, I'm afraid. We had a great hoo-hah the day before we went skiing last New Year. She couldn't find her passport anywhere. The French won't let Sri Lankans in without a visa and we just didn't have time to get one, so we thought we'd have to cancel the holiday. We turned the house upside down and finally found it behind the sofa.' He smiled. 'Heaven knows how it got there.'

'Have you had a break-in recently?'

'No.'

Wessex held up the passport. 'So where?'

'She's been filling out applications for university at school,' Mrs Brooks said. 'They ask for all sorts of identification these days, so she's had to take in her passport a few times to get it photocopied.'

Mr Brooks gave an apologetic smile. 'It's her Achilles' heel – the organisation thing.'

Wessex nodded. 'Could you call her and tell her that we have it. Ask her if she has any idea where it might have been stolen.'

Mrs Brooks glanced at her watch. 'It's the middle of the night over there.'

'First thing in the morning – their morning.' He pulled a card from his pocket and passed it to her. 'Call me on my mobile, as soon as you've spoken with her, please. It's important. Very important. And I'm going to have to ask you to keep quiet about this. If you talk to anybody about what I've just told you, it may compromise our investigation.'

'Of course,' they murmured in unison.

Mrs Brooks dropped her gaze to the card in her hand. 'So the girl you found?'

Wessex shrugged. 'Now? I don't know. I don't know who she is.' He looked at the photo of their daughter again. Then he held out his hand. 'Thank you for your time. I'm very sorry for the mistake.'

13

Jacqueline Rong's life in the last few months had been defined by a series of choices. Confess her condition to the people who knew her, or hide it for as long as she could. Beg for help, or withdraw into solitude and keep her own counsel. She was self-reliant by instinct. But she had made one mistake. And it was a mistake she had come to love very much.

Now she had a new choice to make. She knew she was bleeding, that a shard of wood from the old broken fence that ran like a spine through the jungle had sunk deep into her thigh. There was pain, but something worse too, an electric zing in the muscles around the wound. Gritting her teeth, she scrambled on to her knees – the shocked response of her wounded leg made her shout, once – and felt frantically through the sludge of mud and rotten leaves for her baby son. His blanket was gone – the blanket with the embroidered teddy bear that the woman from Médecins Sans Frontières had given her – and his little body was cold and slippery from leaf mulch. The fall had winded him, and for a moment he was silent. But she heard that familiar in-suck of breath, and she knew what was coming.

His scream echoed through the dark jungle. It sounded different out here, raw, the noise of an animal in pain. She hugged him to her chest, jiggling and shushing him as quietly as she could. He gasped again, but another sound came before his next cry – so soft she wasn't even sure she'd heard it – a twig breaking in the undergrowth at the edge of the little clearing? And then it was lost in Chhaya's next shriek, though she pressed her hand over his mouth to muffle him. Mercifully, he seemed to sense her desperation for him to be quiet because after a few whimpers he fell silent, breathing quickly.

Jacqueline scrambled to her feet, clutching Chhaya with one arm, clawing the air with the other, as if she could swim forward through the murk, but her injured leg gave way again, and she just had time to wrap both arms around Chhaya before she fell hard on to her knees. She wanted to scream with frustration. She wanted to scream for help too: both impulses were there. But it was too late to give in to that other voice. She was a mother now, not a little girl. She was the protector. And if she did scream, no one would come.

She had spent many hours in the jungle collecting firewood to barter for food to keep herself and Chhaya alive, and had always felt secure in the privacy it afforded, something that hadn't been hers since her pregnancy had begun to show. But the place seemed different at night, through the prism of her fear, and she realised that she was hopelessly lost. She had no idea which way led back to her village, or which direction to take to reach one of the other settlements. She started to crawl forward, hauling Chhaya as best she could, dragging her leg behind her, adrenalin diluting the pain.

Then something slid across her back and she suddenly knew exactly where she was. Mine tape. It was the edge of the Koh Kroneg field. Mined land. Her heart lurched again, but nothing could be worse than what was behind her.

Every few scrambled paces, she looked over her shoulder,

and the mine tape receded, five metres, ten. A curl of moon showed in the canopy of branches beyond. And then, in its light, something else. A pale figure standing in the roots of the banyan, on the very edge of the jungle. She stopped and sat still, next to the hollowed-out stump of a tree, clutching Chhaya's tiny, shivering body, muffling his whimpers against her ragged T-shirt, feeling the cool mud oozing between her thighs. The shape in the banyan hadn't moved. But it was there. It was real.

She was being hunted.

Hot tears spilled. Koh Kroneg. Her beauty had brought her to the edge of this abyss. It had captivated Arun, ten years older than her and still without a wife. Jacqueline's father had disappeared, eaten by the minefield, when she was four years old; the dominant memory of her childhood was her mother's incessant fear of not being able to keep them both alive. Hunger had followed them every day. To be flattered and appreciated by Arun was an escape, and she had allowed herself to dream.

Now, through her own stupidity, she had written herself the same history. But where her mother had had a husband and honour, she had none. It was her fault, of course, not Arun's, that she had fallen pregnant, and the consequences were hers to bear. Hers, and Chhaya's. Her son would have to shoulder them too: the stigma and isolation, the constant hunger. By bearing him, she had cursed him. Now that he was here it felt an impossible betrayal to wish him gone, but before he had been born, she had prayed constantly for his growing life to vanish from inside her.

She blinked. How long had it been? Minutes? Time passed differently out here at night. She had been sitting in her hut preparing for bed. The best time of day, Chhaya asleep, safe, tucked inside the wooden crate she had found a couple of months before his birth and saved. Her thoughts losing their definition, she had been about to remove her dress when she heard the bottom step creak. No one ever came to their door, and she hadn't heard approaching footsteps. Lifting Chhaya out of his crate, she backed away, drawing the curtain she used to fence off their sleeping area from the rest of the room quietly behind her. Holding her breath, she peered around the edge of the fabric. Nothing there, she thought for a moment, and then she realised there was something on the doorframe after all. A hand, bloated and pale.

She shot backwards, felt in the gloom for the loose planks in the back wall. She had been meaning to repair them for weeks, but had neither the tools nor the skills, and no one would help her. They turned away when she tried to explain that on monsoon nights, Chhaya would wake, pale and shivering, his chest thick with mucus. Forcing the planks apart, she slithered through the gap, reached back for her baby and ran fast and silent into the trees.

Burying her face into Chhaya's heaving tummy, she jammed her eyes shut. Who would miss her and Chhaya? No one. Both her parents were dead. When their bodies were carried out of the minefield, the villagers would nod and turn away. The White Crocodile had decided.

Anger surged suddenly. Chhaya would die, before his life had even begun. A sudden memory from a few days ago rose. She had been walking back from the jungle with a bundle of firewood, Chhaya in a sling on her back, when she had encountered Arun's new wife on the path, cradling the swell of her stomach. Jacqueline's first inclination had been to duck into the jungle, melt into the faceless trees until she had passed.

But something stopped her. Perhaps it was the noise Chhaya made as her head dipped. It was probably just because her spine had arched and made him uncomfortable. But for that fleeting moment, she felt he was admonishing her. Suddenly ashamed, she kept her ground, looked Arun's wife in the eye and smiled, held her gaze until she had lowered hers, stepping to one side of the path to let Jacqueline past. She had swung Chhaya into the crook of her arm as she walked away, holding him like a prize.

The memory emboldened her. She did have one choice left. Turning, she gently lowered him into the bole of the hollow tree. There were leaves and moss inside – it was soft in there. She covered him with more leaves.

'*Oun sra-lun bong na*,' she whispered. I love you.

She hesitated, but only for a moment.

Unable to meet his gaze, she heaved herself to her feet, turned and stumbled away – not looking back, not once – the physical pain meaningless now. She began to shout and wave her arms, drowning out the high-pitched, keening cry she could hear fading behind her.

Numbness had spread up her leg and her T-shirt was torn and soaked with mud. She was shaking so hard her teeth were chattering. Pressing her hands to her ears to stop the rush of noise, she stared desperately ahead. All she could hear was her surging blood and the fluttering of mine tape. Mine tape! If she could reach the edge of the minefield, she could run. Run fast, without Chhaya to slow her down. Reach one of the other villages, hide until morning.

The tape was so close. Barely the length of her hut away. She would make it. Morning would come. The clearers would find Chhaya.

Jacqueline's foot sank deep into a puddle; she crashed on to her stomach and swallowed water tasting of mud and leaf mulch. She tried to push herself up, but her wrist was snagged. She groped with her other hand under the water, expecting to find a vine. Instead her numb fingers felt something hard and sinuous.

Metal. A metal wire.

Terror mounted, as she scoured the darkness around her. And there, just a couple of arm lengths away. *Manath*. A pine-apple. She had tasted one once – Arun had given her one when he was trying to get her to lie with him – and it was sharp and sweet, unlike anything she had eaten before. But this one was dirty green, not the rich yellow she remembered, and instantly she knew what it was. If she could avoid panic, she would be able to free her wrist. Not all the mines were still live, she knew that. She couldn't lift her hand to see, in case the wire snagged taut; her fingers were slippery and numb, and so cold it felt as if both arms finished at her elbows. Holding her breath, she dipped her face into the water, chewed at the wire with her teeth, rancid water and blood filling her mouth as the wire sliced into her gums. Spitting blood, she straightened, panic beating around her now like wild wings.

It was there, sitting next to her, huge and pale. Its smell settled over them like a cowl.

'*Ta loak chong baan avwai?*' She choked the words out through her tears. What do you want?

It sniffed, as if it was scenting the air.

'*Suom mehta.*' Please. 'For my baby. *Suom—*'

And then the figure spread its arms and embraced her.

Day 4

14

Tess awoke with a jolt, to a juddering noise. Her first thought was: *Christ, the anti-tank mine.* She'd brought it back from the field and shoved it under her bed because that seemed as good a place as any to hide it until she decided what to do with it, who to tell.

Groggily, she sat up. It felt as if she'd only been asleep for five minutes. Her gaze found the patio doors. They were open, the white curtains billowing in the breeze, backlit with an orange-yellow glow from the rising sun. Rolling out of bed, she grabbed her mobile phone.

She took a moment to recognise the voice. 'MacSween?'

'I've just had a call. Some bairn – some baby – in a minefield.'

What was he talking about? Her mind, still sluggish, struggled to comprehend.

'A *baby*?'

'Aye. A baby.'

'What's a baby doing in a minefield?'

'Welcome to Cambodia.'

'But how did it get there?'

'I have no idea.'

'Where's the mother?'

'*They* had no idea.'

'Who are they? Who called it in?'

'Médecins Sans Frontières. They're out there giving malaria

jabs. They like to start even earlier than we do.'

'Is it in the—?' *The White Crocodile field – again?* She didn't need to voice it.

'Aye. The baby is in Koh Kroneg. But don't you start on that crap too, love. I've got enough superstitious idiots at MCT to fill a cathedral and then some.'

Tess bit her lip. 'Is it near to where Johnny was injured?'

'Near enough. It's a small village, on the western edge of the field – Johnny was north – about five kilometres from there. Médecins Sans Frontières were out at the village last week making a list of all the babies needing jabs, and when they went back this morning one was missing. Belongs to a teenage girl who got herself knocked up. Worse than death in a country like this, even with all the prostitution that goes on. They've been living alone in a hut on the edge of the village. Clive from MSF said it looked like they just upped and left right before bedtime. Sleeping roll laid out, but unslept in. They've spotted the baby abandoned in the minefield, but there's no sign of the girl.'

A pause. Tess remained stubbornly silent.

'Look, love. I'm not too stupid to know that the last thing you want to do after Johnny's accident is to face another tricky situation in that minefield, but as I already told you, I've given the teams a couple of days off. Jakkleson's got the paperwork to do on Johnny, Alex has gone AWOL, and I can't do it alone. If nothing else it'll teach you not to answer your phone when you see my caller ID. Grab a quick coffee and a bite. I'll see you outside the lovely Madam Chou's in twenty.'

*

Standing on the balcony, the cool morning air eddying around her, Tess watched the sun rise. As she took a sip of coffee, she realised that her hands were shaking.

It had been mid-May, her father had told her years later, spring in England, the trees in bud, when her mother had walked out on them. She had an image of being trapped in her pram in a hallway, staring at a trapezoid of daylight through an open doorway as her mother stepped out of it, into the sun. Then the door swung shut, and she was alone. The recollection couldn't be real. She hadn't even been two. And that wasn't the way memory worked anyway – it wasn't a series of little films you might record on your smartphone, available to reassemble any time you wanted to view them. And yet sometimes these images were so clear she could almost reach out and touch them: feel the material of her mother's cotton dress slipping through her fingers, the lift of the wind as the door opened, the scent of cut grass on the suburban spring air. At other times that image – the leaving – was so blurred as to be unrecognisable. Just abandonment, followed by an endless stream of faceless nannies, by long-forgotten friends' houses at Easter and Christmas when her father was away on his tours of duty. And sometimes her mind, her memory of that phase of her life was just a blank. As if she was looking through a camera lens with the shutter still on.

Her father never said the words, but Tess could see it in his face, when she caught him standing in the hallway, looking around him as if searching for something he had misplaced. She knew that, even now, her father was waiting, stuck in limbo. Tess didn't know how much he needed from her – what compensation he wanted from her for being the one who had driven his wife away with her baby neediness, her ceaseless demands for time and attention. Now and then, in spite of the carapace of toughness she had built around herself, she found herself almost crippled by loneliness.

The diesel rumble of MacSween's approaching engine cut through the dawn silence. Taking a last sip of coffee, she tossed the remainder over the balcony railing just as he hit the horn, a short businesslike blast. But her hand must have been damp because the handle of the mug slipped through her fingers and she watched it cartwheel away from her. It hit the grass below with a dull thud, cartwheeled again, once, before landing in two pieces.

Another blast of the horn. She turned from the balcony, pulling the glass doors closed behind her.

*

Alex's eyes flicked open, and for a moment he couldn't work out where he was. Groaning, he pushed himself upright. The back seat of the Land Cruiser. Last night. It was all coming back to him.

He had been drinking Johnnie Walker in a vain attempt to anaesthetise himself to sleep. Around midnight, he'd been dozing on the sofa in his living room when he had been jolted awake by a memory.

Luke, drunk, out of control. Johnny, laughing and laughing.

He'd sat up, his gaze finding the bookshelf in the corner of the room where a miscellany of objects from the course of his life mixed with the books; searching out the darkness at the back of the middle shelf and the flat piece of wood hidden there. Looking at it, he remembered Johnny's voice: *Fuck off back to the Land Cruiser then, Alex, and try not to be such a miserable bastard in future. We're only having a laugh.* The line of mine tape had just been visible in the darkness, stirring slightly. He had heard the rush of the evening breeze over the ruined paddy fields and through the tangled elephant grass behind, a sense of invisible distance, of being on the edge of something. Like an abyss.

Johnny was standing in front of the mine tape – on safe ground. He was jiggling from foot to foot, wired, because he loved this kind of thing. *Loved jokes.* He was holding a black sign in his hand, held away from his body because the paint on it was still wet. The ends of his fingers were tinged in black and white where he had held the paintbrushes. Luke was standing next to Johnny, his shirt off, laughing. He had a hammer and some nails in one hand and a can of beer in the other. He was drunk by then, very drunk. The only one of them who was. It had briefly occurred to Alex that Luke was acting out of character: he was usually so ordered, so controlled, like an overwound clockwork toy. Alex had worked with him for a couple of months by then and he didn't know him any better than the first day they'd met.

Got the cork jammed in too tight, was what Johnny said about Luke.

Alex had turned then, and gone back to the Land Cruiser; found the second sign that they'd left on the passenger seat and shoved it in his bag, so that they would only put one up.

Luke, drunk, out of control. Johnny, laughing and laughing.

Midnight. He should have knocked it on the head then: tossed the bottle of Johnnie Walker in the bin, had a shower, tried to get a grip. But he hadn't. Instead he'd headed straight to the Bamboo Train to grab a pizza and shoot some pool with Vannak, the restaurant's owner and one of Battambang's characters, who always had good stories to tell, none of them tethered in reality. The rest of the evening – morning – spent at Paradise Night Club, sinking Johnnie Walker and chatting up the bar girls, who were sweet and beautiful and tempting, and would do pretty much anything for a price, but that was one promise to himself he wasn't breaking, irrespective of how drunk he was, and how shit he felt. He couldn't even remember why he hadn't just driven home, but it was probably because the hospital was only a couple of minutes on a straight road from the nightclub.

Dawn was spreading across the sky as he climbed out of the Land Cruiser: the buildings and trees in the hospital courtyard diverging in the gathering light. He lit a cigarette and leaned against the tailgate. He was apprehensive, he realised, and that realisation caused a twinge of guilt. He didn't want Johnny to be conscious – couldn't yet face the overwhelming devastation Johnny would feel once cognisant of his injuries – knew that he would enter that hospital building only out of a sense of obligation, rather than a desire to see his friend.

The lights from the common room behind him lit his way as he walked towards the dark hospital building. He stepped on to the veranda. Deserted. As he reached for the door, he caught movement out of the corner of his eye: someone was standing in the shadows at the far end. The figure's head tilted to follow his movements. Unhurriedly, Alex opened the door.

In the reflection from the glass, he saw a shadow flit between the posts holding up the veranda roof and approach from behind. Footsteps coming. He paused with the open door clasped in his left hand and counted slowly to three. With his right, he reached for the Browning tucked into the front of his belt. Letting go of the door, he spun around, reaching out in one smooth movement with his left hand, catching the figure by the neck, dragging him sideways, slamming him against the wall and thrusting the muzzle of the Browning into his cheek.

'Were you waiting for me?'

Alex's captive tried to free himself. But he was tiny, much smaller than Alex, and after a few moments of futile squirming he gave up.

Slowly, Alex's vision grew accustomed to the half-light. A skinny young Khmer boy stared up at him, winded and shocked. His ruined hands were clamped defensively in front of him; Alex glanced down, saw the stumps of fingers, gnarled skin, withered thumbs, and recognition dawned. He let go quickly, stepping back.

'Ret S'Mai,' he managed. 'Jesus, I'm sorry.'

Ret S'Mai remained rigidly against the wall, as if still held there. He reminded Alex absurdly of one of those old-fashioned china dolls he used to see in the posh shops of Sarajevo before the town was trashed in the conflict – almost unreal.

'I'm sorry,' Alex repeated. 'I didn't know it was you. I'm just jumpy at the moment.' Looking down, he realised his hand, still gripping the Browning, was shaking. Shoving the gun back into his belt, he pulled his shirt over it. 'Did you want to talk to me?'

'Yuh.' There was a thin, shrill tone in Ret S'Mai's voice.

Reaching out, Alex touched his shoulder. Ret S'Mai jerked his head up. Alex almost took a step back: the kid's eyes were hot with rage.

'What the hell—'

He broke off as Ret S'Mai's mouth opened.

'I seen—'

A moped in the street roared.

Alex cupped a hand to his ear. 'What? What have you seen?'

Ret S'Mai repeated it, but Alex still couldn't hear.

The moped passed with a high-pitched scream. Alex turned back to Ret S'Mai, gave a start as he realised that Ret S'Mai had taken a step forward, was leaning into him, barely a centimetre away.

'I seen him. He die.'

Alex grasped his arm. 'What the hell are you talking about?' But in that one movement, he realised that he had lost the kid, frightened him. Wrenching himself from Alex's grasp, Ret S'Mai bolted down the corridor.

'Fuck.'

Alex turned towards Johnny's closed door and stopped. He couldn't face seeing Johnny yet, he realised. He'd come back later. When he'd had some proper sleep. When he wasn't hungover. Stepping silently back out on to the veranda, he crossed the courtyard to his Land Cruiser.

*

Mist drifted in from the river. At the edge of the jungle, pale-faced villagers stood in knots, shaking their heads and whispering, as MacSween carried the baby back into safe ground, wrapped securely in his jacket. The team from Médecins Sans Frontières were there too, full of questions for the villagers about what had happened, not getting any answers.

The little boy was blue with cold, eyes dull. He must have screamed himself silent, because he didn't make a sound; just sucked in little gulps of air, his head flopping from side to side as if it had become too heavy.

They had found him tucked into a knoll in a rotten tree fifty metres into the minefield, naked, but blanketed under a pile of leaves. But they still hadn't answered the question of how the hell he had got there. Or where his mother was. MacSween and the team from MSF wanted to call off the search. They had scoured the village, interviewed the villagers – who professed to know nothing, and MacSween and Clive both felt they were telling the truth – checked the minefield around where the baby had been left and found no trace of her.

*

But Tess wouldn't let it go. Not yet.

She walked into the trees. It was quiet. She paused and glanced around. The jungle was intensely thick and dark, the light from the midday sun swallowed up in the canopy far above her head which moved slowly, constantly, as if it were breathing. The only sound was the insect hum of the metal detector. She dropped her gaze to the coil, forced herself to keep walking, passing it softly across the ground in front of her. Being isolated from the silence by the hum of the detector should have given her a sense of security. But it was the opposite. The knowledge that she was the only source of uninterrupted noise in the jungle made her feel exposed, vulnerable.

There was only a single, narrow track and she followed it, step by careful step as it wound deeper into the jungle, the ground alternately hard then soft with leaves and damp.

Sudden movement. She stopped and held her breath, staring hard into the dimness between the trees. Something flashed past her face, so close that she felt the rush of air.

Her heart stopped.

A bird. *Christ.* She heard the clatter of wings off to her left, quickly eaten by the silence. Slowly, she let the air out of her lungs. *MacSween was right. Fuck this.* She turned to go back. Took a step and stopped. She wanted to get out of the jungle as fast as possible, forget this whole mad plan. But she knew that she had seen something. Static, unmoving, anomalous in the patchwork of jungle green. She turned slowly back – and saw it again. A flash of incongruous colour.

She approached watchfully. A twist of fabric protruded from a pile of leaves, and she bent and pulled it out, knowing already what it was.

A pale blue woollen baby's blanket, a teddy bear em-broidered in one corner. The blanket was old, frayed and faded, the silken threads of the teddy torn so that it had only one arm.

At that moment she felt it again – the sensation that she wasn't alone. Instinctively, she ducked down, clutching the blanket to her chest like a talisman. *Don't let it happen. Don't. The Crocodile isn't real.* Forcing herself to her feet, she walked forward; the jungle opened out in front of her suddenly, and she stopped stock still.

It was the baby's mother, must be. She stood at the other side of the clearing, serene and proud, looking at Tess without blinking. Tess's first thought was that the girl was afraid to walk back because they were in mined land. She was standing sharply upright, as if propped there. A fly buzzed lazily around her head. Tess took a step closer, and the sunlight fingered the delicate metal wire running around the girl's neck, tethering her to the tree behind.

Tess's second thought was that she was wearing a hat, something droopy and unformed. Then she realised that the top of the girl's head had been struck so hard that the dome of her skull had lost its shape. Tess moved a few paces closer and the girl's body, which had been half hidden by the leaves of the tree, came into sight. Her clothes were shredded, her body slashed in places, the wounds black and clotted with blood. *Tortured*. The smell hit her, so powerful she nearly staggered.

MacSween answered as soon as Tess pressed the call button.

'Where are you?'

'I've found her.'

'And? Is she OK?'

No. Tess spoke the word but no sound came out.

'Tess, TESS . . . stay there. I'm coming. I'll follow the track to find you.'

The radio clicked off, and again she was plunged into silence. Just her and the baby's mother, facing each other. The eyes were wide and staring, focused on a spot just behind her. Tess backed up against a tree and waited. Thinking that she had almost forgotten what it was like to be this scared.

15

The room Dr Ung entered was cool and shady: the morning sunlight diffused by the mosquito mesh covering the windows. Trees outside cast shifting patterns against the screen. For a second the image reminded him of New York, and he couldn't think why. Then he had it: a shadow-puppet show he'd seen one Hallowe'en in a theatre in SoHo. He often felt as though his entire experience in Manhattan was a figment of his imagination. Though he had grown up there, the legacy of wealthy parents who had bought their way on to one of the last helicopters leaving Phnom Penh as the Khmer Rouge stormed the city, America seemed to recede further every year. He could barely imagine returning now.

Ung moved over to the bed. Johnny's eyes were closed and his body was perfectly still under the crisp white cotton sheet draping it, save for the slow rise and fall of his chest. Sitting down on the chair beside the bed, Ung eased it closer; its metal legs screeched across the wooden floor. No matter. He was the only person in the room who would hear it. Reaching out, Ung touched the tips of his fingers to Johnny's forehead. He felt warm and smooth. The antibiotics were working, keeping the infection at bay. Early days, but this was one he might win. Physically at least.

Slipping his glasses off, he wiped his forehead on his sleeve. Luke.

And now Johnny.

And even among his orderlies, a new name for that minefield. Or an old one, perhaps. *White Crocodile.* But Ung was an empirical scientist. In the ten years since he'd come back from New York he'd seen many things. Hundreds of land-mine victims, many less recognisable as human beings than Johnny. Some of his patients stuck in his mind; most didn't. He'd operated on a pregnant woman sliced through the abdomen by a fragmentation mine, her dead baby curled in her uterus like a sleeping cat. He'd seen a three-year-old girl reduced to a legless torso by an anti-personnel mine, slopping in a lake of blood in the back of a bullock cart, her father unaware that he had been driving a corpse for the last few kilometres of the journey to the hospital.

But as the breeze picked up outside, and the pattern of leaves danced and plunged on the window mesh, he realised that the hairs on his arms were standing on end. Getting to his feet, he checked the IV line quickly and turned towards the door. Usually, he left the patients' doors open, so that, back in his office at the far end of the hospital building, he could hear them call. He pulled Johnny's closed; there would be nothing to hear for some time yet.

16

An hour later, Tess sat on the step of the dead girl's hut, cradling her baby and listening to the crackle of the radio and the shouted commands as MacSween called in to MCT to report what they had found, and to ask Jakkleson to telephone Battambang orphanage, tell them they'd soon have another arrival.

On the doorframe beside her was the crude carving of a crocodile, gouged into the damp wood with what looked like the tip of a knife. MacSween had said nothing when she had shown it to him. Just shook his head and cast a quick gaze behind him at the field, silent and still in the swelling heat.

'Don't make a big deal about it. We'll talk later, OK?' he murmured as he walked away.

Médecins Sans Frontières were sending an ambulance to evacuate the body of the mother; the villagers had refused to arrange a funeral for her – a simple pyre in a field, it would have been, nothing more, and still they wouldn't do it. No one was interested in taking her little boy either. MacSween had asked, cajoled, pleaded, got nowhere.

'So the poor bitch is an outcast, even in death,' Tess had heard him mutter.

The baby was quiet now, settled, staring up at her with huge shining dark eyes, his face unperturbed. He held her little finger in his fist, nibbling on the tip gently with his four tiny teeth. Hugging him close, Tess rested her cheek against his warm tummy and shut everything else out. The crackle of her radio as it tracked communications; MacSween's footsteps as he paced backwards and forwards issuing instructions; the image of the baby's mother tethered to that tree; the acid taste of vomit still on her tongue. For a while there was only the heat from his little body, the milky, baby smell of him, the silence, the sunlight spilling on the ground.

Despite everything – all the precautions she had taken to ensure she didn't – she had fallen pregnant. Fourteen months ago now. She hadn't been expecting it, hadn't kept an eye out for signs. When her period had stopped she had assumed that it was stress-related: her recent tour in Afghanistan, the physical toll of her job. Luke's unpredictable violence.

It had only been a month or two after they were married that he had first hit her. A slap around the face for having stayed out too late with her friends, for having got drunk: *You're a married woman now. Behave like one.* As if having tethered her to him in law, he no longer needed to maintain a veneer of self-control. With the benefit of hindsight, she realised that it had been there all along: the dark side to the characteristics she initially found so intoxicating.

One evening, a couple of days after she found out that she was pregnant, he had come home, furious. She hadn't told him, was still agonising over what to do. Whether to tell him and see if it changed things, or whether just to leave – which would mean leaving her life, her job, her home, everything.

What had set him off? She'd forgotten – could this be true? – to buy a Christmas present for his company commander, a chore he had allocated her the previous week. The company commander, an alcoholic fuckwit Luke would rail about in the pub. But Luke always needed everything precise, everything worked out. Nothing was trivial as far as he was concerned. Details mattered. There was more to it than that, of course. These were technicalities. She'd become a sort of conduit for the rage that was there anyway, she understood that now.

He had caught her at the top of a folding stepladder, as she was hanging the nativity star on their Christmas tree. He came up behind her, silent in his rage, and kicked the ladder from under her feet. She had no warning, no time to prepare herself for the fall. Crashing to the floor, she slammed hard on to her stomach. He stood above her, as she lay, winded and shocked, delivering hard, calculated kicks into her side, aiming for the soft flesh between the bottom of her ribs and her hip. It was only when he saw the blood pooling between her legs that he stepped back. There was suddenly so much of it.

He disappeared for a moment, and when he came back he was holding the receiver of the phone in one hand, a bunch of tea towels in the other. He dropped them beside her, and over the burring of the dial tone in her ear, she heard the front door slam. She called an ambulance, the first time she had ever done so. Every other time she had just limped upstairs and cleaned herself up, quietly, alone. This time, though, the blood made her frightened, and the pain in her abdomen was crucifying.

The nurse who broke the news that her baby hadn't survived also talked to her about domestic violence.

'There is no *type*,' she said, busying herself by the side of Tess's bed, checking the drip, smoothing the sheet, tucking and tidying. 'It's so widespread. Before I worked here, I thought that abused women were weak and pliable, people who couldn't stand on their own two feet. If anything the opposite is true. I see so many clever, beautiful, brave women with bruises all over their faces and broken bones. Their partners think they'll lose them, so they start subjugating them, destroying their confidence, just so they can hold on to them.'

Tess had listened to all this, lying still as a corpse, her eyes jammed shut. 'You were *four months gone*, my love. A little boy.' The nurse had held her hand as she wept, sitting quietly on the edge of the bed, the tilt of the mattress and the warm pressure on Tess's hand the only indication that she was still there. Some time later, she had left, seeming to sense that Tess needed to be alone.

After she'd gone, Tess had opened her eyes. She was in a hospital room, clean and white, cold winter sun cutting in through the net curtains on to the bed, a drip stand next to her.

Four months gone.

*

She had made a shrine for her unborn baby in the corner of the graveyard – next to the grave she had chosen for her mother – a navy-blue teddy bear she had picked up in the hospital shop, already sodden and bedraggled, seated on a small pile of stones.

When she was old enough to begin to analyse people's motivations, it had become easier to pretend to herself that her mother had died, rather than to think she was out there somewhere, knowing that she had a daughter. It made her feel less worthless, imagining a mother who couldn't come back, rather than one who didn't care enough to want to. So she had found an old grave in the far back corner of Amesbury graveyard, the headstone cracked, carved letters obscured by lichen.

She left Salisbury District Hospital in the middle of a sudden shower, caught the bus out through the rush-hour traffic on Fourmile Hill. By the time she reached Amesbury the rain had stopped as suddenly as it had started and the sun had come out, light glinting on the ruffled surface of the Avon, casting long shadows of the low brick buildings in the high street.

The only things that moved in the graveyard were wild rabbits, but they skittered for cover as she drew near. She exchanged smiles with an old woman standing by another grave. The corner where she had imagined her mother buried was overgrown, snarled with bracken and blackberry bushes. It was hard going – the grass was wet and unkempt. By the time she reached the stone, the shadows were getting long, and her flimsy ballet pumps were sodden and studded with seed heads.

She had nothing to bury. Four months wasn't viable, not really a baby, the nurse had said. Her little boy had been what is termed a foetus, a miscarriage, without the right to a proper funeral. While she had been lying in the hospital bed, refusing to surface into her new reality, he had been tossed into the hospital incinerator along with the rest of the hospital's refuse.

She sat there for a long time, still and silent, a pair of stone angels watching blankly from a nearby monument. After a while her thoughts curled in on themselves. What was she waiting for? Luke? Her mother? God? She looked at the sodden teddy bear on its pile of stones. It was stupid and pointless and not enough. She had lost and there was nothing left, and she nestled in the cold wet grass clutching the teddy and cried, wishing she could no longer feel.

17

Ten p.m. It had rained heavily for an hour just after the sun went down, and the air was cool and fresh; vapour steamed from the surface of the road. Behind her, shanty huts lined the riverbank. The smell of charcoal, a cooking fire, drifted over the water. Down the street there wasn't a soul to be seen. Tess glanced each way again, just to be sure, then monkeyed over the padlocked gates and dropped with a crunch on to the gravel drive. The key to MCT House was hidden under the fallen statue to the side of the door – all the platoon commanders had been told this, in case of emergencies. She felt around until her fingers brushed its shaft, and slid it out.

The air that met her in the hall was musty. The house had a peculiar smell, damp but with a sweet undertone, like incense. A slant of memory intruded: the candied smell of rotting flesh, sunlight fingering the wire tied around a woman's neck, and the feeling – so intense for a split second, it was almost as if she was back in the jungle clearing – of being too frightened to move, even to breathe.

She backed against the wall and stood still, taking slow, deep breaths, flooding her lungs with oxygen. It was twelve hours since she had found Jacqueline Rong's body, and she had kept herself busy since then, knowing that if she stopped occupying her mind even for a moment, it would find its own entertainment.

She knew now that she couldn't afford to wait passively for answers. She had to be proactive, take control, before another person died. But in the solitude of this house, with its smell and that stifling silence, the morning came back to her: Jacqueline, propped, eyes wide. She had an almost physical ache to switch on the lights, illuminate every corner of the house, but she couldn't risk anyone knowing she was here.

A centimetre at a time, she felt her way across the hall to the stairs, where she started to climb, keeping her feet to the edge of the wooden treads to minimise the sound of her ascent. She reached the landing and stopped. A break in the clouds admitted a faint square of light through the picture window behind her. Shifting into the milky glow, she called, 'Hello,' into the emptiness, quietly at first, then louder. No response. Not that she had expected there to be.

She turned to the window. The garden was deserted, lit by a wash of moonlight which outlined the faint shapes of the trees and unkempt grass. Transposed over it all, in the glass, was her reflection, just the ghost of an imprint, like the negative of a photograph. Reaching out, she touched her image, trailing her fingers down the side of her cheek – hollowed from lack of sleep and missed meals.

She continued up the stairs to the next floor, past MacSween's office – deserted, the stacks of papers arrayed on his desk like abstract chess pieces – along the narrow, dim hallway to Jakkleson's door. The handle resisted, screeched thinly and then gave. His office was a small, square space tucked at the back of the building, one window facing the garden and the high stone wall beyond it.

Now, finally, she allowed herself some light. The single bare bulb flooded the room, illuminating four clean white walls, a filing cabinet, a computer on a large teak desk, the plastic of its monitor and keyboard cracked and yellowed with age. No papers, no mess, nothing out of kilter, the notices on Jakkleson's board pinned in careful rows, an identical gap between each. A smell of the outdoors – of fields and pine forests – despite the closed windows.

A vase of orchids nestled on top of the filing cabinet, alongside the only personal thing in the room – a single photograph in a silver frame. A sleek blonde woman and two pale-skinned, azure-eyed girls, layered in wool and fur against the Swedish winter, Jakkleson standing behind them, his features flushed with cold. Her gaze moved to the vase. A hint of coral tinged the base of each sculpted white petal. She reached out and fingered one. It felt delicate, feminine, an alien presence here.

She sat down at Jakkleson's desk and placed her hand on the mouse. The screen flickered, changing resolution, and an egg timer appeared, turning itself over a couple of times, emptying and refilling. The screen flickered again and a white skull and crossbones replaced the timer, the words 'Danger!! Mines!!' spelt out in blood red below it. A 'File open' icon drifted in the middle of the skull's tombstone grin. *Jakkleson's idea of a joke, maybe?*

Moving the mouse to click the icon, Tess surveyed the list of folders. At the bottom, a line caught her eye: *Safety Records.* Her fingers moved across the keyboard and with a click she dropped lightly into the still water of the file.

Two icons this time, each with a name. The first, 'Jonathan Douglas Hugh Perrier (injury) 18/10/12'.

And the second?

Quickly, she looked – away – back. 'Luke Martin Hayder (death) 29/04/12'. Words jumped out at her from the block of text on the screen.

Anti-tank mine.

Booby trap.

Koh Kroneg.

Conclusion: Accident. Action: none

It sounded so formal. As if a piece of equipment had been lost in that minefield, not a person.

Sitting back, Tess rubbed her eyes. Dropping her hands, she read the document carefully, ignoring the confusion of emotions, trying to see if there was anything that could help her.

But there was nothing. Just that Luke had been killed in a fuck-up with a booby trap. Totally plausible if she hadn't been sure, beyond question, that there was more to his death than a simple, wholly believable accident.

Why didn't I listen to you when you telephoned? Find out what was scaring you?

'Luke,' she said suddenly, dropping the mouse and turning towards the door. Her sudden sense of him was almost as if he'd walked into the room. *Luke, it's because* – she curled her hands into fists on the desktop, digging her nails hard into her palms – *it's because of what you did to me. What I let you do to me. It's my fault too . . .* She stopped open-mouthed, gazing around the empty room. Turned quickly and looked at the blank white wall behind her, ducked and scanned under the desk – she couldn't help herself. *I'm going mad.*

Dropping her hands back to the desktop, she fixed her gaze back on the screen, took the mouse in her hand, guided it firmly back to the first of the two icons. And in this document was everything they had discussed in the meeting yesterday morning. That Johnny had gone in the minefield to check out a skull, that the field had been muddy but not waterlogged, that the marker hadn't been seen (may have been passed/lost during the explosion). *May have been passed.* She'd told them that she hadn't passed it, but Jakkleson hadn't believed her, hadn't been certain at least.

Conclusion: still open (most likely missed mine).

Action: speak to Huan Rae (has not returned to work and has been uncontactable since).

Huan. A face on the team-room wall. A serious, circumspect face. *Huan.* Vital now that she knew there was more to Johnny's injury than a simple missed anti-personnel mine. Where had Huan been the day Johnny was injured? And why hadn't he been in contact with MCT since? Closing the file, she slid the keyboard and mouse into exactly the positions in which she had found them.

Then she began to search Jakkleson's desk: opening and closing each drawer in turn, filtering carefully through its contents. But there was only the usual detritus: paperclips, a stapler, ruler, pens, pencils and rubbers, a stack of Mine Clearance Trust headed writing paper, all neatly ordered.

The filing cabinet then. But where would he keep the key? She hadn't found one. *Probably on a chain around his neck.* Never mind. One of her boyfriends – chosen mainly to wind her father up – had taught her to pick bicycle padlocks when she was fifteen. The principle extended to any shitty lock. Taking two paperclips from the holder on Jakkleson's desk, she straightened them and moved over to the filing cabinet, meeting Jakkleson's cool celluloid gaze. Flicking him the finger, she eased one paperclip into the lock. Once it was as far in as it would go, she pressed it gently but firmly against the roof of the cylinder where she could feel the row of five pins. It wasn't a sophisticated mechanism. They clicked softly as she nudged them into position. Jamming the second paperclip into the lower half of the cylinder, she twisted. The lock stayed stiff and unyielding. She repeated the process, trying not to get frustrated. *Keep calm.* Locks were almost like living things, her boyfriend had told her, could sense impatience and never gave in to it. Finally the cylinder turned with a satisfying click, and breathing a sigh of relief, she pocketed her makeshift tools.

The top drawer contained files labelled A to L. She flicked through them quickly, just to make sure, but wasn't surprised when Huan's file wasn't there. *Rae – Huan Rae – the drawer below then.* But just as she was about to shut this one, she noticed a file which had slid off the runner, lying flat against the drawer's base. It wasn't labelled. She lifted it out and slipped her hand in, felt the familiar sheen of photographs against her palm and thought of the MCT mugshots on the notice board in the team room. Turning, she emptied the file's contents on to the desktop.

Her mouth fell open.

Photographs certainly, but not the ones she had expected. These were personal snaps. *Mementos.*

The first showed a young Khmer woman lying on a grubby bed, naked, her brown legs spread. Her gaze was vacant. Unseeing eyes turned away from the camera. Tess had seen that expression before on children with rough parents, about to be smacked for something they hadn't done. The light from the flash had illuminated the walls of a tiny room: the wooden slats of a hut, barely a foot of space between the edge of the single bed and the wall. The bed was covered in a filthy sheet, stretched tight over its frame. The flash had also caught a poster pinned up behind the bed. The baggy carcass of a condom, the words 'Protect yourself from AIDS' written in capitals beneath it, with a Khmer translation below.

Another photograph showed Jakkleson standing – too close to the camera, as if he was holding it himself – out-of-focus arm, torso and erect cock, the girl lying back on the bed, her hips jacked up. She could tell it was Jakkleson from the gold wristwatch that had slid from the cuff of his shirtsleeve yesterday morning, when he had shaken her hand.

As Tess gathered them up hurriedly, she realised something else. The photos were not of the same woman. They were similar, incredibly so. All Khmer. All teenagers, she guessed, some barely into their teens from the look of them. All with wide, innocent faces, dark eyes and long, dead straight black hair. But they weren't the same girl.

Oh, God. She felt sick. Dirty herself having touched them. She remembered what MacSween had said: '*Corruption. Exploitation. Sexual tourists and paedophiles from the West.*'

It was happening right under his nose.

*

Johnny opened his eyes, sticky with mucus, stared through the crack of his vision at the white of the ceiling, at the rattan fan spinning above him – thwack – thwack – thwack – tilted his head towards the window, to the leaves of the trees outside casting shifting patterns of light and shade over the mosquito mesh.

He felt secure in this cool, tranquil room. Safe.

Safe?

The thought surprised him, and he frowned groggily. What was there to be afraid of? He tried to think but his thoughts were grains of sand slipping through his fingers.

He closed his eyes. That smell. What was it? The gunpowder smell of TNT. Another. Raw, metallic. Blood.

And something else. Emptiness. An absence – the vacuum left by sheared nerves. As though he'd been bitten.

His eyes snapped open.

18

Amesbury, Salisbury Plain, ten months ago

It was well past midnight when Tess got home. The house was dark and silent, but she knew that Luke was upstairs, in their bed, sleeping the sleep of a man who was capable of forgiving himself for anything. Slipping off her shoes, she laid them quietly by the front door. Then she stood in the hall and lifted her face to the air, eyes half closed, smelling the perfume of cut flowers – bought to atone for his attack, no doubt – mingling with the smell of cleaning fluid and furniture polish.

He had cleaned up the blood then. Of course he had.

Vague notions of fear skittered through her brain, but they didn't coalesce. It felt strange to realise that she wasn't afraid of him any more. It was a simple equation. He had taken everything. She had nothing left to lose.

A sudden noise. She turned around.

He was standing on the stairs, shirtless, his pyjama bottoms hanging loose around his hips. She took in the bed hair, the hard stomach, the smattering of dark hair on his chest. Three years ago, the first time they had made love, when they had peeled each other's clothes off item by item, kissing and laughing, just the look of his hard body had telegraphed itself straight to her groin. On their honeymoon in a tiny, isolated croft in the Scottish Highlands, they had made love on every piece of furniture that was big enough. She was sure then that she was the luckiest girl in the world.

'What are you doing?' There was menace in his voice. 'It's almost one in the morning.' He gestured to the front door. 'And why the hell have you left the front door open?'

She stopped and faced him. 'Where's the sock? The pink sock?'

'Why are you asking me that?' His eyes were grey and cold. 'I've got it. It's upstairs.'

She nodded slowly. 'I didn't tell you.'

'Tell me what?'

'I was pregnant.'

He looked confused.

'The sock wouldn't have been any use though. Little boys don't wear pink.'

'What the fuck are you talking about?'

'I was four months pregnant with your son when you kicked that ladder from under my feet.'

She watched the range of emotions playing themselves out on his face: confusion, doubt, incredulity, disbelief, hurt, and then anger. Always anger.

'Why didn't you tell me, you stupid bitch? If you'd told me, I wouldn't have—'

'Wouldn't have what? Kicked a ladder from underneath me when all I was doing was decorating our Christmas tree? What would you have done instead? Been *nice*? Tried to resist the temptation to kick the shit out of me?'

Walking to the front door, she scooped up her shoes. Why had she come back here?

'*You fucking bastard*,' she shouted, as she stepped on to the doormat.

His face twisted with rage. 'What? *What* did you call me?'

She couldn't be bothered with this. She wasn't frightened of being hurt any more. Physical pain was meaningless. '*You fucking bastard!*' she screamed at the top of her lungs.

'You're crazy.' He stared at her in disbelief. She'd never stood up to him like this, and she could see how shocked he was. 'For Christ's sake think about the neighbours.'

She spun around on the path, her arms outstretched. 'Listen to this, lovely middle-class neighbours. He beats me up for *no reason.*'

'Tess, please—' Standing in the threshold, naked from the waist up, looking tense now, he stretched out a hand. 'Come back inside.'

She tore off her wedding ring and threw it at him. 'He stamped on my foot and broke my toe. He snapped my finger for not wearing his fucking ring.' Her voice kept breaking into a scream now. A light went on in one of the houses on the opposite side of the street.

Cold air eddied around her, chilling her bare arms and legs. Tarmac grated her soles as she stepped from the garden path on to the pavement.

Confusion and uncertainty flashed across his face, and then recognition, understanding that she was not going to play the victim for him any longer. Dropping his hand, he tilted his head and gave a contrite smile. 'We need each other. We're meant to be together.'

'*You're insane.*'

'You *need* me, Tess.'

'I don't need you.'

'You have no one else. Your father doesn't love you, and never did. I'm all you've got, Tess.'

She didn't turn.

Behind pale, lifting curtains two neighbours watched a skinny girl with wild red hair, wearing woollen tights but no shoes, stalking down the middle of the street, a ballet pump in each hand.

'No, I don't need you,' she yelled.

Tossing her sodden ballet pumps over a garden wall, she started running.

'Tess,' Luke shouted, but his voice was small. She glanced over her shoulder at the figure of a man, lit by a porch light, almost too far away to see now.

'I loved you,' she whispered, sinking to her knees on the kerb. A car passed her, and she heard it slow for a moment – felt the eyes of its occupants sizing her up, their indecision plain from the idling engine – heard it accelerate away again. Pushing herself to her feet, she turned the corner and started to walk, rubbing the backs of her hands fiercely across her cheeks to wipe away the tears.

I don't fucking need you. I am enough. I only need me.

19

Tess slid Jakkleson's photographs back into the file and re-turned them to their secret place at the bottom of the drawer. She slid the drawer shut, leant for a second against the cabinet, trying to make sense of what she'd seen. She was tempted to leave now: just walk straight out of the room, with its ludicrously prim facade and its dirty little secrets.

But she had come to Cambodia for a reason.

Crouching, she turned her attention to the bottom drawer, and in here, the files she had been looking for, M to Z. Huan Rae's file should be here. She went straight to the Rs – there were only three – and none of them was Huan's. She checked again, taking each file out in turn to make sure that Huan's hadn't slid inside one of the others. But it had not. Putting them back, she moved to the front of the drawer, working through each file in turn, taking it out, flicking through its con-tents, putting it back in its correct place so that nothing was left out of kilter to give her away. When she had gone through the last file and still found nothing relating to Huan, she pushed all the files to the back of their runners and felt around under them, running her hand back and forth across the cool metal base of the drawer. Nothing. Huan's personnel file was missing.

Shutting the drawer, she straightened and locked the filing cabinet, the muscles in her jaw tensing with frustration. Jakkleson was the admin man, known to be pedantic to a fault, and he kept records of everything. *Think*. There must be something of use in here. She just hadn't found it yet.

She stood still and emptied her mind of any expectation, as she had been taught to do when clearing mines. *Look with an open mind.* She went through the cupboard, each shelf in turn, rummaged through the notices on the board, lifting them to see if anything was hidden underneath, pulled all the books from the bookshelf and shook each one by the spine to see if anything had been slipped between their pages. It was only when she was putting the last book back that it occurred to her she hadn't checked the waste bin. Reaching into the dark space beneath Jakkleson's desk, she retrieved it and placed it on the desktop. At the bottom of the bin was a mess of curled, blackened paper and ash. Enough to have been something substantial that Jakkleson had burned – a whole file, not just a sheet or two of paper. So this was it, surely? Huan's file. She picked through the burnt remains, but they all crumbled to ash in her fingers. He'd been thorough.

She took one last quick look around the office to make sure everything was where it should be, and switched off the light.

Closing the door carefully behind her, she headed back down the stairs. She paused for a moment on the landing, as she had on the way up. A full moon hung low in the sky. Turning from the window, she started towards the flight down to the hallway. And froze.

Footsteps, and then a voice. 'What the hell are you doing here?'

She recognised the accent before she made out the figure standing in the pale wash of moonlight below.

'I was emailing my father. He doesn't like speaking on the telephone.' She'd prepared this answer before setting out, but it suddenly rang hollow and mechanical even to her ears.

The man in the hallway didn't reply, though the expression on his face made it clear that he didn't believe her. One measured step at a time, Tess made her way down. *Attack is the best form of defence.*

'So what about you, Alex? What are *you* doing here?' She stopped in front of him, taking in the undone shirt, the messy hair.

He ignored her question. 'Come into the team room.'

'Why?'

'I want to talk.'

She didn't move. 'We can talk here.'

'There are chairs to sit on in the team room. I only want to talk and I . . . would like to sit down.'

He clocked her hesitation and put out a hand to touch her arm. She jerked away and he let his hand fall back to his side, the movement weary, dispirited.

'Johnny's accident has hit him hard,' MacSween had said yesterday. 'They're good friends.' What did she have to lose?

'OK. Let's talk.'

As he turned, she noticed the butt of a pistol stuck into his belt. A Browning nine-millimetre. Her father had one just like it, bought on the black market in Iraq during the first Gulf war and smuggled back to England in his kit bag. He kept it in a tin in a kitchen cupboard, rolling around with its bullets. She had discovered it when she was nine years old, tall enough to reach the cupboard door. He never was one to make allowances for mundane things, like his daughter's safety. It occurred to her that perhaps she should be worried Alex was carrying, but she felt strangely ambivalent.

Alex didn't switch on the light when they entered the team

room. So he too didn't want to be seen here. The thought buoyed her with some confidence. He leaned against the window ledge and motioned her to a chair opposite him.

'Sit.'

She stayed where she was. 'I'm not a Labrador.'

'Please. Sit down, *please*.'

She did as he asked, hooking a chair back into the darker depths of the room with her foot before she sat down, so she wasn't framed in the moonlight washing in through the window. 'What do you want to talk about?'

'What are you doing here?'

'I've already told you.'

'Ah, yes.' He glanced away, a grim smile pulling at the corners of his mouth. 'I might feel like shit but I am not an idiot. Do you always break into offices after ten at night to send emails?'

'I could ask you the same question. Because I guess there's a reason we're sitting here in the dark?'

He nodded. 'You could.'

'So what *are* you doing here?'

Looking out of the window into the wild garden, he didn't speak for a few moments. Watching his back, she noticed the same tense set of his shoulders she had seen at the hospital the day before yesterday, and it dragged her straight back there, to the hurt and fear.

'You don't think that it – Johnny – was an accident, do you?' he murmured.

She drew in a breath, held it for a couple of beats of her pulse while she thought, made a decision. 'No, I don't.'

She saw his knuckles whiten as he tightened his grip on the windowsill. 'Why?'

Should she tell him the whole lot? About her connection to Luke? About the White Crocodile drawing on the envelope containing the pink sock she had been sent from Cambodia? About the anti-tank mine she had found under the anti-personnel mine that maimed Johnny? But she knew that she wouldn't tell him. What was the point in sticking her neck out any further than she already had? She was in a dangerous enough position as it was.

'Because it just didn't feel right.'

'So you came here to look around? Find some evidence, some proof?'

'I wanted to see if I could find Huan's file. It was his lane. He was off sick that day. He hasn't been seen or heard from since.'

'So you think he's responsible?'

'I don't know. But the mine Johnny stood on was in ground that had already been cleared by Huan.'

Alex straightened, rubbing a hand over his eyes. 'In the meeting with MacSween the day after Johnny's accident, you said you didn't know whether the mine was in cleared ground or not, and now, suddenly, you remember it clearly?'

'I've had time to think about it. There were a couple of scorched craters in Huan's lane beyond where Johnny was injured. So mines had been cleared further along the lane.'

He shook his head. 'It was . . . crazy out there. There's no way you could remember details like that.'

'I can, because I remembered that tree,' her voice rising against his. 'That lone tree in the middle of the minefield, that creepy fucking tree that's bent and twisted. There were shadows – the shadows of the leaves on Johnny's face. His face was in shadow and his lower body, his . . . his injured leg was in sunlight. And then I looked beyond him, further down Huan's lane, while I was waiting for the medics, I remember, and I saw a couple of burnt-out craters. I thought they were shadows, but they weren't – couldn't have been – because that tree was the only thing out there casting shade.'

'Big fucking deal. So the mine was in cleared ground. Missed mines happen.'

'There was also the skull. In the middle of a field, right next to a live mine? It was a come-on. There to draw Johnny in.'

A hard light shone in his eyes. 'This is Cambodia. Two million people were murdered by the Khmer Rouge, in fields just like that one. The skull means nothing.'

'Bullshit. It's not that easy to miss a mine. And the skull was just sitting there on the earth – it wasn't buried or anything. You've done this job as long as me, Alex. You know what this is about. Laying mines is a game of wits, us against them. If something looks like a come-on, that's exactly what it is. Someone set a trap for Johnny.'

He shook his head, but with a little, almost imperceptible delay before he did it, as if he was weighing up alternatives, making a decision. 'I talked to his troop. They said that you were panicking, shouting at his clearers, yelling at the medics. You can't *possibly* remember things so clearly. Your version of events is fiction.'

Tess met his gaze. 'I acted *entirely* professionally. I walked down the lane to prove to the medics it was clear. That saved your friend's life. What the fuck would you have done?'

She wondered if she'd made the right decision to confide in him. Now he knew almost as much as she did. She looked past him to the window and the wild garden beyond. Thick foliage, indistinct in the moonlight, the stooping shapes of the trees. There wasn't a soul out there, not in the garden or on the road beyond the gates. It was just her and Alex. Her eyes dropped to the Browning in his belt and she thought again of her father. He had drummed into her from an early age that emotions were weakness, that it was unacceptable to cry in public or let others see that you were hurt or scared. Female emotions were a Pandora's Box to him. One day, aged seven or eight, she had come home with a bloody nose and a black eye, having had a fight with a couple of boys in the park who were kicking a pigeon with a broken wing around as if it was a football. They'd turned on her. It had taken her half an hour longer than usual to walk home that day. Dawdling along, crying all the tears that she wanted to cry at the pain, the humiliation of having been beaten, so that by the time she got home she could be dry-eyed and stoic, just how he expected her to be. At times like this she ached for her mother. The idea of a mother anyway; what she imagined having a mother might be like. Her dad had been so proud when she told him what had happened that he almost burst. For him, stoicism and bravery were the only attributes that really mattered.

Then she had met Luke, Luke who'd been through so much himself that he saw through her immediately, through the accreted layers of defiance and stoicism, seen her terrible need for someone she could confide in.

'I know that mine Johnny stood on was planted.'

Alex shook his head, but didn't reply.

'I think Huan laid a mine and planted a skull beside it to draw Johnny in.'

He still didn't reply.

'I drove out to Koh Kroneg, last night.'

He dropped his gaze and met hers. 'You did *what*?'

'I drove out to the field.'

'Are you crazy? This is Cambodia for Christ's sake, not – where the hell do you come from – England? – this is not England. This place is dangerous.'

'It wasn't dark. It was evening, still light.'

'It was stupid.'

Her eyes flashed. 'I can look after myself.'

Alex shook his head and said almost gently, 'You could have asked me to go with you.'

'Oh, please. We barely know each other. And you haven't exactly been engaging company, the couple of times we have met.' She moved away. Went to stand by the window, staring through the dusty glass. A white Land Cruiser drove down the street, and she tensed, but it didn't slow as it neared the gates to MCT House and drove straight past.

A moment later she heard a movement behind her, felt his hand brush her arm. 'What did you find, Tess?'

She turned slowly to face him. 'I found an anti-tank mine, laid under the anti-personnel mine that maimed Johnny. Fuse out. Set to sympathetically detonate.'

'*What?*'

'It would have vaporised him if it had worked.'

'Jesus.' He groaned. 'Are you certain it was an anti-tank mine?' His dark eyes scrutinised her face.

She gave a grim smile. 'It's under my bed at the boarding house if you need proof. And I do know an anti-tank mine when I see one, whatever the hell you might think.'

He held up his hands defensively. 'OK, OK, so why didn't it work?'

'Maybe the distance between the two mines was too great, or maybe the explosive in the anti-tank mine just failed. It was a Russian TN52, fucking ancient. Either way, it does prove that the "missed mine" theory is bullshit, unless Huan forgot to switch his detector on at all.'

Alex rubbed a hand across his eyes.

'Planted deliberately, Alex. Someone tried to kill Johnny.'

'Planted by Huan? That's what you think, isn't it?'

'He couldn't have missed an anti-tank mine in his lane, he *couldn't* have done. He was "off sick" the day Johnny stood on the mine. If he had been there, he would have gone in to check out the skull, not Johnny. And he hasn't been seen since Johnny was injured. Why? Where is he? If he had nothing to do with it, why doesn't he just come back?'

'Johnny wasn't worried about Huan.'

'Does Johnny worry about anything? OK, you know him better than me. But I don't think he was brought up to think that anything impinged on his world.' She met his gaze. 'Do you know Huan, Alex?'

'I know Huan, but I don't *know* him. I don't think anyone does, except Johnny perhaps.'

'Because Johnny was his platoon commander?'

Alex nodded. 'He was one of the quiet ones. Worked well. Johnny said he was a good clearer. Reliable. Nothing else.'

Tess looked down at her hands, pressed together. 'So what do you think, Alex?'

'I don't know.' His voice was tight. 'Have you told anyone else, Tess? About what you're doing out here? About what you found last night?'

'No.'

'Good. Don't.'

'Why? In case the White Crocodile hears me?'

He gave the suggestion of a smile. 'No smoke without fire. Isn't that what you Brits say?'

She was struck by how the smile transformed him, made him boyish. But it was gone, as quickly as it had appeared.

'You found that woman, didn't you? This morning?'

'Yes, I found her. Jacqueline, she was called. Jacqueline Rong.' Her gaze dipped to the floor. 'I found her, and then MacSween drove her little boy to the orphanage.'

'She's not the only one.'

Tess looked up. 'What do you mean?'

'There are others. Ten, fifteen gone missing, a couple killed, all from villages surrounding that minefield.'

'Surrounding Koh Kroneg?'

He nodded. 'MacSween didn't tell you?'

'No.'

'The locals think that the White Crocodile has possessed the place, that it's taken these women.' Alex gave a short, harsh laugh. 'MacSween doesn't want to freak out our Khmer mine clearers. MCT's history if they get scared. So he's playing everything down. But that's going to get harder, with Johnny's accident, plus the other we had six months ago—'

Silence – a silence which quickly began to feel awkward.

Alex broke it. 'Go back to your apartment and pack your things. You're leaving tomorrow.'

'What?' *Where the hell had that come from?* 'Fuck off. No way.'

He bent nearer to her, lowering his voice. 'You need to listen to me, Tess.'

'*No.* Who are you to tell me what to do?'

He placed his hands on her shoulders. 'Listen to me, Tess.'

'Get off me.' She tried to pull away.

'For Christ's sake, listen to me.' There was only a thin veil of control in his voice.

'Get your fucking hands off me.' She shoved him with the flat of her hands.

'You need to leave. Before you get in too far.'

'You've got no right to tell me what to do. You don't know anything about me.'

'That's where you're wrong.'

'What the fuck does that mean?' She suddenly felt desperate to be away from him. Twisting sideways, she bent her head and sank her teeth into his hand. Swearing, he let go of her shoulders. She turned and ran for the door.

'Do you think Luke was murdered, Tess?'

His words stopped her in her tracks.

'I know that you were married to Luke, and I know why you're here.'

Slowly she turned back to face him; his gaze locked with hers.

'You don't know anything about this place, Tess. Go home before you no longer can.'

20

Tiep Thilda liked to get up early, to tend to her animals before anyone else in the village was awake. She hated the sideways glances from the other villagers and the woman she seemed to be when she saw herself through their eyes: someone to scorn, barely out of her teens, stuck with six-month-old twins – neither of them a boy – left by a husband who had vanished into thin air one night when she was seven months pregnant. At first there had been sympathy, but that had hardened into suspicion and, lately, outright mistrust. She knew they talked about her, questioned whether her 'husband' had left payment and disappeared once her allure had vanished with her swelling belly. How else could she afford two goats for milk and six healthy laying chickens?

Four in the morning; she was alone. The one light she could see shone from a hut at the far end of the village, well out of her way. She crossed the damp expanse of grass to the small, muddy corral where she kept her animals, walking carefully to avoid tripping, navigating by the light of the full moon. She had built it near to the edge of the jungle, fifty metres up a shallow hill from her hut, so that the animals had shade on hot days, but were still close enough for her to keep an eye on them. She came to the corral, put the feed bucket down and bent to slide through the parallel bamboo poles of the fence.

A noise behind her. She wasn't a girl who scared easily, but it irritated her to think that someone had taken to spying on her. It was the same noise she had heard yesterday morning. And the morning before. She had searched the tree line behind her carefully on the previous occasions and seen nothing.

Straightening up on the other side of the fence, the goats jostling her for food, she scanned the edge of the jungle again, the foliage drained of colour by the moon's light. For the first time now came creeping unease. She had heard whispers of a girl disappearing from a neighbouring village, bordering the same minefield, a few nights ago. She didn't know if they were true: nobody spoke directly to her any more and what she knew was pieced together from overheard snatches of conversation as she had collected drinking water from the well. A wind stirred the leaves, and suddenly her mouth felt completely dry.

She looked down the hill to the village. A man had come out of one of the huts near hers. She could see the light from his lantern as he moved around. She could make it back to her own hut – it was an easy downhill run – in less than a minute. Shunting herself back out of the fence, she broke into a jog, barely managing to stay on her feet in the slick of mud. She could no longer hear the rustling of leaves in the jungle behind her; everything was masked by her own heaving breath. The lantern had disappeared, but she could see a pale glow reflected on the ground near the village. Tiep was nearing the huts now, only a few metres to safety. But as she came down the slope her momentum threw her weight forward and, losing her footing, she came crashing down and half slid, half rolled on to her face.

Someone was looming over her. Hands grasped her arm. She twisted on to her back, ready to aim a vicious kick in defence. It was just the old man, wearing a pale woollen cloak against the early morning chill.

'*Daa neh sok sabbai te?*' he asked. Are you OK?

She sat up groggily, let him help her to her feet.

'*La'or, arkhun,*' I'm fine, she said, '*la'or, arkhun,*' staring past him into the black, silent chasm of the jungle, hugging her grazed arms tightly across her chest.

21

A hand had shot up. One of Alex's mine clearers must have found something; he had pulled his teams back to safe ground while he went to investigate. Tess watched him walk up the clearance lane, the Khmer mine clearer trotting behind, trying to keep up with Alex's stride. He looked confident, in control.

Her teams had found ten anti-personnel blast mines this morning, but since the last break three-quarters of an hour ago, nothing. That was how it was with mine clearing. Nothing for ages and then—

'Tess!'

She swung around. Alex was waving, calling her over. He had returned to safe ground and was instructing his mine clearers to pull back to the knot of Land Cruisers, two hundred metres from the near edge of the field. He must have found something difficult. Something big. Tess crossed slowly towards him.

'I need your help,' he said, when she reached him.

Tess nodded, eyes cast somewhere over his left shoulder.

'Tess?'

She felt him staring hard at her.

'Yes, I heard what you said. You called and here I am, at your service.' She said it lightly. That he knew of her relationship to Luke made her feel horribly exposed.

'OK, as far as I can tell it is two anti-personnel fragmentation mines, one a stake mine, the other a bounding mine. The guys, my guys, don't have enough experience to handle it.'

'It's fine. Like I said – I'm happy to help.'

'Thank you.' He hesitated, dragged his fingers through the rough stubble on his chin. 'The mines are hidden in thick scrub, so I might not have seen everything. There could be anti-personnel blast mines in addition, maybe anti-tank, though that isn't likely. Call your clearers back from the field. If this goes there will be carnage.'

Tess returned to her teams and instructed them to join Alex's by the vehicles, well into safe ground. As she walked back to Alex, she tested her detector, shook her belt to check that her tools were secure, tightened her flak jacket, lowered her visor.

'Ready?' He flashed her a tense smile.

She nodded.

'Let's go then.'

They walked down the clearance lane, Alex leading, Tess jogging occasionally to keep up. The lane wound down a dirt road on the edge of a paddy field. On the left side it dipped under the cloudy surface of the half-flooded rows. To their right, undergrowth banked the road for a hundred metres or more. Alex stopped suddenly, crouched, waving at Tess to stay behind him.

'See that trip wire?'

He pointed to a spot just in front of them, on the fringe of the vegetation.

Tess stared hard.

'No.' She was tense, struggling to concentrate. Alex was uncomfortably close. Shifting sideways, she edged away from him and cast her eyes up the track again, trying to pick out the trip wire against the mess of colours and textures in the background. 'No, I can't see it.'

'There. From the trunk of that first palm. The fragmentation mine – a POMZ-2 – is hidden in the undergrowth at its base. The trip wire stretches over the dirt road and is anchored in the paddy field.' He looked at her to make sure she understood. 'Under the surface of the water.'

Tess followed the line of his finger, and then she saw it glint: a length of wire, thin as gossamer.

'Got it.' The POMZ-2 it was anchored to was an unripe pineapple packed with explosive, fitted to a wooden stake. Snagging the trip wire would free the striker's retaining pin, releasing the striker into the detonator assembly and initiating the main charge. The explosion would shatter the steel body, blasting lethal fragments for fifty metres. Tess traced her eyes along the trip wire, from where it broke through the algae on the surface of the paddy field towards the POMZ-2, then, 'Christ, there's—'

'Another one. Running from a bounding fragmentation mine.' Alex indicated a second palm tree, just beyond the first. A fat olive-green finger of steel was just visible amongst the grasses clogging the tree's base. The second trip wire crossed the first in the middle of the dirt road.

'What do you think it is?' he asked.

'The frag mine?'

He nodded. She glanced at him quickly. Was he trying to test her? 'Maybe a Type 69 – looks like it from what I can see. Could be an OZM-3 or 4, but I don't think so. I think it's a Type 69 because of the colour and shape of the plunger.'

A Type 69 contained a propellant and a main charge. Tripping the wire would release the striker, initiating the fuse; the fuse's flash would ignite the propellant, blowing the mine into the air and igniting the pyrotechnic delay element in turn.

Before the mine reached 1.5 metres – groin height – the main charge would detonate, fracturing the steel body.

'I think you're right.' He pointed back to the first palm tree. 'And if you look back to the POMZ-2, right of it, you can see the trip wire continuing into the wood. I think it passes through the safety-pin hole in the striker and keeps going – tensioned – wired to blow if it's tripped or if it's cut. I am pretty sure that the one from the Type 69 runs away only and it's slightly loose, so it's only armed to operate when tripped. We'll have to trace both ends of it though, to make sure before we cut it.'

'That's a pretty dodgy arrangement for whoever laid it. They were either very good or very stupid.'

'Maybe both.'

Tess glanced over and met his gaze. His dark eyes were warm, alive. He was a different animal from the one she had encountered last night. She looked away, unable to hold his gaze.

'I'm going forward for a closer look,' she heard him say. He was kneeling now, reaching to the battery pack of his detector to switch it on. 'Then I'll wire the fuses to neutralise the mines and we can cut the trip wires. You OK with that?'

She nodded. It was vital to neutralise a mine before cutting its trip wire; this way, if while cutting the trip wire you accidentally triggered it, the safety pin or wire you'd wrapped through the fuse would prevent the striker being released into the detonator assembly and initiating the mine.

'Good.' Alex straightened and made to move forward.

Tess grabbed his ankle. 'Watch for blast mines, Alex. There could be blast mines buried where the trip wires cross.'

She caught the flicker of a smile that crossed his face as he looked down at her.

'Thanks,' he said.

She dropped her hand quickly, feeling foolish. A moment later, he had stepped forward and was running his detector slowly left to right across the muddy soil in front of the trip wires. Silence. Crouching, he extended his reach, stretching his detector directly under where the two trip wires crossed. A shrill electronic whine cut through the heavy air. He glanced over his shoulder at her, nodded. She'd been right. There was something there at the nexus between the wires.

Sliding carefully on to his stomach, Alex pulled his prodder from his belt and began to snake forward. Tess inched after him, eyes on the trip wires stretched just in front of him. One touch was all it would need. *Don't think about it.* Instinctively, she reached forward and laid her hand on his back, pressing into it, keeping in contact with him. For a long moment, the only sound was the soft slush slush of their bodies through the mud.

'PMN-2.' A half-circle of black and green plastic in the muddy ground, tilted slightly to its side. A PMN-2 anti-personnel blast mine: it could take a leg off. Tess watched, almost holding her breath, as slowly, gently, Alex began to uncover it from its bed of soil, brushing his hand over its top without placing any pressure on the plate, gouging a hole next to it big enough to bury high explosive.

A crack of thunder sounded suddenly, jerking them from their absorption. The sky had turned from blue to dusty black. Tess hadn't noticed, but now that she was aware of the sky, she felt the heaviness in the air, the moisture on her skin. It would soon rain. Rain destabilised the ground, made tools and hands slippery, clouded visors and impaired vision.

Alex cast a grimace at the sky. Sliding his forearm under

his visor, he mopped his face with a sleeve. As he dropped his hand, Tess saw another wink of green in the soft brown earth. Almost invisible.

'Alex, *stop*.'

His hand froze in mid-air.

'I think there's another mine.'

'Where?' He sounded oddly calm. But she could see his raised hand trembling – a muscle spasm in his jaw. She reached forward, tensing her muscles against the shaking in her own hand, and pointed.

'There. Where you were going to put your left hand.'

Alex looked hard, muttered – 'Fuck' – and began to slither backwards, dragging himself carefully over the ground he had already crawled through. He stopped and lay still, breathing hard. Tess squatted next to him, heart jumping against her ribcage.

Another crack of thunder, louder, closer. The sky broke and fat drops of rain speckled the surface of the road.

'We have to move fast.' Alex took a deep breath. 'I'm going to have another look.' He slithered forward again, prodder in hand, and started easing it into the ground around the flash of green. Contact, immediately. 'It's another mine, for sure. Bastards.' Laying the prodder down, he started digging at the soil with his fingers, carefully excavating.

The rain was lashing now, hammering against their visors, soaking their clothes. The surface of the paddy field was a boiling explosion of circles and bubbles. Alex's fingers were muddy, slippery. Tess moved her hand to his back again, sliding it to the bottom of his flak jacket, grabbing a tense handful of his shirt in her fist. He glanced behind him and they exchanged tight half-smiles.

'A Type 72 anti-personnel mine.' Alex's voice, firm, objective, but she could hear the catch in the words, the choppy sound of his breathing. A Type 72: tiny, minimum metal, incredibly hard to detect. Buried next to the PMN-2, so that it would be missed. So that a mine clearer would nudge it accidentally while clearing the PMN-2 and blow his hand off. 'I'm going to wire the fuses on the frag mines and cut the trip wires,' he said. 'Then we can lay explosive and detonate them all at the same time.'

Tess nodded. 'I'll wire one, you wire the other.'

'No.' He turned. 'You get the explosive.'

'Alex, I'm not going to leave you now—'

'Just go and get the explosive.'

'Alex—'

'It's an order,' he snapped. He looked embarrassed. 'Look, there is no point both of us risking it here.'

'That's my job.'

'Please . . . just . . . go.'

Reluctantly, Tess climbed stiffly to her feet. Cast him one last look before turning and trudging back down the lane.

When she returned with the plastic explosive and detonator cord, Alex was standing, hands in his pockets, staring through the curtain of rain out across the paddy fields. As she approached, he turned, reaching for the explosives with a brief smile. But instead of taking them, he closed his hand around hers. Their eyes met.

'Last night,' he said. 'I behaved badly.'

She shifted uncomfortably; couldn't decide whether to yank her hand away or to leave it where it was and hear him out.

'You were sleep-deprived. You felt like shit,' she said eventually.

'Yes. I still feel like shit.'

She smiled, despite herself.

'And I . . . wanted to apologise.'

'Go on then.'

He looked confused. 'Go on what?'

'Apologise. You said you wanted to apologise, so apologise. Saying "I wanted to apologise" isn't an apology.'

Alex gave a low whistle. 'Jesus! You don't make it easy, do you?'

She felt a sudden stab of real anger and was surprised by it.

'It's getting late. The guys are waiting.' She held up the explosive. 'Let's just finish the job.'

Together, in silence, they laid the explosive. Running a length of detonator cord in a circle to make the ring main; taping four lengths of det cord, one for each mine, to it; knotting the other lengths' other ends and moulding plastic explosive around each knot; laying the explosive in small craters excavated next to each mine. Finally they crimped a long length of safety fuse to a flash detonator and taped the flash detonator to the two ends of the ring main, completing the circle.

'Let's go,' Alex said, rising to his feet and trailing the safety fuse after him.

They trudged slowly back down the track towards the vehicles, slipping on the muddy bank, heads lowered against the driving rain, playing out the safety fuse until they reached its end. Alex lit it, and they jogged further back, well into safe ground. Turning, they squatted down to watch. A second later, the high explosive blew, detonating the mines. A massive, beating pulse hammered through the rain as the mines exploded fractionally apart in a lethal shower of metal fragments fifty metres wide.

When the explosion had died down, Alex stood and brushed

at the front of his shirt. It was caked in mud, his shirt and shorts plastered to his body. Tess knew she looked the same, worse maybe.

'Good job,' he said mildly. 'I'm glad you were with me.'

'No problem. Don't take it personally, but I have to say it was absolutely no fun at all.'

'No.' Alex shook his head solemnly. 'It wasn't the best.' He wiped a hand through his dripping hair, then, without warning, reached over and took hold of a strand of hers. 'You've got mud in your hair.' He dragged his fingers through it, almost absent-mindedly. Tess stood stock still, staring at her feet. But when she glanced up out of the corner of her eye, she realised that he wasn't even looking at her. He was gazing out across the minefield, a stricken look on his face.

'What's the matter, Alex?'

He shook his head, refocusing on her. 'I meant what I said, about you going back to England.' He paused. 'I made a mistake.'

'Mistake? About what?'

He sighed, and she felt sure he was about to answer her, but then the expression on his face changed, a shutter falling. She laid a hand on his arm.

'In MCT House last night, you asked me if I thought Luke was murdered, and you know my answer. But what about you? What do you think?'

He shuffled his feet. 'Does it matter what I think?'

'It matters to me. And I'm pretty sure that it would matter to those women – and to Johnny. Because they're all related, aren't they? I don't know why yet, but I do know that these attacks are related. It doesn't take a genius to work that out.' She dropped her hand from his arm. 'I came to Cambodia to find out who murdered Luke. It's bigger than him now. But I'm still not going to stop until I find out the truth. I'm not going to sit tight and be good and do nothing. And I'm *not* going home.' She paused. 'So what *do* you think, Alex?'

He looked up and their eyes locked. 'I think you're right, Tess. I think that Luke was murdered. I also meant what I said in the office. Christ knows what's going on, but nothing good can come from it, and if you don't have to be here, *go*. Go home. Get on a fucking plane, and go back to England and then you'll be safe. I should never have—' He broke off, shaking his head.

'Never have what?'

'Nothing.' He wouldn't meet her gaze. 'It's nothing important.'

Turning, he started walking back up the lane into the minefield.

'For fuck's sake, Alex, stop talking in riddles,' she shouted after him. 'Tell me the truth. I can take it.'

He kept walking.

*

There was someone standing next to the bed. He knew, but he didn't want to turn his head.

'Johnny.' A soft voice, familiar. Johnny remained silent. He heard the scrape of a chair, the creak of wood and an exhalation as Dr Ung sat down, then pressure on the edge of the mattress, and a light touch on his arm. 'Johnny.'

He was staring at the patterns of light and shade on the mosquito mesh. They were leaping and twisting. It must be windy outside, and wind meant the coming of rain – never one without the other in Cambodia. He hadn't noticed, hadn't felt the slight dip in temperature, the swell of moisture in the air, because his fan kept turning night and day.

He turned his head slowly and looked at Dr Ung. 'What?'

He reminded Johnny of a little bird, with his slight build and neat, precise movements.

'Ah.' Dr Ung pressed his hands together. 'Sorry to wake you,' he murmured, with mock apology.

Johnny said nothing. He stared blankly into Dr Ung's face.

'You look better,' Dr Ung said. 'How do you feel?'

How do you think I feel? After a long pause he said, 'Fine,' in a tiny, weary voice. He tilted his head back to the window. It had begun to rain. The rhythmic patter of drops was just audible over the beating of the fan.

He heard Dr Ung sigh. 'Johnny. Johnny, you have to . . .'

'No,' he hissed, twisting back. 'I don't want your advice. I don't need counselling. I just want you to make me better, so that I can get out of this fucking hospital.' Jamming his eyes shut, he stared hard into the colours blooming on the inside of his eyelids, trying to empty his mind of everything. The fear that he was being hunted, that this was just the beginning. That the Crocodile would eat him by increments. And there was not a damn thing he could do to help himself.

22

Manchester, England

Walking into the autopsy room, Andy Wessex always felt intensely aware of his own body. It was to do with the antiseptic quality of the place: white tiled walls, lino floor, white plastic dissecting tables, a white painted ceiling inlaid with rows of fluorescent lights; air so chill that on late autumn days like this his breath condensed. Every condition of the atmosphere in here was meant to throw the human body into relief, leave no room for ambiguity. The place smelled of disinfectant layered over something brutally primal. Iodine and meat.

Jane Percival was leaning over the table closest to him. A glance at the corpse in front of her, opened from neck to pubic bone, told Wessex that this was his victim. The hair and the skin colour were recognisable, and the rest he would have been happy to gloss over, if he'd had the choice. Percival turned around at his footsteps, laying down her scalpel and holding up a gloved, splattered hand.

'DI Wessex – nice to see you again. I'd shake your hand if I could.'

She was small and slim, late fifties, grey hair pulled back into a neat chignon, her mild blue eyes intelligent and warm. Wessex liked her best of all the pathologists he knew. She was frank and direct and he'd tried hard to imagine what had led her to choose this career. So he'd asked her once. She'd told him that forensic pathology was the most extraordinary puzzle. All the pleasure of the most complicated diagnoses. 'But it feels purer than any other branch of medicine, because we don't prescribe. We don't have that responsibility. We just observe.'

Now she gestured to the girl on the table. 'Have you ID'd this poor soul yet?'

Wessex shook his head. 'The passport led me to an uncomfortable conversation with a couple of good folks in Altrincham, but nowhere else. It was stolen from a half-English, half-Sri Lankan girl who's staying with her uncle in Colombo, saving turtles. So we're back to square one, and I need all the help I can get from you.'

Percival's gaze refocused on the corpse. It was small and painfully thin, like the drug addicts Wessex picked up in Moss Side, who'd go without food for days if it meant they could save up for a hit. Where her eyes and nose should have been there was a ragged hole, the rich cream cartilage of the nose standing proud. Whatever was left in the eye sockets was the colour of burgundy.

'Foxes most likely,' Percival said, catching his gaze.

Wessex steadied himself. 'Not the fat old Staffie then?'

'No. We've got a few teeth marks around the wrist which match the dog, but nothing else. I'd say it was just being inquisitive.' Percival gave a grim smile. 'You'd better let the owner know. He probably hasn't looked at the poor creature in the same way since.'

Wessex's eyes closed for a moment. 'How old was she?'

'Teenager from the length of the long bones. Sixteen. Seventeen.'

'Do we have time and cause of death?'

'Yes and no.'

146

'And that means . . . ?'

'Entomology will be more exact, but I can give you a pretty good time of death. Given the fact she was found outside and the state of the weather – which luckily for us has slowed decomposition right down – she's been dead for around eighty hours, give or take.'

'OK. So that means middle of the night, three days ago. Sunday night . . . actually Monday morning. One or two a.m.?'

Percival nodded. 'That would be about right.'

'And the cause of death?'

'That's the "no" part.'

'What do you mean?'

'Frankly, I'm confused.' She indicated the mass of bruised intestines pooled inside the chest cavity. 'It's a very similar pathology to that which we see in road traffic accident victims. Massive internal injuries. Her insides are basically mush. And here . . .' Jane Percival slid her hands under the corpse and tilted her. 'A huge bruise on her back, and her spine is broken just above the pelvis. Also her left femur is shattered. The right leg's bruised, but no breaks.'

'So she was hit by a car?'

'I'm not sure. You found her in the middle of a wood, didn't you?'

Wessex nodded. 'Rose Hill woods. It's surrounded by roads, but you'd struggle to get a car up near to where she was found. Could she have been beaten, with a baseball bat or something like that?'

She shook her head. 'No. Look. It's one huge bruise, not lots of them. Even if they blended together, I'd be able to tell that each was inflicted separately. They wouldn't be as uniform in colour as this.' Percival slid her hand back out from under the body. 'Her clothes were torn and the skin is badly scratched all over, and I pulled some splinters and bits of bark from some of the scratches, so it's wood – living trees – that made the scratches. I also found some spruce needles in her skin.'

'Rose Hill woods is predominantly conifers.'

'That makes sense. So she was probably running through the trees, through Rose Hill woods.'

'To get away from someone?'

Percival shrugged. 'That's your department, Sherlock.'

Wessex grimaced. 'OK, OK. So she was hit by a car in the wood. Or she was hit and then staggered through the wood.'

Percival shook her head. 'Not with the extent of these internal injuries, or a shattered femur.'

Wessex rubbed a weary hand over his eyes. They hadn't found any tyre tracks, though the weather wasn't helping to preserve the crime scene.

'Doesn't make sense,' he muttered.

The smell of the opened body hit him in a wave, made his own insides lurch for a moment, and he shivered, refocused. Sexist though it might be, women and girls always affected him the most.

'Could she have been carried and dumped there?'

'Perhaps. But I didn't find any foreign DNA on her body. No hairs, no blood on her skin or under her fingernails, nothing – though the slushy rain and sleet over the past few days has pretty much washed it clean. She doesn't have bruises consistent with being carried over a significant distance.' Percival stepped back from the table. 'A body gets heavy after a while, even one as emaciated as this. Carried over the shoulder, she'd have faint bruises on her stomach and thighs. In the arms, well, it would have to be a pretty solid guy, so maybe you're looking for Popeye.'

Wessex gave her a grim smile. 'You're not giving me much, Jane.'

'You're the detective, Andy. I'm just a middle-aged lady who likes dead people.'

Wessex bent down, indicating the victim's right thigh with the tip of his index finger. 'Something to go on at least.' A plain black tattoo – a symbol – nothing he recognised as one of the Manchester gang tattoos, but new gangs were being formed all the time, so that didn't mean much. The ink fuzzy where it had leached into the skin around it. 'An old one by the state of it.'

'Not old. Just an amateur job. I'll have the ink analysed and I've already sent off the DNA samples and taken a blood sample for testing. I bumped into Viles this morning and she said you didn't have much to go on, so I've asked the lab to be quick.'

'You're a sweetheart.' He rubbed a hand across his eyes and yawned. 'Give me a call if you find anything else.'

'We've still got a bit to do, so we might turn up something useful.'

Wessex peeled off his gloves, dropped them into a yellow biohazard bin and made his way over to the sink.

Percival held up a finger. 'There's one other thing, though, that might interest you.'

Wessex looked back. 'Yes?'

'She's had a child.'

'I know.'

'What?'

'I know. Barely more than a child.'

'I said she's *had* a child. She's given birth.' Percival cast him a stern look. 'You'll be doing her a favour if you get some sleep, Detective Inspector.'

23

There was something about Jakkleson's office which invariably made MacSween intensely uncomfortable. The orderliness. The obsessive, damn womanly fastidiousness of the place. He always suspected that he wouldn't be able to find what he was looking for in here and usually he was right. Now, after a desultory minute of searching through the desk drawers and a quick scan of the cupboard, when he realised that Jakkleson had probably stored the personnel files in his filing cabinet, to which he had the only key, MacSween went back on to the landing, leaned over the banister and yelled down the stairs.

'Jakkleson, for Christ's sake come up here and find something for me, will you.' He leaned against the window – watching the flowers in the garden wilt in the heat, a bent figure shaded under a checked krama scarf and straw coolie hat making its enervated way down the potholed road outside the gates – while Jakkleson's light tread approached on the stairs. 'Huan's file?' he asked, when he heard the footsteps stop. 'Any ideas? I can't find a damn thing in this museum of yours.'

Jakkleson paused in the doorway. He raised a hand to his ear. 'It's . . . all the personnel files are in there.' Stepping forward, he pointed to the filing cabinet.

'Get it out for me, will you,' MacSween said, remaining by the window. 'I want to trawl through, see if I can work out where Huan could have got to.'

MacSween waited, fingers tapping a restless motif on his thigh, watching while Jakkleson flicked through the personnel files.

'What? What's wrong?'

Jakkleson had stopped, brows knitted together. He tilted forward and ran his finger along the top of a couple of adjacent files, checking the names, straightened, flicked through the files again.

'*What?*'

'It's missing. Huan's file is missing.'

'Are you sure?'

'It's not here. It is definitely not here.'

'OK.' MacSween nodded slowly. He felt suddenly light-headed. 'Sooo . . . where could it have got to? Is it lost?'

Jakkleson shrugged. His forehead had flushed under the white-blond slick of his fringe. 'I don't know. But I . . . I did notice something this morning. I should have paid more attention to it at the time, perhaps.' He withdrew the key from the filing cabinet and tapped his forefinger on the lock. 'It's dented. See. The lock is dented. I think someone opened the filing cabinet without a key.'

'Oh, Christ.' MacSween raised his index fingers to his temples as if he was suddenly immensely tired. 'This is in danger of turning into a mess. A complete fucking mess.'

When he crossed the room and inspected the lock himself, he saw that Jakkleson was right. Someone had tried to force it. 'It wasn't like this yesterday?'

Jakkleson shook his head.

'You're certain?'

'I notice things like that.'

'Aye, you do.' MacSween cleared his throat. 'Any ideas, Tord? Any ideas who it might have been? Who could have taken that goddamn file?'

Jakkleson remained still, silent, staring at the lock. 'No,' he said finally, rolling his eyes up to meet MacSween's, shaking his head. 'As you know, my office is always unlocked. It could have been anyone who has access to this building. Absolutely anyone.'

24

Battambang airport was one narrow strip of pitted tarmac framed by palms and frangipani trees and lined on either side by military hardware: ancient Russian T-54 tanks, a couple of armoured personnel carriers, three helicopters in muted camouflage. An ageing Royal Air Cambodge propeller aircraft had coasted to a stop on the runway as Tess parked, and a straggle of people were now filing down its rickety steps. Inside the tiny single-storey terminal building a couple of uniformed customs officials stood behind a long table. A policeman lounged in a corner, scanning the new arrivals from the window through mirrored Ray-Bans. Posters lined the wall behind him: one advertising the ancient temples of Angkor Wat, another Lake Tonle Sap, a third warning visitors of the danger of AIDS – the same baggy condom she had seen illuminated in the flash of Tord Jakkleson's camera.

Two civilian helicopters were stationed on the near side of the runway. Tess threaded her way towards them. The rain had stopped and the evening was bright and clear, but it was late enough that the shimmering liquid waves that come with real Cambodian heat had melted to a cooler, dusky haziness. She was still filthy from the minefields – the mud now dried and cracked on her combat shirt and shorts – but she hadn't wanted to go home to change before coming here. She wanted to catch whoever flew the MCT helicopter before they left for the day.

The two choppers looked as if they had been put to bed: windows covered with reflective material, doors locked, caps with ropes attached to them on the end of each rotor blade, tied down to prevent the blades spinning free in a sudden wind. Nearby was a shabby clapboard building with a corrugated-iron roof, white paint flaking from its walls. It looked as if someone had decided to redecorate, taken a paint stripper to it and then changed their mind halfway through the job. But the door was ajar, propped open with what looked like a car battery.

Inside, a young Khmer man in an oil-stained vest and boiler-suit trousers was lounging in a plastic chair, feet on the desk, eyes closed, a full ashtray resting on his lap. Thick black hair, bleached with a badger's streak, hung long over his forehead giving him the look of a rebellious schoolboy.

The room was stiflingly hot, the air so close that when Tess leaned in she felt as if a huge invisible hand was pushing her back. She was aware of a jumble of oddments on surfaces: piles of paper, dirty cups and plates, a radio, assorted bits of metal that looked like engine parts. A fly buzzed loudly against the single window.

Taking a step back, she knocked on the doorframe, and the man's legs jerked as if he'd been slapped. He bolted upright, feet thumping to the floor, the ashtray clattering from his lap. Seeing her, he pushed himself to his feet, sweeping his hands down his vest in an unsuccessful attempt to dust off the ash.

'Hi. Sorry to barge in on you like that.' She stepped into the room, holding out her hand. 'I'm Tess Hardy. Do you speak English?'

His head bobbed. 'Yuh. Some. Some.' He wiped his hand on his thigh and checked his palm before he took hers with a shy smile.

'I'm from Mine Clearance Trust, in Battambang. We share one of the helicopters. I'm not sure which one.'

'Ah, yuh.' He nodded. 'This one. MCT share this helicopter with Médecins Sans Frontières.' He leaned over the desk and tapped his index finger on the grimy glass, indicating the helicopter furthest from them. It was bigger than the other, with a sliding door in its side. Large enough to take a stretcher.

'Do you fly it?'

'Ah.' Again the shy smile, then a shake of his head. 'No.'

Tess's heart sank; the feeling must have telegraphed itself straight to her face.

'Mr Seymour,' he said quickly. 'Mr Seymour fly that helicopter.'

'Is he here?'

'No. Not here.'

'Has he left for the day?'

He looked confused.

'Gone home?' She waved a hand towards the door. 'Home.'

'Ah, yuh.'

'Where does he live?'

'Australia.'

'*Australia?*'

'Yuh. Gone home three days daughter get married, back—' He paused and cast his eyes to the floor, lips moving as he silently counted. 'Tomorrow tomorrow.'

'Friday?'

He shook his head. 'Tomorrow tomorrow.'

'Tomorrow . . . tomorrow? Oh, you mean the day after tomorrow? Saturday?'

His smile this time had a nervous tilt to it. 'Yuh. Saturday.
Late-late Saturday night-time.'

'Look,' she said, trying to keep the high note of impatience
out of her voice. 'I need to know about Monday. They – we –
radioed from the field to say that we had an emergency, that
we needed the helicopter immediately. But it didn't come. It
did not arrive. I need to find out why. Do you know what
happened?'

He lifted his shoulders in apology and shook his head.

'Does Mr Seymour keep a log, a book, something I could
look at?' She put her hands together, opened them flat, shut
them again.

He nodded. 'Ah. Yuh, book. Here.' Beckoning her to follow,
he snaked through the debris to the back of the hut and
stopped in front of a large chipboard desk. A broken plastic fan
was screwed to the wall above it. Surrounding the fan was a collage of posters and photographs: a koala squashed into the fork
of a tree; Sydney Opera House, its white roof lit sunset red;
a blond, tanned family dressed in singlets and matching Ber-
muda shorts on a white sand beach dotted with sunbathers.

'Here. You look.' He opened the desk drawer and pulled out
a large red book, which he handed to her.

'You must have lots of things to do,' Tess said, sitting down,
casting him what she hoped was a convincing smile. 'I'll be fine.
You've been very helpful.' Thankfully, he took the hint and left.

The book was thick, a page for each day of the year. She
flicked over the pages until she reached October, then flicked
back page by page until she found Monday 26th. There in spiky

capitals were the words 'Emergency call – 8.30 a.m.' She lifted a hand to brush the trickles of sweat from her eyes, then read the words again. 'Emergency call – 8.30 a.m.'

She sat back. Eight thirty? Was that right? It felt a bit late. But then she'd been so traumatised that she'd had no real idea what time it was when she had heard someone yelling – 'Helicopter. *Helicopter*' – into their radio.

Whatever. The call was there, logged, official. The call had been received and then what? Nothing. Nothing else written on that page. She flicked back a page and ran her eyes up the lines. The Sunday was blank, but on the Saturday there was another entry: 'Emergency medical supplies drop, Thma Pok, Médecins Sans Frontières.' A similar entry for MSF for the Thursday before but to Banteay Srei this time. On the Monday – exactly a week before Johnny's accident – the helicopter had been serviced. There were no other details, nothing about any mechanical problems or any repairs that might have been carried out, only that a service had been conducted.

Closing the book, she swivelled around in the seat. She was alone. Through the window she could see the young man walking across the tarmac, a bucket swinging from his hand. A whistled version of Lady Gaga's 'Marry the Night' drifted through the door.

Turning back to the desk, Tess began rummaging: through the papers littering the desktop, the single drawer, running her gaze over the notices on the walls, pulling the bin out to check its contents – empty – glancing over her shoulder every few seconds to make sure she was still alone. But there was nothing that related to Monday 26 October. Wearily, she pushed herself to her feet.

Outside the sun was sinking, flooding the runway with orange light. She pulled her sunglasses from her pocket and slipped them on. The young man was running a soapy sponge across the windscreen of MCT's helicopter; he turned as he heard her approach.

'Is OK?'

She half-nodded. 'Thanks, yes, but I've just one more question. Last Monday, in the morning, Mr Seymour's diary says that he did receive our emergency call. But, as I said before, the helicopter didn't arrive. We radioed again, but there was no answer. Did Mr Seymour say anything to you about it? Anything at all?'

'I was not here.' He pointed to the other helicopter. 'Flew Phnom Penh. Left morning, six. Back late.'

'OK.' She held out her hand. 'Thanks very much for your help.'

'Come back Sunday,' he urged, as he shook it. 'Speak Mr Seymour.'

She nodded. Sunday was a whole seventy-two hours away. *Anything* could happen by then.

25

'Fresh air's a good healer,' Dr Ung had said, jamming his fingers under the windowframe and heaving it open. 'And it's a beautiful evening, for the moment at least.' He had turned from the window, adjusting his glasses on the bridge of his nose. 'Tomorrow, we will get you up, Johnny. Ret S'Mai and I will help you.' Underlining his words with a firm nod, Dr Ung had crossed to the door, ignoring the scowl on Johnny's face.

Tossing his P. G. Wodehouse novel on the bedside table, Johnny relaxed back against the pillows and closed his eyes. The shadows of leaves from the trees shading the courtyard moved across his face, and a warm breeze carrying the sweet hint of frangipani flowers drifted through the room. A door swung open, then sucked against its rubber stopper as it closed.

Opening his eyes, Johnny tilted his head towards the window. Two figures were crossing the courtyard to the bench by the far wall, under the trees. One was tiny, a dwarf. Johnny narrowed his gaze. The dwarf was hobbling on his hands, which were wrapped with a protective padding of dirty white cloth. The remains of his legs, hip-length stumps, swung beneath him, the muscles of his arms taut and overdeveloped in relation to the rest of his wasted body. Johnny watched as he made his way over to the bench, shuffled himself around so that his back was against it, and lowered himself to the ground. His companion was a teenager, wearing a mustard-coloured T-shirt with a torn hem and stained khaki shorts. Wooden crutches jammed in his armpits supported him; his left leg was amputated mid-thigh, the skin on his right leg scarred, as if he had been held over an open fire until the flesh dripped from his bones. He hopped across the courtyard and settled himself on the bench, laid his crutches at his side, leaned his head back against the wall and smiled up through the leaves at the sun.

Johnny grimaced and picked up his book again, scanning the words without interest. The murmur of voices, the shrill laughter carried through his open window. The two men had been joined by others. God, how he despised their dumb cheer, their bovine acceptance despite everything that had happened to them – the swollen stumps of arms and legs, the ravaged flesh, and the pitted shrapnel scars peppering faces, necks and torsos.

Ret S'Mai was among them, his pressed olive-green hospital uniform baggy on his slight frame. Johnny hadn't noticed him arrive. He was describing something: arms raised, his useless hands carving excited tracks through the air. Revolted, Johnny tried to focus back on the lines of neat black type, but almost immediately his gaze was pulled back to the group by the bench. Ret S'Mai had stopped talking and was staring in through his window, straight at him, a sly lift to the corners of his mouth.

The novel thumped to the floor as Johnny threw himself flat against the mattress, jamming his hands against the headboard, pushing and slithering until he was below the level of the window-frame. He lay there, muscles trembling with the effort of keeping still. *Jesus Christ. Where is he? Is he still looking?* He couldn't see. Casting a glance at the door, he saw it was shut. *Good.*

Now that he was lying still, he realised how quickly his heart was beating – breath coming in short, sharp bursts through his nostrils, the edge of hyperventilation. Pursing his lips, he sucked a column of air deep into his lungs, his diaphragm contracting with the bubble of air in his abdomen, held it, eased it out, sucked in again. Gradually, his measured breathing, the warmth of the fading sun, the swell of perfumed air calmed him and his eyes drifted closed. Lying quite still, he let his mind waft around the room with the air: stroking the walls, swelling over the ceiling, floating out through the window, flowing across the courtyard and through the hospital gates, to life outside. My life, he thought dreamily.

Johnny.

'The maverick'. He *liked* being a maverick. It amused him. Playing. *There is always someone to play with.*

A sudden sensation that the mattress was tilting made him open his eyes. The white of the ceiling, a motionless fan, skittering patterns of light and shade. His vision blurred and refocused. Something was hanging over him. A face, its tiny eyes glassy. Ret S'Mai.

Johnny met his gaze. When Ret S'Mai smiled, Johnny began to scream.

*

The light was fading as Alex arrived at the hospital. The temperature had dropped, the wind had picked up, and though it was still fine in Battambang, flashes of an electric storm lit up the sky out west.

Through the windows of the common-room building, he

could see patients gathered around the tables drinking and talking, playing cards, a few relaxing on the bench by the wall, smoking cigarettes and laughing together. He stood and watched for a moment feeling an ache – something like envy – for the company. But he knew that in their case he had little to be envious of. Turning, he walked slowly away from the lights and cheer towards the dark hospital building.

As he neared it, he thought he heard another noise, cutting across the others. He paused and listened.

It sounded like somebody screaming.

He crossed the veranda in two steps. As he shoved through the doors into the dark corridor, something hurtled into him, smacking him square in the stomach. He fell back grasping vainly at air. Ret S'Mai, visible in the light coming through the open door, staggered backwards against the wall.

Alex found his feet.

Ret S'Mai's eyes were hooded and unreadable. 'Mr Johnny screaming.'

'Johnny?'

'Screaming. Couldn't find Dr Ung. He *screaming*.'

Alex held up his hands. 'It's OK.'

'*Trying* to help Mr Johnny.'

'Ret S'Mai, it's OK. Johnny's . . . Johnny's had a bad time. He's—' Breaking off, Alex lifted a hand and massaged his eyes. 'It's going to be OK,' he repeated, dropping his hand to his side.

I seen him. He die. What had Ret S'Mai meant? Alex glanced left and right. A dark, deserted corridor. He could take the opportunity to pin the little shit up against the wall and get some truth out of him. Stepping forward, he clamped a hand on Ret S'Mai's shoulder.

'Ret S'Mai, I—'

Johnny called out, his voice panicked.

Alex met Ret S'Mai's gaze for one brief moment, then he glanced towards Johnny's door. And realised his mistake. With breathtaking speed, Ret S'Mai brought his knee up hard into Alex's groin and twisted past him. Alex fell to his knees, groaning and cursing. Ret S'Mai burst through the door to the veranda and disappeared into the twilight.

*

Johnny was crumpled against the metal headboard, arms clamped around his pillow. He was wide-eyed and puce. Sweat stuck his shirt to his body. Seeing Alex in the doorway, he yelped and shrank back.

'It's me,' Alex said in a low voice.

Johnny's eyes skipped wildly around the room. '*Where is he?*'

'Who? Where is who?' He had no intention of fuelling Johnny's terror, not yet.

'*Ret S'Mai,*' Johnny screeched. '*He was in my room.*'

'I didn't see anyone. He must have gone.'

'No!' Johnny hissed, staring past Alex into the dimly lit corridor. 'He's still out there.'

Alex shook his head. The room was hot, breathless. 'Do you want me to switch the fan on?'

'*No.* It's quiet with it off. I need to be able to hear if he comes back.'

Alex limped into the room, shutting the door behind him.

He pulled a chair over to Johnny's bed. 'Ret S'Mai's just a kid, Johnny.'

Johnny's gaze snapped back to Alex. His eyes were bloodshot, the pupils unnaturally dilated. 'Mary Bell was just a kid too, Alex. Thompson and Venables were just kids.'

'I don't know who they are—'

'The Khmer Rouge used the kids in this country to torture and kill. To shop their parents for being too intellectual, for criticising the state. Murder their friends for being unproductive. People were terrified of the fucking kids.'

Alex lit a cigarette. Johnny held out his hand; Alex lit another and handed it to him.

'Ung despises cigarettes,' Johnny said, sucking on it greedily. His contemptuous gaze tracked around the room. 'This hospital is a shit hole.'

Alex took in the cool white walls, the teak floorboards, worn but spotlessly clean, the crisp white sheet that Johnny was feverishly twisting between bloodless fingers. He looked over to the window. He could see the odd flash of lightning through the trees, hear cracks of distant thunder.

'What's going on, Johnny?'

'Huh?'

Alex took a deep breath. 'It wasn't an accident. You – weren't an accident.'

Johnny was fidgeting again; he didn't seem to have heard. 'Give me another cigarette.'

'What?'

'Another cigarette.'

'What happened to the—' He broke off, catching sight of the stub of the first, ground out, barely smoked in the ashtray.

'Here.' He lit another and passed it over.

Cigarette clenched between his teeth, Johnny closed his eyes, hauling smoke deep into his lungs, funnelling it out through his nostrils. A blue fug formed low over the bed. 'What did you say?' Johnny was squinting up at Alex, through the haze. 'About my accident?'

Alex's mouth was suddenly dry. Was he making a mistake? He thought of Johnny and Luke again, arms draped around one another, laughing on the edge of Koh Kroneg.

'It wasn't an accident, Johnny. You were injured deliberately. The skull was bait. Someone put that mine there for *you*.'

Johnny's blood-rimmed eyes met his.

Through pale lips, Johnny whispered, 'He's Huan's nephew.'

'Who? What are you talking about?'

'Ret S'Mai. He's Huan's nephew.'

'Huan? The Huan in your troop?'

Johnny gave an almost imperceptible nod. 'It wasn't my fault. The moped lost traction, swerved into the side of my Land Cruiser.'

'You were drunk.'

'I'd had a few drinks. There *is* a difference.'

Alex sat forward and put his head in his hands. 'So you think Huan tried to kill you for revenge. For his brother's death, for Ret S'Mai?'

Johnny didn't answer. His lips around the cigarette had pressed into a line, and he was staring down at his hands playing restlessly with the seam of the bed sheet.

'What, Johnny? There's more, right?'

After a moment's hesitation, Johnny shook his head.

'Don't lie, Johnny. There's too much at stake.'

Johnny met Alex's gaze. Then he blinked and his eyes wandered over to the window.

'Johnny.'

'Oh, for Christ's sake. Before Keav. Before I moved Keav in, I had a fling with another Khmer girl. She was a teenager, fifteen, sixteen. Unmarried.'

Alex felt his heart sink. 'And?'

'It lasted for a few months. We met each other secretly. She used to come to my flat a couple of times a week. She was sweet, fun.'

'Who was she?'

'Just a girl, Alex. Just another Khmer girl hot for a Western man and his money.'

'Who?'

Thunder muttered on the edge of town.

'*Tell me*.'

'She was Ret S'Mai's sister.'

Alex put his head in his hands. 'Jesus, Johnny. Are you completely fucking stupid?'

'She wanted it, for Christ's sake. She wanted *me*.'

'She was fifteen. The niece of one of your mine clearers. Fuck.' Alex looked back at him. 'So what happened?'

'She, uh, she got pregnant. I took her to a guy I knew, paid for an abortion.'

'And then?'

'Then, nothing. I got . . . bored. She was too clingy, thought there was more to it than there was. She thought I was going to marry her.' He gave a harsh laugh. 'Like hell. I finished it. Gave her a bit of money and that was that—' He broke off with a shrug.

'And the abortion?'

167

'What about it?'

'Did anyone else know about it?'

'She said not. But now—'

'Now you think she told someone.'

'Looks like it, doesn't it?' His voice was barely audible.

'So where is she now?'

'I don't know. She disappeared. I tried to contact her a few times, but never got a reply, so I gave up.'

Alex shook his head despairingly. 'You're a fool, Johnny.'

'Don't be so fucking Bible class, Alex. I was only having a bit of fun, and she was scum anyway. All those girls are.' He reached over suddenly and took hold of Alex's arm; Alex felt his fingers trembling, gripping without strength. 'She's got her revenge now, hasn't she?' A sick smile had crept on to his face. 'You need to get me out of here, Alex. Before they come to finish me off.'

Alex untangled his arm and slid the chair back. 'I'll speak to Ung.'

'No, Alex. You. *You* need to help me.'

Alex held his gaze for a moment then turned towards the door. 'I have to go. I'll come first thing tomorrow.' He felt sick at Johnny. Sick and disgusted.

'Alex! Come on . . . mate—'

When the door had shut, Johnny slumped against the pillow and ground his fingers through his hair with a groan. He had to get out of here.

It was beginning to come back to him, in flashes. The accident. And before – the lead-up to it. A series of jerky images spliced together, jumbled and random.

He hadn't told Alex everything.

He hadn't told him about the ghosts.

26

It was dark, and Tiep wasn't even sure she could remember a time before the storm began. She could no longer stand the sound of the wind rushing in her ears. Her pulse throbbed and her head hurt and every limb ached.

She wished now that she had let her animals be. They would have survived one night without food. She had fed them this morning, checked them again at lunchtime. But they were all she had. All she and the twins had to live on, and she had known that it would just take a moment to run to the corral, toss some food into their troughs, run back to the hut and tuck herself in to sleep. She had told herself there was nothing to be frightened of out there: just wind and rain.

She thought of her twins in their wooden cot. Would they still be asleep, or would they have woken up and begun to cry for her, wondering why she wasn't coming to cuddle and comfort them? The thought emptied her of strength. She would never know the rest of their story. The glimpse she'd had of them as she crept out of the hut, asleep side by side in a tangle of arms and legs, was the last she'd ever have.

She leaned against the trunk of the tree and pressed her fingers against the hot, slippery skin at her throat. Fear, she had imagined, would give her energy, strength. And so it had been for a moment.

Leaning over the fence, tossing vegetable peelings into the

goats' trough, she had neither seen nor heard a thing. The first she knew was the grip on her shoulder. She had struck out viciously with the tin feed bucket she had been holding, swinging it behind her with as much force as she could muster. She felt it connect with bone, heard a crunch and a furious scream, swallowed immediately by the wind. If she had expected to be released, she had been wrong. The bucket was torn from her hand, and then she felt a terrible pressure sliding across the soft skin of her throat.

'*Sohm, te.*' Please, no, she said, and even in those two syllables she heard herself begging.

She raised her hands, felt them covered, hot, and when she held them in front of her, she saw she was wearing dark gloves. And then she was sitting in the mud, heavy footsteps moving away behind her towards the trees.

Tiep pressed hard, feeling the lips of the gash in her throat. Blood filled her mouth and she swallowed it down, felt her mouth fill again immediately. She coughed and spat. Her limbs felt weightless.

She'd been wrong about one thing, though. As the rain lashed down on the crown of the hill, she saw a movement on the other side of the corral. Samnang and Vana, her little girls, were lying there on a pallet of straw, sheltered from the rain by the canopy of branches that leaned over them from the edge of the jungle. Tiep lowered her hands, feeling the rain mingling with the tacky bib of blood on her chest. A fatalism settled on her. She would die here, but at least her children would be the final thing she saw. The girls weren't looking at her, but straight up, into the heart of the storm, their arms and legs moving slowly.

Gradually, her vision closed in. She was terribly cold, colder than she could remember ever having been. She looked to where the babies lay now, but of course they had never really been there at all. Instead there were just the two goats lying by the back fence, fur dark and matted, eyes gleaming. As she watched, one of them got up and walked towards her. Not on all fours, the way a goat should walk, but like a man walks, on its hind legs. Terror filled her. But there was only sadness in the goat's yellow eyes.

'*Ontharai*,' it said, softly, and darkness came as suddenly as it had when she was a little girl herself, and her mother blew out the flame on the shuttered lantern at bedtime.

27

The only remaining lead was Johnny. Luke had been afraid before he died, had obviously known that he was at risk. Did Johnny suspect, as Tess had discovered, that his own injury was deliberate? That he had now become a target for Luke's murderer?

She was halfway across the hospital courtyard when she noticed the Land Cruiser parked under the trees by the wall. *Dammit. Alex.* She couldn't go in to see Johnny with him there; didn't even want Alex to know that she was here.

She turned to retrace her steps, and a movement on the common-room veranda caught her eye. Ret S'Mai was standing in the strip of darkness between two windows, talking with someone.

She started towards him, lifting a hand. 'Ret S'Mai.'

He wheeled round. There was a man standing just behind him. Quickly, she took in the dark skin, the wide flat face, the high soft cheekbones, the crop of short, straight dark hair, the eyes, tiny, black, so similar to Ret S'Mai's. A face staring out from the team-room wall.

Huan.

She broke into a run. Huan leaped off the veranda and sprinted across the courtyard into the darkness of the street. Ret S'Mai remained, big head bobbed forward, eyes cast to the ground.

'Ret S'Mai . . .'

He backed away.

'You know Huan?'

A tiny nod. 'He my uncle.'

'I need to talk to him.'

'Talk to no one. No one at MCT.'

'Why?'

But Ret S'Mai wouldn't meet her gaze. She reached out and touched his arm; he looked up and their eyes met. There was a depth of venom in his gaze that shocked her. Cursing, she ducked away from him, across the courtyard and into the street. She stopped, looked left and right, left again. She couldn't see anything – it was so dark – then a car drove past the end of the road and she caught sight of Huan, bathed for a moment in its headlights, slipping across the intersection.

She started to run. Keeping to the middle of the road. Skipping over the potholes, loose gravel skittering under her boots, calling Huan's name between breaths. At the intersection, she paused – saw there was no traffic – and sprinted across. The street opposite was dark. The houses here were set well back from the road, their high, protective walls draped with foliage. She couldn't see Huan, but she could hear the echo of his pounding feet. At the end of the road he turned right, joining a wider, better-lit boulevard which led towards the river. Tess reached the corner at a sprint, twenty metres behind him. There he was, running hard, bathed in coloured lights from the food stalls lining the riverbank. She sprinted after him, keeping to the side of the road so she didn't get mown down by one of the mopeds. At the end of the road, Huan glanced behind him and dived into the crowd of Khmers thronging the stalls.

'Fuck.' She slowed and crossed the road at a walk, eyes scanning the milling faces. She pushed her way in amongst them, stood on tiptoes to scan over their heads. But clouds of smoke from wood fires and steam from cooking pots had massed above the stalls, held from dispersing in the night air by their plastic canopies; the fog reduced visibility to metres.

She gave up and began to wander among the stalls, gazing at the food, breathing in the smells, ignoring the eager faces and beckoning hands of stall owners, their customers squatting on stools, a steaming bowl in one hand, chopsticks pinched in the fingers of the other, some in groups, others alone, all staring up at her as she passed.

Tess emerged from the end of the food stalls into darkness, the sounds and smells fading behind her as she walked away. The storm had finally arrived. She hauled the collar of her shirt up around her face; rain melted into her hair and dripped down her neck. She jogged over to a tree by the side of the road and stood under it, gazing down at the river weaving through the darkness below her.

*

Standing under the tree, waiting for the rain to stop, Tess felt almost as if she was locked in a cage, the bars of rain fencing her in. She felt intensely frustrated – to have been so close to Huan and still not to have been able to reach him.

It was a feeling she had grown used to in Afghanistan. Always being one step behind: on the edge of achieving, of getting somewhere, but then never actually nailing the target. Securing a supply route, or clearing a village of IEDs – then hearing that the same route had been lost to the Taliban just a week later, or that most of the village had been razed in a Taliban mortar attack. The Afghan children she had seen watching the Engineers' clearance operation from doorways, buried alive under tons of rubble.

What now? She didn't want to go back to her room at Madam Chou's. That would feel like failure, and she wouldn't sleep well knowing that she'd spent most of the evening running in circles, chasing her tail.

Who could help her move forward? Alex was at the hospital, which put Johnny out of the picture, for the moment at least. MacSween was trying to keep the fear contained, and she was pretty certain that he wouldn't open up. So that left Jakkleson. She was loath to have anything to do with him after those photographs she had found, but then she thought back to what he had said in the meeting the morning after Johnny's accident.

You know that Johnny's a complete bloody liability, MacSween. In response, MacSween had exploded, she remembered, silencing him immediately. Jakkleson clearly had strong opinions about Johnny, so what had formed those opinions? He was also the admin man. He had written both reports – on Johnny's accident and Luke's death – and was the centre of information at MCT.

*

The Riverside Balcony Bar was a bar-restaurant on the second floor of an old wooden colonial building by the edge of the river. It was a favourite haunt of expatriate aid workers, and she had recognised it, from MacSween's description, as the backdrop to a couple of Jakkleson's more harmless photographs. It was surrounded by trees and open on three sides, giving it the feel of a treehouse in the jungle.

The bar was full, mainly locals. A smattering of middle-aged Western men: a few sitting around a table drinking, one sitting by the bar, his hand cupping the bottom of a young Khmer girl wearing tight white leggings and a flamingo-pink bra top. Beer girls in their skimpy dresses weaved through the tables, trying to sell their particular brand of beer with their charms. A few Khmer soldiers in uniform were crowded around two tables, pushed together, in the centre of the room.

She noticed Jakkleson immediately, sitting alone at a table in the far corner. He had his back to the room, so didn't see her enter. She slipped through the wicker tables and chairs to the bar and ordered an Angkor beer. Then she walked to the wooden balcony railing, close to his table, and leaned over it, staring at the dark snake of river below, sipping her beer. A few moments later, over the jumbled hum of conversation, she heard her name called. She turned.

'Jakkleson!'

He beckoned her to join him, standing and pulling out a chair for her. Sitting down, she met his pale gaze with a smile.

'I didn't realise you were here,' she said. 'How are you?'

'I'm . . . well – thank you. And what are *you* doing here?'

'I was just up at the hospital. Visiting Johnny. I decided to grab a beer on my way back home. I haven't been to central Battambang at night before.'

'You shouldn't either. Not alone.'

'I'm sure I'll survive.'

He didn't answer her.

'How *is* Johnny?' he asked, after a moment.

Tess shrugged. She wasn't about to explain to Jakkleson that she hadn't actually seen Johnny, or the reason why. 'I don't think he's the type to take an accident like that, a disability like that, in his stride.'

'No. No, he's not the type. I don't think he's ever had to face real adversity.' Leaning across, he touched her arm. 'Did you find what you were looking for in my office the other day?'

The question was so sudden that she was caught off balance. 'I was using the internet. I should have asked, but it was after office hours and you weren't there. I needed to email my father, let him know that I'm OK. He's not a fan of telephones.' She waited, almost holding her breath, wondering if he would press her on why she had been there so late at night.

He nodded. 'That's fine. You're welcome to use it when you need to. All the troop commanders should have offices, but there isn't the space, or the money.' He gave a short, hollow laugh. 'Johnny liked spending time in my office, too. He found my photographs interesting.'

Tess's heart leaped into her throat. She had put them back exactly as she'd found them. Hadn't she? And locked the drawer. *Hadn't she?* Now – on the spot – she couldn't think, couldn't remember.

'My family amused him,' Jakkleson continued, and she felt relief wash over her. 'It amused him to think that I was married. I'm not sure why.' He gave a thin smile.

Tess nodded; she didn't trust her voice enough to respond. Shifting her chair, she turned to survey the room, as Jakkleson

was. The middle-aged man at the bar had been joined by another, also in the company of a teenaged Khmer girl wearing a
strapless white minidress. The men were laughing together, the
women cuddling up to them diffidently. The Khmer soldiers
were drunk now, lolling in their chairs, their tabletop a riot of
dirty plates and empty bottles. Space had formed around them,
as if some imaginary line was forcing everyone else – even the
Westerners – to keep a distance.

'You come here to do good,' Jakkleson said suddenly. 'And
then—' He gestured irritably towards the room. 'Then this
world takes you over.'

Tess twisted to face him. 'This world?'

He nodded, but didn't elaborate. After a moment, she
turned back to the jumble of tables and bodies. The military
men were getting to their feet now. One swayed and knocked
the table as he stood, sending a couple of bottles crashing to the
ground. Another said something to him, something that made
him straighten immediately. Tess looked from him to the man
who had admonished him. He was tall, a head taller than the
rest, pale skin accentuated by jet-black hair, aquiline nose, his
eyes so black their irises merged into the pupils. He had five
stars on his epaulettes. An officer then.

Jakkleson's soft voice pulled her back. 'You go to Phnom
Penh and you see fifty-year-old Western men with eleven-year-
old Khmer girls. Many of these men are from aid agencies.
Their wives will be back home – their eleven-year-old daughters – thinking Daddy is off saving the world.'

Tess tried to catch his eye, but he wasn't looking at her. He
was still staring across the bar. She thought of the family smiling out from their silver frame on top of his filing cabinet.

'What leads people to behave like that?'

'Lack of respect. Power. Opportunity – knowing that they can behave in a way they wouldn't in their own countries and get away with it. Precedents set by others who came before. Perhaps, a combination of all four.' He spread his hands, nodding towards the military. They were leaving now, laughing at the waiter who had brought their bill, waving it away. 'They have power and they use it to exploit their own countrymen. We foreigners come to help and we see this going on. See that people have no respect for each other. When some people see that, I imagine, it is hard for them not to think—' He shrugged, gave a harsh half-laugh. 'Not to think, why not? I'm working hard to help them, so perhaps . . . perhaps I should take a little for myself.' He brushed a thin hand across his brow. 'When you justify in those terms, it becomes easy.' He dropped his hand and touched her arm. 'Be careful, Tess,' he warned softly. 'Human nature is a dangerous thing.' His hand felt cool on her skin. 'Johnny – Johnny was, *is*, a good example of that.' He squeezed, the tips of his thin fingers pressing into her flesh. 'Don't walk around on your own at night again.'

Day 6

28

The sun hadn't yet climbed above the horizon when Tess parked the Land Cruiser by the river and crossed the road to the Psar Nat market. She hadn't been here before – only passed it a couple of times – but she needed to stock up on food.

The market occupied a vast, warehouse-like space on the ground floor of an art deco-style building in central Battambang. Inside, countless wooden tables were crammed together and piled to unfeasible heights with every kind of produce: anise star fruits, pineapples, papaya, bamboo, firewood, sacks of rice, a stall bearing cages of skinny, flapping, squawking chickens – most of them destined for egg production at least, she consoled herself, because the majority of Khmers were Buddhists and therefore vegetarians – wicker baskets filled with spices of every conceivable colour. A nanny goat wandered down one of the narrow twisting aisles, knocking a couple of papaya from a teetering stack with a swish of its tail. The level of noise – haggling, barter, chatter – was deafening.

Tess followed a corridor that cut between rows of stalls, slopping through the muck of rotten vegetables and litter on the floor, taking a right, then a left, another right, zigzagging her way into the depths of the market.

The smell of barbecuing meat filled her nostrils, and she turned towards it. Charred crickets lay on a metal grill above a wood fire in an oil drum. The stallholder, an elderly woman, her thinning grey hair swathed in a checked krama scarf, held up two fingers.

'Crickets, madam. Very tasty. Only twenty cents one cricket.'

Smiling, Tess shook her head and stepped back, came hard up against someone.

'Cambodian speciality, Miss Hardy,' said a voice.

One of her section commanders, Mao, was standing behind her.

'Sorry. I didn't mean startle you, ma'am.'

Mao was in his early forties, older than the average age of the clearers by a good decade. He had a scar running across his cheek, from the corner of his mouth to his left ear, which made him look as if he was always smiling. He had argued with a man holding a machete when he was a boy, he had told her the first time they'd met. 'I think I arguing with the man. But really I arguing with the machete. Never argue with a machete, ma'am, I learn this.' He had a moon face running slightly to fat, and solemn dark eyes.

'It's fine, Mao. I just didn't expect to bump into anyone I knew.'

He was dressed, like she was, in MCT uniform. Smiling, he held up his hands: he was clutching a paper cup of chai and an unlit roll-up in the other. 'I run out of food too.'

'Only twenty cents, madam. Very cheap.'

Turning back to the stall, Tess shook her head. The thought of eating one of those at any time of day made her queasy, but at six in the morning it was an impossibility.

'Ten cents for one,' the stallholder said. 'Only ten cents big bargain. Crickets are lucky lucky.' She laid a flat palm on her heart and grinned, showing teeth stained burgundy by betel nut, the front two missing. Tess noticed a chunk of betel tucked inside her cheek. 'You eat cricket. You lucky inside.'

'Eat one,' Mao said. 'For luck, like the lady say.'

She glanced across. 'Do I need luck?'

'We all need luck.'

'What do they taste like?'

'Cambodian delicacy.'

Tess laughed. 'Yes. But what do they actually taste like?'

Mao smiled. 'Taste like nothing. Like you eat burnt wood.'

'OK. I can do burnt wood.' Tess gave the stallholder twenty cents and picked up two of the charred crickets. Turning, she held one out to Mao. 'For luck – and because there is no way I'm eating one of these on my own.'

'Thank you.' He gave a little bow.

'Now is there any chance you can find me a coffee in this maze?'

Popping the cricket into his mouth whole, Mao turned away. 'Follow me, ma'am.'

He led the way through the warren of stalls towards the front of the marketplace, where a young man was selling coffee and chai from two tin tea caddies perched on a small wooden handcart. A few people squatted on upturned plastic crates, drinking, chatting and squinting against the early morning sun. Buying two cups of coffee, Mao passed her one and they found a seat on a pile of old sacking. Tess was still holding her cricket, cold now, in the palm of her hand.

Mao nodded to the cricket. 'You eat.'

She pulled the cricket in two, wincing at the slight resistance before it gave, and put the back end on to her tongue. Mao was right. It tasted of barbecue, nothing else.

Mao glanced at his watch. 'We need be going, ma'am. It's fifteen minutes after six, and ten minutes' walk to MCT House.'

'I've got one of the Land Cruisers parked outside. We can be there in a couple of minutes. There's no rush.'

She wondered if he felt uncomfortable in her company. She had noticed some of the other Khmers at the chai stall casting Mao looks, as if they were wondering how he came to be in the company of a Western woman, even though they were wearing the same uniform.

'Would you tell me the story of the White Crocodile, Mao?'

He looked surprised.

'The real myth. Not that mad myth that's got everyone going crazy.'

His eyes found the floor, but he nodded. 'What do you know?'

'Probably nothing. Certainly nothing sensible.'

He smiled faintly.

Someone was dragging a metal-wheeled trolley across the concrete floor of the marketplace. The sound of the wheels screeching cut over the ambient hum of barter and chatter, made Tess wince.

'So the White Crocodile is a bad omen?'

Mao's response was quick and clipped. 'The White Crocodile is bad omen in Cambodia, this is sure.' He folded his hands in his lap. 'Cambodian people place a white cloth with a crocodile drawn on it outside their home when someone in their family dies. This White Crocodile is a sign of death. We call it *Tong Kroper* – Crocodile Flag.'

'So in Cambodia the White Crocodile does signify death.'

He nodded. 'Five hundred year ago, Kropom Chhouk, daughter of King Chan Reachea, was eaten by a huge white crocodile when swimming in Tonle Sap River – the river that joins Lake Tonle Sap to our capital city, Phnom Penh. The king order his men to find the crocodile and bring him. After many many weeks of looking, the crocodile found in a river in Ratanakkiri province—' He drew his arm in a wide arc, pointing off across the chaos of stalls into the depths of the marketplace. 'Far in the northeast of Cambodia, a hundred miles from where the princess eaten. The king kill the crocodile and take the body of his daughter from its stomach. Then he order that a Buddhist stupa be built to bury his daughter. The king also order twenty women be executed and buried around the stupa so their souls haunt the stupa and protect it from destruction for all time. Ever since, Cambodian people draw picture of a crocodile on white flags to signify death in family.'

'I was hoping for something a little more cheery than that.'

Mao was gazing at the floor, his expression serious, closed off. 'Cambodians are frightened of many things.' He tugged at the collar on his shirt, flapping it against his skin; there was a large sweat stain on the fabric. 'Bridges even, can you believe.'

Tess smiled. 'How can anyone be frightened of bridges?'

'During the reign of another of our kings – always it is the kings – people believed that to execute and bury dead bodies beneath bridges or temples would help to protect these places from being destroyed. Many Khmers, even to this day, are scared of bridges. So we must swim across the Sanger to get back to MCT House.'

'How about we just lock the doors instead and I won't stop for anything until we're on the other side?'

29

Sitting on the bottom step, staring out across the elephant grass to the string of red-and-white tape hanging limp and still in the early morning air, Lyda swung her legs from side to side. Her feet almost touched the ground. She glanced over her shoulder. Her mother was preparing breakfast; her father had gone to gather firewood; her baby brother, whom she adored and had promised to take care of for ever, was lying on the floor kicking his legs in the air. No one would notice if she slipped away, just for a while.

Lyda slid off the step.

Her parents had told her never to go near the minefield. She had been smacked once, viciously, by her father when she had returned to their hut holding the empty case of a land mine one of the men had given her. He had yanked the stump of her arm, sending searing, burning pain into her shoulder.

She had seen the boy with no legs, pale and silent, who had been attacked by the Crocodile. She had been there when they burned his body on the fire, had cried in fright at the sounds his mother had made. The Crocodile had come for her once, sunk its teeth into her arm, taken a piece of her. But she couldn't remember what had happened. Couldn't remember its face. Her body had been this way for as long as she could recall. She liked the men who came with their tools to work in the field. They knelt down and talked to her, face to face, as if she was important.

She liked the woman who had come too. The one with the green eyes and hair the colour of fire. She had smiled and been gentle, and listened when Lyda had tried to tell her what she had seen. She hoped the woman had understood.

The tyre tracks from last night were filled with rainwater. Lyda stepped into one and the soggy ground closed around her ankles. Mud oozed through her toes, and she clenched and un-clenched them, enjoying the sensation of coolness. Then she stamped her foot, spraying muddy water over her old purple T-shirt.

She walked a little further, slopping along in the tyre tracks, wondering what the people who had come so quietly in the middle of the night had done. Everything looked the same. The elephant grass and soybean were motionless in the morning haze, undisturbed. In the jungle beyond, mist gathered between the trees, silent. The lonely tree, which looked like the trees she drew with a stick in the dirt of the village yard, was dense and still, its shadow stretched by the rising sun. She glanced behind her. Deserted – only the wa-ter buffalo watching her calmly through their heavy-lidded eyes.

The red-and-white tape was close now. Lyda didn't want to make her father angry. She was about to turn back when she noticed something glinting on the ground ahead of her. Taking a few steps forward, she bent down.

It was a coin. A shiny silver coin.

Lyda knew how little her father earned collecting and selling firewood: ten dollars a month, if he was lucky, for work which left him broken and exhausted. Though they tried to hide it from her, she also knew her father and mother often went without food, so that she and her baby brother could eat.

The coin was cold and solid in her hand and Lyda held it tight, terrified of dropping and losing it in the muddy water. She sloshed a little further and her eyes widened. Another silver coin. Resting on the ridge of earth between the tyre tracks, just like the first. Lyda snatched that one up too, glancing quickly around to see if anyone was watching her. She was still alone.

She was very close to the red-and-white tape now, and she knew that she had to turn back. Remaining where she was – moving no further forward – balanced on the ridge of earth between the tracks, Lyda stood on tiptoes and craned her neck, solemn dark eyes searching the ground ahead of her.

Another glint of silver.

She felt a nervous thudding in her chest as she moved forward to pick up the third coin, but pushed it away. She could already imagine how her mother would react when she walked back into the hut and dropped this fistful of treasure into her lap.

She was right under the tape now; it sagged in front of her face. Her heart leaped at the sight. Shuffling back a few steps, she stopped and stared out across the scorched earth and grass of the minefield. She would go back to the village now. Even if there was another coin, she would leave it and go home.

Then she saw the butterfly.

A bright green toy butterfly, sparkling like a gem.

Lyda dropped to her knees and shuffled forward. She wouldn't have to touch the earth below her, not at all. She could crane over it from here, so that only her fingertips came into contact with the butterfly. As the tape fluttered above her, something came into her mind. A memory. Faint. Something horrible and agonising and she didn't know what it meant. The stump of her arm tingled. She looked at the butterfly. Then she heard something, voices, getting louder.

Glancing over her shoulder, she saw her father running towards her, waving his arms. His face was contorted, and he was shouting something, but he was still too far away for her to hear. He didn't seem real somehow – like the hand puppet her grandmother had made for her from a bit of old T-shirt.

The butterfly was so pretty. So green. Like the green of that lady's eyes.

And she had the coins. Her father wouldn't be angry with her when he saw the coins.

She didn't have anything pretty. Anything new and perfect. Anything to call her own at all. Just the hand puppet, now old, tatty and torn. She looked longingly at the shiny green toy someone had discarded so carelessly.

Placing the coins carefully in a little pile next to her, she reached out and closed her tiny fist tight around the butterfly.

*

The field radio flooded the room with the crackle of white noise. Jakkleson sat at his desk, sifting through heaps of paper. Bills. Lots of them, many the red sort with capitals and generous amounts of underlining. Jakkleson knew far more than MacSween realised about the parlous state of MCT's finances. He'd stood listening to MacSween on the phone to the biggest potential donors over the past few months, heard the big Scot struggle to find the right tone, jammed between his natural belligerence and the necessity to pay obeisance. They had trickles coming in from organisations who had supported them for years, but that wasn't enough to keep their heads above water for long.

Jakkleson sat back and tuned his ear to the radio. He could hear all the field radios on this one. One of his many jobs was to listen for any problems out there, give advice when it was needed, keep schtum when it wasn't; call the helicopter in if things got really messy. The babble was pretty much constant today. Nerves, lots of chatter.

'I'm not sure I should have sent the teams back out there so soon,' MacSween had said to him yesterday. Jakkleson had replied with soothing platitudes. He ran Mine Clearance Trust – whatever MacSween thought to the contrary – and he hated not working.

He carefully straightened out a paperclip and began to pick at a speck of dirt trapped under a thumbnail. Not that he had done only that these past couple of days. He had paid a few visits to Akara. But he had been irritable and short-tempered, and had wanted to foreshorten their usual routine. Her caresses, the compliments he had taught her: all of it had felt irritating and cloying. Instead, he had made her crouch on all fours and, clutching her breasts in his hands to stop them from swinging, had fucked her quickly and silently from behind, so that he didn't have to look into her eyes.

Pushing his chair back, he stood and went over to the window. A light breeze had picked up, stirring the leaves of the frangipani outside. Fine, white petals floated sideways on the breeze like snow. The thought of snow reminded him of home. He hadn't been back in three years.

He had been in the Swedish army once, a Major in the Engineers. He had been very good at it. He had always been good at things, ever since he was a kid. He wasn't popular, but that was fine: it was inevitable that envy would stifle popularity. Friendships weren't important to him anyway. But then stories about him started to circulate, that he was using his position to hold relationships with younger officers – female officers. It was all rumour. At least until he had been caught screwing a junior officer over his desk one evening, when he thought everyone else was at the regimental dinner. He was given a dishonourable discharge, and that was the end. No job, no position, no money coming in. His wife, who was already suspicious of his antics, had left him, taking the kids with her.

He was still looking out of the window, his mind off in a small, wooden cabin beside a lake in Värmland where he used to go fishing for the weekend, when he heard his computer ping. Pushing himself away from the window, he went over to his desk.

A 'new message' icon floated in the mouth of a skull and crossbones, a copy of the blood-red 'Danger!! Mines!!' sign he had chosen as his wallpaper. He clicked on the icon and the screen filled with white – only one line of neat black type.

Jakkleson let his eyes hang closed for a moment, exhaled slowly.

Finally.

He had got in touch.

*

She was still moving when he reached her, his beautiful little girl. Her eyes were open, her face amazed.

He couldn't see where she was hurt, there was so much blood. Her purple T-shirt, his filthy T-shirt, was drenched; the soil around her slick and black. He didn't know what to do. He wanted to grab her and never let go. But he didn't want to touch her, to hurt her more. Sinking into the cool mud, he slid his hands gently underneath and tried to raise her. Her little chest hollowed in a gasp of agony, and then he saw the ragged gash, the coil of guts spilling over the sopping cotton. His throat constricted and he couldn't catch his breath.

She was trying to whisper something. He raised a trembling hand to his lips. '*Sngat.*' Quiet.

She was looking past him, trying to focus. She lifted her arm, gesturing; a gush of fresh blood pulsed from the wound in her chest.

'*Sngat, Lyda.*'

Her eyes pleaded with him. He turned to see what she was trying to tell him and there on the ground were three silver dollar coins. Three dollars: more than a week's wage. And now he realised what had led her to defy him. And he hated himself, despised himself for their miserable existence, for his failure to give his child anything good out of life, to find a way of protecting her from the Crocodile.

How could there be so much blood? She was so tiny.

'*Sohm toh, Lyda. Sohm toh.*' I'm sorry.

He raised himself to his feet, clutching her body. She was as light as air. He could feel the flutter of her heart against his chest. He was walking at first, slowly, trying not to stumble, cradling her in his arms and talking into her hair.

The fluttering was fading. He could feel blood soaking into his shirt and trousers. He could hear something now, and he looked down and saw that her teeth were chattering, the sound dry and loud. Her face was pale, her eyes closed.

Her grip slackened, she went limp in his arms, and suddenly he was running.

30

Thirty minutes later, Jakkleson parked the Land Cruiser at the base of the limestone outcrop on which the Sampeau Temple was built. It was half past nine, and already hot. He took his light jacket off, tossed it in the driver's seat, pulled a baseball cap on and started to walk, ignoring the small pack of emaciated kids skipping around him, hands outstretched for 'riel' or better still 'dollar': let me show you temple, beautiful wat, Mr Barang, let me carry bag, stupa, very holy mister, must see Buddhist stupa, watch out for land mines, Mr White Man, I show you where, keep you safe.

He had visited Sampeau only once before, early on in his time in Battambang, when he had had nothing better to do at weekends. The weather had been cooler then, late afternoon, rain clouds sweeping in from the west, but even so it had felt like a long climb up the seven hundred steps carved into the steep limestone hillside. There were several different routes, he remembered now. He chose the track that snaked through the thick jungle: it was longer, but the gradient was shallower and the path shaded. He had time, half an hour still, before he was due to meet Huan, but even so he set off quickly, outpacing the kids, leaving them behind in a small cloud of disappointment and dust.

The jungle closed around him as he walked. Ancient shadows. This was an *old* place – he'd felt it all those months before.

He took a handkerchief from his pocket and wiped the stinging sweat from his forehead. It was like standing fully clothed in a steam room. The Israeli-made Jericho 941 revolver secured in a quick-draw holster in the small of his back – within easy reach, but out of sight – chafed his skin with each step, a presence both irritating and reassuring. But there was no one else on the track.

The thick vegetation that had given him some shade on the climb began to thin as he approached the summit. He stopped and looked around. The sun was so bright after the twilight beneath the canopy of trees that, even with his sunglasses on, his vision was blurred. It made his head ache. The roof of the small hilltop wat was visible a couple of hundred metres above him. Just off to his right he could see the mouth of a cave under a rocky bluff. He had visited it the last time he was here. It was famous locally. The Khmer Rouge had turned it into a killing place. A small staircase led from the cave opening to a floor made entirely of human bones and skulls. A single shaft of light lanced down from above. Men, women and children had been bludgeoned by the Khmer Rouge soldiers above, their bodies tossed through a narrow hole to the echoing space below. Jakkleson had found it difficult not to wonder how many of them had still been conscious as they fell into that blackness.

A man was waiting for him at the top of the hill, as if he had known that Jakkleson would choose the easier jungle path. He was wearing cotton chinos and a white long-sleeved shirt, and he was leaning nonchalantly against one of the wat's crumbling towers, like a tour guide waiting for the coach to unload.

Jakkleson reached behind him and rested his fingertips on the rubber grip of his revolver, slick with sweat, as he walked the last few steps. A couple of metres away, he stopped. Squinted against the bright sun.

'I thought you'd come alone. Never one to share the glory, Jakkleson.'

Jakkleson was stunned into silence.

'Thought you had it all worked out, didn't you?'

Finally Jakkleson spoke, his voice hoarse with the effort of getting the words out. 'You sent me the email? From Huan's email account?'

'I don't think Huan has an email account. Who the hell would he email?' The man gave the suggestion of a smile. 'Actually, I'm wrong. He has one now. I'll give him the log-in details when I next see him.'

Jakkleson's mouth gaped; his brain clunked through the possibilities and ended up with only one. 'Those women? *You* killed them. You killed them all.'

The other stood watching him, his head tilted to one side, a quizzical expression on his face, as if he was studying a colourful insect that had just crawled from the jungle.

'I did.'

'Why?' Jakkleson spluttered.

'Because they deserved it. Simple as that.'

'What do you mean, "deserved it"?' Jakkleson asked, in a voice which broke with tension.

'The life they lived. The choices they made.'

'Why is that your business?'

'This is about morality. I don't expect you to understand.'

Jakkleson's face flushed. 'What about the ones who've disappeared? What have you done with them?'

'You don't need to worry about them,' he said, smiling.

'They're making themselves useful.'

Jakkleson stared. 'And Johnny?'

'Johnny. It's all a game to Johnny.'

'And to you?'

'I am enjoying myself.'

'Johnny's your friend.'

'Johnny's a prick.' A hard light shone in his eyes. 'He always has been.'

'And that's enough?'

'Come on, Jakkleson. I'm not that much of a bastard.' He smiled again, but didn't elaborate.

Jakkleson kept his voice composed, as affable as he could given the circumstances. 'Killing people isn't a game.'

'Ever done it? You should try it some time.' He reached to scratch at his forearms. 'The heat. It's a bitch. I should have just met you in the Balcony Bar for a beer, but it didn't seem to have the same symbolic significance as this place.'

The screech of a baboon rang from the jungle, and the man in front of Jakkleson raised an arm, gestured far over to the left. Without moving his head, Jakkleson glanced quickly out of the corner of his eye, caught sight of the slopes of another hill in the distance, through the haze.

'Crocodile Mountain. It was a Khmer Rouge stronghold during the civil war. They had some big guns up there. Used it to rain shells down on the peasants to keep them in order. I thought it was an appropriate location considering. Meeting under the eye of the crocodile.'

'You're mad,' Jakkleson muttered, regretting the words as soon as they were spoken.

'Without doubt,' the other said with a slight lift to the

corners of his mouth. 'We're all a little mad though. You're mad for believing those sad little whores you fuck don't despise you.'

Jakkleson winced. The man in front of him smiled. 'Everyone knows, Jakkleson. It's one of the world's worst-kept secrets. That Jakkleson is a dirty old bastard.'

Jakkleson mopped a hand over his brow. He was sweating profusely, more than on the climb to the summit.

'You should not have started interfering, Jakkleson. Burning Huan's personnel file. Trying to protect my scapegoat. You're spoiling the game.'

Jakkleson slipped his hand around to his back, made it look as if he was having a scratch while closing his hand around the solid butt of his Jericho 941, lifting it slightly to make sure it wouldn't catch on the belt of his shorts if he needed to draw it quickly. He concentrated on speaking slowly and sparingly. 'You chose a strange place to meet me, irrespective of the significance. Top of a mountain, surrounded in jungle, no access to any vehicles. And it's a tourist destination. There'll be hikers along in a minute.' His gaze, which he held unwavering, was met with a smirk.

'Feeling nervous? That famous Jakkleson cool shaken?'

'Not at all.' His skin felt clammy as a corpse's.

The man facing him glanced at his watch. 'It has been nice talking to you, but I have to leave in a minute. I have things to do. Places to be, people to catch up with.' He gave a short, harsh laugh. 'The thing about killing people, Jakkleson, that's different from killing animals, is that they can imagine things turning out differently. An animal will fight, but at a certain point they give up, switch off. People are different. They always beg. Everyone begs at the last moment. Because they all think there's a chance that you're going to let them go. They want it so much. That's the last thing you see. Not just fear, but hope. Do you think anyone will miss you, Jakkleson?'

Jakkleson saw that the other man's bare hands, hanging down, were empty. His chinos were tight and in the bright sunlight his thin linen shirt was almost translucent: nowhere to hide a weapon. Despite his sedentary lifestyle, Jakkleson was still in good shape, kept himself fit. His reactions were fast and he had learned some solid hand-to-hand combat techniques in the army, which he still practised occasionally. He could draw his Jericho 941 in a split second. It was loaded and cocked, the safety off, and he had never missed a target in his life, stationary or moving.

He realised, nevertheless, that he was shaking.

31

Manchester, England

Unsurprisingly, the lift was broken, the open doors revealing a cube of dull steel covered in graffiti. There was a puddle in the middle of the floor, and the ammonia stench of urine pulsed from inside it.

Detective Inspector Wessex turned. 'Fancy a climb, Sergeant Viles?'

'Do I have a choice?'

''Fraid not.'

They reached the sixth floor of the tower block, both of them panting – Wessex considerably more heavily than Viles, he realised in a moment of uncomfortable clarity – and stopped for a minute, leaning against the metal stair railing to catch their breath.

Viles scratched a hand through her crew cut. 'Do you think he's in?'

'Bound to be. The lift's broken and he's a lazy arse. Years of shooting up doesn't predispose you to fitness.'

She smiled. 'Are you trying to confide in me, sir?'

Wessex rolled his eyes. 'My problem is burgundy and takeaways. Heroin doesn't get a look in.' Patting his stomach, he added: 'I wouldn't have a gut like this if it did.' He paused, raised an eyebrow. 'Now there's a thought . . .'

Crossing the narrow concrete landing, Wessex rapped his knuckles on the flaking, hospital-green door.

The voice from inside the flat was sleepy. 'Who is it?'

Wessex flicked open the letterbox, angled his mouth to the rectangle of light. 'It's Detective Inspector Wessex,' he shouted. 'Open up, Bear.'

'Bear?' Viles mouthed.

'You'll see.'

They waited. They could hear faint sounds of someone scuffling around inside the flat, hurried footsteps, the slam of a door.

'What on earth is he doing?'

'Depositing his skag somewhere he thinks we won't find it,' Wessex said, with a wink. He thumped his fist hard on the door three times, making it rattle on its hinges, stepped back and shouted – 'Police' – into the void of stairwell.

A muffled voice came from behind the door. 'Fuck's sake, I'm comin'.'

They heard the safety chain being unhooked, and the door was whipped open. If a grizzly had slipped on a dirty white T-shirt and torn jeans, it would have looked a lot like Ryan James. It was obvious why anyone who knew him for more than a brief 'hello' referred to him as Bear. Though he was slouching, his head grazed the top of the doorway. Brown hair fell in dirty curls to his shoulders; the bottom half of his face was lost to an untidy salt-and-pepper beard.

'Keep your voice down,' he hissed. 'Do you want the whole of Longsight to know that I'm being visited by the fuckin' bizzies?'

Wessex pushed past him into the narrow hallway. 'Should have got a move on, then. I'm not interested in your smack.'

He looked back, wide-eyed. 'Wot you talking about?'

'Don't give up your day job, Bear. Hollywood won't be beating down your door quite yet.'

Shrugging and muttering, James followed Wessex back down the hall, leaving Viles to close the front door behind her.

The living room was small and filthy, opening on one side to a tiny balcony which looked out on to another of Longsight's slate-grey council tower blocks, and on the other to a kitchen piled with Lucky House Chinese takeaway boxes and cans of Kestrel lager. The brown carpet was threadbare and dotted with cigarette burns. A tattoo gun and some half-empty plastic bottles of tattoo ink sat on a small Formica table against the wall behind the brown PVC sofa, the only thing in the room that was orderly. Photographs of tattoos: all colours, shapes, sizes and designs made a multicoloured collage of the wall, from tabletop to ceiling.

Wessex cast his eye around and decided to remain standing. Viles stayed in the doorway.

'I need your help, Bear.'

'Help? Why the hell should I—?'

'For turning a blind eye to the smack, which I'm sure we'd be able to dig out without having to search too hard.' He tilted his head towards the tattoo table. 'And I have no doubt that social security would like to know about your sideline.'

'Do me a fucking favour,' James muttered, with a sneer. 'That's pennies, that is. Wouldn't affect me social.' Slumping down on to the sofa, which gave out a huge puff of air as he landed, he retrieved a packet of Marlboro and a plastic disposable lighter from the floor. 'Wot you after?'

'I need to know which gang this tattoo belongs to.' Wessex passed over the photograph of the tattoo.

Lighting up, Bear glanced at it. 'I dunno. Never seen it before.'

'Take a better look.'

Bear looked from Wessex to Viles and back again.

'Well it's not a professional job, is it? None of the fucking edges are straight. Cheap ink.'

'And the symbol?'

'Means nothin' to me.'

'Is it a gang tattoo?'

'Nah.' He shook his head firmly.

'Why?'

'Too small, too plain, too badly done. Nah. Never seen a gang with a tattoo like that.' He sucked on the cigarette, blew a cloud of smoke into the room. 'They got more pride than to 'ave something like that on their skin. Can't 'elp yeh.'

Someone in the car park below had fired up a stereo. Grime, the kind of music Wessex had heard hundreds of times as a police constable, trawling around the city-centre clubs arresting pickpockets and breaking up drunken fights. He glanced out of the window: saw three teenagers with matching buzz cuts, gathered around a souped-up black Vauxhall Corsa.

Looking back into the room, he exchanged glances with Viles; she shrugged.

'We're not so busy today, Bear. Just this case. Maybe we should stick around for a while. You weren't going anywhere, were you?' Wessex slumped, uninvited, on to the sofa next to James, crossed his legs and plucked the Marlboro packet and lighter from James's lap. 'Going to get us a cup of tea then? Mine's milk, no sugar. Viles?'

'I'd prefer coffee.'

'Oh, for fuck's sake.' James threw up his hands. 'OK, OK. Some of those hookers up at Cheetham Hill have tattoos like this. Little ones. Not too obvious. Badly done like this one.' Dropping his cigarette into an empty can of Kestrel, he coughed out a harsh laugh. 'Marks out their owners. Like a cattle brand – dumb fuckin' cows.'

His eyes met Wessex's briefly, before sliding away. Wessex resisted the urge to lean over and smack him around the ear.

'You're a quality guy, you are, James.'

'Speak to your vice boys, Officer. They'll 'elp you better than I can.'

32

The day had been busy. Fifteen anti-personnel blast mines found in the rice paddies Tess's teams were clearing and an anti-tank mine buried beneath a dirt road, the main thoroughfare between two neighbouring villages bordering Koh Kroneg. Thankfully, the ox carts that traversed the track were too light to detonate it, so the anti-tank mine had been traipsed over for years by farmers oblivious to its existence. Her teams had worked hard. She was hot, dirty and in need of civilisation.

The swimming pool at the Victory Club was empty except for a tall elderly white man who stood in the shallow end, splashing water over his back like a baby elephant and talking to himself. He obviously viewed himself as an engaging companion because enthusiastic nods and animated facial expressions accompanied his dialogue.

Tess had been surprised by the size of the swimming pool, thirty-five metres long, and reasonably well maintained: white-washed walls and terracotta tiles, a few of them cracked but clean, surrounding the pool, the water clear and smelling faintly of chlorine, a large semicircular bed of tropical plants and palms at the far end which, if she squinted through semi-closed lids, made her feel almost as if she was swimming in the pool of a five-star hotel.

The Victory Club restaurant bordered one side of the swimming pool, the tables spilling out on to the poolside. Two of the tables were occupied by Khmer businessmen in collared shirts and pressed trousers, holding late meetings over bottles of Angkor beer and bowls of cashews; another by four young men wearing Ray-Bans, ripped jeans and fake pastel-coloured Ralph Lauren polo shirts – the only Khmers who could afford the Victory Club's two-dollar entry fee, two days' wages for the average Cambodian.

The whitewashed wall on the opposite side of the swimming pool bore giant posters – the images obviously pirated from American fitness websites – showing buff Westerners in various fitness-related poses. In one, a couple of blonde women in bikinis relaxed in a steam room. Another showed a musclebound man in tight black shorts and a white Nike vest posing on a running machine. It struck Tess as strange that any advertisement for fitness or beauty in Cambodia seemed to feature Westerners; or maybe not so strange, as they were the only ones able to afford the time or energy to exercise.

The club would have been impressive once, no doubt built to entertain the scores of Western aid workers who had arrived to help rebuild Cambodia after the fall of the Khmer Rouge. But, as with everything in Cambodia, it was now in a state of 'use until it falls apart' maintenance, paint peeling off the walls, tiles cracked, the exercise machines in the gym – she had a quick look before she'd changed for swimming – rusting, half of them broken.

She swam a few more laps and then stopped in the deep end, holding on to the side so that she could check her watch. It was getting on towards 5 p.m. and she realised she was hungry and in dire need of a beer. Ducking under the water, she front-crawled back to the shallow end.

Alex was standing by the steps, holding out her towel. She
didn't recognise him for a moment because he was wearing chinos, a white linen long-sleeved shirt and spotless brown suede
desert boots, not his usual grubby mine-clearing uniform, and
his dark hair was damp, as if he'd just got out of the shower. A
pair of aviator sunglasses were tucked in his shirt pocket. He
looked as if he'd just stepped out of a Giorgio Armani advert.

She reached up for the towel before she started to climb out
– she had no intention of letting him see her in a bikini, and especially one that had been bought for her honeymoon with the
express purpose of looking slutty – wrapping it around herself
awkwardly with one hand as she shuffled up the stairs.

'Is this a coincidence?'

'Planned,' he answered. 'Madam Chou told me where to
find you. Beer?'

She met his gaze with a raised eyebrow, but he didn't elaborate.

'Please. I'll just get changed.'

'You don't have to.'

She smiled sarcastically. 'I'll be back in a minute. Make mine
a large one.'

He watched her walk away. Ordering two large bottles of
Angkor from the restaurant, he found a table by the swimming
pool, where they wouldn't be overheard. When Tess returned,
she was wearing a short green cotton dress patterned with tiny
white daisies, and he almost choked on his beer when he saw
her.

'You look . . . different.'

Ignoring his comment, she sat down across the table from
him and knitted her fingers around the ice-cold bottle of beer.

'So what's up, Alex?'

'Have you been here before?'

She was momentarily thrown. 'To the Victory Club?'

He nodded. 'Yes. Swimming. Using the exercise machines?'

He sounded as if he was trawling for lines on an awkward first date.

'No. This is the first time. Madam Chou mentioned it, so I thought I'd check it out. It's nice.' Unlacing her fingers from the bottle, she picked at the label, easing a corner away from the damp glass with a fingernail. 'What's up, Alex?'

He looked away, across the swimming pool, fixing for a moment on one of the posters on the opposite wall.

'A little girl was killed this morning in the White Crocodile minefield.'

'A little girl?'

He nodded. 'Mao radioed me a couple of hours ago. He had just heard. He said you'd already left the field for the day and he wanted you to be told. He said that you knew her.'

Tess felt a growing unease. 'Knew her?'

'Knew is too strong, maybe. Met her. He said you'd met her.'

'Where?'

'He wasn't clear. Her father said she'd spoken to you a few evenings ago. Was it the evening you drove out to the field and found that anti-tank mine?'

Tess sat quite still, staring at him. 'The little girl, with the missing arm? Not her? It wasn't her?'

He nodded slowly.

'What happened?'

'She picked up a butterfly mine.'

'Why? Why did she pick it up?'

'Her father found a pile of dollars next to her.'

'So someone laid them deliberately to tempt her towards the mine?' Her voice broke. 'If she hadn't tried to warn me about the White Crocodile, she might still be alive.'

'No. It wasn't your fault.'

'Why not? Why else was she killed? Because the Crocodile fancied a kid this time? She must have been trying to tell me something important – something more – and I just shooed her away.' She dropped her head, fighting back tears. 'Why did you come here to tell me? Why didn't you just leave a note with Madam Chou?'

'I wanted to tell you in person. In case you were upset—' He tailed off.

Snatching a paper napkin off the table, she scrubbed at her cheeks. 'I already told you I don't need babysitting.'

He kept his eyes fixed on the bottle in his hands. 'I wanted to talk to you anyway.'

'What? Now you know that I'm not just going to turn tail and run away, like you want me to?'

'We're both after the same thing. To find out who is doing this to these women, to Johnny and Luke, to that little girl. We may as well help each other.'

She glanced up at him.

'You don't trust me, I know that,' he continued. 'And you're wise not to. You shouldn't trust anyone. But I know why you are out here and surely, with that knowledge, I'm more dangerous as an enemy than as a friend.' He gave a grim smile. 'What do they say? Keep your friends close and your enemies even closer.'

She dropped the twisted napkin on to the table; took a large slug of beer, then another. She knew that Alex was right. She had no friends out here, no allies, no one to support her or watch her back. If she continued on her own she would get nowhere. Probably just end up getting herself killed. And if she trusted him? She didn't know, but the alternative was most likely worse.

'Another woman went missing last night,' he said, breaking the silence. 'An old man from her village found her this morning at the edge of the jungle. Her throat had been cut open.'

'Another single mother?'

'Six-month-old twin girls. The old man lived in the hut closest to hers. He heard the babies crying this morning, and went to have a look. He found them alone, and got his wife to look after them while he went to search for the mother. He said that he'd seen the woman two nights ago, running from the edge of the jungle, looking terrified. She kept her animals in a small corral there. She told him that something had been out there watching her. He went up there to look for her this morning and found her dead. He was shaking when he told me. He said that no human could have done what was done to her.'

Tess looked across at him.

'But you don't believe that, do you?'

'I come from a small village in Croatia. We believe all kinds of shit out there too. They come from somewhere, these myths. They're not just taken from the air.'

'They come from the lips of people with too little education and too much imagination.'

'Thank you for describing me so perfectly.'

'That's not what I—' she broke off, catching the twitch at the corner of his mouth. It was only momentary, like grey clouds parting to reveal a tiny patch of blue sky. 'We're looking for a man, Alex. Someone very human and very sick.'

Alex's face was expressionless again, closed down. She wondered if he was berating himself for letting a chink of light through.

'Family. It's about family, Alex.'

'What do you mean?'

'Young, unmarried women with babies, rejected by society for messing with society's values. The women disappear or are killed. The children are left. So whoever –' she paused – 'or whatever is doing this, is punishing the women.'

'Maybe they're punishing the kids. And what about Luke? Johnny? Where do they fit in?'

'I don't know. But there must be another link that involves them.'

Alex's eyes flicked up to meet hers for a second.

'What, Alex?'

'There's a kid who works with Dr Ung at the hospital. Ret S'Mai, he's called. He was badly injured and his father killed when their moped collided with a Land Cruiser in Battambang last year.'

'Yes, I met him briefly with MacSween.'

'Ret S'Mai is Huan's nephew – his father was Huan's only brother.'

She thought of the glimpse she had of Huan and Ret S'Mai chatting on the veranda before Huan had run, but held her tongue and waited.

'It was an MCT Land Cruiser that hit them.'

'MacSween told me. It was Johnny, wasn't it? Drunk driving? But MacSween said that Ret S'Mai's father was also drunk.

That it wasn't Johnny's fault.'

Alex nodded, but there was something unconvincing about the movement. 'MacSween was right. Drink-drive laws don't apply out here. They were both in the wrong. Johnny was lucky that he was the one in the Land Cruiser.'

'That's not all, is it, Alex?'

Silence.

'Alex?'

He was looking back across the pool towards the posters, but his gaze was unfocused – looking but not seeing. Mellow orange evening light lit his face as he looked back and caught her eye.

'Johnny had an affair with Ret S'Mai's sister. Made her pregnant. She was fifteen.'

Tess felt suddenly lightheaded. 'Jesus Christ.'

'He paid for her to have an abortion.'

'And just dumped her after?'

'Johnny lost interest, gave her a bit of cash and hasn't seen or heard from her since. He says that he tried to find her, but that she'd disappeared. I can't imagine that he tried too hard, but still—' He broke off.

'So you think she might be one of those women too? One of the disappeared?'

'I don't know. She may just have been sent away to family somewhere else in Cambodia, but it does give Huan another reason to hate Johnny. The accident aside, messing with an unmarried daughter from a good family is madness, particularly the niece of an employee. It would have been different if he had intended a future with her, but he was just playing with her. Once his brother died, Huan became the guardian to his children, both Ret S'Mai and his sister. He is responsible for their welfare, for keeping them safe.'

'And I suppose Huan is also responsible for getting revenge when something bad happens to them?'

'Khmers don't sit and let justice sort itself out, because there is no justice in a country like this,' he said. 'Just like there is no justice in the country I came from. If I was him, I would do the same.'

Tess waited for him to continue, but he said nothing else. Behind him, the sun was dipping below the tree line, turning the swimming pool into a cage of shadows.

33

The potholed tarmac petered out into dirt and grew empty of bicycles and mopeds as they left the outskirts of Battambang. They were travelling through dense jungle now, passing the occasional isolated hut, the odd track cutting at right angles from the dirt road, snaking away through the trees. *You could hide forever out here and no one would find you.* The hot evening air rippled over Tess's face and bare arms, fluttering her green daisy dress around her thighs, drying the last vestiges of damp from her hair.

Over a second beer at the Victory Club, they had agreed to drive out to Huan's village – this evening, now, Tess had insisted, draining her Angkor and standing up – when he wouldn't be expecting visitors. If they couldn't find him, at least they might be able to glean some information as to his whereabouts.

Slipping off her shoes, Tess put her feet on the dash and hugged her arms around her knees, staring ahead into the thickening darkness, the Land Cruiser's headlamps twin cones of light picking out the dirt road.

'Do all of you get involved?' she asked, glancing across at Alex.

'Involved in what?'

'Young girls. Sleeping with young Khmer girls?'

Alex shot her a cold look. 'No, of course we don't all get involved.'

'You just told me, back at the Victory Club, that Johnny did. And Jakkleson does too. I found photographs in his filing cabinet while I was looking for Huan's file. Did you know?'

Alex nodded.

'Did he tell you?'

'No. He thinks that no one knows. Johnny found out.'

'How?'

'I don't know. Johnny finds out a lot of things.'

Tess pulled a face. 'But Jakkleson's married.'

Alex shrugged. 'Marriage doesn't mean dick to most of the guys out here.'

Tess laughed. '"Doesn't mean dick"?' What are you, Alex, Dirty Harry? Did you learn English watching American films?'

He frowned. 'No. Well – yes.'

'How about you, Alex? Does marriage mean anything to you?'

'I don't know. I've never been married.'

Tess watched him quietly for a moment. 'I have. But you know that already, don't you?' She swallowed. 'How did Luke die?'

He seemed prepared for the question. Unsurprised. But he didn't respond.

She nudged his arm. 'You were there, weren't you? At the hospital, the day of Johnny's accident, I asked you if you had ever been injured by a mine and you said "once, almost" and that you had got too close to someone else's fuck-up. It was Luke's . . . the mine that killed Luke, wasn't it?'

Alex sighed. The words that followed were so quiet she almost couldn't hear them over the noise of the engine. 'Yes it was.'

'Except that we both know it wasn't a fuck-up. It was deliberate, planted, just like Johnny's mine was planted.' She scrutinised his face. 'What happened, Alex? I need to know.'

'I'm sorry, Tess. I can't help you.'

'You said you were there.'

'I was there.' A shadow crossed his face. 'But I can't remember anything.'

'I don't understand.'

He opened his mouth, then closed it again without saying anything. Tess tightened her arms around her knees and waited. Finally, he spoke.

'All I remember was that I was walking up the lane towards Luke and he was squatting, his back to me. I was a few metres from him when the mine went off, then nothing. The hospital. Nothing else. I can't remember why we were in the lane, what the problem was.'

Hugging her legs tighter to her chest, Tess stared at him over the bumps of her knees, willing him to continue.

'MacSween told me later that it was a booby trap. Luke, Johnny and I, we were all there, trying to sort it out.'

'Where was Johnny?'

'Where was he exactly? I don't know. But he was there, somewhere.'

'Why were all three of you there? Why was Johnny there?'

'It was Luke's troop. Johnny's good with booby traps. It's his speciality.'

'And you?'

He shrugged. 'I can't remember.' Reaching across her to the glove box, he extracted a packet of Marlboro, shook out a cigarette and lit it. Tess waited while he smoked, wanting him so badly to tell her something – anything almost, just so that she would have an answer. She reached across and took one of the cigarettes for herself.

'I see things,' he said suddenly. 'I see things totally clearly, believe that is how it happened, then it changes and it's something different, but just as real.'

'I need to know, Alex. I need to know what happened.'

'I can't help you.'

'You must.'

'I can't.'

'Alex, please.'

He shook his head; laid his hand on hers in a moment so sudden and unexpected that she flinched. 'I can't.'

Alex braked suddenly and swung the Land Cruiser into a grassed-over track which cut at right angles away from the road through the jungle. After a hundred metres, he switched off the engine. Reaching across her, he opened the glove compartment again and pulled out his Browning. Tess caught his arm.

'Why have you got that with you?'

He shook her off. 'I always have it with me.'

'Are we going to need it?'

'No.' He didn't meet her gaze. 'No. I'm taking it because ... you don't ever know ... that's all. Habit more than anything. Don't worry about it.'

Shoving the pistol in the waistband of his trousers, he held his finger to his lips and eased the driver's door open.

When she climbed out to join him, Tess understood why; she was immediately struck by the quiet. Jungle surrounded them, eerily silent except for the soft aeroplane whine of mosquitoes. Another hundred metres on – walking in single file, the grass muffling their footsteps – they found themselves at the edge of a clearing. On their right stood a bamboo shed, doorless, the stench of excreta pulsing from inside it. Beyond the shed, across trampled mud, they could see the bamboo slat walls of a hut, squat and square, dirty brown sacking framed in glassless windows by the lantern light glowing behind it. Beyond the nearest hut there were three or four more. And now that Tess listened, she realised that she could hear the murmur of voices, the scuff of feet on wooden boards, the clank of metal cooking pots.

She felt Alex's hand close around hers, and then he was leading her, jogging silently across the clearing to the doorway. Their movement disturbed a rat, which scuttled from under the stairs and disappeared into the darkness.

They mounted the stairs. Inside, the hut was cool and shadowy. A dark curtain sagged from a rope strung midway up two facing walls, dividing the hut in two; from behind the curtain candlelight glowed. Alex tapped his knuckles against the edge of the doorway and leaned in to speak.

'*Johm riab sua.*'

The scuffle of feet, murmured voices, their surprise evident from the tone. Tess and Alex waited. A moment later, the curtain was tugged back a fraction and two women slipped through. One was approaching middle age, her round, flat face crossed with shallow lines and tugged downwards by delicate bags of skin. The other was an old woman: tiny and reed-thin, skin diaphanous as crushed silk. She wore baggy black trousers and a ragged T-shirt the same faded grey as her hair.

The younger woman stopped in front of the curtain; the old woman approached, paused a metre from Tess and Alex, and gave a slight, stiff bow.

Alex inclined his head. '*Niak sohk sabaaye te.*'

The old woman looked at him long and hard; her pinched face showed no emotion.

'*Kh'nyohm mao pii* Mine Clearance Trust,' he said. 'MCT.' Again silence followed his words, but now a hard gleam shone in her eye. Alex shifted uncomfortably. '*Huan. Neuv ai Huan?*' he asked.

As soon as the old woman had seen them, she must have known why they had come. But when Alex spoke Huan's name her expression changed, mouth popping open, eyes suddenly frozen. Sensing the change, Alex reached out to touch her shoulder. She shrank away. He dropped his arm, jammed both hands in his pockets. As a man outside the family, he shouldn't have tried to touch her; it wasn't done.

'I'm sorry,' Tess heard him say. '*Sohm toh.*'

The younger woman stepped forward, curling her arm around the elder's, leaning into her.

'*Sohm toh,*' Alex said again, spreading his hands. '*Sohm toh.*' He began to speak then in Khmer words Tess didn't understand, his voice softer than she had ever heard it, hands balled into fists in his pockets, slouching a bit to reduce his height, to seem to them less huge, less threatening.

He stopped speaking. Again there was silence. Tess could sense his agitation in the pulse of a muscle in his jaw.

'*Neuv ai Huan,*' Alex repeated. '*Neuv ai Huan?*'

Suddenly the old woman lurched forward. Lips curled back from yellowing teeth, eyes bright pinpricks in the folds of her lids. Her voice was a hard, angry whisper.

'*Kh'nyohm muhn yuhl te. Sohm niyay yeut yeut,*' Alex said,

spreading his hands, trying to calm her.

Her speech slowed a fraction, but still the words flowed from her, the volume rising with her anger. Alex interrupted where he could, posing questions, pressing for sensible answers.

Tess glanced at the younger woman. She had moulded herself to the wooden slat walls of the hut and was staring at Alex as if he was the devil. Tess caught her eye. They held each other's gaze for a fraction of a second. Tess smiled; the woman looked away.

The old woman had raised a gnarled hand now, index finger pointed as if she wanted to jab it in Alex's gut, but was struggling between anger, fear and deference to this Western man. Trembling, she started speaking again, her words a torrent of uncontrolled emotion. She was yelling now. Her words filled the room, echoing from the pitched roof.

*

'What did she say?' Tess asked.

They were back on the road to Battambang, the packed dirt flowing beneath them.

'Nothing that was useful.'

'She seemed angry. Scared.'

'Of course she was scared. We may be the first Westerners they've ever seen. Definitely the first they've had to their house.'

Tess twisted around in the passenger seat to face him. She had to lean towards him and shout to make herself heard over the noise of the engine, he was driving so fast; the Land Cruiser groaning in protest at the ruts on the dirt track.

'But it wasn't just that, was it? I thought she . . . she said something about you, didn't she?'

Taking a hand from the wheel, Alex scratched at his forearm through his shirtsleeve, his expression unreadable.

'What? What did she say?'

'She said, "He's frightened of you. Huan's frightened of you."'

'You?'

'Me. Us. MCT.' He flicked the wipers on and sprayed some water over the windscreen; mud splatters streaked across the glass. 'Us at MCT. She said that he's frightened of us at MCT.'

'Did she say where he is?'

'No. Just that he'd left.'

A phone rang suddenly. Alex frowned, fumbled a mobile from his pocket. He glanced at the name flashing on its face, hesitated, seemed to be weighing up options. He tossed the phone on the dash. It stopped ringing. A few seconds later, it started again.

'Fuck.' Grabbing the phone from the dash, he flicked it open. 'Alexander Bauer.'

A pause. When he spoke again, his voice had an uneasy edge. 'I'm driving back to Battambang now. I'll be with you by—' He glanced at his watch. 'Seven thirty, eight at the latest.'

Jamming the phone back in his pocket, he looked across at Tess.

'That was Dr Ung. He said that Johnny has gone crazy, he's smashing his room up, won't let anyone in.'

'Go straight there. I'll walk home from the hospital.'

34

As Alex parked the Land Cruiser in the hospital courtyard, Tess glanced through the side window and saw Dr Ung hurrying towards them. Silhouetted in the light from the hospital building, he looked as insubstantial as a shadow.

'Thank you for coming, Alexander.' He clasped Alex's hand in both of his. 'Hello Tess.'

She had only ever seen Dr Ung calm. Now he crackled with nervous energy.

'What's going on?' Alex asked, as they turned and jogged together towards the covered veranda.

'Half an hour ago I was leaving the operating theatre and I heard screaming, the sound of things being thrown. I came out to see what was happening and found Johnny very agitated, out of bed, tossing things around the room, shouting and screaming. He is insisting on leaving the hospital tonight.'

'Why?'

'I have tried to find out, but he won't talk to me.'

They reached the veranda, and turned to face each other. Tess hung back by the Land Cruiser, letting them talk, feeling that she was intruding on something too personal. She wished now that she'd asked Alex to drop her home on the way here.

'Also,' Dr Ung had lowered his voice, but she could just about hear him. 'He has been seeing things, imagining things.'

'What things?'

'Someone in his room.' He slipped off his glasses and pressed the tips of his fingers to the bridge of his nose. 'He thinks that someone is trying to kill him. Paranoid delusions. Not unusual after the sort of trauma he's experienced. But in his case they seem severe.'

Alex nodded wearily, but didn't reply. He wasn't about to open up. Dr Ung had enough on his plate running the hospital with paper-thin resources and Alex had too much respect for what he did to drag him into this mess unnecessarily.

'Perhaps I should have been to see him earlier tonight. Perhaps that would have made a difference. I was . . .' Dr Ung shook his head, the movement slight, distracted. '. . . Busy. We had a new mine victim arrive at the hospital this afternoon, a child. I was operating until almost seven p.m. When I left the operating theatre, I heard the commotion. You must persuade Johnny to stay, Alexander. His leg needs more time to heal properly, while he is resting, and he needs physio. If he falls, he risks damaging the stump, and that will put his recovery back for weeks, months even. Also, he needs help with the psychological issues associated with his injury. Otherwise,' he added quietly, 'I fear greatly for his recovery.'

Frowning, he slipped his glasses back on and led Alex inside. Tess remained by the Land Cruiser.

*

Johnny's room reeked of cigarette smoke and sweat. The table lamp illuminated a jumble of clothes and cigarette packets strewn across the floor. The bed was on its side, the mattress and sheets in a heap in the corner. A shattered whisky bottle lay beneath the window in a golden puddle, and the reek of booze struck Alex the moment he saw it. The mosquito netting covering the window had been slashed from top to bottom, side to side; the jagged edge of a shard of glass from the bottle protruded from it, knotted with brown mesh.

Johnny, wearing a pair of white boxer shorts, was standing, leaning on a pair of wooden crutches, staring down at the chaos on the floor. His stump was swaddled in bandages, the skin of his thigh shrunken and livid with shrapnel scars. The cigarette in his hand trembled, flaking ash into the open suitcase at his feet.

''Bout fucking time you showed up.'

Without answering, Alex moved over to the bed, hooked his hands into the metal frame and hauled it upright. He reached for the bedding and tossed it back on to the mattress, pausing for a second to look down at something in his hand, which he slipped in his jacket pocket, before arranging the bedclothes in some semblance of order. Moving over to the window, he crouched down and started collecting the shards of glass.

'What are you doing?'

'What does it look like?'

'Leave it.'

Alex ignored him.

'Leave it, you cunt.'

Glass clinked as Alex opened his fingers and let the shards fall to the floor. He straightened and met Johnny's gaze. Johnny's pale blue eyes, red-rimmed and unfocused, held his for a second before skipping off around the room.

'This morning. You said you'd come back this morning. Where the fuck were you?'

'Clearing.'

'In Koh Kroneg?' Johnny coughed and shook his head. 'You think you're invincible, don't you? You reckon you can keep clearing in that field and nothing is going to happen to you?'

'It's my job,' Alex muttered, staring through the gash of mosquito netting into the dark courtyard beyond, his hands gripping the windowframe so hard that his fingers turned white. He felt as if he was wrapped up in something and every second he stood in this room it tightened around him.

'You've got to help me, Alex. I'm a dead man.'

'Probably.'

'What? What did you say?'

Alex turned his head slowly. 'Why do I get the feeling that you deserve everything you get, Johnny?'

'How the fuck can you say that?' Johnny bellowed. 'Is it because of that fucking girl? Some stupid little Khmer whore who got herself knocked up? That I deserve this.' He gestured to his leg. '*This!*'

Alex stalked towards him, his face twisted in fury. 'Are there any more, Johnny? Are there other things you haven't told me? Because this is bigger than you. There's other women gone missing. Other "stupid little Khmer whores" – all from villages around that field.'

Johnny took a half-step backwards. 'I don't know what you're talking about. I don't know anything about that.'

'Because I just found this, just now, when I picked up your bedsheets.' Alex flung something at Johnny, who caught it instinctively. He looked down at the stone in his hand. Painted on it was a tiny white crocodile. The crocodile was missing a back leg – the right leg – just like he was.

'And don't tell me it's Ret S'Mai. It's hard to paint if you haven't got any fingers.'

Johnny stared at the object in his hand in silence.

'It was on my pillow. Someone came into my room last night while I was sleeping and left it there,' he said, in a voice that Alex barely recognised. 'That's what I'm talking about, Alex. Someone's got me marked. I'm a dead man.'

35

Alex didn't seem to have heard Tess cross the courtyard towards him. He was standing on the veranda, bathed in the light from the hospital window, his face expressionless. In his left hand he held a cigarette, cupped in his palm. The smoke rose to the veranda roof, a hazy column, undisturbed in the still air.

'How's Johnny?' Then she realised exactly what he was doing with that cigarette. 'What the fuck are you doing?'

He started. He hadn't realised she was there until she'd spoken. Something in him seemed to register the concern in her voice – the command – because he slowly uncurled his fingers and dropped the smoking butt on to the veranda.

'Tess.' His smile was bleak.

'Alex?'

He took a step towards her and held out his hand. The light from the window found the cigarette burn on his palm, a blister already forming. She trailed her gaze over the discoloured pockmarks of older ones, hard to see against his tan, to the knife marks carving their way up his wrist, disappearing beneath the cuff of his shirtsleeve.

Stepping back, she came hard up against one of the pillars holding up the veranda roof. Shifting to her left, she manoeuvred herself to one side of it, curling her arm around the solid wood. 'Why do you do that?'

He shook his head, as though he didn't have an answer to the question. With studied nonchalance, he put his hands in his pockets. She saw him wince as the material dragged against his palm. Her gaze moved from his hand to his face; the eyes looking back at her were absolutely empty. Such control, such stillness – and beneath it all . . . this.

She had seen too much of raw human nature in Afghanistan to judge him. Some of the bravest men she knew had turned out to be the most screwed-up inside.

But she had to put some space between them, get herself some time to think.

'Johnny,' she reminded him. 'Johnny needs you. He must be ready to go by now.'

He didn't respond.

'I'll walk home.' Releasing her hold of the pillar, she backed away slowly until her foot found the edge of the veranda. 'Alex, please don't do that to yourself any more. Just don't.'

He shook his head, but his eyes were still empty. She turned and, without looking back, jumped off the veranda and ran across the courtyard to the gate. She heard him call her name, once, but didn't turn, didn't stop until the darkness of the street folded around her.

*

'You want to go? So let's go.'

'You came back,' Johnny whispered.

Without answering, Alex tossed the few remaining garments

and the packets of cigarettes into Johnny's suitcase, shut the lid and clicked the locks. He lifted the case, clenching his fingers tight around the handle to stop his hand shaking. 'Are you ready?'

Johnny nodded. He held out his hand for Alex to help him up. Ignoring the outstretched arm, Alex walked to the door. The burn on his palm was oozing liquid. His gaze moved from it to the other scabbed craters ringing it, to the knife marks tracking up his forearm. He knew that Tess was right. When someone noticed, commented – and it didn't happen often – he felt a momentary swerve towards objectivity. But looking at his scars now, he felt nothing – no disgust, no regret – just a quiet satisfaction. The pain had sterilised something dangerous inside him.

'I'm ready.' Johnny's voice sounded tiny, timid; Alex could barely hear it. He was standing by the bed, a crutch tucked under each arm.

'Can you walk all right?'

Johnny nodded. Leaving the room with Johnny's case, Alex propped the door to the veranda open. The hospital courtyard was dark and quiet. The air felt unusually cool. He had a quick look around for Tess, but knew, even before he looked, that she wouldn't be there. Just as she had begun to trust him, he'd fucked it up again.

Johnny came outside and shuffled haltingly across the veranda on his crutches. He stopped at the top of the stairs and tried to catch Alex's eye. Alex looked at his own feet. He sensed Johnny start down the stairs, sensed him falter, pause for a second to regain his balance, then start again; he broke into a run and reached the bottom of the steps just in time to catch

Johnny as he stumbled and fell.

Alex installed Johnny in the passenger seat of the Land Cruiser and went around to the driver's side. Johnny was sitting motionless, his hands curled in his lap. He glanced across as Alex climbed in and opened his mouth to speak.

Alex cut him off. 'No more, Johnny.'

He felt tired, tense, at the limit of his endurance. Staring straight out of the windscreen, he started the engine, ground the Land Cruiser into first gear and cruised slowly across the courtyard. But as he pulled out of the hospital gate on to the road, something caught his eye. He stared hard in the rear-view mirror as they drove down the road. A skinny child-man was standing by the gate, watching the retreating Land Cruiser, his broken hands pressed tightly to his sides.

Day 7

'Coffee?'

MacSween twitched in his seat. He opened his eyes. 'Tess?'

'Please tell me you didn't sleep here.'

He straightened behind the desk, rubbing his knuckles into his eyes. He looked dreadful: cheeks paunchy, the one he had been lying on criss-crossed with patterns, the edge of his blotter from the dimensions of the dent, eyes black-bagged and cloudy with sleep.

'In that chair? All night?'

Dawn was breaking. The river was washed pink, the windows in the shops and restaurants on the opposite bank glinting under the low rays of the rising sun. The sunlight hadn't reached MacSween's office, though, which was gloomy and smelt stale. A fly floated in a glass of Scotch on his desk and a half-eaten pizza curled in its open box. Tess laid the mug of coffee in the middle of his blotter.

'Aye, well, I was working on this crossword and I got stuck on a clue.'

'What?'

A creased copy of *The Times*'s international edition lay on his desk. Picking it up, he straightened it out and passed it to her. Tess took the paper from his hand. There was a photograph of Boris Johnson on the front page, looking suitably dishevelled, pushing through a throng of journalists and cameramen. Underneath the photograph was the caption: 'Mophead Boris wows the Conservative Party Conference.'

'Only a matter of time before he ousts that stiff twat Cameron.'

Tess gave a quick half-smile. 'I didn't realise you were interested in British politics.'

'British? English and sheep shaggers it will be soon if the man Connery gets his way. And good riddance.' Pressing the back of his hand to his mouth to suppress a yawn, he reached over, flipped the lid of the pizza box shut and tossed it into the bin under his desk. 'Back page. Three down. Twelve letters. Two words, one five-letter, one six.'

Tess turned the paper over. She had always been terrible at crosswords; could never be bothered to give them the required level of time and attention. Her eye was caught by a photograph and couple of lighter articles on the back page. Jeremy Clarkson, his corpulent figure squeezed into the cream leather sports seat of a Lamborghini Countach.

'An enthusiastic style of worship that might be practised at a Christian Mission,' she heard MacSween say.

A short piece about life satisfaction, the author wondering if modern Western children were too spoilt to appreciate how fortunate they were.

It all felt a million miles away from here. From now. Would she ever be able to go back and just be *normal*? What was normal? Was there even such a thing? The questions made her brain ache. The crossword an easy diversion in comparison.

'Happy-clappy.' Tess dropped the paper on the desktop.

MacSween span it around 180 degrees to face him. Picked up a pen and began filling in the boxes.

'Dammit, lass. You're right.' He sounded impressed, but his body language, the restlessness of his hands on the desktop, betrayed an irritation.

Tess pulled back a chair and sat down across the desk. 'What's up?'

'What do you mean?'

'Something's up. You don't seem . . . you don't seem yourself.'

'What? Being as you know me so well after—' He glanced at his watch, lifting his wrist to his face and squinting to see the date. 'After five days, is it? Or six, mebbe?'

There was an edge to his voice; an antagonism that she had never heard before, even during the meeting following Johnny's accident. She shrugged, took a sip of the coffee she'd brought in for herself, let the silence stretch.

'Sorry, lass. It's . . . it's been a long night.' He looked sheepish.

She found his gaze over the desktop. 'There is something bothering you, isn't there?'

'Apart from another woman and a little girl murdered, you mean? Apart from this whole bloody White Crocodile madness. Apart from the fact that most of my Khmer mine clearers are so fucking jumpy that sending them into a minefield now is tantamount to asking them to commit suicide. Apart from all that, you mean?'

Tess was overtaken by two contradictory impulses: to stand up now and walk out of his office, leave him alone with his fury, or to sit tight and brave it out. Two impulses – only one realistic choice.

'Alex told me. About the woman and the little girl.' She didn't elaborate on her fleeting connection with the latter.

He dropped his head to his hands. A gesture so exhausted, so defeatist that she had to resist the urge to walk around and lay a hand on his shoulder. She knew that he wouldn't appreciate it. That he'd see it as a sign of reflected weakness, would clam up on her. She sat in silence, waiting. A fly landed on her hand; she remained still, feeling the tickle of its feet on her skin.

Finally, he sighed and straightened. 'Jakkleson. Jakkleson has gone missing.'

'What do you mean by "gone missing"?'

'He's not been seen since early yesterday morning. I called his landlady half an hour ago. He didn't come home last night at all.'

'But isn't that—' She broke off. What was she going to say? *But I found his dirty snaps and hasn't he probably just spent the night with one of those poor girls? Turn around and he'll be standing in the doorway with crumpled clothes and a smug expression on his face?* 'Has he never stayed out before?'

'Aye, but there's more. A lot mor—' A pain appeared to shoot across MacSween's back, cutting off the end of the sentence. He tilted forward, wincing.

'Are you OK, MacSween?'

'Aye. Of course I'm OK. I'm not in me dotage yet,' he muttered, squeezing his hand into a fist on the desktop. 'Jakkleson's Land Cruiser was found last night in a car park near a local tourist destination.'

'Which one?'

'Sampeau Temple. It's an ancient Buddhist temple built on a rocky outcrop twenty kilometres southwest of Battambang. You get a great view of the neighbouring mountain from up there.' He paused. 'Crocodile Mountain.'

Tess started.

'The car had been there since early morning,' he continued. 'A couple of tourists noticed it there on their way up the mountain, and a few hours later on their way back down. When they came down, there were kids crawling over it, pulling bits off. They thought it was odd that it had been there so long, particularly as they hadn't seen anyone else on the hill, so they contacted the local police station.'

'OK. But hasn't he maybe just had enough? Wanted a bit of time off? I saw him the night before last. I bumped into him in Riverside Balcony Bar. I hardly know him, but even so, he did sound melancholy. Like he'd kind of—' For some reason her mind flipped to that man she had seen at the swimming pool yesterday evening, holding an intent conversation with himself. 'Like he'd had enough of being out here. Of being in Cambodia.'

MacSween shook his head. 'Every expat gets like that sometimes. Everybody gets like that, wherever they live. Nothing is roses all the time. Jakkleson loved it out here. It suited him.' He clenched his teeth, a grimace tracking fleetingly across his face.

'There's more, isn't there, MacSween?'

He nodded. 'The local police found his Jericho.'

'Found it just discarded?'

'It had been fired.'

'By the temple?'

'Aye. They found an empty shell casing too.'

'Well, maybe—'

'It had blood on the grip.'

'Jakkleson's?' As soon as she said it, she knew it was a stupid comment. There was no way the police in rural Cambodia would have access to DNA profiling technology. 'Sorry . . .

obviously they don't know whose it is.'

'No. But they found his baseball cap. He labelled everything, anal sod that he was, so there was no doubt it was his. The cap also had blood on it. Lots of blood, they said.'

'MacSween, you need to call Battambang Provincial—'

He raised a weary hand, cutting her off.

'Aye, and he left me this. On my desk. It was written on a scrap of paper so I didn't find it until late last night. I was scrabbling around trying to find some information for a donor I'd been speaking with earlier on in the evening, and there it was, slipped under my blotter.' He held it up, so she could read it.

Had an email from Huan. Going to meet him at Crocodile Mountain. Wasn't time to radio you, so went alone. Will report back.

'You've got to call Battambang Provincial Police in, MacSween.'

He spread his hands, let his gaze drift around the room. 'It will mean the ruination of all this.'

'No. Not ruination. Just . . . just postponement. Just for a few days.'

He shook his head.

'Things blow over. Especially out here. You're . . . we're doing so much good. It's not going to end—'

She heard a noise behind her. Turned and saw Alex in the doorway. He was wearing shorts and a khaki long-sleeved shirt. She thought of last night, the sight she had had of his scarred arms.

The chair screeched thinly on the wooden boards as she slid it backwards and stood. 'You have to call in the police, MacSween. You have no other option. You *have* to. For

Jakkleson's sake. For those women, and that little girl.' *For Luke* – she didn't say it. 'It's gone too far.'

Turning, she walked towards the door. Shrugging Alex's hand off her arm, she slid past him on to the landing, heard MacSween asking him to go and tell the staff that mine clearing was suspended until further notice, that they'd still be paid. Jogged quickly down the stairs before Alex emerged from MacSween's office.

*

Johnny woke, head throbbing, mouth mossy and foul. His cheek was sticky and his eyes were sore and stinging. Gingerly, he heaved himself on to his elbows. *Did I pass out?* He couldn't remember. Couldn't remember anything after he'd screwed Keav and told her to bring him a bottle of whisky before she went back to her bedroom downstairs.

Alex had dropped him back home, helped him up the stairs to his bedroom, brought in his suitcase and then left, turning down the offer of a drink. *Sod him*, Johnny had thought. *I can look after myself.*

Reaching over to the bedside table, he found a packet of cigarettes. He lit one and lay back, staring up at the ceiling. Sucking the smoke deep into his lungs, he formed an O with his lips, exhaled and watched the smoke ring fade upwards, spreading out as it reached the ceiling.

Your first day out of hospital, Johnny. The first day of the rest of your life.

He blew another smoke ring, this one crooked, squashed

along one edge. He knew that if he lay too long he would start to think about his accident, his life before it, start blaming himself when he knew it wasn't his fault because he'd just been having a laugh, playing games. How the hell could he have known it would get this out of control? The tobacco rush segued into tingling anxiety.

Closing his eyes, he pressed his head deep into the soft pillow, laid his arms flat by his sides and carried on smoking. The sound of singing floated up the stairs, light and carefree. In his mind's eye, he could see Keav flitting around his sitting room, picking things up and dusting them, placing them back carefully, just as she had found them, her beautiful oval face calm in concentration.

'Keav! Too early. Less fucking happiness please,' he yelled.

The singing stopped. A scurry of feet receding down wooden stairs, the muffled sound of a door being eased closed. Focusing hard to steady his hand, he reached out and stubbed the cigarette carefully in the ashtray.

He wouldn't think about it. He'd bolted all the doors, was safe here in his own home.

He wouldn't think about *it*.

*

As Tess made her way down the gravel drive, slipping through the gaggle of clearance teams loading kit into the backs of Land Cruisers – a sense of hesitation in their movements, the ambient hum of paranoia evident, even though they had yet to be informed that Jakkleson had almost certainly been murdered, that mine clearing was suspended until further notice – she experienced a sensation of pure fear. She stopped just inside the gate and stood for a long time, almost motionless, her stalled brain trying to find the logic in what she had just been told in MacSween's office.

Jakkleson. Could he possibly be dead? Could there be some reasonable explanation? No. There wasn't likely to be. Huan had asked to meet with him, and now he was dead. But what if the White Crocodile wasn't Huan? When she and Alex had visited his family yesterday, his mother had been furious with them; furious and afraid. *Me. Us. She's frightened of us at MCT.* If Huan was the White Crocodile, why was she so frightened?

Slipping out of the gate, she cut across the road, dodging through the stream of mopeds and bicycles ferrying people to work, and joined the throng of chatting, laughing Khmers walking along the top of the riverbank. It was diverting to be among company, but by the same token, she didn't want to catch anybody's eye, be drawn into pidgin chat about 'where you come from, miss'. She stared blankly at the backs of the people in front of her as she walked, her eyes skipping from person to person. MacSween would call in the police, she was certain of that. He had realised, now, that even if it meant the end of MCT, he had no other choice. But what would the police do? They would focus on the Westerner, on Jakkleson, for certain. The women who had disappeared, the others who had been killed, that little girl – they would be ignored, just more statistics in a country where sixty thousand children die each year from poverty and land mines.

The throng of Khmers were heading into Battambang centre, and she followed them, letting herself be carried along by the flow, making no conscious choices about where she was going, what she was going to do. In the centre of the bridge over the Sanger, she stopped, tilting forward over the concrete parapet – in almost exactly the same place she had stood a few days ago – watching the early morning light play across the muddy water, feeling sacks and bags brushing against her back as people shuffled past.

Tess knew that she should go to the hospital, find Ret S'Mai and try and get him to talk one way or the other. But she felt as if she could more easily drop over the parapet of this bridge and walk on the water below her than do anything construct-ive; as if all the energy had been sucked out of her by the fifteen minutes she'd spent in MacSween's office.

The morning was scorching and even standing in the centre of the bridge, soft gusts of cooler air from the surface of the water eddying around her, she was boiling in sweat. Though she pressed herself against the parapet, she was still jostled by the people passing behind her. She felt like turning around and yelling at them all to keep their distance, but on another level she knew that she was safe in their company, both physically and mentally. Slumping down on the road, ignoring the sur-prised looks of passers-by, she pulled off her combat boots and socks, stuffed a sock into each boot, tied the laces together and hung them over her shoulder. The tarmac was chill against her bare soles as she pushed herself to her feet; it had trapped the night's cool.

She started to walk again, turning left when she reached the end of the bridge, away from the Riverside Balcony Bar and its rowdy breakfast crowd, away from the centre of town.

If Jakkleson had been lured out to Crocodile Mountain and

killed, it meant that her own life was in danger too. She experienced an almost overwhelming urge to go straight back to her apartment and pack her things – just as Alex had told her to do – go to the bus station and catch a bus to Phnom Penh. *Go home before you no longer can.* Six hours by road, enough distance, surely, to put her out of harm's way. She could be there by dinnertime, check into one of the faceless city-centre hotels and become just another anonymous tourist until she could book a flight back to England.

Run away. She thought about running away and then she thought about Luke as she had last seen him, a tiny figure on the doorstep of their house. The couple of phone calls they had shared since, shouting over the interference on the line. The knowledge that he had been frightened; that she had dismissed his fears. And what of Johnny? Jakkleson? What of that little girl who had tried to warn her about the White Crocodile?

A young Khmer man with bleached blond hair and multiple ear piercings appeared in front of her suddenly, holding out a flyer with a picture of a boat on the front.

'Boat trip. See beautiful countryside.'

He pointed towards a wooden boat, painted in blue and yellow, tied up to a jetty on the river. The boat was about thirty feet long, an old wooden tub which would have been long since mothballed in a richer country. There was no inside, just a flat deck with a multicoloured sunshade stretched over it.

'No. Thank you.'

'Please come. Lots of fun. Come beautiful lady.'

Without making eye contact, she tried to move past him; he sidestepped in front of her. 'Only two dollar. Two dollar, four hours. No better deal, whole of Battambang. Lot of other tourists.'

She was about to say, 'I'm not a tourist,' but she stopped herself. She looked past him to the other passengers seated on the benches under the awning – only six of them. Two of them, a girl and boy aged about twenty, Gandhi pants and dreadlocks, were poring over a copy of *Cambodia on a Shoestring*; the others, three men and a woman, each sitting separately from each other, clearly not yet acquainted, wearing the ubiquitous traveller's uniform of grungy T-shirt and multi-pocketed shorts. Normality. In some form at least. And space to think. To clear her mind, make some logical decisions.

Sliding her boots off her shoulder and lowering them to the ground, she rooted around in her pocket, held out her two dollars to the bleached-haired man.

'Good choice beautiful lady. You have wonderful day.'

*

The boat motored at a snail's pace through a series of shabby, untended suburbs – if you could call them that – of crumbling white-painted concrete houses mixed with traditional bamboo huts, women washing clothes, krama scarves wrapped around their heads to protect them from the sun, naked children splashing and swimming, the rubbish collected in reeds on either side of the river petering out as they left the buildings behind and floated into the countryside. The dreadlocked hippies were keeping to themselves, but the other four had formed a group at the stern and were chatting and laughing, sharing cans of beer that one of them had brought in his rucksack.

Resting her chin on the side of the boat, Tess watched the banks slip by: paddy field after paddy field terraced up the side of low hills, the workers harvesting the rice dots of primary colour among the intense emerald of the rice plants; a tiny village of crooked bamboo huts on stilts, deserted except for a couple of old people sitting in doorways in the sun, a few chickens pecking in the dirt, and a pack of tiny children who kept pace with the boat for a couple of hundred metres, running along the bank, shouting and waving. They passed a small wat set incongruously in the middle of a field, a couple of monks in orange robes drifting between the temple's intricately carved pillars like spirits. It was stunning countryside, peaceful and unworldly, and she realised that she had never had a chance to look at rural Cambodia like this – just look – with no other motive than to absorb and enjoy.

Would she let herself be driven out of Battambang, out of this beautiful, complex country? Thwarted by some five-hundred-year-old myth?

Her feelings for Luke were so confused that even here, sitting quietly, able to think, to reason undisturbed, she still couldn't order the emotions in her mind. She had loved him once, with an intensity that even at the time she had realised was obsessive, driven by a need to cling to someone, to call them her own. And he had reciprocated, driven by a similar need. He had loved and needed her every bit as much as she had loved and needed him – she was certain of that. But he had also callously exploited her weakness. And now? There was no love left, but there was memory and because of that a muddled, desperate kind of loyalty.

She was her father's daughter too, in the end: the formative

37

Manchester, England

Eleven p.m., and though the night had hardly begun for them, even the prostitutes and drug dealers occupying their patches on Cheetham Hill Road looked cold and weary. Wessex pulled his collar up around his face, glancing up at the snowflakes drifting down from the orange halo cast by the sodium-vapour street light above him. Viles was sitting across the road in a twenty-four-hour kebab joint, reading the *Manchester Evening News* and dragging out a can of Diet Coke and a doner. Wessex caught her eye through the grubby plate-glass window and gave her an almost imperceptible nod.

The brothel was in an Edwardian terrace, jammed between a shuttered grocer's on one side and a branch of Barclays Bank on the other. The only thing marking it out as a brothel was the fact that the facade bore years of city grime and the curtains, a dull shade of crimson, were crying out for a makeover. A Volvo estate was parked outside, its front wheel on the kerb, as if its driver had been in a hurry. Wessex locked eyes with the stuffed bunny discarded on the child seat in the back.

His phone rang.

'Wessex.'

'Jane Percival.' She sounded livelier than he felt. 'Sorry for the lateness of the hour, Detective Inspector. But I know you've been burning the candle at both ends on this case anyway, so I wanted to tell you straight away. We've had a result from our blood test, and from the DNA ancestry test.'

He moved over to the side of the pavement, cupping his hand to his mouth and lowering his voice. 'Great. Go ahead.'

'The blood sample showed traces of diazepam – Valium.'

'So she was drugged forcibly?'

'It's impossible to know how it was administered. She may have been a habitual user.'

'And the DNA test?'

'Well, I didn't get very far with our in-house DNA testing. South East Asia was all they told me. I thought you might want it narrowed down a bit more than that. Seeing as you have nothing else to go on.'

'Right.' It felt uncomfortable to be reminded. 'And?'

'And I won't bore you with too many details because I appreciate that you're standing on a pavement freezing your nibs off. But I remembered a forensics conference I went to last year. We had a speaker, a professor, from the Research Department of Genetics, Evolution and Environment at University College London. He was talking about advances in genetic testing, most of it way beyond our meagre budget of course.'

'Go on.' It was all he could do to stop his teeth chattering.

'The professor was talking about a couple of projects they were doing in conjunction with the University of California and Chiang Mai University in Thailand, identifying the key genetic markers in different language groups in that region. Thai speakers, Malay speakers, Khmer speakers, etc.'

A car shot past, too close to the kerb, its radio thumping R & B; Wessex leapt back as muddy slush mushroomed up.

'Shit.'

'What?'

'Sorry, nothing. Just got a drenching. Go on, go on.'

'Khmer. Our girl was a Khmer speaker.'

'She's from Cambodia?'

'That's right.'

'OK. Thanks, Jane. I really appreciate you pushing the boat out for me on this one. Call if you get anything else.' Flicking the telephone shut, he dropped it into his coat pocket.

'Cambodia,' he muttered, walking back across the pavement to the dirty white-painted front door. He knew nothing about it; just a faint trace of its history under the Khmer Rouge. He had visions of a subsistence existence, ox carts and paddy fields, people who could barely afford a bowl of rice to eat, let alone a plane ticket to England.

The brothel owner, standing behind a makeshift Formica counter in the narrow hallway, was mid-fifties, rat-thin, with bad teeth and a shaven head. He didn't look like a healthy man. Wessex would be surprised if his skin, grey-white as a rain-heavy sky, had ever glimpsed the sun.

He had to pay up front; fifty quid, no questions asked.

The attic room he was sent to had aubergine-coloured walls and a threadbare seventies carpet, a psychedelic pattern of aubergine and yellow swirls. The only furniture in the room was a double bed that sagged in the middle and a heavy dark wood rocking chair in the corner. Pinching the threadbare piece of material covering the bed – a 'throw' it would probably have been called in a more salubrious setting – between the tips of his index finger and thumb, he peeled it off and tossed it on to the floor. Years ago, he had watched a programme during which scientists had tested furnishings in a typical three-star town-centre hotel – a seaside town somewhere down south, he couldn't remember the name – to see what substances they harboured. The sheets had been clean, but the bed cover had carried seventeen different types of sperm and twenty-six of urine. You could quadruple that in this kind of establishment and still fall woefully short.

Sitting down on the side of the bed, he lowered his head to his hands and sucked in a couple of deep breaths, trying to rid himself of the knot of tension in his stomach.

There was a knock on the door. He looked up.

38

Leaving her boots at the top of the bank, Tess picked her way back down towards the river. The afternoon on the boat had been lovely, and she had no compulsion or desire to be any-where else. She stopped and sat when she reached the wall of reeds hemming the water. The noise of the Riverside Balcony Bar hummed behind her. In front of her, the Sanger silently reflected the lights of central Battambang: dancing orange fires from the food stalls, the white beam of a motorcycle headlight sweeping along the road at the top of the bank, the steady yel-low glow from windows.

She had returned from the trip an hour earlier and nipped into the Balcony Bar for dinner, choosing a quiet corner table and sitting with her back to the room, so that no one would be tempted to engage her in conversation. She could have killed for a steak with pepper sauce, but they had run out and what was left on the menu was traditional Cambodian dishes or a selection of right-on traveller food: vegetable stews, salads and stir-fries. She settled for a Khmer curry of chicken, sweet potato and pumpkin in a coconut milk sauce, and a bottle of Kingdom beer. When they arrived, she polished them off in five minutes – she hadn't eaten since breakfast at 6 a.m. and realised, after the first spoonful, that she was starving. After dinner she ordered another bottle of beer and carried it back down the stairs.

Wiggling her toes, she wormed them into the silty earth of the riverbank. It was quiet here, the air warm and still. A faint smell of sewage rose from the water below her. She closed her eyes and tuned in to the sound of the river slipping by – and then another noise, footsteps on the embankment behind her. She looked around, saw Alex making his way towards her out of the darkness.

'Hello, Tess.' He sat down.

'Hello, Alex,' she said coolly.

'How are you doing?'

'Good, thanks. Just escaping—' She broke off with a shrug, letting the words hang in the air. 'Enjoying the view. It's beautiful down here.'

'Yeah, it is beautiful.' His voice was soft.

She glanced over. His shirt was unbuttoned. Quickly, she traced her gaze down the smooth muscles of his chest and stomach, to the butt of his Browning sticking out from his belt. He was sitting too close. She could smell him. She leaned back against the bank, edging away a little, and cast her eyes along the river again following the darkness to where it transitioned to streets and lights.

'How did you know where I was?'

'I've been looking for you. I had just given up and was walking home, when I found these at the top of the bank.'

He held up her boots; she took them from him.

'Breadcrumbs.'

'Huh?'

'Nothing. Just a fairy story.'

'Oh.' He nodded, not understanding.

'Why were you looking for me?'

'I wanted to talk to you.'

She looked back down at her toes. The nails were blackened with mud. There were two lines of tiny dents on the bank where she had wormed them into the soil.

'The police want to interview all of us tomorrow. MacSween has suspended the operation. No more clearing until all this shit is sorted out.' He paused. 'One way or another.'

'Until someone catches the White Crocodile.'

'Until *we* catch it.'

'There is no *we*.' She looked him in the eyes. 'How did you know that I was Luke's wife, Alex? I didn't think anyone knew.'

'I don't think anyone else does know,' he said casually, his gaze drifting away from hers.

'So how do you?'

He didn't speak for a long moment. Tess waited, watching him, the doubt written in his features.

'Tell me.'

With a sigh, he reached into his pocket and pulled out his wallet. Flipping it open, he slipped out a folded sheet of paper and dropped it into her lap. The paper was thin, pale yellow, faded white at the creases. Though she didn't need to – she already knew exactly what it was – Tess picked it up and slowly unfolded it. A photo-booth photograph was stapled to the top right-hand corner of the paper: her tongue stuck out, red hair in pigtails, too much lipstick on, 'I love you, Luke' scrawled across the page, a big heart slashing through the words. She remembered writing it the day before they got married, re-membered scrawling the heart in thick red ink. She looked up. Alex held her gaze for a brief moment before looking away. Re-folding the paper, she threw it back at him.

'Where did you get that?'

'Luke showed it to me once when we were in a bar together.' His voice was little more than a whisper. 'Not long before he died.'

'And?'

'He was drunk. He never talked about his private life because he didn't think it was anyone else's business. He had told us that he was single.' Tipping his head back, he stared up at the starry sky. 'Though he lied about that.'

Tess nudged her hand against his thigh. 'Tell me, Alex.'

'He was—' He turned to look at her. 'Melancholy, I suppose.'

'Why? Why was he melancholy?'

'He used to get like that. He was very aware of his own mortality. Afraid of dying.'

'Did he *know*? Did he know he was going to die?'

'I don't know. I didn't think about it at the time, but looking back, maybe he did.' He met her gaze; shadows filled his eyes. 'Probably. Probably he did.'

'How did you get my letter?'

'MacSween had Luke's landlady pack his stuff into boxes. He put them in the cellar at MCT House because he didn't know what else to do with Luke's things. I went through them, took your letter.'

She felt her breath catch in her throat. 'Why did you take it?'

'Because I wanted it.'

'A dead man's things? That's sick.'

'It wasn't like that.'

'It's sick, Alex.'

'Are you still in love with him, Tess?' he mumbled.

Staring straight past him to the slick black snake of river in front of them, to the black trees on the far bank hanging heavy in the hot night air, she knew exactly what the answer was.

'No.' She formed the word, but no sound came out. 'No, I'm not. But . . . it was complicated.'

Twisting on to his side, Alex reached out suddenly and laid a warm hand on her arm. Tess shivered.

'He loved you so much. I was jealous of him. I wanted to love someone like you.' He trailed his thumb over her skin. She knew that she should pull her arm away, that this was going somewhere she couldn't afford to go, not with him. But she didn't move away. 'Buddhists believe that everyone has an aura,' she heard him say. 'The colour that your body exudes which tells everyone what kind of a person you are. Blue is happy, pink is loving.' He twisted a lock of her hair around his fingers. 'Red is passionate.'

She tugged it out of his grasp and smoothed it down with exaggerated care. 'Red is for "Danger!! Mines!!". Red is for blood.'

'Why did you run out today?'

'Why do you think, Alex?'

'I was looking for you. I wanted to . . . help you.'

'*You* wanted to help *me*? I'm not the one who stubs cigarettes out on their own skin, Alex.'

He didn't say anything, but she heard the catch in his breath.

'You didn't need to be jealous of Luke, Alex. He used to beat me up. I suppose you didn't find a hint of that in his boxes, did you?'

She glanced across, met his horrified gaze.

'He broke my finger once because I'd taken my wedding ring off to have a bath and forgotten to put it back on again. Just bent it back until the joint dislocated. He was smiling while he did it.' She bit her bottom lip. 'I told the doctor at A & E that I had slipped in the bath, like some geriatric old lady.'

'Jesus Christ.'

He reached for her hand; she shook him off. A fish must have broken the surface, because the reflected wash of light from the bars behind fractured for a moment.

'I only went to hospital if I really needed to – when something was broken. I was too ashamed otherwise. Because everything he did to me was my fault, of course. I'd made him angry.' Her voice broke. 'He believed it, and in time I came to believe it too.' She paused, swallowed. 'I was so needy when I met Luke. So desperate for someone to love me, and to be able to love someone back with everything I had. And the funny thing is, I did love him so much early on.' She dragged an arm roughly across her eyes. 'So what about you, Alex? Why do you self-harm?'

A pause. Over the choppy sound of her own breathing, she heard him sigh. 'I'm sorry, Tess, but that's my business.'

'I've just told you all . . . that, and it's still your business.' She shook her head. 'No, Alex. Not if you want me to trust you. If you want me to trust you, I need to know why you do it. Why you're here. You know about me, now I want to know about you.'

'I said that it's my business.'

She pulled her knees to her chest and wrapped her arms around them. 'Guilt?' she asked softly. She heard the pattern of his breathing change, quicken, and twisted to face him. 'Are you punishing yourself for something?'

He shook his head, but his eyes were unreadable. He reached for her hand, took it in his, and she felt the stippled surface of his burns against her skin. She shivered. He raised her hand to his mouth and kissed the back of it. She felt the warmth of his lips, and shivered again. She glanced away at the lights of the city floating on the surface of the water, suggesting a shape, something she couldn't quite name.

'No, Alex.' She wrenched her hand away. 'It doesn't work like that. You can't do this. This . . .' she gestured to his arm, ' . . . then just . . . make it all go away.'

His face was pale, his dark eyes guarded. She dropped her gaze to the butt of his Browning, reached for it, closing her fingers around the rubberised grip of the handle and yanking it out of his belt before he could react.

'Why don't you just put yourself out of your misery?' she said quietly, feeling the weight of the gun in her hands.

'Don't play around with that, Tess. It's loaded.' He tried to take it from her, but she pulled it clear of him.

'Loaded and cocked. Just put it to your head.' She closed both hands around the butt and held it out in front of her, squinting down the sights towards the black of the river. 'Put yourself out of your misery.' Her voice was trembling, but her hand was steady.

He shook his head and made a noise, something quiet but bitter, bitten off before it was finished. Then he caught her wrist with one hand, pulled the Browning out of her grasp with the other. He jammed it back into his belt and pushed himself to his feet.

'I'm going home.' His face was hard; his voice controlled.

'OK, Alex. Just run away.'

He turned silently and began picking his way up the bank. She twisted around on to her knees to watch him go.

'Run away, Alex.'

He kept walking, refusing to turn.

She stood up and shouted, 'You're a sick boy, Alex.'

But by then he had disappeared into the darkness and she wasn't sure if he had heard. She turned back to the river, slumped down and dropped her head to her hands.

39

Manchester, England

A South East Asian girl slid into the room wearing a baby-pink faux silk dressing gown. She smiled at him shyly and let the dressing gown fall from her shoulders. She wasn't wearing much underneath: only a hot-pink G-string and a matching bra that sat flat against her chest. Wessex had bigger breasts than she did.

God, she couldn't have been more than sixteen, seventeen tops. She hardly came up to his chest, and he was not even six foot. She was so thin that if he moved her in front of the window – not that there was one in this grotty attic – he would have been able to see the fluorescent orange from the street lamps cutting straight through her body.

There was something funny about the light in the room; it cast shadows across her face and body, but even so he could tell that she was beautiful. His eyes dipped to the tattoo on her thigh. He recognised it immediately.

The wooden boards creaked as she padded across the carpet to stand in front of him. She reached out and laid a soft hand on his cheek. Wessex found that he couldn't look at her.

He felt her hand slip to his shirtfront, her fingers undo his top button. She was halfway down when he roused himself from his stupor.

'No.'

He looked up. And saw. It wasn't shadow that had criss-crossed her body. It was bruises. On her cheek, striping her arms, a huge one, fist-sized, right in the middle of her stomach.

'No,' he repeated. 'I don't want to.'

The fear he saw in her eyes was intense.

'Please, I good. Very good. Make you very happy.'

She propped her hands on her hips as she spoke; tilted to one side and jiggled self-consciously. The wretched attempt to make herself more attractive transported him back to Christmas Day: watching his eleven-year-old niece trying to copy the moves from the Rihanna DVD he had bought her. Standing up, he buttoned up his shirt, bent and retrieved her gown, held it out to her. She pushed it away, her eyes filling with tears.

'Please. I make you happy. I very good. Make you very happy.'

He shook his head.

'It's not because I don't like you. You're—' His voice caught. 'Beautiful. I'll say we had sex, I promise. I just want to talk to you. Just talk.' He slid the gown around her shoulders, his gaze fixing on that huge bruise on her stomach, blue-black in the middle, yellowing around the edges.

'Do they beat you up?'

She shook her head.

'You can tell me.' *I'm police.* He couldn't say it. Couldn't afford to give himself away, even to her.

She shook her head again, but with such resignation it made his chest tighten to watch her. Her voice, so quiet that he had to lean towards her to hear, sounded like it had been programmed in some kids' toy.

'Good men. They good men who keep me here.'

40

A shot. The noise that cut through the still air down by the river sounded like a shot, but then there was silence, and Tess had no idea if she had heard right. She glanced over her shoulder and back along the riverbank. It was dark, deserted. Her eyes found the bar behind her, an oasis of lights. The tables that she could see – the ones close to the front edge of the balcony – were still jammed with drinkers, the hum of noise as consistent as it had been all night. No one else seemed to have been disturbed by the sound. It could have been anything. The backfire of a moped engine. A celebration.

Turning back to the river, she folded her arms around her legs and rested her chin on her knees. She knew that she should go home, but she couldn't quite face it. So she sat and stared into the darkness, and gradually something else broke through the hush in her mind. A disturbance in the rhythm of sounds from the bar: raised voices, an urgent shout, the scrabble of feet and the scrape of chair legs.

The scene that met her gaze when she glanced back had changed in the few moments since she'd last looked. The tables close to the front edge of the balcony had emptied; a stream of people bottlenecking towards the exit, pushing down the stairs. A jostling line of heads and shoulders filled the road that ran along the top of the riverbank – a crowd forming. She thought of the noise that sounded like a shot, then immediately of Alex.

The feel of his Browning in her hand. *Why don't you just put yourself out of your misery?*

Jesus, what had she done? She had sensed that he was close to the edge, but her fury at his refusal to open up to her in return had made her cruel. What the *hell* had she done?

Slithering and sliding on the muddy bank, she clawed her way to the road.

The Riverside Balcony Bar was empty now, its customers crowded by the roadside. Some were talking loudly, others whispering, others just standing there, watching, sickly-faced and silent. Grabbing the arm of a Westerner standing to the outside of the group, she pulled him around.

'What's happening?'

His face was pale. 'Someone's been shot.'

'Who? Do you know who?'

He shook his head. She pushed her way to the front of the crowd. Another, smaller circle of people was huddled in the road fifty metres away. A moped cruised out of the darkness beyond them; it slowed, its driver interested. What he saw made him swerve and accelerate. The insect buzz of his engine shrieked as it sped past the crowd in front of the restaurant, fading, swallowed again by the night.

Tess ran along the road. She skipped sideways as a police vehicle screamed past her. It braked by the group, tyres spitting dirt. Four policemen in bottle-green uniforms and black combat boots, wielding wooden batons, spilled out of the doors and ploughed their way into the circle of people. Tess heard the sickening crunch of wood on bone, a couple of high-pitched, surprised cries of pain.

As she reached the circle's edge, it began to part and separate.

She caught glimpses of the police: shoving with their batons, baying orders, faces hard, arms outstretched. People began to peel reluctantly away from the group and drift back down the road, their attention still locked on what they had left.

*

In the photograph, Johnny was standing with two other guys; he couldn't even remember their names now. The grey earth and shrubs of Angola spread out behind them, a flat, featureless landscape as far as the camera lens could see. He was smiling, his expression innocent and open. His two legs were tanned and muscled and he looked so damn young.

His first day of humanitarian mine clearing, fifteen years ago now.

Almost all of your adult life, Johnny.

Picking the photograph up, he held it close to his face and studied it, unable to take his eyes from the image of his own younger, perfect self. Turning it around, he slammed the glass frame against the edge of the bookshelf. The glass shattered; slivers rained on to the wooden floor. A jagged triangle of glass was still hanging in the frame. Closing his fingers around it, he pulled it out and used the end to slice through the photograph, top to bottom, left to right, corner to corner.

Dropping the frame on the floor, he ran his eyes along the other shelves, over the photographs, the souvenirs, a decade and a half of mine clearing. The first mine he had ever cleared lay on the middle shelf. A PMN anti-personnel blast mine, its brown plastic body and black pressure pad glossy as a priceless museum exhibit where Keav had polished it.

The PMN produces a substantial fragmentation hazard within a few metres.

Reaching out, he put his finger on the pressure pad, pressed it gently.

It was a game. It had started out as a game. He had just been playing with those women, playing with their lives.

The large explosive content, combined with the fragmentation, leads to very serious injury and can prove fatal.

His hand was trembling.

For fun. Just because it was fun, and their position in life, their choices, made them irrelevant to him.

Once armed this mine cannot be neutralised.

He tensed his arm, trying to steady his hand, spread his fingers and gripped the sides of the pressure pad. It wasn't his fault. How the hell was he supposed to know it would go this far? That he was playing the game with a mad man?

Explosive type: TNT. Operating pressure: 8–25 kg.

He lifted the pressure pad, teeth clenched against the jitters in his body, and peered inside. It was empty.

He was still staring into the empty case of the mine when he heard Keav come into the room and cross the wooden floor towards him. He dropped it.

'I told you to get rid of this mine-clearing stuff.'

'I will get rid.'

'I don't want to think about this shit any more. I'm out of it. I want it gone from my life. *All of it.*' He closed his hand around the glass shard.

She gasped. 'Johnny . . .'

'*Now,*' he bellowed. 'Get rid of it all *now.*'

He saw her hesitate, then turn for the door.

Blood was seeping through the gaps in his fingers. He opened his hand. The glass was embedded in his palm. He stared at it, detached, then he was suddenly aware of the quantity of blood. It had run down his arm and was all over the sleeve of his shirt. Huge globs had fallen to the wooden floor. Pinching the top edge of the shard between the fingers of his other hand, he tried to pull it out. The skin of his palm sucked on to the edge of the glass, lifting with it; he felt a nerve connection all the way up his arm. He tugged again and the glass pulled away, releasing a fresh gush of blood.

Keav came back into the room carrying a wooden box. She saw the blood and the box slammed to the floor. Ignoring her, Johnny turned and shuffled to the bathroom, leaning heavily on one crutch.

Pulling a towel from the rail below the sink, he pressed it to his hand. His palm felt numb, his fingers swollen. Curling his palm over the rim of the basin, he picked up one end of the towel and then the other, wrapped them over the back of his hand. It took him some time to make a knot: gripping the towel with his teeth, tightening, gripping, tightening.

His palm was throbbing now, fingers bloated and stiff. He held his hand up in front of his face, catching his reflection in the mirror beyond it. Alcohol-washed blue irises, marbled with red, stared back at him from a pale, haunted face, stubble beginning to soften and curl into a beard.

Hobbling back to the sitting room, he slumped down on the sofa.

'Get me some more whisky.'

Keav had almost emptied the shelves. 'I just finish.'

'*Now.*'

Dropping the box, she scurried out of the room. By the time she came back, he had staggered around the room again, checking the window locks, bolting the door to the balcony. He had found his Makarov and was loading rounds into the magazine, his left hand lying impotent on the sofa beside him. Wedging the pistol between his knees, he slipped in the magazine, cocked it, checked the safety, and jammed it in his waistband.

He could look after himself.

Glancing up, Johnny saw Keav gaping at him. He put his hand out for the whisky and she handed it to him at arm's length. He lunged for her and she jumped back with a startled yelp.

He sat slowly back on the sofa, hands trembling.

*

Craning her neck, Tess tried to shove forward through the crowd. Suddenly she heard a sharp exchange in Khmer, one of the voices familiar. Jumping, she caught sight of Alex's face. She stood on tiptoes and shouted over the heads of the people between them.

'Alex.'

He saw her and raised a hand; he was talking to one of the policemen. The man was waving dismissively, his face devoid of emotion. Alex shook his head, clearly exasperated, and turned away. She watched him push his way through the crowd. When he reached her, he pulled her to him.

'What the fuck is going on?'

'You shouldn't be here. Come on, we're leaving.'

'Alex, who is it?'

'A Khmer man. I never saw him before.'

There was something in his face that frightened her, and she suddenly realised that he knew exactly who was lying on the tarmac.

'Bullshit.'

She tried to tear herself from his grasp, but he held her tighter. She felt the tension in him.

The crowd had thinned, dispersed by the police; people were flowing past, back towards the restaurant. One of them bumped into Alex hard and he staggered. She took her chance, twisted herself out of his grasp and slipped past him.

The man was lying flat on his back, arms and legs splayed as if he had been picked up by a huge hand and flung on to the road. His face was calm, eyes open and blank. Blood had pulsed from a huge hole in his chest, wound in thick rivulets down the slope of his shoulders and pooled in the cleft of his throat.

She realised that she knew him too, from his photograph on the team-room wall, from that quick glance she'd had of him at the hospital with Ret S'Mai before he'd run.

'Huan.' Unable to find her voice, it came out as a whisper. She took a breath – 'Huan,' she yelled and ran forward. A policeman whirled around and swung at her with his baton. She felt the blunt wood whistle past her shoulder. Heard Alex shout at the man in Khmer, felt the force of his body as he jammed himself in front of her and shoved her back.

'Alex, let go of me. I have to see him.'

'He's dead, Tess.'

'He might know something. Have something.'

'He's dead.' He tightened his arms around her. 'Huan is dead and if you keep shouting like that the police will start asking you questions, and you do not want that to happen.' Looking down at her, he stroked the back of his hand gently across her cheek. 'We need to get out of here now.'

'Alex, for Luke, I need to . . .' Irritated by his touch, she grabbed his wrist and pulled his hand away from her face. 'Please let me—' She broke off. 'What have you got in your hand?'

'Nothing. Let's go.'

She gripped his wrist, saw him blanch from the pain as she tightened her grip. He tried to pull his hand away, but he still had his other arm wrapped around her waist and was constricted. Forcing his fingers uncurled with her other hand, she grabbed the tiny metal tube in his palm.

She'd seen dozens of these littered around the shooting range on Salisbury Plain. 'It's a bullet casing.' Had fired plenty of handguns that used this calibre. 'Nine-millimetre.'

'Tess.' His voice was strangled.

She pressed it against her cheek. It was warm.

'Huan was dead when I got to him. I saw someone running away. I shot at him.'

She started to shake. 'But you missed?'

'He was thirty metres away before I even had the safety off.'

She was shaking all over, like she used to when Luke beat her up. She felt Alex's arms restraining her, and made a physical connection from Alex to Luke that she had never made before. She looked past him to Huan, lying on the ground with that gaping bullet wound in his chest, and she felt sick. 'I picked up the casing because I didn't want the police to find it. You can't trust the police – not out here.'

She looked into his face. His eyes were dark and totally expressionless. She thought of the scars on his arms. *Guilt. Punishment.* Thought of the lie he had just told her. *Just a Khmer man. I don't know him.* Thought of a terrified old lady who would outlive her son. *Why would Huan be frightened of you?* She forced herself to relax. The shaking slowed. *Me. Us. Us at MCT. She said that he's frightened of us at MCT.* She smiled up at him, and thought the smile must look sick and twisted.

'You believe me?' she heard him ask.

She felt herself nod, heard herself reply, 'Of course.' Felt herself reach up and put her hands on his chest, start to lever herself away from him.

'Are you OK now?'

'Absolutely.' She felt herself step away from him. *I've been lucky. But once, almost. I got too close to someone else's fuck-up.* He was there. Alex was there when Luke died. She sensed his grip on her arms loosen. Willed him to let go. 'I'm going to go home now, Alex.'

'What is it, Tess? You don't believe me, do you?'

'I'm going home.'

'I didn't kill him.'

'I didn't say you did.'

'I found him. I tried to save him.'

'Who was it? Who shot him?'

'A man. I don't know, Tess. For fuck's sake, it's dark. I couldn't see.'

'You're a fucking liar.'

'Tess, stop it.'

'You were there when Luke died. You were there, and I've

only got your word for it that you weren't involved. Only your word.'

She was pouring sweat, and the stench of the river and the blood and the gabble of voices behind them and the bland lights of the hostels lining the road felt malevolent. 'You're sick.'

'Tess, stop it. Please.'

He tried to catch hold of her; she slapped his hand away.

'Get away from me.'

He tried to shake his head, but he couldn't find the motion. 'Let's go back to my house. I'll tell you everything.' His voice was strangled, his face wrung out.

He held out his hand to her. Turning away, she sprinted off down the street.

41

Manchester, England

The sleet must have turned to rain. Wessex could hear a ghostly patter from the rooftop above them. He glanced at his watch. He had been allotted half an hour and was allowed to 'get happy', as the rat-man at reception had put it, twice in that time. The half-hour was almost up. Soon he would be joining Viles across the road in the café, a warm cup of tea on the table in front of him.

Get happy. Eight men every night, she had told him. She didn't have good enough English to explain how she had wound up in Manchester, but she kept repeating the same word. 'Battambang.' He'd committed it to memory, would find out what or where it was as soon as he got back to the office.

'Why don't you go home? Back to Cambodia?' he asked her. 'Go home and be with your son?'

A tear ran down her cheek. 'No passport.'

He fought the urge to whip his warrant card out of his jacket pocket, slam back down the stairs and ram it down rat-man's throat.

'You need to go to the police.'

She shook her head. 'Police bad.'

'Not here. Not in England.'

'I no get out.' She raised a hand and pointed dispiritedly to the door.

'I can go to the police for you.' It was as close as he could get

275

to admitting who he was. He thought it would give her some reassurance.

Instead, she gripped his arm. 'Please no.' Her voice cracked. 'Happen before, another girl. Hid her. Police go, they kill her. Show us body.' She started to sob. 'They kill me too. Please no police.'

Still sobbing, she slid her hand into the pocket of her gown. When she pulled it out, she was holding a small black-and-white photograph. She held it out to Wessex. It showed a little boy. Two or three he must have been, sitting in the dirt, all distended belly and stick arms and legs. The shiny surface of the photo was cracked, one corner faded entirely where she must have held and held it, looking at the image of her little son, frozen in time. He was four now, she had indicated, holding up a hand, fingers outstretched, the thumb tucked into her palm. She hadn't seen him for three months.

'I can't take it,' Wessex said. 'It's too precious. I'll remember his face.'

She raised her head and thrust out her chin, her gaze meeting his directly for the first time.

'Please.' She looked desperate. 'If you take it you remember. Remember help me.'

Someone had put some music on downstairs. Tom Robinson's 'War Baby' floated up through the boards, drowning out the sound of the rain. Wessex tucked the photograph into his back pocket.

'What's his name?'

'Dien. Dien Yathay.' She indicated herself. 'Me, Jorani Yathay.'

'I will find out what has happened to him and I'll come and

let you know.' *Come back with the cavalry.* He pulled out his wallet and emptied it of notes. 'A hundred pounds. It's all I have.'

She looked shocked. 'No.'

'Take it. Please.' He pressed the notes into her hand. 'And I will find your son. It might take some time but I will find him.'

I'll get you out too. He couldn't say it; couldn't afford to give himself away. *All of you. And I will nail those bastards who imprisoned you and killed that girl.*

Her smile looked so sad, but at least it was a smile.

42

When Tess slotted her key into the lock and pushed her apartment door open, she half expected to see Alex sitting on the sofa, cradling his Browning on his lap and watching her with those black eyes. But the room was empty, neat and impersonal, just as she had left it this morning.

Unzipping her dress, she let it slide to the floor and climbed straight into the shower. Turning up the water as hot as she could bear, she scrubbed herself from head to foot, and then again, as if she could scrub hard enough to scour Alex's touch from her skin. Then tugging on light khaki cotton trousers, a T-shirt and her trainers, she ran downstairs and out into the dark street.

Battambang Provincial Police occupied a low brick building on a dusty plot of red earth fifteen minutes' jog from Madam Chou's. She knocked on the front door and waited. It was a couple of minutes before she heard movement from inside, footsteps making their way towards her. The lock clicked and the door inched open. A strip of bottle-green beret and a fleshy cheek appeared in the crack, the wood-coloured eye blinking blearily. It widened briefly on seeing her. The policeman hauled the door open, smothering a yawn with the back of his hand. Smoothing his shirtfront, he adjusted a couple of buttons where the material had strained around his middle and straightened his beret. Then he pulled back his shirtsleeve, gesturing to the Rolex on his wrist.

'Late. Station closed.' He had a smoker's voice, heavily accented. 'Three in morning.'

'I'm sorry, but I need to speak to you. It's urgent.'

'Who are you?'

'Tess Hardy. I'm one of the mine clearers who works at Mine Clearance Trust.' She gestured behind her, in the general direction she imagined MCT House to be.

'Interviews tomorrow morning. Arranged with Mr MacSween. You ask him. Come back then.' Withdrawing, he shut the door.

Interview? What was he talking about? Then it dawned on her: Jakkleson. She jammed her foot over the threshold – 'No, please—' and was thankful that she wasn't wearing sandals as the door ricocheted off her toes. 'It's about something else. Please. It won't take a minute.'

The policeman remained where he was, blocking the doorway, one hand resting on a meaty hip. He studied her from top to toe without embarrassment. She would not have put up with such scrutiny in any other situation, but this felt like the end of the road. The bullet that killed Huan was the only thing that led back to the Crocodile.

Finally, a gruff nod. 'Follow me.'

He turned and beckoned her down the hall. She followed, past a couple of grainy black-and-white photographs dull with dust, a line of uniformed men standing to attention in front of the police station; a statue of the Buddhist god of fortune, Kuvera, perched on a wooden shelf nailed to the wall; an Asian sunset vividly portrayed in batik print. On her right were rooms, offices from the scatter of paper on the desks, all of them dark, except for the second, where another uniformed man leaned back in his chair, feet crossed on the desk, a telephone jammed to his ear. The policeman went slowly, glancing over his shoulder every few steps to study her face, to click his tongue against the back of his teeth.

They entered another office at the end of the hall. A desk covered in papers faced the door, a large window behind it looking out on to darkness. A fan rotated in the middle of the ceiling, stirring the ash in a heavy glass ashtray on the desk with its rhythmic thump. The room smelt of incense and tobacco. Indicating a chair across the desk from him, the policeman sat down.

'Provincial Officer Prak Long. Please sit.'

Tess caught sight of her reflection in the window behind him as she lowered herself into the chair; her face was ghostly white.

'What do you want?'

'A good friend of mine was killed in Battambang a few hours ago. I want to find out where his body has been taken.'

The policeman was watching her closely. 'Why?'

'I want to see him. To say goodbye. It's, uh, it's an English thing.'

'English, eh?'

She nodded.

'You know Liverpool Football Club?'

She nodded again. 'Steven Gerrard – great player. Peter Crouch – should have gone for basketball maybe, but still a great player.'

A half-smile tilted the corners of his mouth. 'It is not usual for us to give out this information, even to the English.'

'I appreciate that. But I would really like to see him. Just one last time.' She held his gaze, fighting the urge to dip hers to the desktop.

'Your friend's name?'

'Huan. Huan Rae.'

'My colleague, he deal with this murder. I will ask him – see if he help you.' He shrugged. 'But I doubt.' Holding up an index finger, he added: 'Minute. One minute.'

He left the office, and she heard his footsteps receding down the corridor. She waited and waited, the muffled sound of voices, a phlegmy smoker's cough, drifting back to her. Standing, she went over to the window. The offices backed on to a rectangle of land, surrounded by low buildings – she could just make out the outlines of their roofs against the midnight blue of the sky. No hint of sunrise yet.

She turned back to the office. Minutes ticked by. She could still hear the policemen chatting and laughing.

Provincial Officer Prak Long's desk was messy; it reminded her of MacSween's. A few sheets of paper had slipped on to the floor. She bent and picked them up, looking at them before she slid them on to his desk. They were written in curving Khmer text, meaningless to her. She took a stack of papers from his desktop and flicked through them. All in Khmer. The other stacks, the same. She was looking for anything written in English – the international language. If MacSween had communicated with Battambang police, or if they had communicated with Jakkleson's home country, it would be in English.

She realised that she was abusing his trust, but felt no guilt. If he returned with the news that his colleague was not prepared to help her – as she expected he would – she would curse herself for having wasted this opportunity.

Putting the papers back, she pulled open the desk drawer. Like MacSween's, it was a miscellany: pens and pencils, a stapler, a couple of pads of lined paper, an ancient Motorola mobile phone wrapped in a tangle of headphones, a well-thumbed copy of the *Official Liverpool FC Annual 2008* – how the hell had he got hold of that? In the bottom of the drawer she found an unopened packet of tissues, a tin box containing betel nut, one shoelace, a dried slice of pineapple and a layer of crumbs and lint. Rearranging the contents more or less as she had found them, she closed the drawer.

His computer screen flared into life when she nudged the mouse. He had been looking at www.rolex.com. Online porn for middle-aged men who would need to work a lifetime to be able to afford one – a real one at least. There was another tab open. Glancing up, she scanned the doorway – empty – tilted her head – the mutter of conversation from down the corridor was unchanged. She clicked.

Battambang Provincial Police's email inbox opened in front of her. She scanned the page quickly. Just a list of emails, every one in Khmer script. Moving the mouse to the bottom of the page, she clicked the back button. The inbox flicked to the second page. She scanned the list quickly. Scanned it again, more slowly. Stopped. One email stood out. The title was written in Khmer – just one word. One of only three Khmer words that she recognised, along with the words for 'Danger' and 'Mines'.

'Help!' – an exclamation mark after the word. Her eyes flicked to the email address it had been sent from: awessex@gmp.police.uk.

Police? UK?

The policeman had obviously Googled the Khmer word for 'Help' and then copied and pasted it into the title box because when she opened the message it was written in English. She scanned the email quickly. Saw that it was from a Detective Inspector Andy Wessex of the Greater Manchester Police. Something about a body they'd found. DI Wessex was asking Battambang police for help. The words 'dead woman' and 'orphan' jumped off the screen. There was a photograph attachment on the email. She double-clicked on the attachment and the computer started whirring, the little egg timer turning over and over. Over and over. She looked around the room frantically, searching for a printer. There wasn't one.

The computer was still opening the photograph; it seemed to be stuck. Pressing the back button to cancel the operation, she scanned the menu bar above the email. Which one of those elaborate Khmer words meant 'forward'? She pressed one and the email disappeared briefly, then reappeared underneath the GMP email address. She had pressed reply. *Shit!*

As she closed the reply, reopened the original email and moved the mouse to another of the words, she realised that the chatter from down the corridor had stopped. She looked up quickly. The doorway was empty, the dimly lit corridor behind it silent. She would hear him coming back down the corridor surely? Hear his tread? She knew that the sensible thing would be to return to her side of the desk, sit and wait patiently until he came back, but now that she had seen those words – 'dead woman' and 'orphan' – she just couldn't.

Forward.

A cough. That phlemy cough, and footsteps approaching.

Hurriedly, she typed in her own email address:

thardy@hotmaiil.com. Was just about to press send when she realised she'd hit the 'i' twice. Deleted one, hit send.

The footsteps had come to a halt. She looked up from the screen, met his surprised gaze. Smiling, she straightened. 'Were you able to find out—'

He spoke over her. 'What are you doing?'

Tess felt the fear in her gut, tugging at her like the grinding ring of the unanswered telephone she could hear from the neighbouring office.

'I, uh, I picked up some papers that had fallen on the floor. When I put them back, I must have touched the mouse by mistake.' She indicated the screen. 'Rolex. I've always wanted one. I noticed the one you have. The Submariner, isn't it? It's very cool.'

His face was unmoving. Tess stared back at him, an instinct for self-preservation driving her to hold his gaze steadily. Provincial Officer Prak Long breathed in deeply. His eyes were very black in the darkness of the corridor.

Suddenly, he laughed – so loudly that she almost jumped.

'Oyster Perpetual Submariner.' The words were laboured. 'You know watches?'

'I've always wanted a Rolex.' She smiled and shrugged.

'One day.' He held out a piece of paper. 'Municipal Hospital. Hospital for poor. Your friend taken there.'

43

December 1990, England

The little boy was woken by a noise. A brief cry. Silence followed, so complete he wondered if he had dreamed his mother's voice. But sleep wouldn't come, even when he tugged the duvet right up to his chin and closed his eyes.

He could picture Mummy sitting motionless on the sagging faux-leather sofa in the lounge with that empty stare she got in her eyes sometimes, on those afternoons when he would call and call her and she wouldn't hear. Opening his eyes again, he saw the black night framed in the curtainless square of window above him, a few flakes of snow circling past. It was Christmas in two days' time.

Pushing his duvet aside, he climbed out of bed and went out into the corridor. His mother's bedroom was dark. He tiptoed silently into the room. The moon slid from behind a cloud, lighting the unmade bed, the duvet in a heap on the floor, six cans of Special Brew and four of Stella – he counted them carefully, was proud for a moment that he could count that high – littered on the carpet, a spent wrap of foil and a syringe on the bedside cabinet.

No Mummy.

He turned back to the door. The corridor beyond was still and dark.

'Mummy?' Just a whisper.

He strained to listen. 'Mummy?' There was no answer, but

he heard noises coming from the sitting room. Familiar noises. Hugging his arms around himself, the little boy tiptoed towards the sitting-room door.

Through a crack of the doorway he saw a shirtless man, jeans and Y-fronts around his ankles. His legs were hairy, like the old donkey at the city farm. The man bent forward over the sofa and his bare buttocks twisted. A thick groan. He began to thrust his hips backwards and forwards. From the sofa in front of him protruded a pair of legs spread wide. The boy could only see the soles of the feet, the rail-thin ankles with the damaged, bruised veins. But he knew they were his mother's legs. And he knew what she was doing. Just like he'd seen in those magazines the men she brought home left lying by the toilet.

He sank to the floor outside the door and shivered. He felt sick for a moment and then realised it was hunger. He couldn't remember the last time he had eaten. Yesterday, he thought. Baked beans yesterday evening. The thought of them made his stomach growl. His pyjamas were too small, the trousers barely past his knees, the sleeves exposing the dimples of his elbows. Though he could hear the old heating system in the tower block creaking and shuddering in the belly of the building at night, the air in the flat was freezing and stale.

Again and again the man's buttocks twisted as he thrust. The man was shoving his willy inside her, and she was groaning and gasping like she did just after she had slid one of those needles into her arm.

He stared through the crack. His lips were moving, though he didn't know it. Get off her. Get off her. His heart was racing. He let out a sob: 'No.' Jammed himself blindly forward into the crack between the door and its frame. 'Get off her.'

The man stopped. He turned around and the boy saw his willy bobbing grotesquely in its nest of dark hair, the startled face of his mother beyond, her mouth hanging open, lips wet.

'I mean it,' he sobbed. 'Leave her alone or I'll kill you.'

Silence. He realised his teeth were chattering.

The man hauled up his pants and jeans, looked down at his mother, and then walked towards the little boy.

'Well, good evening there, son!' he said, and his accent was funny – a Scottish accent his mum called it, like the little girl who lived across the hall. 'Did you ever hear about knocking before you walk into a room?'

'Sweetie . . . baby . . .' his mum drawled, and the little boy didn't know whether she was talking to him or the man.

'Because your mum and I were just in the middle of something.' He was standing right in front of the little boy now. The little boy could smell his foul breath. 'In fact, it's probably safe to say –' the man's face, which had been smiling, twisted with rage – 'that you couldn't have come in at a worse time.'

The little boy shot back, slammed hard up against the wall. Scrabbling sideways, he tried to find purchase on the thread-bare carpet of the corridor. But he wasn't fast enough, and the man's hands gripped the lapels of his pyjamas. He struggled to free himself, panicking. The man slapped him around the face, and the back of his head struck the plaster.

'Sor . . . sorry—' he struggled to say through his tears. 'P . . . please, no—'

Day 8

44

The Municipal Hospital, the hospital for the indigent, was a crumbling concrete block with glassless windowframes, filling one side of a narrow street on the outskirts of Battambang, where the town gave way to patches of farmland. Opposite was a string of run-down guesthouses. There seemed to be no door facing the road, so Tess edged around the facade, looking for a way in. She followed an alleyway between the flank of the building and a rusty wire fence. It led into a concrete court-yard which smelt of urine. A couple of bicycles leaned against one of the walls, and propped in a corner was an old but well-maintained moped, its rear wheel secured with a heavy chain. Open concrete stairs snaked from the courtyard up the outside of the building. She looked around, and when she couldn't find a door on the ground floor, walked over to the staircase and started to climb.

The stairs opened from the first-floor landing into one enormous room. Fifty or more patients dressed in ragged scraps of clothing were lying side by side on mattresses without sheets or blankets. A few others were curled immobile on the stone floor. The air seethed and flickered with flies, and the room stank of sweat and iodine. There were no doctors or nurses to be seen.

Pressing her hand to her mouth, Tess made her way through the ward, trying not to breathe or stare. Most of the patients were unmoving, looking blankly up at the ceiling. Others watched her, faces lifeless as masks. At the far end of the ward children occupied a bed, four little bodies layered horizontally across a foam mattress. Slipping the bottle of water she had been carrying from the pocket of her shorts, she laid it on the bed, but none of them acknowledged it was there, let alone moved to take it.

The ward on the second floor was identical to the first, crammed with bodies, the air thick with the smell of infection. A man in a white knee-length coat leaned over a bed in the near corner of the room. He must have heard her approach because he straightened and turned. He was unusually tall and lanky for a Khmer, with greying hair and mahogany eyes. His face was hollow and gaunt. He looked as she felt – knackered, taut to breaking point, then ratcheted a few notches tighter.

Tess held out her hand. He gave a curt nod, but made no move to take it.

'One of my friends, a local man, was shot early this morning, close to the Balcony Bar,' she said. 'I was told he would have been brought here.'

'Shot dead?' He spoke English slowly, with a heavy French accent.

She nodded.

'I spoke to the police. They said he had been brought here.'

He nodded slowly, then turned back to the bed. The figure lying on it was almost unrecognisable as a human being.

'I found 'im lying at the bottom of the stairs when I came into work two days ago. 'E was covered in sores, crawling with maggots.' The doctor bent down and began to peel the bandage away from the man's face. 'The 'ospital does not provide medicine or food. If a patient 'as no family to bring them what they need they will die.' The bandage came away soaked with pus; the face underneath was a patchwork of bloody sores. The doctor pulled a clean bandage from his pocket and began to unwrap it.

'Your friend was brought in this morning at about two a.m. The police said that 'e 'ad been attacked for money. Mugged. 'E was dead on arrival. There was nothing I could do for 'im.' He leaned forward and began wrapping the new bandage gently around the patient's head.

'Where is he?'

'In the morgue.'

'Can I see him?'

He shook his head dismissively. '*Non.*' Then after a studied pause, and in a softer tone, he said, 'Believe me, you don't want to see 'im. Are you a tourist?'

'I'm a mine clearer. I work in Battambang.'

'Ah.' He finished what he was doing and unpeeled himself from his crouch. 'So you are used to the realities of life in Cambodia?'

Tess nodded. She felt sick. The lack of sleep and the smell. She rubbed her hand across her eyes and her head started to spin. Dropping her hand, she steadied herself on the bedstead.

'Are you ill?'

'No.'

'Sure?'

She nodded.

'It is not easy to lose a friend, even if you are a tough mine clearer.' He smiled, a tight-lipped smile. 'The police, they said mugger. Myself, I feel that muggers are using very sophisticated weapons these days. Come with me.' He turned and went out the door to the stairs. She followed, grateful for the fresh air that engulfed her as the door swung closed behind her.

''E was a real mess, an 'ole the size of a fist in 'is chest,' he said back over his shoulder, as he picked his way down the stairs. 'Much blood lost.'

'Was it a pistol wound?'

'*Non.*'

'Are you sure?'

'Of course. I 'ave seen plenty of pistol wounds.'

She stared at his back and bit her lip. If it wasn't a pistol wound, then it wasn't from Alex's Browning. Though she hadn't even realised she was holding her breath, she felt a balloon of air empty from her lungs.

'What was it then?'

'Rifle, I imagine, though the 'ole was big enough to 'ave come from a bazooka. I 'ave never seen a bullet wound like it.'

He reached the bottom of the stairs and crossed the courtyard to the other, smaller building. The door into this building led to a short, dimly lit corridor. Dirty grey laminated tiles covered the floor and peeling cream paint the walls. The doctor stopped halfway down the corridor, pulled a bunch of keys from his pocket and unlocked a door.

'This is my office. Come in for a moment, please.'

The office was small and cramped, a desk piled with papers and twin metal filing cabinets taking up most of the space. Above the desk was a photograph, yellowed with age, of the doctor wearing medical scrubs, standing in front of one of the Sorbonne university buildings in central Paris. There was no glass in the office's one window, but a double layer of metal mosquito netting had been tacked untidily to its frame with sturdy U-shaped nails. The doctor went over to his desk, opened the top drawer and rummaged around in it.

Straightening, he turned and held out his hand. A large, gold-coloured bullet nestled in his palm.

'It spinned,' he said matter-of-factly.

'*Spinned?* Spun? You mean spun?'

'Certainly. It looks like it started spinning when it 'it 'is chest. The entry wound was in 'is chest, the bullet finished in 'is lower back. The bullet did not go straight through, but it *spun* . . .' He emphasised the word. 'Changed direction many times. This left a very big mess of 'is insides. A special bullet, I would say. One shot, no chance to survive. Here.' He held it out to her. 'Take it.'

45

Alex lived in a small, white-painted wooden house on a corner plot near the river, surrounded by a mess of untended garden. It reminded Tess of a fairy-tale cottage hidden deep in an enchanted forest. Flowering vines had scaled the walls and crept over the roof.

He was sitting on the sofa, reading, and the sight looked incongruously domestic and peaceful, given the circumstances the last time she'd seen him. He didn't realise she was there until she had been standing in the open doorway for a few moments, and then he seemed to sense rather than hear her because he glanced up suddenly, startled. She reached out and grasped the doorframe to steady herself. He looked terrible. Wounded, totally beaten.

'Tess.'

'Alex.'

'I didn't expect you.'

He was naked except for a pair of white boxer shorts, and had a bandage wrapped around his left arm, from wrist to elbow. Patches of blood had soaked through the bandage.

'You're not asleep,' she said. 'After last night – this morning – I thought you'd still be asleep.'

'No.'

'Have you slept?'

'No.' Dropping the book, he rose from the sofa and padded

over the rug towards her. She held up a staying hand.

'Stop, Alex. Stop there.'

He stopped walking.

'I just want to talk.'

'Come and sit down then. Let's talk.' He indicated the chair on the other side of the table and retreated back to the sofa.

Tess sat down in the chair, tucking herself deep in its sagging cushions. The room was comfortable, personal. She hadn't expected it to be. The linen-covered sofa and two chairs ringed an old teak coffee table, piled with books and a half-finished mug of coffee. A bookshelf leaned against the far wall, crammed with more books, some English, some Khmer, others with Cyrillic text. One of the shelves held a jumble of assorted objects: photographs, a dark, serious family, arms around each other, father, mother, daughter, son – the son younger, softer-looking but unmistakably Alex – a large, white house in extensive grounds, photographed from the air, a knife, a pot plant, its leaves curled and brown.

'What have you been doing today?' she asked.

'Nothing much. How about you?'

'I went to the Municipal Hospital to try to see Huan's body.' She paused. 'It wasn't a pistol wound.'

He looked at her silently.

'But you knew that already, didn't you?'

He continued to watch her across the table in silence, his face expressionless. She sat forward, tried to keep her voice steady.

'I'm sorry about my behaviour last night. But what did you mean when you said, "I'll tell you everything"?'

He spread his hands. 'You're right to have your doubts about me. I have killed someone. But it was in another life, Tess. Not in this one. In Bosnia, not here in Cambodia. It's not relevant to anything here.'

'I still want to know. I *need* to know, Alex. I have to be able to trust you.'

He nodded. 'I'll tell you. I wanted to tell you anyway.' He leaned back, crossed his arms over his chest and stared up at the ceiling.

'He was an aid worker,' he said finally, looking back to her. 'With one of the agencies in Bosnia. One of the humanitarian agencies that moved in after the war, to hand out kindness and sort our problems out for us. It was a short while after I found out that my family had been killed. My sister and I had been sent away to live with my aunt in Greece when the war started, to keep us safe. I hadn't wanted to go. I wanted to stay with my parents. I was twelve, old enough to fight I thought, but they wouldn't hear of it.' He was speaking quietly, dark eyes fixed on hers. 'They were killed when I was in Greece. The Serbs shot all the men in our village. All of them – even the little boys. The older women were also killed, the younger ones taken away. I don't know where.' A pause. 'But I can guess why. My mother was young, and beautiful. Really beautiful. When the war was over, I came back and tried to find her, but I couldn't. I spent months and months looking. I'm pretty sure, now, she was killed . . . once they'd grown tired of her.' He broke off, looked down at his hands, his expression blank. 'It was while I was looking for her that I killed the aid worker. I was sleeping in the open, in a forest. He was raping a young girl, twelve or thirteen. She was screaming. So much fucking . . . pity in that sound. I saw everything bad you can think of when I was young, but that was the moment that it hit me somehow. This girl. Some mother's baby. Someone's precious daughter who only wanted to live and be happy. And this fuck has her pinned down on the floor of his Land Cruiser, with the tailgate open. He jumped when he heard me, climbed off her and slid out of the back, stuffing his dick inside his trousers. He was fully clothed, in some fucking aid-agency uniform, I can't even re-member which now. The girl was naked. She crawled away, pressed herself against the back of the seats, shaking and crying, trying to cover herself up. She was . . . bleeding.'

He stopped talking and glanced over towards the balcony doors. Tess followed his gaze, and for a brief moment their eyes locked.

'He asked me if I spoke English. I told him that I did and he said it was OK, that he owned her. "I just bought her," he said. "Seventeen hundred dollars. Not cheap, but she's a virgin. She would have been forced to work as a prostitute if I hadn't bought her." He was jumpy. He kept glancing over his shoulder at the girl and at his handgun, which he had left on the dash-board. "From your lot," he said. "I bought her from one of your lot." Your lot – like we were all the same.' Alex sat forward and put his elbows on his knees, his head in his hands. 'We committed huge atrocities in our countries. The international community watched and sent people to save us from ourselves. Many of the people they sent committed atrocities themselves. They think they're doing us such a big favour and because we're all savages they can leave their morals at home. Countries like ours are easy to betray. We're so fucking grateful that we put up with anything.' He shook his head, suppressed fury in the movement.

'How did you kill him?'

'I hit him.' He sat back, put his feet on the coffee table and knotted his hands behind his head.

'Once?'

'No. At least I doubt it. I don't really remember, but I broke my hand while I was hitting him.' A grim smile touched his mouth. 'I thought it would sort everything out, make it all fine, for her and for me. But it didn't. Afterwards, I felt as if I was the one who had died.'

'What about the girl?'

'She was terrified. Terrified of me. I crawled into the Land Cruiser to try to pull her out and she started screaming, lashed out at me with a piece of metal and cut my hand.'

'Did it hurt?'

'Yeah, it hurt.'

'But it helped?'

He didn't say anything. Just watched her.

'Why do you do it? Why do you harm yourself?'

'Because it's *easy*. Physical pain is an easy distraction. It takes everything away. All the pain, all the anger, *everything*.'

'You've got to stop doing that to yourself.'

'Pain's . . . so much easier than pleasure. You have to work hard to make someone feel good. Pain . . .' he shrugged. 'Just a flick of a knife, or a twist of a cigarette.'

'Look, I know it's not simple. That you can't just—' She broke off with a distressed shrug. 'I want to say that I understand, but I don't. And I don't know what else to say, how to help.'

'It's my problem, Tess.'

'No. It's—'

'I don't want to talk about it.'

They lapsed into an uneasy silence; eventually, Tess broke it.

'Would you do it again?'

'What?'

'Kill him.'

He nodded. They sat looking at each other across the table, wary, uncertain.

'You can go if you want,' he said quietly. 'Obviously you can go.'

She shook her head. 'I travelled through Europe with a friend when I was sixteen. We caught a train from Vienna to Athens, through the former Yugoslavia. We had a carriage for eight to ourselves for most of the way, then in Croatia the train stopped and some Croatian soldiers and sailors boarded. Six of them came into our carriage. They were young, some about the same age as us, some a bit older. We talked all day, and when it was night they insisted on sitting on the floor so that my friend and I could lie down flat on the seats and sleep. We would have been happy just to sit, but they wouldn't take no for an answer.' She smiled. 'I remember them so well. How polite they were. How shy and funny and gentle.' She stood up, padded around the table and sat down next to him on the sofa. 'Circumstances can drive people to do terrible things, Alex. You had the chance to help someone who couldn't help herself and you did.'

'I couldn't help her enough.'

'You tried.' She reached out and stroked her hand across his cheek, then dropped it to his chest. 'At least you tried. And we need to try again now.' Her hand, on his heart, felt the beat of a jackhammer.

Taking her hand, he raised it to his lips, as he had done by the river. She felt the warmth of his kiss and shivered. This time, she didn't pull away.

46

Sitting cross-legged on the grimy concrete floor of an over-crowded dormitory, Dien used his body to shield from view the object he was holding in his hand. He didn't want the other boys to see it, knew that as the youngest and smallest, he would have it snatched from him immediately – punched and kicked until he let go – if they found out he had something he treasured. He glanced over his shoulder. Without air conditioning or a working fan, the temperature in the room was already overwhelming. Most of the other boys were lying on their mattresses, two to each one, three for the smallest like him – panting like dogs, eyes closed, limbs lolling – and paying him no attention. He watched a couple kicking each other as they vied, hot, irritated and half-asleep, for more space on the mattress. Relieved that he had time undisturbed, he returned to the object in his hand.

Closing his eyes, he tried to bring a picture of his mother to his mind, just her face, her eyes or her mouth. But even in these snatched moments when the orphanage was quiet and he could creep into a corner by himself, he strained to call her face to mind. He held an image of her in his head, slight, beautiful and happy, eager to cuddle him, to comfort him. He would climb into her lap and curl up – like a cat, she used to say, and laugh and bend forward so that her body was covering his, her arms wrapped the whole way around his body, and hug him tight.

She had made him feel safe.

And then that morning he had woken. Alone. He didn't know how long ago it was now, but it had been before the rainy season. A few days after Māgha Pūjā, the Full Moon of Tabaung celebration, the day hot and calm. The dried boards of their hut, still soft and green with sap, had creaked as they withered and shrank in the heat. Three months, Chanthou had told him. He had been here in the orphanage for three months and in that time his mother's face had become little more than a blur to him.

The thing that hurt him worst of all was to think that he would soon forget everything about her: her face, the sound of her voice, the feel of her touch on his skin. That his memory of her was no more substantial than his breath, floating away from him, out of the window and into the blue sky. Every day, these things faded a little more.

He curled himself into a ball – 'like a cat, Dien' – hugging her necklace in his hot palm, and closed his eyes, turning his little body to the wall, curling against it. Tears flowed from his eyes and he felt them trickling through the grime on his baby cheeks, hot and salty on his tongue.

*

Johnny could hear the barking, tugging, insistent. He hadn't been sleeping. Couldn't sleep. Memories filtered in at night. He kept on thinking of faces. Women's faces, hard and crystalline, crowding his dark windows.

And something pale behind them.

The White Crocodile hunting at night.

He had to stay awake, had to keep his brain occupied. He had tried kipping on the sofa during the day, but Keav was there, moving silently around the room, cleaning, watching, spying.

The barking continued.

'Shut up,' he screamed. What the fuck was the dog barking at? They had sixth senses, dogs. Could it sense the women out there? He jammed his fingers in his ears, could still hear the barking, pulled them out again. He looked down to his lap, at the pistol gripped tight in his right hand. It was daytime; he was safe. The pistol was trembling like an animal. It's trying to tell you something, Johnny. The ghosts, the Crocodile, the dog, the ghosts, the dog. Fucking dog. *Fucking dog.*

Using the arm of the sofa for leverage, he hauled himself to his feet. Too quick; he slipped and fell. His crutches clattered against the hard wooden floor, the rest of him landed soft. He banged his left hand. It was swollen, infected, stank. He didn't want to look at it. The towel was crusted to his skin. He hauled himself up again – slowly this time – found his balance, started to hobble across the sitting room to the sliding doors, made it to the balcony, rested against the railing for a moment, panting, straightened and began to shuffle left. The balcony went around the corner and ran down the side of the house. He followed it.

The dog was tied to a chain in the yard next door. It was straining at the chain, feet planted apart, ears and tail erect, eyes fixed on something – but there was nothing there – barking. It glanced at him quickly, looked away, carried on barking. He raised the pistol. His arm was trembling. The barking was driving him crazy. He was sweating, shaking – *fucking dog.* Tightening his finger on the trigger, he took the slack, felt it snag, squeezed some more. The sound of the shot was deafening. The dog yelped, leaped and spun, the chain around its neck yanked taut, then it fell, limbs scrabbling in the gravel.

He heard screaming. A woman. Women screaming. He squeezed off another shot, then another. One bullet hit the dog's prone, twitching body. The other missed, ricocheting off the concrete yard and splintering into the side of the house. Johnny stood, staring. The dog's back legs paddled, twice, as if it were dreaming. He saw movement out of the corner of his eye. A man. The dog's owner, he realised, coming out of his house. Johnny saw his face, the shock and fear. Saw him raise his arm. Something whined past him, so close he could feel its breath on his face. Plaster showered over his shoulder as the bullet slammed into the wall behind him. He leaped back, pressing himself against the wall. The man couldn't see him; he was hidden by the lip of the balcony. He shuffled left, hugging the wall, heard another shot – way off target – edged around the corner, felt the cool glass of the balcony door behind him, and then its metal frame, grabbed it, turned, his back pressed against the frame, and slipped inside.

Keav was standing in the living room, her hands on her face, staring at him, frozen in shock.

'The ghosts,' he hissed.

Suddenly the house, the street, were horribly silent and still.

'The ghosts were out there.' He stumbled forward, stretched out his left hand, swollen, throbbing, reaching for her. 'Those women – they're coming back.' She backed away, started to scream. Barking. Screaming. The dog. The ghosts. He brought the pistol up, right arm stiff, closed one eye, squinted along the barrel. Screaming. Barking.

'*Help me.*'

The sound of the shot filled the room.

*

When Tess woke it was hot, the air in the room close; she felt sweaty, her head muggy with snatched sleep. Kicking the sheet off, she sat up. The sun was high in the sky. Bright rays poured through the open bedroom window and flooded the bed. No curtains. A man's smell, musty with sweat and aftershave, but Alex wasn't there.

Reaching over, she put her hand on the crumpled dent in the sheet where he had lain, where they had made love. It was warm, but a crisp, dry warmth from the sun. She reached the other way to the bedside table and grappled for her watch. It was half past one – she'd been asleep for nearly four hours.

Sliding off the side of the bed, she padded into the bathroom. The window was open in here too, but the air was cooler, damp and woody, the leaves from the trees in the garden shading the room. An emerald-green gecko had crawled in through the window and was clinging to the white tiles of the shower, tongue flicking in and out, tasting the moist air. She stepped into the shower, switched the tap on and gasped as the cold water hit her; the gecko skittered up the tiles and disappeared out through the open window.

After her shower, she dressed, made herself a coffee and went into the sitting room. Alex wasn't there either and yet he was everywhere. The coffee table was littered with his things: an empty packet of Camels; a spare magazine for his Browning; a Khmer phrase book, the pages thumbed and curled; his white boxer shorts crumpled on the floor where she had tugged them off and thrown them. His scent on everything.

She wandered over to the bookshelf. Most of the shelves were tightly packed with books; the middle shelf held a few photographs in solid wooden frames. Some of the books were in English. She tilted her head to read the titles: *The Psychology of Behaviour*, *Human Instinct*, *Logical Chess*. Nothing military, or about mine clearing. Another life he had lived.

Dropping her gaze to the middle shelf, she studied the photographs. One was of a large white house at the end of a curving drive. Big picture windows looked out over a sweeping lawn; bougainvillea climbed up the walls from a flowerbed beside the front door and spread outwards above the porch, its flowers deep pink in the sunlight. The villa looked American – Palm Beach – or Spanish or Italian. Not Croatian. At least not what she would have expected Croatian to be from the news coverage of the Balkans conflict. Alex was right. She had watched and thought, as he had predicted, that they were all savages. All the same.

Was that what was happening out here in the White Crocodile minefield? Someone making judgements about those women, someone who thought they understood what was going on in their minds, their imaginations? Using the myth of the White Crocodile to terrify, kidnap and kill?

Family. It's about family, she had told Alex. Was she right, or was that just her own past, the unfinished family business in her own life, talking?

Putting the photograph back, she ran her eye along the shelf. There was another photograph, unframed, lying on its face. Picking it up, she turned it over, and started.

The photograph showed Alex and Luke in a beer garden – the Riverside Balcony Bar – she recognised the wicker chairs and tables, the huge spreading trees shading them which made you feel as if you were sitting high up in the middle of the jungle. Luke had his hand up, two fingers raised in the victory sign, and he was laughing. He looked drunk. Alex, sitting across from him, was tilted back in his seat, arms folded across his chest. He wasn't looking at the camera, he was looking at Luke, and the expression on his face was one of contempt. There was a cluster of empty beer bottles in the middle of the table, and something else. Tess shifted sideways so that the light from the window fell on to the photograph and lit the object on the table. It was baby pink, and she knew instantly what it was.

She heard something behind her and spun around. Alex was standing by the patio doors; he was staring at the photograph in her hands.

'You shouldn't look at people's things.'

'You shouldn't leave people alone in your house if you don't want them to look at your things.'

'I'm not sure that it's supposed to work like that, Tess.'

She held his gaze for a moment, turned and put the photograph back on the shelf, face down as she had found it. 'You sent me the sock, didn't you?' There was challenge in her voice. 'The pink sock.'

He dropped his gaze. 'I wanted you to come to Cambodia. I wanted to meet you.'

'And then you wanted me to leave again.'

'I had no idea that things would escalate like this.'

Tess bit her lower lip. 'How did you know I would come?'

'Because I knew you before I met you. You're a female mine clearer – there are precious few of those. And from what he . . . from what Luke said about you. You didn't seem the type to leave well enough alone.'

'You were right.' She smiled. A smile that didn't touch her eyes. 'But perhaps I should have done. Though it's too late now, isn't it? For either of us.'

47

The sun was high, the sky clear. Heat shimmered off the tarmac of the airport's runway as they drove past it, melting the outline of the buildings and vehicles beyond. Half a kilometre further on, Alex slowed and swung the Land Cruiser left to join a track which ran up a densely wooded hill towards Battambang's orphanage.

Tess clutched the email she had forwarded herself from the police station. Alex had waited in the Land Cruiser while she ran into the King Fy Hotel and slipped the girl behind reception a couple of dollars to print out the email and the photograph. As Alex negotiated the throng of bicycles and mopeds clogging the town centre, she read it out loud to him. Detective Inspector Wessex, from Greater Manchester Police, wanted help in identifying a Cambodian woman who had been found dead in south Manchester. 'Could you look at your missing persons lists?' DI Wessex had written. Alex laughed.

'Missing persons lists. Who does he think he's dealing with? Interpol? The only list Battambang Provincial Police will have is a list of local businesses who haven't paid their protection money.'

'Don't be such a cynic, Alex.'

The description DI Wessex had provided could have fitted eighty per cent of the teenaged Khmer women Tess had seen since she'd arrived in Battambang. Oddly, there was no photograph of the woman. The photograph was of a little boy, Dien Yathay, four years old. DI Wessex had also asked Battambang Provincial Police to see if they could track Dien down, and then call or fax him to let him know if the boy was safe.

'I promised his mother,' he had written.

Dien's mother, Jorani, was working as a prostitute in Manchester. The fax didn't make it clear how Dien or his mother were linked to the dead woman they had found.

'I can't believe you stole that email,' Alex muttered, glancing across. 'You would have been strung up if the policeman hadn't believed your crap about Rolexes.'

Tess shrugged. 'Well he did. Testament to my great acting skills.'

'It doesn't have anything to do with the White Crocodile.'

'Why are you so sure? Another dead Khmer woman, a teenager, who has given birth.'

'Found in Manchester. Thirteen thousand miles away from here.'

'And another little boy missing his mother. Here, in Battambang.'

They almost missed the turning in the trees. Alex had to brake and reverse, then swing the Land Cruiser into the grassed-over drive. The ground was ridged with tree roots, and tangled undergrowth on either side created a natural alleyway, dragging against the doors of the Land Cruiser as they drove down it. After a hundred metres they pulled into an open grassed area in front of a squat two-storey building which reminded Tess of a Second World War bunker. It was austere and institutional-looking: beige paint peeling from its concrete walls, corrugated-iron roof dented and rusting, thick mosquito netting covering the small square windows.

'Jesus, it's a grim place,' Tess said.

'I imagine it's cheap.'

They parked and climbed out of the Land Cruiser. They could hear voices from inside the building, and shouts and snatches of laughter, slightly louder, which sounded like they were coming from the far side. In one of the rooms a tinny radio played Kylie Minogue, accompanied by a warble of voices.

Inside the building was dark; it took a moment for their vision to adjust.

The hall was a rectangular space with a corridor that ran off it, left and right. A window at the back of the hall let mottled, rust-hued light through the mosquito netting. The walls of the hall were a dull coffee colour, the floor concrete laid with a couple of straw mats, worn to nothing in patches by too much tread. The air in the building was hot: a heavy, claustrophobic heat, and there was a strong smell of disinfectant, masking the slightly weaker tang of faeces and urine.

'Can I help you?' From the corridor to the left, a middle-aged Khmer woman had appeared. She was a head shorter than Tess, straight black hair cut into a neat bob and a gentle, open face. She was dressed in plain black shirt and black trousers: practical clothing.

'Sue-saw-day.' Tess held out her hand. 'I'm Tess. Tess Hardy.'

'Sue-saw-day.' The woman shook it. 'My name is Chanthou Long. I run the orphanage.'

Tess indicated Alex. 'And this is my, uh, my friend, Alexander Bauer.'

The woman smiled and gave a half-nod towards Alex but made no move to take his hand.

'We just wanted to talk with you, if you have a moment.'

'Of course. Please.' She turned.

Tess followed, down a narrow, dimly lit corridor which cut through the centre of the building. Doors opened off either side of it at intervals of a couple of metres, some closed, others ajar. Tess glanced into the rooms as they passed. Four metal-framed bunk beds were laid tightly together in each room, crammed into the four-metre-square space. The beds were mostly occupied, some children squashed together in sleep, others sitting on the floor, playing with plastic toys and chattering. They passed a room full of cots: twenty or more babies lying like little brown dolls, silent and unmoving.

They were quickly encircled by a clamorous pack of little children, in torn, stained T-shirts or dirty sagging shorts, but never, it seemed, both. The children pulled at Tess's clothing, their little hands finding their way into her pockets, grabbing at her legs, trying to hold her hands.

Chanthou turned and tried to shoo them away, but Tess smiled and shook her head. 'It's fine.'

She clasped the hand of one little girl – four or five, she must have been – and the little girl grew a couple of centimetres in height in the short walk down the corridor, swelling with pride at being singled out for adult contact, her face split into a huge grin. Tess smiled down at the others, patted a couple gently on the arms, but kept walking, feeling as if she was pushing through a tide of children. She glanced behind her at Alex; he looked uncomfortable with the attention. He had his hand pressed to his stomach and for a moment Tess didn't understand why, until she realised he was trying to keep the children from grabbing at his Browning.

The room they entered was large and in contrast to the hall and corridor, the air was cool and fresh. Double doors in the far wall opened out on to a patch of grass behind the building, where Tess could see a plastic swing set and slide, and a large window at the front looked on to the courtyard where they had parked. A few small children played on the slide, while others lolled on the grass in the sun. An elderly white woman was sitting under a tree, reading a book to a group of older children.

'Please.' Chanthou sat down behind a large teak desk covered in papers and indicated a chair across from her; it was the only other one in the room. 'Sit down.'

Tess sat. She could sense Alex hovering somewhere behind her.

'We don't get many visitors out here, and particularly not Barang . . . Westerners,' she corrected. She had a pleasant, almost melodious voice and spoke English virtually without an accent. 'How can I help you?'

'This might sound a little strange, but one of my friends met a Khmer woman, Jorani Yathay, in England – that's where I come from. She's . . . she's working there. She said that she had left her son Dien in Cambodia, that he might be in an orphanage. My friend promised her that he would find out what had happened to her son. He asked me if I could look for him, make sure that the little boy was OK.' Tess slid the printed photograph across the desk.

Chanthou took it. She was silent for a few moments. When she looked back up, Tess saw that her expression had changed.

'Yes, her son is here. He has been here for a couple of months, ever since his mother—' She tailed off. 'His mother . . . she was a young single mother, living in a rural village near one of the huge minefields, out west of Battambang. She left . . . three months or so ago.'

'Left?'

'Disappeared. She is one of the disappeared. You've heard?'

Tess nodded.

'Taken,' Chanthou continued in a murmur. 'By the . . . by—'

'By the White Crocodile?'

Chanthou blushed. 'It is ridiculous to believe these tales in this modern day, but they are buried deep.' Pressing her hand to her chest, she continued. 'Somewhere right in here, the heart, not unfortunately up here –' she raised her hand and tapped a finger on her forehead – 'where logic and reason would enable us to see sense. Come and I will show you where he is. He is one of my favourites. So little to be left.' She shook her head. 'So little.'

Chanthou led them back down the corridor, shooing the children out of the way as she went, and across the hallway into another, almost identical corridor. She walked slowly, reaching back to touch Tess on the arm, talking non-stop about the orphanage, the challenges they faced: the lack of interest from most Khmers in the children's plight and the lack of money to do anything but keep the children as clean and well fed as they could, and teach them to read and write, little else.

'We have some Western donors – small charities which support a number of Cambodian orphanages and send Westerners over here to work. And your Bob MacSween, of course. He comes here on a Sunday, once a month or so, to help out with odd jobs. And he gives us what money he can.'

'MacSween?' Tess couldn't hide her surprise. 'How did you know that we were from MCT?'

'The Land Cruiser. The MCT logo. MacSween always drives an MCT Land Cruiser when he comes here.'

'And he's given you money?'

'Not much.' She smiled. 'But when you have as little as we do, every cent is precious.'

Tess glanced back at Alex, but he didn't seem to have heard. He was walking a few paces behind, his gaze cast to the floor, his mind somewhere else entirely by the look of him.

She looked back to Chanthou, who had stopped.

'In here,' she said, pushing a door open.

This room, like the others, was oven-hot and crammed with small bodies pressed tightly together in a mosquito-bitten, overheated, testy doze. In the far corner of the room, beneath the window, was what Tess thought for a second was a little brown dog curled in sleep. But when she crossed the room, she realised that it was a little boy, limbs curled into his chest, hands pressed tightly together, and twitching slightly as if he was dreaming.

'That's him – Dien,' Chanthou whispered from the doorway. She didn't seem fazed that he was asleep on the floor and when Tess knelt by the boy she realised why. Though it was dirty, it was also cool – the deep, permanent cool of concrete.

Dien had thought that he heard the dried boards of their hut creaking as they withered and shrank in the heat, but the sounds had faded as he drifted back to sleep. It was only when he heard his mother's voice calling his name that he opened his eyes. His mother was kneeling on the floor next to him.

Dien sat up. He reached his arms out for his mother.

'*Meak*,' Mummy, he said, and he smiled dozily waiting for her to fold him into her arms, to hug him. *Like a cat, Dien, like a cat.*

Tess heard his sleepy mumble, watched the range of emotions playing across Dien's face as he sensed her presence and began to wake: happiness, the corners of his soft mouth tilting upwards, then his forehead furrowed and he seemed to lose himself for a moment in uncertainty. He looked up at her and his eyes, unfocused with sleep, met hers.

'*Meak*.' Mummy. A huge smile spread across his face as he uncurled, his arms stretching out to her. '*Meak*. *Meak*.' Mummy. There was something clutched in his fingers, a gold necklace bearing a tiny purple amethyst in the shape of a heart. He was trying to give it to her, she realised. She put her hand out and touched his arm, shook him gently to try to wake him fully.

'No. I'm not your mummy, sweetheart.' And she watched as he finally remembered where he was, why he was here. Recognised that moment between sleep and full cognisance where the brain was still living in the past – a self-constructed, dream-like, perfect past – before reality cut in. Saw the joy at believing he was still safe at home with his mother fade into naked fear as reality dawned.

48

Alex turned the Land Cruiser on to the main road. The potholed tarmac felt smooth after the rigid hammering of the track. In the distance Tess could see the white prefabricated terminal building at Battambang airport, shrouded by the trees ringing the runway. She rested her head against the seat and closed her eyes. Chanthou's words came into her mind: *And your Bob MacSween, of course. He gives us what money he can.*

She opened her eyes. 'Alex, Chanthou told us MacSween gives money to the orphanage. Why would he do that?'

Alex shrugged. 'Wouldn't you give them money if you had any to give?'

'That's not the point. MacSween is obsessed about mine clearing and he's always complaining that we don't have enough money to do the things he wants to do. So why is he giving money away, even if it is for a great cause?'

'Because he has been there and seen the place. He's seen the place and he's human.'

'But in his mind mine clearing is the most important cause of all. Lots of those kids in the orphanage are only there because their parents have been killed by land mines. It . . . it—' She tailed off as she remembered more of Chanthou's words – *the Land Cruiser, the MCT logo* – and with them rose, unbidden, an image of a little girl standing by a minefield in the fading light, the curtain of her hair falling across her face, whispering something about the Crocodile.

She twisted around to face Alex. 'The little girl that was killed by the butterfly mine, the one who tried to warn me about the White Crocodile. She was talking about the Crocodile and night-time. But she also used another word that I didn't understand. I just dismissed her. I said that I was a mine clearer and that I knew what I was doing. But now, I don't know. She could see that I was a mine clearer because I had my kit on and I arrived in an MCT Land Cruiser. She would have seen MCT mine clearers in that field and would have known that we know about the White Crocodile. She must have been trying to tell me something else.'

Alex glanced across. 'What word didn't you understand?'

'I, uh . . . oh God, let me think.' Shutting her eyes, she pressed the tips of her fingers to her forehead, physically willing the word to come. The little girl whispering: Whie Crocodil, night-night. The curtain of her hair falling across her face. The scars on her upper arm ridged and ugly like elastic. Tess dropped her hands to her lap. '*Laan* something.'

'*Laan ch'nual?*'

Tess closed her eyes again, focusing her whole being on an image of the little girl, her lips moving, her voice as quiet as the whisper of wind. 'Say that word again, Alex.'

'*Laan ch'nual?*'

'Yes, that was it.'

'You're sure?'

'Yes. Yes, definitely. What does it mean?'

'It means bus.'

'Bus?'

'Bus. A large vehicle that carries people.'

'Yes, all right, ha, ha. White Crocodile – night-time – bus.' She said the words slowly, fighting for clear thought. They were drawing close to the airport. Just ahead and to the right the thin black line of the runway cut through the trees. 'White Crocodile bus came in the night-time.' On either side of the runway the military hardware was rippling in the intense heat, which had not dissipated with the onset of evening. At the end of the line were the two civilian helicopters. *Came to do what?* – she thought, then a second after – *oh, Christ* – as clarity flooded the places where a moment ago there had been none.

'*Stop at the airport, Alex.*'

'What?'

'Stop at the airport. It's Sunday afternoon. The guy who flies the MCT helicopter got back from holiday last night. I need to speak to him because he answered our radio transmission requesting the emergency helicopter to evacuate Johnny, and he also must have taken the transmission from whoever cancelled it. And the bus, it must be a Land Cruiser. For a child, a Land Cruiser would seem huge.'

He glanced across and she saw the understanding in his eyes. 'No, Tess. He can't be the Crocodile.'

49

December 1990, England

The man grabbed the little boy's arm and dragged him towards the sofa.

'Hello kitten.' His mother smiled. She was lolling back on the sofa, naked. There was sticky gunk on her thighs. 'Were you spying on us?'

The little boy looked up at her, frozen with shock. Tears had made white tracks through the dirt on his cheeks.

'No, Mummy.'

'You're as good a liar as your mum, you are,' the man said.

'Mummy,' he sobbed. 'Please Mummy—'

The man was very angry and the little boy knew he was also drunk, could smell it on his breath. He knew that drink made people angrier, made them hit harder. The man held him tight by the arm and punched him in the mouth. The little boy's head slammed backwards and he tasted blood. The man punched him hard in the side of the head, and once more in the stomach. The little boy doubled up, sobbing.

The man was very matter-of-fact about his violence, as if he was used to doing it and it was no big deal. He let the boy drop to the floor, and disappeared from the room. The little boy was on his hands and knees, and he was shaking and crying and trying to crawl to his mother.

'Mummy—'

His mother reached over and her hands fluttered over his

cheeks where the man had hit him. Then she gently smoothed his hair back with one hand. She wasn't looking at him, the little boy realised, but past him, into the shadows in the hallway, gaze unfocused.

When the man came back in he was carrying the broom handle. He walked over and smacked the little boy in the ribs with it, knocking him flat.

'Mummy, help me,' he said, trying to get up, but the man hit him again, knocking him back down, and through his tears he saw her watching, an odd little smile on her face.

50

Those voices. They were ghosts' voices.

'You're going to die,' they whispered.

Johnny sat up. It had been day, but now it was dark. Night had come. He thought he'd been awake, but he must have drifted off. He was imagining the voices, he knew he was imagining them.

Sitting on the floor, his back to the sofa, he couldn't keep himself quite upright. He was aware of the smell of vomit and he thought it must have come from him, that he had thrown up, but he wasn't sure, couldn't remember. He felt feverishly hot. He couldn't feel his hand, but his arm throbbed.

'What do you think happens next?' the ghosts whispered.

His gaze snapped around him. He felt his lips moving, trying to form words, to answer. Sounds came from his mouth, but something in his brain must have been broken because he couldn't seem to assemble the sounds into anything sensible.

'. . . leavemealoneImeanitleavemealone . . .'

He tried to stand but his good leg wouldn't respond. Didn't matter, he could still get to the door, check the door was locked. Pressing his throbbing bandaged hand to the floor, biting back the pain, he dragged himself forward. He felt the flesh tearing in his palm, heard the pop of scabs, noticed, in some small part of his rational brain, the stench of decaying meat, but in three pathetic lunges he was there, grasping the door handle, tugging it, checking the lock, drawing the curtain tight. He dragged himself around the rest of the room, reaching up to pull the shutters closed, locking them, lurching from one to the next, checking, checking, frantically checking.

'We're already here,' the ghosts whispered.

Johnny jammed his eyes closed, the darkness in his head flashing and flickering. *I'm imagining it. It's a dream. For God's sake, leave me alone.* Scrabbling for purchase, his good leg cycling manically, trying to get a foothold on the wooden boards, he flung himself blindly back against the sofa. He could hear panting, whimpering. Fumbling around on the floor, he found his pistol, closed his hand around it, felt the pain in his hand, almost unbearable, but didn't let go, couldn't let go.

Had to protect himself...

Close by someone started screaming something in a thick voice he couldn't understand. 'LeavemeleavemealoneImeanit-pleasepleaseleavemealone.'

He wrenched in a breath and this time he heard the words clearly. The voice. His voice.

'Leave me alone, I don't deserve this, I don't, *please*, Jesus have mercy.'

*

As he turned the Land Cruiser into the airport car park, Alex's mobile rang. Cutting the engine, he pulled it from his pocket. Tess watched his face darken as he listened to the voice – a man's voice, she could hear from the muffled tone. She could also hear from the pace and the rise and fall in timbre that whoever was speaking was very upset.

'That was Johnny,' he said, tossing his phone on to the dashboard. 'He's shot his next-door neighbour's dog. He's lost it. I have to go.'

*

MacSween sat at his desk in silence, staring blankly at his computer screen, a bottle of Glenfiddich at his elbow. The heat was intense, the pressure in the air made his head throb and he couldn't get rid of the feeling, no matter how many shots he downed – or maybe, he pondered with a sick dry chuckle, because of them. His gaze drifted down to his blotter, to the note laid on top of it.

Had an email from Huan. Going to meet him. Wasn't time to radio you, so went alone. Will report back.

It hadn't been Huan.

'You've got to call the police in,' Tess had told him. And she had been right, of course. Irrefutable logic. A logic that he had denied for too long, because he had known what would happen to MCT if he acknowledged it.

But after Jakkleson's suspected murder, he knew that he didn't have a choice. He had hardly left his desk since making the call and suspending clearing, speaking to no one, just sitting, thinking.

He took a slug of Glenfiddich, winced as the acid liquid scorched down his throat. As he raised the glass to his lips for another, it slipped from his fingers, and although he made a grab for it, his co-ordination seemed to be off, and instead of catching it he just knocked it sideways. MacSween watched dully as the copper-coloured liquid spread over the desktop, soaking Jakkleson's note.

It hadn't been Huan.

Suddenly he swept the computer screen from the desk, sending it crashing to the floor. He had expected it to shatter, but it just bounced a couple of times and then lay there, intact, as if it was laughing at him for believing he could wipe away history, the White Crocodile, with one sweep of his arm.

Slumping forward in the chair, he dropped his head to his hands. For several seconds he remained like that, rocking backwards and forwards, grating his fingers across his scalp. Staggering to his feet, he grabbed the whisky bottle, stumbled over to the window and threw it open. He stood quite still, feeling the cool swell of unsettled air, listening to the thunder rumbling in the distance.

*

A light was on in the clapboard hut. As Tess neared it, the door swung open and a middle-aged man wearing an oil-stained vest and shorts emerged. His mop of blond hair was tied back from a tanned, lined face, and a smoking roll-up hung from the corner of his mouth. He squinted sullenly at her as she approached, with her hand outstretched.

'Hi, I'm Tess Hardy, from MCT.'

He took a drag from the roll-up, blowing a cloud of smoke over her, and shook her hand briefly. 'Dick Seymour.'

Tess took a step back. 'I wanted to ask you about an emergency call we made to you on Monday morning. Monday just gone.'

He nodded slowly, his expression non-committal.

'Early, around half past eight. You received a radio transmission from MCT asking you to evacuate a casualty from Koh Kroneg minefield.'

'Yeah, I received the transmission.'

'But the helicopter never came.'

'I got another call cancelling the helicopter less than a minute after the first one. I hadn't even started the rotors.'

'But we didn't cancel it. We needed it.'

He squinted past her, out across the runway. 'You may not have cancelled it, love, but it was cancelled by MCT nonetheless.'

'But we radioed again about ten minutes later, and there was no answer.'

'I was in the air by then, answering an emergency call from Médecins Sans Frontières which came in a few minutes after your first one, so I wouldn't have got the second call.'

'Can you check?'

'Check what?'

'Your paperwork. Just to confirm.'

'I don't need to check any paperwork, love. I've got it all stored right here.' He tapped a nicotine-stained finger to his temple. 'I got a call from MCT House saying that the casualty wasn't bad and that you'd take him to hospital by road instead.'

'From MCT House? Not from the field, then? The call cancelling the helicopter wasn't from the field?'

She saw a look of fraying patience cross his face. 'From MCT House.'

She stared at him incredulously, her mind accelerating. 'Who was it, sorry? Who phoned?'

Hawking some phlegm into his mouth, he spat on to the tarmac.

'Your boss.'

Tess thought she hadn't heard him right. 'Who, sorry?'

'Your boss. MacSween.'

'Bob MacSween?'

'That's right.' He gave a short laugh. 'Or if it wasn't him, it was someone who can put on a bloody good Scottish accent.'

*

He could have taken any of the Land Cruisers: they were all his in the end, paid for with his sweat.

But he chose this one. *Jakkleson's*. Returned this morning by the police, minus its wing mirrors, a perfect round coffee-coloured stain on the passenger seat where they had tossed Jakkleson's baseball cap.

Penance.

For letting it get this far. He had put MCT, the clearance operation, above everything. Above Johnny, above Jakkleson, above those women and their babies. Been obsessive in his belief that nothing – *nothing* – was more important. Would lives have been saved if he had capitulated and called in the police earlier? If he had sat at his desk, like he had for the past twenty-four hours, and just thought – worked step by step through the possibilities – worked out who the White Crocodile could be? He knew what the answer was.

He twisted the key in the ignition and the engine fired with a boom so loud that it made him flinch. He felt like shit: headachy, sweat pooling in the cleft of his neck and ballooning under his arms despite the air conditioning which rattled and spat lukewarm air at him. He wasn't sure what he was going to do, where he was going to go. To the police first, to tell them what he had worked out. And then? Home? Did he have a home any more?

All he knew was that he needed to escape from here, from the collapsing edifice of his life. But escape to where, to what?

He stared blankly ahead through the windscreen. He didn't notice the pale figure standing in the middle of the drive until it was too late.

Manchester, England

The POLICE – DO NOT CROSS tape was still in place, hanging limply between the trees. Despite the familiar hum of the cars on the M60, the twinkling of office lights from Sharston industrial estate where nine-to-fivers would now be tidying their desks, there was a denseness to Rose Hill woods this evening, a night world, folded into the daylit landscape of south Manchester.

Shivering, DI Wessex ducked under the tape. He didn't have a clear idea of why he had come back to the crime scene; hadn't challenged the niggle in his mind that had pulled him back here, with logic.

Forensics had combed every centimetre of the woodland around the girl's body. They had found nothing. No broken twigs, no footsteps, no tyre tracks. No signs at all, in fact, to indicate that she or anyone else had run through these trees.

He had been happy to sit out the raid on the brothel. Happy to let DS Viles direct the vice boys. If he scaled a tree, he fancied he would see them now, lined up on the pavement outside the brothel on Cheetham Hill Road, kitted up and psyched up, ready with the steel tubular Enforcer to take down the door, an armed unit for back-up – just in case.

It was warmer this evening than it had been for the past couple of days, and he felt clammy in his wool coat and scarf. Pulling off the scarf, he wrapped it around his hand and tapped his padded fist against his forehead a couple of times. How the hell had the girl got here?

He ducked instinctively as an aeroplane roared overhead suddenly, its belly almost grazing the tops of the trees, its landing lights casting the wood around him in cold white light as it passed. Heading towards Manchester City Airport, just a few miles south.

It's a very similar pathology to that we see in road traffic accident victims. Massive internal injuries.

He looked up through the branches as another aircraft rumbled towards the airport. This one was smaller, not a jetliner but a private turbo-prop plane, perhaps owned by one of the executives who had colonised Manchester for its cheaper labour and office space. Or by one of the drugs gangs who could slip unchallenged through a busy commercial airport like Manchester in their £1,000 designer suits, while the baggage handlers and customs officers they'd paid off expedited their packages' flight past customs.

The skin is badly scratched all over . . . it's wood – living trees – that made the scratches.

It was as if her body had been teleported from Cambodia, straight to this urban wood.

That's your department, Sherlock.

A private plane.

Jesus. How the hell could he have been so stupid?

52

Alex wasn't sure what he had been expecting, but it wasn't this. A dark, silent house. He knocked loudly and waited. The hum of voices and traffic from the street behind him was loud, but from inside there was nothing.

Stepping back, he surveyed the facade: a small, detached French colonial villa on a busy residential street near the centre of Battambang. Johnny liked the life, the fact that whatever the hour of the day or night there was always something going on in his neighbourhood. Alex remembered sitting in the garden with Johnny only a few weeks back, drinking whisky shots and discussing what the neighbours got up to at night. The gambling, the fucking, the drinking and the wife beating that Johnny witnessed in this microcosm of Battambang society. *Rear Window* from Hell, he called it.

But tonight the surrounding buildings were dark and quiet.

Pulling his collar up against the smattering of rain that had begun to fall, Alex walked down the side of the house, checking to see if any windows had been left unlocked: kitchen, dining room, Keav's bedroom, a box room overlooking the side alley. He expected to see her sitting on the bed, reading or sewing, but though her light was on, the room was empty, her bed unslept-in. He reached the back garden. The doors and windows at the back of the house were also dark, the huge plate-glass doors which led into the sitting room shut and bolted by the looks of it. No way in, unless he smashed a window, which he didn't want to do. Johnny's call had given Alex an idea of the state he was in and the last thing he wanted was a bullet through the brain as a result of breaking and entering.

Stepping on to the patio, he pressed his face to the glass and looked into the sitting room. A woman lay on the floor, her head resting on a cushion. She could have been asleep, but there was something about the arrangement of her limbs that told Alex that he was too late to save Keav.

His gaze rose from the floor. What looked like a single black eye stared straight back at him. It took him a moment of squinting through the dark and rain to see Johnny's face behind the eye, white and bloated and sick-looking. His eyes, washed-out blue shot with red, stared straight back at him, as if they'd seen a ghost. It took Alex a fraction of a second longer to realise that the black eye was the barrel of a pistol.

An avalanche of glass covered him as the bullet passed through the window. His chilled skin was slow to register the pain. Then the concrete slammed up to meet him.

*

The grounds of MCT House beyond the gate and the building itself looked, as she had expected, deserted. Glancing each way down the rain-drenched street to make sure that she was alone, she hauled herself over the gate and lowered herself silently on to the gravel drive.

The front door was unlocked. She hadn't expected it to be.

When she stepped into the hall and locked the door behind

her, she recognised the sounds and smells that met her. Those of an old, empty house, familiar this time: hot, dusty air; whispered creaks and groans magnified by the silence and by her own tension; the hollow echo of her footsteps on the wooden boards as she crossed to the stairs; the slide of the banister underneath her palm as she started to climb.

She tried MacSween's office, but the door was locked. She knocked – couldn't stop herself, though what the hell would she do if he opened it? – rested her ear against the rough wood and listened, but there was no sound from inside.

When she reached Jakkleson's office, she switched on the desk lamp instead of the bare overhead bulb, so her presence would be less obvious to anyone outside. The weak cone of light illuminated a room as absurdly tidy as the first time she had seen it. The desk clear of documents, the notices on the board perfectly aligned, his family still smiling out from their silver frame, the vase of flowers, frangipani this time, drooping and sick.

Déjà vu.

Lowering herself gently into his chair, she flicked the on switch, waited for what felt like an eternity for the computer to boot up. The miniature egg timer emptied and refilled itself a couple of times before the 'Danger!! Mines!!' sign replaced it, casting a red glow in the darkened room.

Déjà vu.

A sudden shiver ran down her spine, a fleeting sense that someone was standing in the doorway behind her. *MacSween?* The doorway was empty, the dark landing beyond it quiet. Noiselessly, she breathed out, took a long draught of air back into her lungs, willing herself to relax. But she couldn't shake

53

December 1990, England

The little boy's ribs hurt when he breathed, but he didn't think that any of them were broken. They had hurt like that before, but the hurt was just bruising and it had gone away after a few days. His head throbbed at the back where the man had held his hair and smashed his head against the floor.

But he couldn't cry. Was too scared to make a sound.

The hitting and the loneliness felt much worse than before because this time his mother had done nothing. He was used to her lolling on the sofa with her eyes half closed, mouth slack, but she would protest, a bit at least, when the men beat him too viciously. Would stumble over and pull on their arms, tell them to leave the kid alone. He was used to her taking him to the doctor, saying that he had been in a fight at school, or fallen down the stairs – different doctors, different reasons – and he would nod when the doctor questioned him, because he loved his mummy. Was desperate for her to love him back. Now, he knew, there would be no more doctors' trips.

He began to cry, but then he stopped himself. He took a breath and held on to it, looking out through the cracked window pane to the darkness outside fading into flinty winter daylight, snow falling hard now, imagining that he could fly out through the window like a bird, go anywhere he wanted, disappear into the grey sky for ever. But his gaze was caught by the bloodstain on the windowsill, where the man had cracked his head too hard and it had bled. Now that he'd seen it, his mind just gave up and refused to imagine, refused to take him anywhere. It left him in his room with his pain and fear and loneliness.

And it was much worse this time because he had seen the look on his mother's face and in her eyes, and he knew that she had gone. Gone somewhere she wasn't coming back from.

54

'Jesus fucking Christ, Johnny, it's Alex.'

His face was pressed to the concrete and he was breathing in blood and rainwater. He dared not move a muscle, had no idea if Johnny could hear him. He knew he had been hit in the left side, had felt the searing heat of the bullet as it passed through his flesh. But the adrenalin had dampened his feeling and the pain was bearable.

Reaching down gingerly, he felt around his middle for the wound, yelped when his fingers found the hole. It was a flesh wound, bloody and painful, but he had been lucky. A centimetre to the right and he would be living with one less kidney.

'It's me – Alex,' he yelled again. 'Put the fucking gun down.'

Warily, he raised himself on to his elbows – no second bullet, no sound at all over the whoosh of rain – and scrambled backwards fast until he was shielded by the wall of the house. He climbed slowly to his feet, clenching his teeth against the pain, crossed himself – God knows why, because he didn't believe in any fucking God any more – and tilted sideways, so he could scan the room out of one eye. He couldn't see anything for a moment, only bulky outlines in the darkness, but gradually his vision adjusted and his gaze found Johnny. He was sitting, leaning back against the sofa, but tipped to one side, as if he had been propped into position by someone else, then, like a rag doll, had slid off centre.

'Johnny.'

Alex slapped his hand up and down the wall inside the door, groping for the light switch. He found it, and harsh electric light flooded the room. Johnny remained motionless, head sunk into his chest. He was still holding the pistol, but it was sagging against the floor, the fingers gripping it loose, almost as if he had forgotten it was there. His other hand was lying in his lap, the towel bandaging it mottled with dried blood and pus.

Alex stepped inside the room. He passed by Keav's body, and this close it was clear how she had died. A neat bullet hole in the centre of her forehead had turned her into a beautiful, alabaster Cyclops. He cursed himself for his stupidity. Could he have saved her if he had listened to Johnny's plea for help earlier? Taken him back to the hospital and asked Dr Ung to give him drugs to calm his paranoia? He knew that the answer was probably yes, that he was almost as culpable for Keav's death as Johnny was.

Dragging his gaze from her gelid features, he knelt in front of Johnny, wincing at the pain in his side, feeling a fresh gush of blood released by the movement.

'Johnny.'

'Alex. Mate.'

Johnny smiled and lifted his hand in a limp salute, let it fall. Alex glanced down. The muzzle of Johnny's pistol was pointed straight at his groin. Slipping his hand to Johnny's wrist, he twisted the pistol away from him. With his other hand he tried to uncurl Johnny's fingers from the butt. Johnny flinched and jerked it savagely away.

'NO! Need it!' He raised his eyes to Alex's. The whites were shot with red. 'Need it . . . need to defend myself.'

'You don't need it. No one is going to hurt you.'

'Hurt me? *Kill me.*'

'No one is trying to kill you.' Reaching out, he laid his hand over Johnny's, on the pistol. Johnny's eyes sparked with fury and he wrenched his arm away, but Alex held on.

'Kill me,' Johnny wailed.

Shaking his head, Alex uncurled Johnny's fingers from the pistol: the index finger first, taking the tension in it against his own finger, releasing the pressure from the trigger.

'Coming to kill me.'

'Who?' Alex asked. 'Who is coming to kill you?'

Uncurling the last finger, he pulled the pistol from Johnny's grasp, ejected the magazine and the cartridge from the chamber, and slid them across the room.

'Wh . . . white,' Johnny muttered, groping after the pistol. 'White Crocodile . . . trying to kill me.'

Alex met Johnny's dull gaze and felt nothing beyond the throbbing pain in his side, and complete and utter exhaustion. He realised now how close to the edge he was. He looked at the sofa behind Johnny, wanted to curl up in those cushions, close his eyes and just shut down: no pain, nothing to resolve, no more fighting, no more dying.

'White Crocodile wanted to kill me. Screwed up.' Johnny made a strangled noise, deep in his throat. 'Won't screw . . . next time.'

Alex shook his head, but without conviction.

'And I –' Johnny started to choke; it sounded as if an obstruction in his throat was keeping him from catching his breath, '– deserved it.'

Alex's gaze snapped back to Johnny's face.

'What the hell do you mean?'

Johnny cupped his hand over his bandaged stump. 'It was a game,' he whispered. 'Playing. Playing with those dumb as fucking oxen women.' His fingers turned white with the pressure of his grip. 'Their fault, he said—' Johnny gave a pathetic chuckle. 'He said it was OK because their lives were shit anyway.'

'What?'

Johnny let out a gasping sob. 'Keav. I helped her, didn't I?'

'What did you just say?'

'Keav. *Keav.* I helped her.'

'Not Keav. You said something else. A man. Something about a man.'

'A man?'

'Yes. You said "he" – "he said it was OK because their lives were shit anyway." Did you mean MacSween?'

'MacSween?' He looked wide-eyed, guileless as a baby.

'*Johnny.* You said "he"—'

'*I didn't.*' He shrank back against the sofa. 'I didn't kidnap anyone.'

Alex gritted his teeth.

'Keav. I helped Keav, didn't I? Didn't I?' Something had happened to Johnny's face, like a curtain falling at the end of a play, bringing the action to a close. All expression was gone: mouth sagging and lifeless, blue eyes washed to nothing. 'She hates me now, I know she does, but I helped her, didn't I? She would have been a common whore if I hadn't taken her in. I helped her, didn't I?'

Alex felt jaded, angry, bone-deep exhausted and he knew he had lost it – that he wouldn't get anywhere with Johnny tonight. 'Yeah, you did. You helped her.' *You fucking prick.*

'I helped her. I know. I'm not so bad.'

*

His accent, thick Mancunian, was difficult to understand, interspersed with the manic crackle on the line.

'You're going to have to speak slowly, Detective Inspector. The line's terrible.'

It had already taken five minutes of interruptions, of speaking over each other and of him twice threatening to put the phone down on this hoax call, for her to explain who she was and why she was calling. He was in the office, thankfully, and was able to Google 'Mine Clearance Trust' to check that it was a legitimate organisation and that she was who she said she was.

She glanced down at the fax in her hand. 'Can you tell me more about the woman – Dien's mother? Who she is? Where you met her?'

'I went to a brothel.' He sounded embarrassed. 'Official, of course.'

'Yes, of course.' A pause. 'And—' she prompted.

'This young Cambodian woman was working there. She couldn't speak much English, but she showed me the photo of her little boy. Christ, he's only four, just a baby.' She heard him clear his throat; the tense dry cough of a machine gun. 'Did you find him, love?'

'Yes. He's in an orphanage out here.'

'Is he OK?'

She thought of Dien, curled up like a little dog on the grimy concrete floor, thinking, for that brief moment on waking, that he was still safe at home with his mother.

'As OK as a kid in an orphanage out here can be.'

'I see a lot of nasty stuff in my job, but I have to confess that that girl got to me. She really got to me.' He paused and she could hear his terse, uneven breathing.

'How did she wind up in a brothel in Manchester?'

'We're pretty sure that all the girls in the brothel and our murder victim were kidnapped and trafficked, though we need to interview them through interpreters to get a full picture. We think that our murder victim was in the process of being trafficked when she was killed. Tossed out of a private plane. We've known the drug-smuggling gangs have used them for years, shuttling between big European ports like Rotterdam and Manchester, bringing in heroin and cocaine. They have a ton of airport workers on the payroll. We arrest one and ten others crop up in their place.' He gave a humourless laugh. 'These gangs all diversify in time. Big business could learn a lot about diversification and developing new income streams from criminal gangs. I'm sure when I finally get to the bottom of this, I'll find some of the familiar old drug-smuggling faces are involved in the trafficking of these women too.' He paused. 'We'll probably never know why, but perhaps she became hysterical and fought with her traffickers. It finally occurred to me after listening to endless bloody planes roar over the patch of woodland she was found in. We're following that line of enquiry at the moment. But it would really help me get justice for her if I could identify her.'

'I'm sorry, and I know this sounds harsh, but there's not much chance of that. Not without a better description. And even then you'd be very lucky to find her. It would take a lot of trawling around all the local villages with a photograph to have any chance.'

'We don't have a photograph.' He didn't elaborate. 'What about a missing persons list?'

'It's not like that out here. They don't keep track of missing persons. Too many people die of land-mine injuries, illness and poverty. They hold a funeral in their village, an open cremation in a field, and that's it. No one keeps track.'

Beyond the line's static crackle, Tess thought she heard the crunch of tyres on gravel.

'Is there anything else, DI Wessex, before I go?'

He didn't answer immediately. When finally he spoke, his tone was grave. 'Look, love, I want you to listen to me. The people involved in human trafficking are entirely without morals or humanity. They enslave these women for money. *Just for money.* They beat them, rape them, mutilate them. Kill them if they step out of line. And these, as you know, are young, *young* girls. I appreciate your help, I really do, and if you find out who is running this trafficking operation from your end, you'll be doing me a huge favour. But you must remember that these people won't mind killing you, love, I promise that.'

'I can't stop now, but I'll be careful.'

'Wait, love, wait. There's one more thing.'

'Yes?'

At that moment, she noticed a change in the way the light fell on the landing outside Jakkleson's office; a light had been switched on in the hallway downstairs.

'DI Wessex—'

'We went in a couple of hours ago, mob-handed.' His voice

was urgent. 'Busted the place. We have fourteen women under our protection. But the woman I talked with originally – Dien's mother – she wasn't there. The brothel owner told us finally, after we exerted a bit of friendly pressure. He said that she's dead. She killed herself.' He made a bitter noise. 'So that little boy of hers is now an orphan for real.'

*

Dr Ung was sheltering under a tree by the gate, waiting for them. Bathed for a moment in the Land Cruiser's headlights, he looked tense and distracted. He was wearing his trademark suit trousers, shirt and tie, but the knot of the tie hung loose and the top few buttons of his shirt were undone revealing a pale, skinny chest. Shielding his eyes from the glare of the headlights with one hand, he lifted the other in a listless greeting. Alex parked by the hospital building and walked back to join him, clasping his hand and shaking it before he spoke.

'Johnny's stump is infected,' he said, in a low voice. 'He cut his hand a couple of days ago and that's also badly infected.' He paused, rubbed a hand over his eyes, avoiding meeting Dr Ung's gaze. 'And he's, uh, he's mentally bad, very bad.'

'He shot you?' Dr Ung indicated the bloodstain covering the side of Alex's shirt.

Alex nodded. 'It's only a graze.'

'I was afraid that he would degenerate further mentally, but not to that extent.'

'It's worse than that.'

'What?'

'He killed his housekeeper. Shot her in the head.'

Dr Ung's face displayed several dramatic changes as he listened. 'You must tell the police, obviously, though I am sure they will do very little. Deaths of Westerners' housemaids hold little interest for them. An occupational hazard, I'm sure they would call it. I will operate again first thing tomorrow morning, on both his leg and his hand. He can stay here until he recovers enough, and then it will be up to the police what happens to him.'

Alex nodded.

'Help me get him into the hospital, Alexander, then let me clean you up.'

'I'm fine,' Alex said, more aggressively than he had meant to.

They faced each other for a moment.

'Well at least go home and bandage that wound yourself, then get some sleep. I will take care of Johnny now.'

Johnny was slumped in the passenger seat, eyes rolling back in his head. Alex grabbed him under the arms and, staggering under the dead weight, hauled him out. With Dr Ung grasping one arm and Alex the other, an orderly his legs, they managed to carry him into his old room. The blast of the fan seemed to revive him for a moment because he opened his eyes. When he realised where he was, he started to struggle.

'No,' he muttered.

Dr Ung held his arm. 'It's OK, Johnny. You're safe here.' Dr Ung indicated to the orderly to hold Johnny down on the bed while he slid a line into his arm.

Johnny cried out: 'Alex, help—'

Ignoring him, Alex turned away. Walked over to the window and looked out into the dark courtyard.

'Alex, help me—'

Rain was hissing against the mosquito mesh. He could hear something loose banging out in the street. Dr Ung's voice was raised.

'Ketamine. *Ketamine. Aylow.*' Now.

The sound of Johnny struggling faded; his voice died down.

Alex felt as if he could stand here all night, just looking at nothing.

Dr Ung called his name, and he turned reluctantly from the window.

'I have given him a drip to help hydrate him,' Dr Ung said. 'It contains mild ketamine – only mild – just to calm him and help him sleep. As I said, I will operate first thing tomorrow morning. Come tomorrow evening, if you have time, but not before, please. Some time to rest alone after the operation will do him good.'

The orderly left, and Dr Ung held out his arm to shepherd Alex out of the room.

Alex hesitated. 'Give me a minute.'

'He will sleep all night with the ketamine.'

Alex nodded. 'Just a minute. Please.'

Dr Ung looked irritated. 'A minute.' He laid a hand on Alex's arm, the grip stronger than Alex would have expected given his slight frame. 'But then I insist that you go home and get some sleep. And make sure that you put some proper disinfectant on that bullet wound.' Turning, he left the room.

*

Tess placed the phone silently back into its cradle, looking at the doorway. There was nobody there. Slowly, she raised herself from the chair, sliding the legs back fraction by fraction so as not to make a sound. She had nothing to defend herself with, so she grabbed Jakkleson's envelope opener, a gilded knife, five centimetres long, the national emblem of Sweden, three gold crowns, inlaid into its handle. It looked as if it wouldn't be able to cut through butter, but it made her feel infinitesimally more secure.

She moved silently towards the doorway. Out on the landing, the air was cooler than in Jakkleson's office, so that she shivered slightly. She had been right – the light in the hallway downstairs was on. Easing forward, she leaned over the banister.

Quiet.

'MacSween?'

She stood motionless, counting to fifty.

'MacSween?'

Still no answer. Only the blood pulsing in her ears. Cautiously, she made her way down the first few steps. Rounding the staircase on to the landing, she paused beneath the huge picture window. The moon hung low over the garden, casting her in a faint wash of light. The hallway below was empty, all the doors off it closed. She carried on down, one step at a time, walking at the very edge of each stair to minimise the potential for creaking, clutching Jakkleson's letter opener in front of her. At the bottom of the stairs, she stopped and backed against the wall. She could hear a low humming sound.

'MacSween?' Her voice was threaded with panic and she

hated herself for it. 'Is that you?'

No reply. Just that rhythmic hum. She realised it was coming from the team room. The light was switched off, she could see that from the crack under the door.

'MacSween?'

Oh, Christ.

As she pushed the door open, her heart was beating so hard in her chest that it hurt. She couldn't see anything. The room was dark, but the hum was intense. And the smell was almost overpowering. Pressing her sleeve to her mouth, she fumbled blindly for the light switch. Found it and flicked it on. *Why the hell isn't the light—* Something brushed against her face in the dark, and she jumped.

A fly, it's only a fly.

Then there was another, and another.

*

Johnny looked dead. Alex stared down at his supine body, laid out on the bed. He was too wrecked, mentally and emotionally, to think clearly, but there was one question he still needed answering. Who had Johnny been talking about? Had he been talking about MacSween? Was Bob MacSween the White Crocodile?

Leaning over the bed, he shook Johnny by the shoulder.

'Wake up.'

Johnny's brow furrowed and he gave a little moue of dissatisfaction, but his eyes remained closed.

'Johnny! For fuck's sake *wake up!*'

His eyes opened a crack, fluttered closed, opened again, his pupils rolling around in his head as he focused blearily on Alex's face.

'Mate.'

'Who did you mean when you said "he" back in your house? I need to know now.'

'He?' His lips formed the word but no sound came out.

'You said: "He said it wasn't so bad because their lives were shit anyway."'

Johnny shook his head feebly and closed his eyes.

'Johnny. *Johnny!*'

Alex straightened, trying to swallow his anger because he knew that if he lost his temper now he would annihilate any chance he had of dragging the truth out of Johnny. Suddenly he registered the clear sac at his eye level across the bed, its translucent hose trailing into Johnny's arm. Still pumping Ketamine. *Shit.* Vaulting over the bed, he tore off the plaster and yanked the IV needle from Johnny's forearm.

Johnny's eyes snapped open.

Alex met his gaze. 'I need to know, *now.*'

*

MacSween was there, sitting in the middle of the team room, on one of the stiff-backed chairs. He was facing her, she thought, could tell by the domes of his knees, and his shirt, the front of his black shirt – it was the front, because she could see his collar and the top button, but it was moving – why was it moving?

Oh, Jesus. The front of his shirt was moving; a black, crawling mass of flies.

She couldn't see his face, *because it's too dark*, she thought. *Or maybe his head is tilted to the side.* She tried to take a step forward, but her body wasn't obeying orders, and she just stood there, rooted to the spot, swaying on unsteady legs.

There *was* no face, she realised. There was a body – a body of rippling, feasting flies and nothing – nothing above.

And now she felt it.

The fear.

MacSween was dead.

He had been tied to a chair and someone had blown his head off with that gun, that P90, she recognised it now – the P90 that was lying near him, but not so near that he had shot himself and dropped it there. The same P90 that had killed Huan. *A bullet that spun, a very sophisticated weapon, I would say.*

But if MacSween really was the White Crocodile, then who had killed him?

A noise behind her and the light in the hallway went out.

55

'Someone hated you enough to try to kill you, Johnny. Who was it, and why?'

'I'm not involved,' Johnny hissed. 'Not any more.'

'Not involved in what?'

Silence.

'Not involved in what, Johnny?'

'Trafficking,' he muttered through clenched teeth.

Alex didn't move. 'Trafficking?'

Johnny gave an almost imperceptible nod.

'Of women?' Alex demanded. 'You're telling me that you were involved in human trafficking?'

Johnny nodded feebly.

Alex slammed his hands on the bed's metal footboard. 'Trafficking them where? To do what?'

'Prostitution,' he whispered. 'We provided prostitutes to a criminal gang in Europe.'

'*Prostitution?*'

Johnny squeezed his eyes closed.

'*You sell those women as slaves?*'

'I'm not involved any more. Couldn't do it.'

Alex could feel his stomach knotting itself. The girl in the Land Cruiser, years ago now, but not one day went past without him thinking about her – he had the evidence scrawled over his arm. *I bought her from one of your lot. Seven-*

teen hundred dollars. Not cheap, but she's a virgin. Jesus. He turned away, fighting to keep calm. 'And you haven't tried to stop it?'

'I'm not involved any more. Keav. Keav was one of the first. I saved her.'

'Keav's dead, and you killed her, you fuck.' Alex spun around and slammed his boot against the base of the bed, ricocheting it into the wall. Johnny cowered against the headboard. 'Why did you do it?' Alex yelled.

'For the money.'

'But you . . . you told me that your parents have millions. How much fucking money do you need?'

Johnny didn't answer. He had started to sob quietly. Alex knew he would hurt Johnny badly if he stayed where he was, so he retreated, shaking, to the window.

'They had miserable fucking lives, in a miserable fucking country,' he heard Johnny croak. 'It's not as if they left anything behind. They're probably better off where they are.'

'They left their children, their babies, behind. Without even having the chance to say goodbye.' The mosquito netting was right in front of him, hard and thin. He placed his hand on the cheese-wire mesh. 'You are fucking scum, Johnny.' Clenching his hands, he scraped his fingertips down the mesh, grazing their ends. He imagined slamming his fist through it, and the jagged hole that would leave, the sharp metal ends scoring into his flesh. He imagined dragging his wrist against them so they would cut into him, tearing them up the soft flesh of his forearm, still slashed and bloody from the last time. 'Is it MacSween? Is that who you're working with? Is he running things?'

'MacSween?'

He forced himself to turn from the window to stop imagining harming himself, but he couldn't get the picture out of his mind. His whole body was trembling with rage.

'Did MacSween sell these women to fund MCT?'

He looked down at the scars on his forearm, realised he'd been scraping them with the nails of his other hand, had ripped some of the scars open. Blood was dripping on to the floor.

'MacSween? No. Not MacSween. Dr Ung. Dr Ung sold those women to fund this hospital.'

*

Tess held her breath. Someone seemed to be breathing in and out with her. No, not someone. An animal?

All her senses had been on high alert, quivering with the effort of listening, straining to see in the dark, feeling any change in temperature, but the breathing sounded so close. How could it have got so close to her without making any noise?

She spun around, slashing the letter opener wildly in front of her. Aiming for a wall to press herself against so that at least her back would be covered, she stumbled backwards in the dark, felt something behind her, solid and unyielding. Grateful for that small mercy, she grasped it.

Pulpy under her fingers – *pulpy?*

Her brain, expecting rigid plaster, struggled to comprehend what she was feeling. Something pappy and moist, and it was undulating under her fingers, rippling against her skin, and suddenly that humming sound that had become background noise filled her ears and the air was alive with flies. The stench of opened flesh was so intense she felt she would drown in it.

Rigid with fear, she stumbled away from the body. All sound had gone except for that mad ceaseless humming – she couldn't even hear her own breathing – the animal she'd heard could be an arm's reach away from her and she wouldn't even know.

A pale blue stripe of moonlight cut suddenly across the boards to her left, a window, and she blundered for it, falling to her knees, clambering on all fours to the edge of the room, squatting against the skirting board, trembling and panting. A hand surged out of the darkness – the fingers huge and very white. She struck out blindly with Jakkleson's letter opener, felt it slice into something soft, a grunt, and then something hit her on the head so hard she felt as if her skull had been cleaved in two. Blood ran into her eyes, blinding her. She didn't register the second blow, but from the sound her head made as it bounced off the rough wooden floor, she realised that it must have knocked her flat. She felt the weight of something pinning her down, warm breath on her neck.

And all she could think was: *It is real.*

*

He was sitting at his desk, his back to the door, doing some paperwork. Alex pulled out his Browning. Though he made no noise, Dr Ung must have sensed his presence. He turned. Their eyes met.

'So Johnny has remembered?'

'Is it true?'

Dr Ung half-shrugged; there was something almost apologetic in the movement.

'Why?' Alex croaked.

'Because I am fighting a war, Alexander. And in war people are sacrificed for the greater good.'

'A war?'

'Against the suffering caused by land mines. The human suffering they cause in this country is incalculable.' Slipping off his glasses, he rubbed at the elliptical imprints they had left in his nose. 'We are the only hospital in this region that saves the lives of land-mine victims, gives them back a future.'

'People trust you. You're a fucking doctor.'

'What do you think I'm doing?' Anger flared in Dr Ung's voice. 'How do you think I pay for all this year after year?' He spread his arms irritably. 'I tried to get funding from legitimate sources and it was *impossible*. Western governments and most charities see mines as a way of life for countries like Cambodia. I had to make this hospital happen by myself. All of it.'

'By sacrificing those women?'

'This is bigger than they are. Those women had nothing to live for.'

Alex stared back at him, his finger frozen on the trigger.

'They had their babies.'

'What future did their children have, born out of wedlock in a place like this?'

Alex felt the solid butt of the Browning in his hand. It would be easy and quick. There were no ballistics tests out here. They could never link Dr Ung's murder to his gun.

'Kill me and all this,' Dr Ung spread his hands, 'all this crumbles to dust. The land-mine victims in this region will have nowhere to go. No one to save them.'

'What about Johnny?'

'He threatened to expose me. Johnny is a restless man. Never satisfied with his cut.'

'But why did you then save him, when the mine failed to kill him?'

'I made my point. And I'm a doctor, Alexander. It's my business to save lives.'

'What about those women who were found dead in the White Crocodile minefield? The ones who fought. What about Huan and Jakkleson?'

'I have taken the Hippocratic oath.' Dr Ung's face was patient, unperturbed. 'I save lives. I don't kill.'

'Oh, for fuck's sake. You might have saved Johnny in a fit of misplaced conscience, but you've murdered—' He broke off. Dr Ung was always in the hospital working. When would he have had the opportunity?

'I didn't murder anybody. And I didn't plant the mine for Johnny.'

Alex lowered the Browning. Whatever Dr Ung had done, he couldn't kill him in cold blood. He met Dr Ung's gaze, and saw that he knew the same.

'Where is Tess, Alexander? At MCT House? Alone?' With a faint smile, Dr Ung slipped his glasses back on. 'I am not the White Crocodile, Alexander. I only pull the strings.'

*

I'm not going to die. Not now. Not like this.

Pressing her hands flat to the floor to give herself leverage, she slammed the sole of her combat boot backwards, blindly, as hard as she could. The crunching sound and the howl of pain told her she'd connected with bone and muscle. The weight on top of her shifted slightly, and it was enough.

She scrambled away, tipping and weaving in the dark like a drunk, hoping she was moving towards the door. Luck was with her and she felt the frame of the doorway in her hands. She plunged through it, aiming left – the front door was left out of the team room – and in the hallway there was a faint light from the moon shining in the picture window above her. She stumbled again, found her balance and ran for the front door.

She yanked the door handle. Nothing. She heard herself yell, desperate, heard the sound of feet approaching – slowly – grabbed at the handle and pulled and kicked, but it was no good because the door wasn't stiff, it was locked. Locked not only with the bolt, but also with a key.

The Crocodile's voice was a whisper in her ear: 'My beautiful wife. How nice of you to come all this way, just for me.'

56

January 1991, England

The little boy clutched the plastic bag containing his spare pair of underpants and his pyjamas, and looked at the black door in front of him, the building it was set into towering over him, so tall he felt as if it might topple over and squash him. He started to cry. He wanted to turn away, run somewhere – he didn't know where – but it was freezing cold, slushy rain falling hard from a winter sky, and he didn't have a coat. He was soaked through and shivering.

He was frightened of what was behind the front door but he was more frightened of what was behind him.

'This is your new home, kitten,' Mummy had said, twisting around to look at him from the front seat of the man's car, with that glassy vacant look she had in her eyes almost all the time now. 'It's a children's home. A home for children like you.'

The little boy looked at her without speaking, tears making white tracks through the dirt on his cheeks. He was frightened of her too now, but he still loved her because she was his mummy. He didn't want to get out of the car.

'Get out of the fucking car.' Jonjo leaned over the back of the seat and shouted right in his face.

'Mummy—'

'Get out.'

'Mummy,' he sobbed.

Jonjo was drunk and angry and his mummy was high. The

car was so rusty that the door stuck and he got frightened as he struggled with the handle. Frightened that Jonjo would lose patience and hit him again, like he had hit him every day since he moved in with Mummy. He was so frightened these days that sometimes he wet himself accidentally, which made both Jonjo and Mummy furious.

They drove off as soon as he was out of the car. He watched them through the rear window, thinking that Mummy would look back at him. But she didn't. Not once.

He began to cry, but then he stopped himself. He took a breath and held on to it, half closing his eyes so that he was looking at the great black door through tiny slits, so that everything around him was dark too and slightly fuzzy. In that way he found that he could imagine it was a black hole in space, and he could step through it into a whole new world of stars and moons and aliens. He was free then. Free to go where he wanted, to be on his own, to fly through space like a rocket ship and find a planet where no one else lived. A new home – just for him. Alone. Alone and safe.

Imagining helped him and he stepped forward. He couldn't stretch high enough to ring the bell, so he just tapped with his fist on the door, hoping that someone would hear him. It was a long time before anyone did. A grey-haired woman with mild blue eyes, wearing a big brown cardigan, opened the door.

*

Anna didn't realise there was anyone on the doorstep for a moment. She had been expecting a delivery of bread and was looking around at head height for a delivery driver in a crisp white coat. Finally, she looked down. The little boy on the doorstep was tiny and shivering. He wore a filthy white sweatshirt and jeans that finished halfway down his calves. His shoulders stood out from the sweatshirt like a wire coat hanger. He had a black eye and she could tell from the angle his left arm was hanging at that it was broken. In his other hand he held a plastic Tesco carrier bag. She looked beyond him, either way down the street. There was no one around. No people. No cars. He was alone.

'Why are you here, sweetheart?'

No response, no change in his expression. His eyes were alert for any sign of danger.

'Come inside out of the cold and then we'll talk.' She ushered him into the hallway and shut the door. Then she knelt down in front of him. 'Who brought you here?'

'Mummy,' he whispered, his voice so tiny and timid she had to tilt her head towards him to hear. 'This is my new home.'

The woman looked confused and the little boy felt desperate. Desperate to make her understand him. He dug deep in his brain to find the right words. The words that would make her like him. He knew that it was important for her to like him, but he didn't know how to make that happen.

'Mummy said . . .' He was struggling not to cry. 'She said that this is my new home.' It was warm in here and the woman had a kind face. He didn't want to go back outside. It was beginning to get dark, he could see the light outside the hall changing to grey and he didn't want to be outside in the dark and the rain. 'Can I live here? Please.'

'It doesn't quite work like that. We'll need to speak to social services, the police.'

The words were meaningless to the little boy.

'We'll sort you out, sweetheart. Let's get you to bed now and we can sort everything out in the morning. Where are your things?'

The little boy held out his plastic bag. Inside were a pair of grey underpants and a pair of pale yellow girl's pyjamas with Minnie Mouse on the front, size 3 to 4 she noticed from the label. He looked embarrassed when she took them out of the bag.

Anna knelt down beside him; slipped an arm around his shoulders.

'How old are you?'

The little boy smiled for the first time at that question. She saw that one of his front teeth was missing. 'Six,' he said. 'I'm six today.'

The woman's eyes were bright and furious and when he looked up at her, she looked away. He started to shake again, thinking that a smack or a punch was coming.

'No, sweetheart,' she said, pulling him against her. 'It's OK. We'll look after you. You're safe now.'

The warm air in the hall moved over his skin, he could smell food cooking, and the sound of children playing somewhere above him, running feet and their laughter. He could hear laughter. The woman's arms were soft and he hadn't been cuddled for longer than he could remember. It felt so good that he started to cry, great shuddering sobs that felt as if they came all the way up from his toes.

'Shhhh.' She kissed his cheek and hugged him tighter. 'Shhh, it's OK. You're safe.' Levering him gently away from her, she stroked a hand over his face. 'Can you tell me your name?'

He nodded and smiled, knowing that for once he was sure to get something right.

'Luke.'

57

She heard the familiar sound of leaves rustling, the creaking of wood, the hiss of rain. The air was cooler, the smell mellow and damp – not the stuffy smell of a closed room. She thought that she must have left her bedroom window open, which was good because she liked to sleep with the outside close by. She opened her eyes a crack. Darkness.

Still night, she thought, relieved.

She closed her eyes and felt a dull ache in her head, like a hangover. She twisted and shifted. The mattress was hard – hard and cold – a cold that seeped through her skin. She wondered why. Her tongue felt thick and heavy, and she could taste something chalky and metallic. She tried to swallow, but her mouth was so dry . . . and the taste, what was the taste? She just wanted to sleep. Curling herself into a ball, she shut her eyes again.

'Tess.'

A whisper.

'Luke?'

She tried to open her eyes, but her lids felt too heavy.

Luke? Luke was dead. Wasn't he?

She stretched her arms above her head. She recognised the taste in her mouth – *blood* – and now she was moving the pain in her head was almost unbearable. Lying still, she gulped in air, fighting a tide of nausea.

When the feeling had subsided, she hauled herself to sitting. The surface behind her was rough. She shifted against it, trying to get comfortable, but it was the same wherever she moved – grooved and knotted. She looked up; her head thumped and her vision swam. Holding herself still, she breathed hard, willing the spinning to stop. Slowly her vision refocused and she made out dark shapes above her: branches, a bobbing, twisting mosaic of leaves. A tree, its bark rough against her back. Through the leaves she could see a sliver of moon.

Lowering her gaze, she stared hard into the darkness around her. Muted outlines began to form. An undulating landscape, puddles of water reflecting the moonlight, elephant grass swaying in the wind, and closer to her, the dark sides of a crater, too deep for the moonlight to penetrate.

Further away there was something else, something twisting and fluttering in the darkness. She had heard that sound so many times before in different places around the world, when the wind was up and the red-and-white striped mine tape was lifting and dancing.

*

Johnny lay back against the pillows and knew that he was dead.

Johnny the joker.

Johnny the dead man.

In some other plane, somewhere else entirely, he recognised that he should feel some guilt, some shame. But he couldn't bring himself to feel guilty. It hadn't been like that at the time.

The rain rattled against the mosquito mesh.

It was time. He knew it was time.

Shifting on to his side, he reached to the bedside table for his trousers, which Dr Ung had folded neatly and laid in the drawer. He found what he was looking for in an instant. The penknife was small, but the blade was sharp.

Better to do it now, while he had a choice about the *how*, than to wait.

Blinking, concentrating hard to make sure he didn't fuck it up, he drew the blade down his wrist, breaking open the tender skin, slicing vertically through veins. Blood bloomed, bright, but instinctively he knew that it wasn't enough.

Tilting sideways so that he could lay his arm flat on the mattress, he nudged the point of the knife into the wound. He winced as the blade met open flesh. Jamming his eyes shut, his brain fumbled for an image, something to take him away from the abhorrent things he had done. *Something to leave with*—

Shropshire: open spaces, grass beneath his feet and a crystal blue sky above. *Home. I'm home*—

The image was perfect and he held on to it. Shifting sideways, he leaned the full weight of his body on to the hilt of the knife. The blade slipped smoothly into his wrist, neatly severing the muscles and tendons, the network of veins and artery. He held the image of home in his mind like precious china as he watched his blood jet across the white sheets.

Shropshire. Rolling fields. Late afternoon, he realised. The sun just dipping behind a copse of trees. Bitten, then bisected. Then gone.

58

Luke smiled at her.

'I've missed you,' he said. 'I've missed my beautiful wife.' He leaned forward, and even though there was no one to overhear them, whispered right in her ear. 'And I've missed her tight cunt.'

She struck out, but he had been expecting that because he caught her wrist in the air and twisted her arm up behind her back, so high that she felt her shoulder would pop out of its joint. Shoving her against the tree trunk, he grabbed her hair and smacked her head viciously against the bark.

'NO.'

Just the one word, but it was enough. She stopped struggling, let her body go floppy, her mind float off, following the familiar tracks she had learned when they were married. He gave her a soft kiss on the cheek and released her.

'I'm sorry, my darling. But you know how you wind me up. You've got to stop winding me up.' He smiled. 'I heard you talking to that detective inspector on the phone. I presume that he was talking about my women, was he?'

Her stomach knotted.

'Jorani, perhaps?' He smiled. 'It means radiant jewel.'

He placed a hand lightly on her shoulder. She tensed.

'So beautiful. Just perfect.' He tightened his grip. 'He's met her, has he? Used her?'

'Take your hand away,' she said, with fierce restraint.

Luke dropped his hands and smiled in mock surrender. 'Sorry.'

'So it was you who set the mine for Johnny, and murdered Jakkleson and Huan?'

'Johnny was helping me at the beginning, but he got greedy and threatened to expose me.' He gave a wry half-smile. 'Unfortunately for him, he underestimated my commitment.'

'You didn't feel the need to finish him off?'

He shrugged. 'Didn't need to. I paid him a visit at the hospital, left a souvenir from the White Crocodile, and his own pitiful mind did the job for me. It would have been far less satisfying to kill him.'

'And Jakkleson? Huan?'

'Jakkleson didn't know who the White Crocodile was, but he was pretty sure it wasn't Huan – that Huan was the scapegoat. He destroyed Huan's personnel file so I couldn't find out where he and his family lived. But there's more than one way to skin a cat. I was always going to get to Huan eventually. Shame that Ret S'Mai disappeared before I got to him too.'

'Why Ret S'Mai? What the hell did he ever do?'

'He saw me in Johnny's room at the hospital one night. He didn't know who I was because he'd never met me, but he knew that something wasn't right. He told Huan, and together they worked it out.'

Tess bit her lip. 'So why have you brought me here?'

'Why? Because this is the White Crocodile's hunting ground. My spiritual home, I suppose.' He shrugged again. 'The White Crocodile put the fear of God into those women, made the hunting so much easier. They were terrified before I even got to them. Fear makes people compliant. Almost everyone imagines that they'll be brave in the face of terror, but in the end – it's always the same.'

'And I'm next.'

He shook his head. 'Not you.'

'What do you want then?'

'I still love you, Tess. I want to be with you.'

Wrapping her arms around herself, she looked away from him, across the deserted minefield.

'And to explain.' His voice cut into her consciousness. 'Tell you why. I think I owe you that. You've had to live with me being dead for six months. It must have been hard. I'm sorry, but I had no choice.'

'So you weren't frightened, were you? When you telephoned me from Cambodia. You were just pretending to be.'

'I'm sorry, but it was necessary.' His voice was soft. 'I became very good at pretending as a child. Pretending was the only thing I had.'

'How did you survive the mine?'

'I rigged a radio-controlled anti-tank mine at the edge of the jungle, so I could slip away and trigger it remotely, and everyone would think I'd been vaporised.' He held up his twisted hand, encased in a white leather glove. 'I wasn't quick enough. My hand got badly burnt and I lost a couple of fingers.'

'It's a shame you weren't slower.'

A flash of anger crossed his face, and Tess tensed, knowing what was coming. But instead he raised a hand, the undamaged hand, and stroked a finger across her cheek. She winced, repulsed.

'That's why I love you, Tess. None of those women were fighters.'

'Only the ones you killed, you mean? I presume they fought or you wouldn't have killed them.'

'Those women were worthless. All of them. Imbecilic whores who got knocked up by some fucking loser, and the kids are the ones who suffer. Those little children, who've never done anyone any harm, get shitty lives, barely surviving in some filthy shack without enough food to eat. No prospects. No love.'

She felt his fingers slide over her face and closed her eyes, trying to block him out, his voice, the feel of his fingers on her skin.

'They were loved. Jorani loved her child. And he loved her. I met him. He was crying for his mummy.'

'Of course he loved her. Just like I loved my mother. I never told you, did I? I never told you because I just wanted to leave it behind, pretend that it had happened to another little boy.' He laughed bitterly. 'But I couldn't, of course. You can't just shrug off your past like a coat – because it's here.' He planted a fist on his chest. 'Right here, inside, part of you, just like your heart or your lungs. My cunt of a mother let her boyfriends beat me virtually every day of my childhood. And the more they beat me the more I loved her. I would have done anything to make her love me back.'

Luke was breathing heavily; his voice caught as he spoke.

'It was my sixth birthday when they dumped me at that children's home. She drove away with the cruel fuck and didn't look back. Not once. I stood there on the pavement, in the freezing rain with my shitty girl's pyjamas in a plastic Tesco bag and the cunt didn't look back once. Those women are the same as my mother. They can't keep their fucking legs closed for five minutes. They'll jump from one man to the next and because the kids aren't theirs, the men will just abuse them. You have no idea what it is like trapped as a child in a dysfunctional family. You have no escape, no options, and the feeling—' He paused and the catch in his breath made her eyes snap to his face. There was nothing there – his features blank. His voice was a monotone now.

'The knowledge that whatever you do, however you behave you will suffer. That there is *nothing* you can do to save yourself. And that it will just go on and on and on and never stop.'

Tears ran down her cheeks: for the women he had killed and trafficked and for their children, but for Luke too, she realised, for his childhood self. For the life he had endured, and for what that life had done to him.

'These women don't deserve to have children. It's always the children who get punished for their whoring. It was time for the mothers to be punished, not the babies.'

Tears strangled her voice. 'It's not the same, Luke. They weren't the same as your mother.'

He didn't seem to have heard what she said. He continued to talk, as if to himself. 'I enjoyed it, Tess. Watching those pathetic women cry and beg and grovel, just like I cried and begged when my mother's boyfriends beat me. And I've saved their children, Tess. For once I've done something good. I've saved their children from the life I had. The children's home was the best thing that ever happened to me.' Fury shone in his eyes. 'When a parent mistreats their child, they plant a seed in that child. Maybe in some kids the seed just dies as they grow, but not in me. I can't help getting angry, Tess. You know I love you. You know I don't mean to hit you.'

Tess blinked. The field, his voice, all of this felt unreal.

'I've done what I needed to do now. I've found some peace and I've done something positive for a change, something that I'm proud of. I'm not stupid – I know you don't want to be with me, but I need to be with you. You're the only person who has ever loved me.' His gnarled hand stroked her face. 'It meant so much to me, Tess, being loved by you. I can't let you go. I need to be with you, and I know how I can make that happen.'

*

Alex left his Land Cruiser skewed across the drive and ran up the stone steps. The front door of MCT House was ajar, the hall in darkness. All the doors opening off it were shut. He stopped and listened, but he couldn't hear anything over the hoarse sound of his own breathing. Pulling his Browning from his belt, he made for the stairs. The sound of his feet slamming on the wooden boards as he took them two at a time echoed through the house.

It was the sound of an empty house and he knew – *knew* – that he was too late.

*

He was standing in front of her, so close that his features had blurred. His breath misted warm and wet on to her cheek, mixing with her tears. She felt calm because she had discovered

372

something strange. She wasn't frightened of him any more. All she could see when she looked at him was the little boy he had been.

'It's time,' he whispered into her ear.

*

Alex went straight to Jakkleson's office. The desk lamp was on and the window was open. A wind had picked up and the garden bristled with noise. He went over and shut the window.

He wheeled around, the sudden silence jarring. The chair was slid back from the desk, at a slight angle, and now that he listened, he could hear the purr of Jakkleson's computer. Tess had been here, for sure.

He sprinted back down the stairs.

*

He slid his hand into his pocket and when he pulled it out, he was holding a tiny green mine in his palm.

A butterfly mine.

PFM-1. Her brain started churning. An anti-personnel mine intentionally shaped and coloured to look like a toy so that young children would pick it up, thinking that it was a plaything. Luke was holding a mine made specifically to maim and kill children.

'We won't feel anything. Except each other.'

I'm not going to die, she thought. *Not now. Not like this. And*

I'm not going to let him hurt anyone else.

Luke slid his arm around her waist, and she let him, offering no resistance as he pulled her towards him. He held the butterfly mine between them at head height, in that gnarled, burnt hand of his.

'I love you, Tess.'

He leaned forward and she felt his lips on hers. Digging her blunt, bitten nails hard into her palm to stop herself recoiling, she let him kiss her, let him slide his tongue into her mouth. His lips on hers, arm twisted around her waist, she rocked backwards, taking him with her, just enough so that he was slightly off balance. In one sudden movement, she lunged forward and aimed, slamming her fist into the bridge of his nose, following hard with her elbow, driving it right into his solar plexus. He fell to his knees. She kicked him hard in the stomach and watched him tip sideways, groaning in pain. She had been planning to run: straight down Huan's lane, which she knew was clear because she'd cleared it herself, and out of this sick damn minefield.

But something was wrong. She felt herself falling with him. Grabbing the tree trunk for support, she staggered, trying to stay on her feet, but the force dragging her down was too strong – *he* was too strong. He had a chunk of her shirt twisted tight in his fist. She squirmed and struggled, kicked out as she fell, catching him hard in the stomach again, watched him double up and retch hot yellow bile, but his grip on her shirt was like iron.

He raised the hand holding the butterfly mine between them.

'The White Crocodile is fate.'

*

In the doorway through which he had passed so many times to join team meetings, Alex stood, half stiff with shock. Flies had settled to sip from the bloody gashes on his forearm; he didn't swat them away.

He stood and stared at MacSween and time stood still. It was only the noise of a moped passing in the street that woke him from the trance.

Tess. He was here to find Tess.

Batting away the flies, he backed out of the room, pulling the door shut behind him.

*

The inside of her head exploded with sound. Her left hand felt as if it had been bathed in fire. She couldn't see; her vision was clouded blood-red.

She was hurt. Her hand was white-hot with it. *Fuck, her fingers.* She'd lost the index finger, the middle finger. Bending double, she pressed her hand to her stomach, dousing the pulse of blood against her shirt, compressing the pain.

She had taken a risk – a calculated risk. As he had raised his hand between them and tightened his fist around the mine, she had wrapped her hand around his and rammed the butterfly mine up towards his throat. The noise of the explosion was deafening.

She dragged her sleeve across her face, feeling the hot slick of blood on her cheeks, opened her eyes, saw nothing but a red haze. Scrubbing at her face with her sleeve, she blinked. And saw him.

His face was dead white. Blood snaked from the corner of his mouth. The butterfly mine had taken off his hand, left a ragged hole the size of a fist in his throat. His eyes met hers for a brief moment and the reproach in them was intense. She saw straight through to the little boy, covered in bruises, lying shivering and alone.

'I loved you once,' she whispered, pressing her hand to his throat, feeling his hot blood pump from between her fingers, the flutter of air against her palm. But she wasn't sure if he had heard her. Bending her head, she laid her ear against his chest, listening for the beating of his heart. There was nothing.

She heard the sound of a Land Cruiser engine, heard it splutter and stop, a door slam. She stood, wiping her bloody hand down her shirt.

Giving Luke one last look, she turned and walked back down Huan's lane, out of the White Crocodile minefield, and into Alex's outstretched arms.

Acknowledgements

Huge thanks to my amazing agent, Will Francis, who has been incredibly supportive and without whom this novel would never have seen the light of day. Thanks also to the rest of the team at Janklow and Nesbit (UK).

I would also like to thank Katherine Armstrong, crime editor at Faber & Faber, for her conviction, enthusiasm and commitment. Also thank you to the whole fantastic Crime and Thriller team at Faber.

I was lucky enough to have Mo Hayder as my mentor early in the writing of this novel and she has always been hugely supportive and incredibly helpful. I owe you!

Thanks to my wonderful mother, Pamela Taylor, who has always supported me. Thanks also to my sister, Maggie Knottenbelt, who was my first reader, and to my sister-in-law, Jo Medina, for all her help with the kids. Thanks as well to some of my great friends including: Bettina and Sean who need to come back, Nancy Le Roux and Tor Crumby for my champagne celebration, Yani Nayman for always being there, my Devon crew, Crocks, Liz and Nome for wet weekends, Lindsey Pitt my original writing buddy, my friends from Bath Spa, Aengus and Sophie, Tor, Ana, Belinda and Steve (the fabulous Chickens), my NCT buddies, Tracy Grass, Judi Faithful and Jo Manley, my godson Will Creffield and his mum, Katie. To the friends I haven't mentioned by name, thank you for all

Acknowledgments

your support.

In loving memory of my late father, Derek Taylor, who appeared in this novel with a fat Staffie!

Most of all, lots of love and more thanks than I can ever express, to Anthony Medina, Isabel, Anna, Alexander and Pandy.

About the Author

While studying for a degree in Psychology, K. T. Medina joined the Territorial Army where she spent five years, first as an officer trainee and then as a Troop Commander, in the Royal Engineers.

After leaving the TA she worked in publishing as Managing Editor, Land Based Weapon Systems, at Jane's Information Group, where she was responsible for providing information on small arms, armour, artillery and land mines to global militaries. Whilst at Jane's she spent time in the Middle-East and in Cambodia, working with mine clearance charities in Battambang to provide them with information that would help mine clearers deal with complex mines and IEDs more safely in the field.

She has also worked as a strategy consultant with McKinsey and Company, and has lectured in business and consulting at London Business School and the London School of Economics. She recently obtained an MA in Creative Writing from Bath Spa University and now writes full time.

White Crocodile is her debut novel.

MULHOLLAND BOOKS

You won't be able to put down these Mulholland books.

Visit mulhollandbooks.com for
your daily suspense fiction fix.

Download the FREE Mulholland Books app.